LGBT Fiction

I0610218

Violence Begets...
A Gay Young Adult Novel

Indie Artist Press

VXV

LGBT Fiction:
Violence Begets...
A Gay Young Adult Novel
P.T. Denys
Published by Indie Artist Press
First Print Edition
copyright © 2015 P. T. Denys
All rights reserved.
ISBN: 978-1-62522-058-5
September 2015

PRAISE FOR VIOLENCE BEGETS...

"THIS BOOK GRABBED ME RIGHT FROM THE BEGINNING BECAUSE I COULD SEE IT WAS TOTALLY NEW AND DIFFERENT, AND THAT IT WAS SO UNPREDICTABLE ALL THE WAY THROUGH, THAT I JUST KEPT READING AND READING. THE CHARACTER DEVELOPMENT IS INTENSE AND COMPLETE." ~ **GAY GUY READING AND FRIENDS**

"IT TAKES A TRUE AUTHOR TO BE ABLE TO AFFECT READER'S DEEP SEATED EMOTIONS. P.T. DENYS DOES THAT IN DROVES IN THIS BOOK." ~**LOVE BYTES**

"THE DIALOG, THE IMAGERY, AND OVERALL INTENSE EMOTIONAL FEEL THROUGHOUT WERE SIMPLY MAGNIFICENT." ~ **THE BLOGGER GIRLS**

"IT SUCKED ME. IT SPIT ME OUT. I LOVED. I HATED. I STRUGGLED. I CRIED. I HAVEN'T FELT SO DEEPLY IN QUITE AWHILE."
~ **FANGIRL MOMENTS AND MY TWO CENTS**

"WITH MY EMOTIONS IN THE LINE, I COULDN'T THINK ABOUT ANYTHING BUT HOW AMAZING THIS READ WAS." ~ **MY SWEET FETISH**

"NOT AN EASY READ - BUT A MUST READ. A REAL MUST READ."
~ **BOY MEETS BOY REVIEWS**

"5 STARS - THE WRITING DESERVED IT. THE STORY DESERVED IT."
~ **PRISM BOOK ALLIANCE**

"BRUTAL. RAW. VISCERAL. PAIN. A LOT OF IT. THE IN BETWEEN. OH GOD, THAT WAS LIKE A SYMPHONY." ~ **SHEREADSALOT**

"WITHOUT A SINGLE DOUBT, MY BEST AND MOST MEMORABLE READ. EVER."
~ **NICOLA HAKEN - AUTHOR OF BEING SAWYER KNIGHT**

Violence Begets...

For TK

To All Who Have Chosen Love

Acknowledgments

Thanks and love to Bean for listening to me obsess about these characters for the past thirteen years. Schmunchkin for the strength, courage and love she brought to our home—laboo! Myra, my editor, for her attention to detail and amazing insight. Ruth for inspiring my return to writing. Melissa for beginning the story and Katie for being there from start to finish. Jae Jay, Pagan, DJ, Dan and Tony for their time and feedback. Diane, Mary, and Cassie for their amazing proofreading skills. Josh for brainstorming and my family for always putting love first. And most importantly, to every child and adult who has suffered pain at the hands of another—there is always a choice.

Prologue...

Kevin

Dirk's bar smelled like a fucking casino, like a goddamn stale ashtray. I sat at the back in my usual spot, slouched on a barstool at a high table between the pool tables and the john. I waited. It wasn't long— it never was—before a guy approached me. He could've been twenty or forty years old, fuck if I cared.

Years ago, the differences between them had started to fade and this one was just one in an unremarkable string looking to get lucky. He paused in front of me. I cocked an eyebrow. He nodded subtly and disappeared. I smashed out my smoke, knocked back a shot of Wild Turkey and followed him. The dented and faded bathroom stall locked behind me as his hands grabbed my ass, pulling me towards him.

"What's it you're lookin' for?" I hummed into his neck.

"The usual."

I expertly snapped open the button on his jeans,

pulling them down slightly as I crouched in front of him and went to work. I knew I only had to get a few more guys off to get the money I needed. With my good looks and talent, it wouldn't take long. Shit, most guys at Dirk's dreamed about someone like me, and it wasn't often they got the opportunity to make their dreams come true. The man above me fisted his hand into my charcoal-black hair, yanking hard and thrusting as he came.

I stood slowly, taking my time meeting his gaze as his eyes took me in hungrily. I let him linger on my chiseled features and athletic body in a long-sleeved, tight black shirt—always black. I had it going on, pure muscle that came from fighting, not lanky and skinny like most guys my age, and an ass that made men cream themselves. God, even I'd pay for the opportunity to be with me, and I didn't pay for shit. I offered him a half smile and a shy look to close the deal. *Like taking candy from a baby,* I thought as I left to rope in my next trick.

Rick

Blood covered everything. I could see a crumpled body lying on the street...

... Flashing red light colored the dark sky. I looked into the face of a young paramedic.

"Where's Jason?"

"Son, do you remember what happened?"

I tried to understand him but couldn't. I blinked several times before I finally pushed out the questions racing through my head. "Where is he? Where's my brother? Where's Jason?" Something wasn't right.

"Was there anyone else in the car with you?" he asked in

response.

"Jason. He was with me. What's going on...?"

...Waking in the hospital. Someone said my dad and Sylvia were on their way...

...A silhouetted figure stood in the doorway; head hanging, my dad didn't enter the room...

"What happened? Where am I? Where's Jason?" Why wouldn't anyone tell me what was going on? ...

.... Days later, the sun felt hot on my face and my black suit jacket absorbed the heat. I could feel the sweat dripping down my back as I stared at the thick blades of grass between my dress shoes. High school girls I didn't know cried hysterically around me. I didn't cry...

Jolting awake, my eyes fought to adjust to the darkness. I rubbed at them, trying to make sense of my surroundings. There wasn't anything on the walls and there were boxes everywhere. As recognition settled in, I curled back into my blankets, gripped the pillow to my chest, and rolled over, letting the tears come.

One...

Rick

At just after four in the morning, I gave up on getting back to sleep, buried my head in my pillow and tried in vain to stop the tears from coming. I squeezed my eyes shut, attempting to block out the bloody images, but my mind kept throwing memories of Jason at me, and as the tears tore to the surface I scolded myself harshly. No amount of tears would bring him back. I battled until the sweet sound of the alarm cut through my torment. Although I dreaded starting a new school, it was better than what the night held for me.

I lay in bed listening to Sylvia help Emma get ready for her first day of second grade. I knew my stepmom would be leaving early to drop her off at her new private school before heading in to work at the hospital. I hoped Emma would like school but was sure she'd let me know if she didn't. I smiled slightly thinking about her. She was the only thing that really made me smile anymore. After they left, I knew it was time for me to get going for the day. Of course, I tripped over the corner of a box that hadn't fully been unpacked yet, stubbing my toe as I made my way to the bathroom.

As my dad got ready for work, I could hear him moving about the kitchen. The smell of bacon, coffee, and cigarette smoke filled the air. For the briefest second, I wondered if he'd made me breakfast like Jason used to do, but threw that idea out as fast as it'd occurred to me. Despite the new house, things weren't going to change.

I pulled on a pair of jeans and the red and gray t-shirt my brother had gotten me for Christmas in ninth grade. He had enjoyed shopping to buy me clothes—either that or he knew the mall was a good place to pick up girls. Since he wasn't around anymore and I was never much of a shopper, I was stuck with clothes that were several years old.

"What's wrong with your eyes?" my dad asked accusingly as I walked into the kitchen, like he didn't know.

"Didn't sleep well," I replied, embarrassed that the swelling and redness were so easily noticed. He didn't look so hot himself. I was surprised to find him still home but not surprised to find no breakfast waiting for me.

He glanced at me uncomfortably. "Have you seen my keys?" he asked distractedly as he put his dishes next to the sink.

"I think they're by the box of books in the front entryway."

"Make sure these are cleaned up before you go to school," he said, glancing at his dishes as he hurriedly made his way towards the door. I heard him grab his keys and make a quick exit. As usual, he couldn't get away from me fast enough, but his silence stayed behind. I sat at the empty kitchen table, glancing at the unpacked boxes surrounding me. I knew this house would never be my home. As I glared at the vacant walls, I wondered what Jason would've thought of our new digs. He probably would've thought the house was pretty cool. He'd thought everything was pretty cool.

After rinsing my dad's dishes and putting them in the dishwasher, I grabbed a too-wet rag and wiped down the counter, noticing the streaks it left behind. Heading out, my stomach growled as the door shut behind me. Jason had always cooked breakfast for the both of us.

I'd walked the route to school the night before so I wouldn't get lost and be late. I tried not to notice everyone walking around me with their new clothes and their old friends. After the accident I'd pushed away most of my California friends, so leaving there hadn't been terribly hard, but still, the thought of not knowing anyone made my stomach turn with anxiety. I passed house after house with perfectly manicured lawns and sprawling driveways. My new neighborhood was much nicer than the one in California. I'd overheard my dad and Sylvia talking about a better housing market in Utah, and I guess that meant we could afford a bigger house.

I approached the school from the back entrance, weaving my way through the parking lot full of Jeeps and Mercedes. It seemed the cars of my new classmates were just as nice as the houses in my neighborhood. *Good thing I won't be driving anytime soon,* I thought. I'd hate to imagine the snide remarks about the kind of car I'd likely be given the opportunity to drive.

Taking a deep breath to still the slight shaking of my hand, I opened the door to start my first day as a junior in my new high school.

All things considered, by the end of the day I had concluded that it could've gone worse. I was only late to three classes, but I didn't fall down with a lunch tray in front of everyone or some mess like that, partly because I never found the cafeteria. I did learn that when asking for directions and someone says turn left at the end of the hall, they're full of it. The school was a maze of circles, a figure eight within another eight, and there were no "end of the hall" turnoffs, just a tangle of curves.

Emma, always the sunshine in my day, barged into my bedroom as soon as she and my dad arrived home that night.

"Hey schmunchkin!" I said, laughing as she threw her arms around my neck. "How was your first day of school?"

As she prattled on about all the things that thrill and excite a seven-year-old, I smiled and watched the light dance in her eyes.

"Sounds like you had quite the adventure! And daycare after school? Do you think you'll like it there? Make any friends?" I asked, experiencing a silent pang of jealousy for her easily found joy, even though I was thrilled she was getting along so well.

"Yeah, I love it there! There's a girl named Melanie, she tripped right in front of me and I gave her some gummy bears and she's my best friend," she said quickly, fitting it all in one breath.

"That sounds great." And before I could get out another thought, she was skipping off down the hall to her room to get lost in some new toy dad and Sylvia had bought. Shutting the door behind her, I thanked whatever god was out there for at least letting me have her in my life.

The next day at school was an improvement over my first day. I made it to lunch on time but realized immediately that I was going to have to sit alone to eat. As I found an abandoned table in the back of the room, I was sure every single person looked at me at least once, trying to guess what the new loner's story was. I could handle the laughter I saw on their faces, but the pity for me — the guy without any friends — reminded me of the looks I used to get in California, and it made me want to close my eyes and scream. I put my earphones in, cranked up Zeppelin and ducked my head, wishing I could just run away.

As bad as things were at school, I began to prefer the isolation there to the tension at home. At least during the day I could disappear and drift through the crowds of people. Sylvia had pretty much made it clear she didn't love being a stepmom from the moment she'd married my dad eight years ago, so nothing was new with her. However, my dad's avoidance and disgust with me were rising to unbearable levels.

I'd developed a routine of playing video games in the front room before he got home. After Jason died, I had stopped doing much of anything for months, including eating. By the time a year had passed, however, I'd finally somewhat gotten my appetite back, but because my dad seemed to like it better when I avoided meals with the family, I typically fixed myself something to eat right before he got home. As soon as I heard the garage door, I'd escape to my bedroom for homework, which always included welcome interruptions from Emma with reports about her day.

Just like in California, I thankfully didn't see much of Sylvia. She typically kept long hours at the hospital as a neurosurgeon. And now, with my dad's increased avoidance, I was able to spend more time on my homework. I'd always been a good student. My sophomore year had been really hard, but the teachers at my school in California understood what I was going through. I didn't want my new teachers to take pity on me, so I planned on working twice as hard to stay on top of things.

I was working on a history report about the assassination of Lincoln, and as I stared at the flashing cursor on the blank page, it reminded me of my empty life—no words or thoughts to fill it up and make it complete. I could hear my dad downstairs, cooking dinner for him and Emma, cracking a beer, and settling in to watch a game. In the beginning she had always begged me to join them, but had eventually given up as I had withdrawn into my world without Jason. I plugged both of my earphones in to distract myself from their presence.

After long, stressful days as some sort of VP at American Express, my dad kept his distance. It wasn't unusual to find him with a Miller Lite and a cigarette in hand, and whatever sport was in season turned up loud on the TV. While he was zoned out and Sylvia was at the hospital, Emma and I began to unpack as much as we could each night. We started with my room and moved through the rest of the house until we had all the boxes unpacked and even a few paintings hung on the wall.

Even with the familiarity of our old stuff around us, I still fell asleep as tears were swallowed by my pillow. If my nightmares didn't wake me up, my dad's always did. Between the haunting of Jason and the daytime loneliness, I felt myself being swallowed by the pain, and I found that I really didn't care.

In a rare show of mother-like caring, Sylvia knocked on my door one night during my second week of our new routine. After slipping in, she asked how I liked my new school.

Hesitantly, I replied, "I guess it's okay."

"Well, I'm glad to hear it. We could all use a fresh start, I think."

"Yeah," I nodded, not sure what else to say to her.

"And your classes are going well so far?"

"So far."

"Make any new friends yet?"

"Yeah, a few," I lied.

"Good. So, I think we're going to watch a movie tonight as a family, and Emma would love it if you joined us. Interested?"

I looked at my homework, knowing everything I needed for the next day was already done. "Yeah, I guess," I said, looking back to her. "Just give me a minute to wrap things up and I'll be right down."

"Great." She smiled easily at me, something she didn't do often. "I'll see you in a few."

After packing up my schoolbag, I made my way downstairs to watch a movie with my family. It may have been the first movie we'd watched together since my dad and Sylvia had gotten married, and I wondered if things might really turn around like they hoped.

Kevin

Shit, I'd much rather be fucking someone at Club Normandy than here at school. I smiled, remembering the hot guy I'd gone home with the night before school started. Man, he'd so been worth a hangover on the first day.

I picked at my food on the lunch tray, disgusted with the meat (that couldn't possibly be meat) covered in clumpy gravy. I glared at the guys sitting next to me; they thought they were my friends but I didn't have any friends. Mike, Brett and Jeremy were talking bullshit about whatever girls they were pretending to have fucked. They didn't have the balls to fuck anyone, so I tuned them out. I was so over all of it, yet still had two fucking years left!

I was scanning the room, aware as always of potential threats, when I noticed him walk through the double doors—not a threat by any means. I'd been watching him since the first day of school. He seemed insecure, distracted, and utterly hopeless. It hadn't taken me long to place him with the moving van that had come and gone around the corner from my house. New kid with no friends. I knew he'd be a perfect addition.

I watched as he walked into the cafeteria. The short blonde hair cropped close to his forehead made his eyes stand out against light skin with a spattering of freckles across his cheeks. His blue eyes were almost always swollen and red, I guessed from crying, which would make my job easier. The weak ones were always quick to follow. He carried himself hesitantly and awkwardly, sat alone and ate very little. He never looked around or smiled at anyone. He came, he ate, and he disappeared.

I knew he'd be my next target, and I felt confident he'd be an easy one. Jeremy, Mike and Brett had long since been initiated as my so-called friends and were stable. They followed my rules and didn't push me. This was how I'd trained them, but I was bored. I needed to exercise my talents, my ability to focus and control.

If I waited too long to approach him he might find a better offer. Only a couple of weeks into the new school year and I could see he was drowning. I had to throw him a lifejacket before someone else beat me to the punch. If he had other options, he might not be desperate enough to fall in line with me. I could offer him a lot, but I demanded much in return.

As usual, I paced myself along with the guys on the short walk home from school. I'd intentionally waited until the new kid left, making sure we were close behind. He walked slowly, with his eyes to the ground. I wouldn't have been surprised if he'd seen the inside of a locker a time or two. He was so far gone that he didn't even look over his shoulder every now and then. I almost fucking shit myself when two guys walked past him, elbowing him out of the way. Since he hadn't seen them coming he stumbled to the ground, his belongings scattering around him. I couldn't have planned it better.

Mike, Brett and Jeremy immediately started laughing and mocking him.

"Shut it!" I hissed at them. Exchanging glances, they snapped their mouths closed. I jogged up to him and offered my hand.

He glanced up at me. It was perfect. He was embarrassed, and I could see the touch of shame shading his eyes.

"Thanks," he said, slowly reaching out and gripping my hand to help himself up. His hand was hot, surprisingly so for the cool autumn day. He proceeded to gather his stuff, shoving papers and books into his worn backpack. I waited, standing patiently until he faced me. When he finally did, I was ready with a pack of cigarettes.

"Wanna smoke?" I offered. He glanced at the pack but didn't move. The guys had caught up and were standing quietly behind me, my army to be reckoned with.

"The name's Kevin," I said, allowing a small smile to ease his obvious discomfort as I awaited his decision. He looked at the smokes in my hand. They were an offering of friendship, acceptance, and a life no longer spent alone and drowning. I could tell by the emotions playing on his face that he knew this. And yet he hesitated.

"Do you want one or not?" I asked as casually as I could, but I was wondering why the fuck he was taking so long. If I'd miscalculated and he said no, it'd be the first fucking time I'd ever read a person wrong. I didn't do well with being wrong. As a last attempt I pretended not to care, shrugged my shoulders and started to pull the pack back.

"Sure, why not?" he finally said coolly. Something about the way he said it set my instincts on edge. It felt like he knew the game I was playing and had made the decision to play back, and I briefly wondered if he'd intentionally made me sweat the whole cigarette thing. My irritation fought to be recognized, but I shoved it down. He tugged a smoke from the pack. I didn't smile.

"So again, I'm Kevin, Kevin Vincent. And you are?" Of course, I already knew, but it was a formality.

"Rick," he said plainly.

"Got a last name?"

"Uh, St. James."

"Well, here you go, Saint Ricky," I said as I tossed him my lighter and noticed his hesitation again. I paused before moving on to introduce the rest of the guys. I wanted to make sure he lit up before officially welcoming him into the group. The moments dragged on, but I could wait him out. It was all part of my game.

He looked at me as if weighing his options. Then something flashed in his eyes, and for a second I thought he'd back out again. Fuck, I hated doubting myself. When he slowly brought the flame to the smoke and lit it, I found myself letting out the breath I'd been holding. God help him if the other guys noticed my tension. He choked out a cough, pegging himself as a new smoker. I laughed a little. It had been nearly perfectly played, with the exception of my damn second-guessing.

"First time?" I said, turning away from him and moving on to introductions. "This is Jeremy, Mike and Brett."

Jeremy nodded, Mike reached out for a handshake, and

Brett barely looked at him.

"So, you're new, right?" Jeremy asked.

"Yeah, just moved here a few weeks ago." His voice was quiet, but steady.

I started walking again, and the others followed me obediently. I glanced at the smoke in his hand. He hadn't taken any drags since the first one.

"Not your flavor, Saint Ricky?"

"What? Oh no, it's fine." He brought it back up and took another drag.

Rick started talking about what classes he had, and Mike and Jeremy let him know which teachers were assholes. I watched them carefully, gauging how well he'd fit in. Mike and Jeremy seemed to warm to him okay, but Brett was making it clear he didn't like him. I'd have to watch the two of them. I also had to be careful of them getting too friendly or they might start talking and try to challenge me. Bringing in a new person was always a risk to the balance of power, but I needed a challenge.

Rick

Kevin had tension rolling off him in waves, like the feel of an electric current right before it sparked. I wasn't sure I was going to like him. He certainly thought a lot of himself. They had left me standing in front of my house, not inviting me to hang out with them, wherever they were going. I watched as he raked his fingers through his dark hair, not looking back as he walked off. He was tall and fit. The Mike kid looked like a football player, and I wondered if any of them played sports like Jason had. Jeremy seemed nice enough. He was small but had an edge to him that made me not to want to cross him. They all seemed like pretty tough guys. I could tell I was going to have problems with Brett; there were some guys I could tell were jerks right off. Despite all this, I wondered where they were going. I hated to admit I was bugged they hadn't invited me. It had been the first time anyone had really talked to me since I moved in. The interaction with Kevin had brought my quiet isolation into shocking awareness, as if he had removed my earphones and left me surprised by the silence. I watched as Mike turned back and gave me a small nod before quickly looking at Kevin and then forward again. For a second, I wondered what would've happened if I'd invited myself to go along. "Yeah, right," I muttered to myself. I knew I didn't have enough balls to do that.

I stared at the cigarette still burning in my hand. Jason and I had promised each other that we'd never smoke. Growing up with it always in the house disgusted both of us. This was one thing we had in common with Sylvia. She hated the fact that my dad smoked. He'd tried to quit dozens of times, but it'd never worked. I brought the smoke to my lips again, considering the fact that Jason would never find out about my broken promise.

The next morning, exhausted from no sleep again, I left the house, wondering if I'd run into the guys from the day before. I passed the corner Kevin had said he lived around but didn't see anyone. I continued down a hill and around another corner and found all four of them standing near a street sign, talking. Kevin was leaning against a cement wall that came up to his lower back.

He took his time raising his eyes to meet mine. After

an irritated puff on his cigarette, he mumbled, "You're late." I looked around and found I was the only one he could be talking to.

"Uh, me?"

He looked at me, not saying anything.

"Sorry, late for what?" I added into the silence.

"Be here by 7:40. That's when we meet," he said angrily. I bit back a bark of laughter. He had to be kidding.

"But school doesn't start 'til 8:30." He didn't seem to be joking, and when he didn't respond, I added, "Why so early?"

"We usually get to school early so we can have a few smokes at the catwalk," Mike offered.

I wanted to ask how I was supposed to know I needed to be anywhere at a certain time, what the catwalk was, and why I'd want to get out of bed earlier than I had to just to smoke. But instead I said, "Oh, ok."

"Well, we don't have a lot of time now. Can we go?" Brett asked, looking to Kevin.

He nodded, pushed himself off the wall and started walking. As soon as he did, the rest, including me, started to follow him. What was it with this guy?

The catwalk was a cemented path between two houses and was secluded by trees. Obviously a walkway meant to give the neighborhood access to the high school, it also seemed to be the meeting place for every kid who smoked.

Kevin walked up to a small, good-looking girl with black, spiky hair and dark makeup. He wrapped his arm around her waist, leaning in to kiss her.

"That his girlfriend?" I whispered to Jeremy.
"One of dozens," he laughed.

Two...

Kevin

I had timed the cab arriving down the street from my house almost perfectly. Once settled in for the ride downtown, I swallowed two hits of E and waited for the exhilaration to come. I flashed my fake ID at the door and made my way to the bar. Franko knew me and slid a shot of Wild Turkey across the counter.

An hour later, salty sweat burned my eyes and the colors bent and moved with the music. Smoke swirled mystically in and out of red and yellow rays of light. I rolled my head from side to side as the music moved my mind. Every cell reverberated with the drumming of the bass. Shirtless male bodies gleamed with sweat as they pressed their hard bodies against my own. The hands of strangers caressed me, and my mind was overloaded with the intensity of my surroundings.

"You rollin'?" a husky voice shouted in my ear over the music.

"But of course," I yelled back.

"Wanna line?" he asked. I opened my eyes to take him in. He wasn't bad. Hell of a rack, nipples pierced, tan arms that could probably break me in half. He'd do.

"Depends. Whatcha got?"

"Coke."

"Works for me."

I followed him to the back of the club and into one of the restrooms. In the stall, he laid out two thick lines of coke. I closed my eyes and felt the music as he rolled a dollar bill and took the first line, then tapped me on the shoulder.

"Your turn." I sniffed up the powder and handed the bill back.

"You here alone?" he asked.

"Maybe, why? What'd you have in mind?" The coke immediately sent my heart racing and sharpened my focus.

"There's an after-hours party tonight at a friend's house. Wanna come?"

"I always wanna come. But we'll see about the party." I flashed a half-smile as I wrapped my arms around his neck and pulled my fingers through his hair. I knew I was going to end up at the party, but I wanted to make sure he didn't know it yet. I backed him up against the wall and kissed him roughly, feeling myself get hard as he ground his body against mine. He unbuttoned my jeans and I took a step back.

"Not so fast. All in good time." I kissed him briefly, left the bathroom and returned to the dance floor, expecting he'd find me again. Until then I lost myself in the rhythm of the music that surrounded me.

"So, what's your name?" he asked as he reappeared over an hour later.

"What do ya want it to be?" I asked, moving my body with his to the music.

"Oh, you're going to play it like that?"

"I'll play it however you want."

"Really? I could get used to that."

"Well, I wouldn't get too used to it. You never know how long it will last," I teased him.

"So, have you made up your mind whether or not you're leaving with me?"

"Depends. When ya leaving?"

"Soon. They're about to close."

I remained silent, knowing he was hanging on for my answer. He liked my game, so I played it out for him. He eventually got impatient, reached out and kissed me. It was gentle — not really my style — but nice.

"Maybe that'll help convince you," he smiled mischievously.

"I think I'm convinced. Let's get outta here."

"Perfect!" He grabbed my hand and headed towards one of the exits. "Do you wanna take your car or just ride with me?"

I loved that he assumed I had a car. "I'm good to ride." He had drugs, a car, and a nice body. The night was going to be just what I wanted.

The house was close-by, and I was pleased to walk into a dim, candle-lit front room with a dozen or so hot, sweaty men moving to a variety of techno beats. I knew I had made the right decision to come when I noticed two gorgeous guys going at it on the couch, and right next to them was a coffee table covered in an assortment of alcohol and drugs.

"By the way, in case you're wondering, my name's Dan," he said, handing me a beer. "And are you going to tell me your name?"

"Kevin." I wrapped my arms around his waist and pulled him into a demanding kiss. He responded nicely to the touch of aggression and I stepped it up a notch. He matched my intensity, which was a good sign. I pulled away from him, not wanting to give him too much too soon.

"You are so hot!" he grumbled at me. "You look barely old enough to be in the bar. How old are you anyway?"

"I'm as old as you want me to be." Looking to change the subject quickly, I kissed him again and the conversation was forgotten.

The night proceeded to move in slow motion, yet hours went by in what seemed like seconds. The more alcohol I consumed, the more I faded in and out of my surroundings. Dan found me and kissed me, then I found myself kissing some guy I hadn't been introduced to. I was doing a line of coke off another guy's chest when the effects of the E finally led me to reach out for deeper physical contact. The early hours of the morning found several hot bodies in a bedroom. I noticed Dan was missing, but I didn't care. I'd come to find darkness, naked men, strong arms and hands, kissing, touching, and fumbling towards getting off, and I had.

After passing out for a while, I woke to tangled bodies on the floor and empty bottles of alcohol strewn around. My shirt was still on and I was able to find my jeans and shoes in the kitchen. I called a cab to get me home before my father woke up.

After the cab dropped me off, I went around the side of the house to the storage shed. I always kept a spare change of clothes in a box of Christmas ornaments on a shelf in the back. One could never be too careful about the smell of booze and smoke on clothes. I pretty much had to change every time I came home. After quickly swapping out my shirt and jeans, I used a few squirts from a bottle of cologne to mask the smell of smoke in my hair. I then quietly snuck in the window of my bathroom, listening intently for any sound from upstairs. With the coast apparently clear, I locked the window behind me and smiled. Another night's adventure had been a success.

Rick

Kevin showed up just a little before 7:30, and I was already waiting at the corner.

"You're early," he grumbled.

"So are you."

"And?"

"And I couldn't sleep." It was the first thing that came to my mind. I tried to cover the slip by adding, "What's your excuse?" As it came out, I immediately knew it was the wrong thing to say to him. I'd noticed that the others never really talked back to Kevin.

"Do I need a fucking excuse?" he snapped, pulling out some cigarettes. "Here," he said, handing me the pack. I unraveled the plastic wrap and tugged at one until it came loose. When I tried to hand the pack back to him he told me to keep it. I slid it into my pocket and watched as he opened his own and pulled one out. He handed me his lighter so I could light mine first.

"Don't we usually do this at the catwalk?" I'd thought the whole point of meeting at this ungodly hour was so we could get to school early to smoke. I couldn't tell if he looked at me through his sunglasses, but he didn't respond. I tried a few more small-talk conversation starters, but he never responded, so I finally took the hint, shut up, and smoked.

A little later I about dropped my cigarette when he suddenly yelled, "Hey, Jessica! Come here." I looked around and saw a girl with straight brown hair almost to her waist glance our way and smile as she walked towards the corner we were standing on. She held a worn mug, and as she got closer the smell of coffee floated up around us. "This is Jessica."

I fumbled with the cigarette as I tried to switch hands so I could shake hers and introduce myself. Before I could do anything but look like a complete idiot, she smiled warmly and came up on her toes, her arms wrapping around my neck in a hug.

"I don't shake, I hug," she said as she took a step back. Again, I wasn't able to find any words. Girls didn't hug me, especially ones as hot as Jessica. "Nice to meet you, Rick."

"Let the guys know I'll be at the catwalk," Kevin said shortly as he walked off. I stared after him, mortified he'd left me alone.

"He's a bit of a jerk, but you'll get used to it." Jessica said, her voice solid. It wasn't unsure or giggly like the girls I heard talking in the halls at school. "So, you're new, right?"

"Yeah," I said lamely.

"I live next to Kevin, and you live just around the corner?"

"Yeah." Again, I sounded like a stupid idiot.

"Didn't you move in just before school started?"

"Yeah." *Okay,* I thought, *if she'd stop asking me yes-or-no questions I might be able to stop sounding like a broken record.*

"Any siblings?"

"Yeah, a little sister."

"Me too, my brother just started second grade. How old is your sister?"

"Same, second grade."

"She going to Carter?"

"No, a private school across town. I think it's called Hanson's Summit."

"Yeah, I've heard of it. I moved here a few years ago. I guess Salt Lake is okay. Like I said, Kevin can be a complete ass at times, but he's not all that bad. You've met Mike, Brett and Jeremy, right?"

I nodded.

"Brett's a creep. Have you met anyone else yet?"

I shook my head.

"Well, I could introduce you around. I expect Kevin will keep you pretty busy, but if you ever feel up to it, we should hang out." I wasn't sure what she meant by Kevin keeping me pretty busy, but I just nodded again.

Our conversation continued in the same pathetic manner, with me shaking my head or mostly mumbling one-syllable responses. Her eyes were dark brown but danced with animation as she talked. She easily carried on a conversation with me, as if I were an interesting person. She reached out and touched my arm lightly at one point. As I watched her hand fall loosely to her side again, I found myself wondering what it would be like to hold it.

Her spell was broken when Jeremy showed up, followed soon after by Brett and Mike. She chatted just as easily with all of them, asking them questions, and, like me, they seemed to hang on her every word. They weren't flirting with her like I'd seen them do with other girls; I could tell they just wanted to be around her.

That afternoon at lunch I asked her if she wanted to sit with us. She said she was going to lunch with some friends but invited me to go with her. I was about to agree when I noticed a look from Kevin. He didn't say anything, but after a quick glance to the guys, a disapproving nod from Mike and a smile from Brett, I declined her invitation. She didn't seem surprised as she sailed off to meet her friends.

As we neared my house after school that day, Kevin let me know they'd all be sneaking out to go to a place they called Zarahemla. He didn't ask me if I wanted to go; he just told me what time to show up. I was excited to be trusted enough to be included. I felt like I had passed some sort of test when I'd told Jessica no, and I didn't want to screw it up. They still left me at my driveway every day and walked off without me. I was dying to know where they were going. If I could pull off this sneaking-out thing, I was sure they'd start letting me go with them after school as well.

Sneaking out of the house brought back horrible memories of the last time I'd left my home in the middle of the night. The memories were always there in one form or another; I just had to work a little harder at keeping them shoved aside. I didn't dare sneak out through the front door, so I scoped out a good route while it was still light. There was a huge tree next to the house, perfectly set with a limb stretching and curling right towards my window. I could easily swing out and let myself down the tree.

After checking out my escape route, I dreaded going back inside. My dad had been in a particularly rotten mood after work, and I really didn't want to get into it with him.

"Where the hell have you been?" he asked as I came in the front door.

"Just out front. I haven't been gone that long," I said, glancing around for Emma. I found her sitting on the couch, watching cartoons.

"Are you sassing me?"

"No, Dad. I was just in the yard. Sorry." I tried to make my way to the stairs, away from Emma. I knew my dad yelling at me scared her.

"You're an ungrateful little shit," he mumbled, and I could tell he'd already had a few beers.

"I know." I bit down on my lip, darting my eyes towards Emma, who seemed oblivious.

"What was that?" His voice rose to a concerning level.

"What do you want from me?" I snapped. Sensing things were already at the breaking point, I was still leading the argument out of the front room. "You tell me to stay out of the way, to disappear. You're constantly telling me it should've been me! Then you get pissed that I'm not around?" I could see his temper flare, his square face beading up with sweat and turning red. "Tell me what will keep you off my back and I'll be happy to oblige."

"Don't you raise your voice to me!" he screamed. "I'll ground you for the rest of the year if you don't shut that trap of yours."

"Grounding me would only keep me here more, and we both know that wouldn't work for either of us."

Faced with the obvious logic of this statement, he fell back on his favorite phrase. "If your mother were still alive, she'd be so disappointed."

"More disappointed than now?" I asked. "It's kinda hard to outdo killing your brother."

His jaw opened and then closed a few times as he clamored for words through his anger.

I ducked past him and ran up the stairs to my room, gripping onto the wooden handrail. I was about to crack, and I didn't want him or Emma to see me. As I slammed the door, my anguished words racked through my body, stabbing at my heart with their truth. I twisted and locked the door behind me as I crumbled to the floor, barely hearing his pounding as I curled into a ball and disappeared into my memories.

It must have been hours later when the text message from Kevin rang and lit up my phone. *You're fucking late.* I hadn't even realized I'd cried myself to sleep. I shot up, grabbed a jacket and was out my window in less than a minute. I thought of eye drops only as I landed on the grass. I debated going back up, but counted on the darkness to work in my favor.

"Nice of you to join us." The sarcasm dripped from Kevin's words.

"Sorry, my dad..." I started but fell silent when he took a step towards me, glaring into my obviously puffy eyes.

"I let you walk to and from school with us, you don't sit alone anymore, and I practically handed Jessica to you on a plate this morning. On top of all that, you get the privilege of coming tonight. So shut up before I give you a real reason to cry."

I flinched and took a step back, not sure if this was because of his words and his anger or the feeling he was about to hit me.

"Okay, you got the message," Kevin relented, smiling as he placed his hand lightly on my shoulder. My mind started swimming. "Let's forget it. Come on. Jeremy, how's that science class with Barney? I have him next semester," Kevin said as he started walking down the street, dropping the intimidating attitude immediately. I was on edge waiting for him to freak out on me again, but he continued like nothing had happened so I convinced myself that I'd imagined his threat.

To reassure myself of this, I put on the best show I could and tried to join the conversation. "So how'd you come up with the name Zarahemla?" I asked as casually as I could, hoping my voice didn't betray my nerves.

"It's the name of a place in the *Book of Mormon*," Mike replied. Kevin looked right at me, but I couldn't tell what he was thinking.

"The what?" I asked, completely unnerved.

"*Book of Mormon*. It's a book like the Bible, but it's for the Mormons." Brett actually sounded like he didn't hate me. Maybe he was taking pity on me and my swollen eyes.

"It's our own little holy land," Jeremy laughed.

"So, you guys Mormon or something?" Things felt like they were getting easier.

"It's Utah, we're all Mormon," Mike laughed.

"Not so fast. I'm not," Jeremy protested.

"Do you actually go to church and all that?"

"I do. My father insists," Kevin said evenly, slipping back into his normal nonchalant-but-edgy mood.

After following an alleyway—well, as much of a secluded road as you get in the ritzy suburbs of Salt Lake City—the place they called Zarahemla appeared. It looked like an old horse barn, obviously deserted and trashed.

"Sit." Kevin motioned me to a cinderblock as they each settled on other left-behind remnants. Kevin perched himself on what appeared to be the remains of an old wall. He leaned back against another adjoining wall, and I noticed that it immediately gave him higher ground, almost a regal setting.

"So, I have a treat for you guys tonight," Kevin said, setting his backpack between his legs and unzipping it. He pulled out a bottle of what looked like dirty water and a six-pack of beer.

"Where'd you get that?" Mike asked excitedly.

"I have my ways. Here, Jeremy, why don't you do the honors? You've been quiet tonight and I think you need something to loosen you up," Kevin said, tossing him a beer.

"I'm not really sure, Kev. I have a test tomorrow." Jeremy had an edge to him with everyone else, but when face-to-face with Kevin he acted like a scared puppy. The uncertainty in his voice threw me.

"What, afraid of the calories or something?" Kevin said, laughing as Jeremy turned red. I couldn't help laughing until Kevin turned to me and tossed the water bottle.

"As my guest, you can do the honors," he smiled. I wasn't about to piss him off again, so I pulled open the top with my teeth and squeezed a bunch in my mouth. The second it hit my throat my gag reflex pushed it right back out and I spit it all over the ground.

"What the...? It tastes like rubbing alcohol," I coughed. Everyone was laughing at me and I felt myself turning red like Jeremy had. I was blowing it. "I'd like to see you take a swig of this. It's disgusting." I threw the bottle at Brett, who was in tears laughing at me.

"It's not supposed to taste good, you idiot." He put the bottle in his mouth and took a long drink. "Sweet Lord! That's brutal," he said, grinning as he handed the bottle to Mike.

"Not up for the beer?" Kevin said, bringing the attention back to Jeremy, who cracked it open and took a sip. Kevin reached for the bottle from Mike. Both he and Brett had downed the mixture without much problem, and I realized that none of them were new to this like I was. After Kevin took a shot he handed it back to me.

"Wanna try again, tough guy?" The thought of putting

that concoction back in my mouth made my stomach churn.

"What exactly is in this?"

"Whatever was in Jeremy's parents' liquor cabinet."

"What? You got that from my house? They'll kill me if they find out!"

"Don't worry about it. I just took a bit off the top of all the bottles. They'll never miss any."

"So, what's in it?" I asked again.

He laughed, "A bit of this, a bit of that. I don't know. Whiskey, wine, vodka, rum, Jagër, whatever was there."

"And you mixed it all?" I ask, astonished.

"Well, what would you like? Me to make you a martini or something? It's not supposed to taste good; it's just supposed to fuck you up. Go ahead." A command was hidden there, and I held my breath and put the bottle as far back in my throat as possible. As I swallowed, I felt the fire all the way down to my stomach.

"That stuff is just wrong," I gasped.

I handed the bottle off to Jeremy as Kevin nodded at me to do so. I was still coughing and trying to keep the mixture in my stomach. The way it burned I expected to feel drunk instantly. I wondered if something was wrong with me because I didn't feel drunk at all.

Suddenly, a flash of Jason's face tried to crowd into my head. *He isn't here*, I reminded myself. I had to pull this off. I couldn't go back to eating lunch alone, and somehow I knew this was just another test.

"Hey, Kevin, can I have one of those beers?" I asked. A rare smile crossed his lips as he handed me the beer.

Thirty minutes and several swigs later I was drunk. I

looked around to find that Kevin had disappeared, and I stumbled outside to find him.

"Whacha doin' out here all by your lonesome?"

"Trying to get away from you drunk fools," he replied. I put my arm around his shoulders to try to keep my balance. He immediately shrugged me off and I fell down.

"What'd ya do that for?" I laughed from the ground.

"Don't fucking touch me," he said coldly and walked back into Zarahemla.

So that's what a buzzkill is, I thought. I wasn't going to let him bring me down. He had nothing on the memories I fought with. What could he possibly say or do that would hurt me more than what I'd already done? I followed him back in and grabbed the bottle of alcohol, adding to the fire burning in my stomach. As I got to know the guys better, Kevin faded back into the silence.

At the end of the night, I stood at the base of the tree next to my window. I looked up and immediately lost my balance, falling back onto the grass. There was no way I was going to be able to climb the tree, and I was glad the keys to the house were still in my pocket. After letting myself in and taking what felt like an hour to get to my room, I remembered Mike had said something about taking some aspirin and drinking water, but the only thing I could think of was making it to my bed.

I woke the next morning with my shoes and all my clothes on. My mouth was dry and felt like I'd been chewing on cotton balls and onions all night. The sunlight was coming through my window and it was like a bad scene in an alien movie—far too bright to be natural. I dizzily stumbled to the bathroom and tried to throw up in the toilet, but I couldn't. My head hurt more than it had after the car accident. I found my way back to my bed and buried myself under the blankets, trying to shut out the sound and light of day. I now understood why Kevin had said he'd excuse me for not making it to the corner in the morning. He knew there was no way I was going to be able to go to school.

Three...

Rick

"Aren't we going to wait for him?" I asked the guys the next day at the corner. Kevin was late.

"He wasn't here yesterday either," Mike said as if that explained everything. They started walking. I joined them but kept looking behind me to make sure Kevin wasn't coming. I didn't think he'd like us taking off without him.

"And we know he's not coming today?" I questioned.

"He's never late. If he's not here on time, he's not coming," Jeremy supplied.

"Besides, two days in a row, he'll be out for a few more days." Mike pulled his jacket a little tighter around him.

"What?" I was not catching on.

"He does this. He takes off and doesn't show up for a few days, sometimes a week," Jeremy offered.

"Where does he go?"

"Off partying, shacking up with some chick, don't

really know. He doesn't talk about it, and we don't ask," Mike continued.

"Don't his parents get mad?"

"His dad," Brett said shortly.

"What?" I asked again, trying to catch up.

"It's just him and his dad," he threw at me, making me feel like I should've known this.

"Kevin's dad is pretty strict, but Kevin never mentions getting grounded or anything, so I guess he just deals with it." Jeremy offered as an explanation.

"My parents would totally freak," Mike said.

I couldn't help but wonder where Kevin was. I pictured him someplace with hot girls and alcohol, which immediately reminded me of the party where I'd picked Jason up. Trying to push thoughts of Jason away, I focused on the good times Kevin was likely having.

Several mornings later, he was back at the corner. As usual, he leaned against the cement wall in dark contrast to the colors of the leaves changing around us. His dark hair, black long-sleeved shirt, dark pants, black boots, stance — everything about him screamed back-off to me.

"You're back," I offered hesitantly.

"Yep."

"Where've you been?" I couldn't help my curiosity.

"Wouldn't you like to know?"

"That's why I asked."

He stared at me without saying anything, and I wondered if the right thing would ever come out of my mouth at the right time. It seemed that it didn't matter if it was Jessica, one of the guys, my dad or Kevin; I was always saying the wrong thing. I was glad he let it go, and I stood there awkwardly, waiting for the others to get there. I slipped my hands in my jeans pockets and listened as the fall leaves tumbled and rustled down the street in the wind.

After school that day, I didn't feel like being left behind again as they all went off to hang out. There was only so much I could take. If I killed enough time, walking home alone wouldn't be so bad because the streets would be empty. I wondered for just a second if I should let the guys know I had a test or something, but they probably wouldn't care. I mean, if they cared, they'd invite me to hang out with them, and they still didn't.

I was right; none of them said anything about it. Over the next week or so, I walked to school with them in the morning, ate lunch with them, and even got invited to sneak out with them one night but after school I made myself scarce and avoided walking home with them.

I was surprised one day when Kevin said, "So, you too good to walk home with us now?" He was passing out packs of smokes to the four of us at the corner. I watched curiously, wondering if he'd ask us to pay for them. He never did.

"Uh, me?" I asked, stalling. He raised an eyebrow. He knew I was stalling and wasn't going to humor me. "No. Why?" Another stall.

"Well, it's been a week since you walked home with us. Just wondering why."

"Got in trouble. Detention. Why? You miss me?" I swallowed hard, foot in mouth. I just couldn't help myself. I felt so defensive around him.

He paused for several seconds, his irritation evident,

obviously considering his reply. "What'd you do?"

"Told a teacher to mind his own business." I'd already over-stepped, might as well slide in a subtle 'mind-your-own-business' statement for him. Half of me hoped he'd catch on. The other half wondered what he'd do to me if he did figure it out.

Without hesitation he answered back, "What's that get ya, a week?"

"Sure, somethin' like that."

"Well, good. That means you will be walking home with us again on Monday."

He had cornered me, and I had no place to go with my excuse. The smirk at the corner of his mouth proved that he knew exactly what he was doing.

"Yeah, that's what it means." And I began walking home with them again, experiencing the embarrassment every time they continued on without me.

Kevin

Shit, he was good. I didn't know if I liked that or despised him for it. He was quick and had balls. He was never stupid enough to call me right out, but enough to let me know he wasn't going to sit back and take my shit. I think I admired him because it would be all that much more satisfying to see him break.

I was curious about what he'd been doing after school. I knew damn well he hadn't been in trouble, but I wasn't overly concerned. When pressed, he gave in to what I wanted, but I was curious as to what buttons I could push with him. His eyes were a dead giveaway, but I'd tried several times to get to the bottom of that shit, and he was like a goddamn fortress. All locked up and shit. Like all of them, he worried about being cool and that was working, but it wouldn't work forever. I couldn't quite get him to show me his weakness. It infuriated the fuck outta me. I'd wanted a challenge, and I'd gotten one.

One thing I'd noticed was his annoying habit of being nice to everyone, even people who didn't owe him the time of day. While it wasn't the gem I was looking for, I was itching to get him to crack just a little and not pull off his quick responses so easily. On the first day he started walking home with us again, I spotted Beth walking by herself. A plain girl without any of her friends around, she was the perfect target.

"Hey, Beth?" She turned and eyed me suspiciously. "My buddy Saint Ricky here wants to fuck you."

"What? Hey! That's not true," Rick stammered out quickly, then, noticing Beth's hurt expression, he said, "I mean, it's not..." Then he pulled his quick recovery shit and shut up. I was going to have to push him.

"Well, hell, if he won't, I will. Why don't you come over later and I'll fuck ya."

She rolled her eyes, turned her back on me and kept walking. Normally, I wouldn't let her get away with this, but my target was Rick, not Beth. Everyone was laughing.

"Seriously, Kevin, have some respect," he spat at me just as I'd hoped. I'd found one of his buttons. It seemed Rick was a bit of a gentleman. A soft heart would be easy to exploit.

"What exactly is respect, Saint Ricky?" I slipped into a very calm place in my mind and carefully weighed every word I spoke. This was his first big lesson, and I had to leave an impression. "Because, the way you are talking to me is not very respectful."

"Seriously, what's your problem?"

"Well, look who has grown some balls," I said as I walked towards him.

"Listen, no disrespect. I don't want any problems, but come on, you shouldn't talk to her like that." I heard a collective deep breath taken by the guys. They knew what was coming. They had all witnessed it before.

"Well, look who is quite the gentleman," I said, advancing on him, and for a brief second I saw a shadow of fear cross his face. He was good at hiding his shit.

"Okay, I'm sorry. It's just, well, she's a girl."

"And you think that makes it okay to disrespect me?" I took a few more steps forward, and he backed up.

"Listen, I'm sorry. I didn't mean anything by it." His sense of self-preservation was spot on. His instinct told him he was in trouble, and he was listening and trying to get out of it. Well played.

"I know you did not mean anything by it," I smiled, "but..." I slammed my shoulder against his chest and shoved him. A second later, I slammed my fist against his jaw and watched his eyes haze over. I tightened my fingers around his throat and my voice came calm and low, just loud enough for everyone to hear. "But," I paused for effect, "I do not appreciate being told when I should and should not say something. Got it?" He failed to respond quickly enough and my fingers tightened around his throat. "Got it, Saint Ricky?" He nodded the best he could. He'd submitted nicely and I could reward him. Like a fucking animal, punish when being a shit but reward to encourage good behavior.

"We're headed to Zarahemla now. Let's go." He was officially initiated.

Rick

He scared me. I knew he'd lash out if pushed, but I thought he'd just be a bigger jerk. I didn't expect him to actually hit me. Then to turn around and invite me to go with them to Zarahemla after school, I didn't know what to think. I'd gone, of course. Completely off balance and confused, I hadn't thought twice about drinking the alcohol he'd offered.

From that moment forward, I knew he was not to be crossed. The look in his eyes when he had wrapped his fingers around my neck—that look was not a teenage punk being a jerk. That was controlled, malicious, and downright evil. He'd sent a very loud and clear message to me. Want the perks of being friends with Kevin? You deal with Kevin.

The days that followed were not easy. Crossing him was not a good idea, and because of that, I couldn't help wanting to. The part of me with a death wish insisted that I push back.

When he allowed us into his bedroom after school one day—one of eight bedrooms in his massive house—I looked around, speechless. I didn't know what I'd expected. I guess I'd expected crumpled jeans tossed in the corner, dirty plates on his nightstand, sheets falling off his bed, and in general, things in a mess, but his room was immaculate. I felt fearful walking in. The thought of him shoving me against the wall if I touched something practically stopped me in my tracks. I gauged the actions of the others and tried to do what they did. It didn't surprise me that they acted with reverence. None of them sat or touched anything; they all just stood around talking. I noticed Kevin hesitate just a second before opening his closet doors, then busy himself hanging his jacket. He glanced subtly behind him, and I noted the corners of his mouth pulling into a pleased smirk.

"Hey guys, relax. Sit," he said abruptly with a smile. It wasn't so much a gesture of manners as a command. He tossed Jeremy a bag of what looked like weed before cracking several windows and lighting some incense. My stomach clenched. How was I going to get out of this one? Cigarettes and booze were one thing, but drugs were a whole other story.

"You up for this, Saint Ricky?" Kevin asked, and I knew immediately that this was another test.

"Sure, it's not like it's my first time." I lied, instantly regretting it. He wasn't stupid.

"Sure it's not," Mike snickered.

"Whatever, fool." I glared at him.

"Well, in that case, would you like to do the honors?" Kevin tossed me a pack of small papers, like I had any idea what to do with them.

"Don't ya have a pipe?" I asked, figuring it would be easier to put some in a pipe than roll a joint.

Kevin smiled. He didn't move, just nicely said, "Of course, I do. But what's wrong with a joint?" It was always a battle with him.

"Well, I prefer a pipe, that's all." My mind reeled with ways to figure out what to do with a pipe. I didn't think it could be that hard. I was sure I could figure out how to use one. It had to be easier than rolling a joint. Kevin sat for an instant longer before going back to his closet. He located his pipe, strolled casually back and handed it to me.

"Well, isn't that your luck? It's already loaded. Go ahead and do the honors. Take the first hit." He smiled at me. He knew I had no clue how to light or smoke a pipe. And he was going to make sure everyone else knew it. The guys watched me with curiosity. After several moments Jeremy spoke up.

"Come on, if you're not going to hit it, let me," he said, reaching for the pipe.

"Jeremy," Kevin snapped, and he stopped instantly. I'd seen this done in the movies and I thought it couldn't be that hard. I put the pipe up to my lips and held the flame to the weed. As the dry, harsh smoke assaulted my lungs they immediately began to burn, and I started to cough. Remembering what I'd seen in movies, I strangled the coughs in my throat and did my best to hang on to any smoke that was left. When I couldn't take it anymore, I met Kevin's stare and, with controlled effort, blew the smoke in his direction. It was a challenge. *Go ahead*, I mentally dared him. *Try to convince yourself I'm not for real*. He narrowed his eyes questioningly and then smiled at me.

"Well done. Just like a pro." He took the pipe from me and took a hit off the still-lit weed.

Kevin

The hell with him, was the only thing I could think. So

he knew how to smoke weed. Big deal. I'd been wrong. It hadn't happened before, but everyone had a first. The piece of shit was a punk. He knew that. I knew that. The guys knew that. Then what the fuck was the big deal? I didn't have time to second-guess myself. I needed to fucking control something. Saint Ricky was proving to be more of a challenge than I was comfortable with, and I was not okay with my lack of confidence about the situation.

I glared at him from behind the pipe as I took a hit, letting the smoke ease the tension I was feeling. After another round, I hid the pipe back in my closet and watched as Rick slowly faded with the weed. Even if he had smoked before, he hadn't done it a lot. The effects certainly hit him harder than the others. I kinda felt bad when I kicked them out. It sucked not being able to ride out a high like the one Rick was feeling. But I knew my father was due home soon and having friends over without permission would not go well. After a quick change of clothes and a spray or two of air freshener, I closed and locked the windows before heading upstairs.

When my father sauntered in shortly after seven in his finely tailored suit, I was at the kitchen table doing homework.

"Keeping those grades up Kevin?" he greeted me shortly.

"Yes, sir. All A's as expected." He rode me hard and I learned early on that meeting his expectations was one way of keeping him off my back.

"Good. Don't let them slip. Have to get into the Ivy Leagues for a decent education." I nodded at the familiar conversation and continued working. Eventually he went to his room, closing the door behind him. I heard him flip on the TV and started packing up my books, knowing he wasn't likely to come back out.

I knew the evening would proceed like fucking clockwork. He'd stay in his room, turning off the TV and lights at 10:45 after the news ended. I'd wait until 11:30, then quietly sneak out the window and head to the club. On this particular night, I was still pissed about the fact that I'd been wrong about Rick, and the fact that he'd smoked out before. After calling a cab from my personal cell phone, the one my father didn't know I had, I planned to stop off at Dirk's to earn the money I needed to have a good time at the club. By the time I made it to Normandy I was turned on and itching for release.

Right away I noticed Quinn on the dance floor with some of his friends. I'd been around the scene long enough to know he was a bottom and liked it a little rough. He was perfect for what I had in mind. After several more shots of Wild Turkey at the bar, I approached him.

"Can I buy you a drink?" I asked, turning on the charm I knew he'd find irresistible. He took a step away, obviously checking me out. I was proud of the tight black shirt that showed off my well-defined chest. I knew what I had to offer, and it was something he wouldn't be able to walk away from.

"Sure," he smiled, following me off the dance floor.

"What's your poison?"

"Blue Hawaiian."

I ordered his drink and another shot of whiskey for myself. "My name's—"

"Kevin," he interrupted me, "I'm well aware. And I'm...?"

My turn. "Quinn," I supplied, as my lips curved into a mischievous grin.

"I see our reputations precede us," he smiled knowingly.

I laughed. "I sure hope so." I'd heard he liked to be courted, but I wasn't really in the mood. Sensing he liked a guy who took charge, I leaned in and lowered my voice so he had to strain to hear me. "So, why don't we head out back and cut to the chase?" He narrowed his eyes, smiled, and made quite the show of sucking his entire drink down through his straw.

"Let's go," he laughed as I grabbed his wrist and pulled him behind me out the back exit.

It wasn't my first time in the dingy alley, and I knew it wouldn't be my last. On more than one occasion I'd run into other guys who had the same idea. A few times I had even hooked up with some couples who were already in the midst of things. But most often I continued with what I was there to do, while the chorus of others getting off around me heightened my arousal. On this particular night, it was early and we found ourselves alone. It was cool for an October night, but I planned on heating things up real quick.

To hell with foreplay. I knew what I wanted, and I was sure Quinn wanted the same thing. I immediately spun him around and pushed his chest into the wall. I came up behind him and shoved my fingers into his thin, straight hair, gripping and pulling his head back towards me.

"You ready for me?" I asked harshly. I didn't wait for an answer before I began and I knew by his reaction this was just fine by him.

Shortly after, I left him at the bar with a thank you and another drink. I never left on bad terms. The gay community was too small and word spread quickly.

I made my way to the dance floor. I wasn't opposed to leaving with someone else, but it wasn't my main priority. Right then I wanted to lose myself in the music, surrounded by sweaty masculinity. Saint Ricky was nearly forgotten.

Four...

Kevin

I banged on his window again. Goddamn earphones. He startled this time and spun to look at me, pulling the buds out of his ears. As he approached, I noticed his pathetic red eyes again. He'd been crying. I was glad I'd changed my mind at the last minute and come to his house instead of Brett's. I made it a habit to check in with all of them from time to time, ensuring they were doing exactly what they'd said they'd be doing. I'd have to kick some serious ass if I ever caught them lying to me.

"You shouldn't lock this shit," I said as he pulled up the window, clearly letting him know I didn't appreciate being locked out.

"You ever heard of a door?" he snapped. I took a deep breath and steadied my temper. The point of my visit wasn't to scare him.

"Doors have parents. I don't do doors," I said as I grasped the upper edge of the sill and swung myself in.

"But you do two-story trees and locks?"

Again with the mouth. I could feel my anger and turned away from him so he didn't see it in my eyes.

"Again, you shouldn't lock it."

"And maybe you should try calling first."

I heard myself mutter, "Hell!" as I turned on him. "Listen, are you trying to get me to hit you, or are you just that fucking stupid?" I blurted out. Shit, damn and fuck, I said to myself as I felt my control slipping. I didn't blurt, and I sure as hell didn't accidently mutter things I was thinking.

He took a step back at my obvious threat. Now that it was out, I couldn't really back down. I'd actually come over to play nice. Well, yeah, I was patrolling, but I'd meant it to be a friendly visit. I was an ass, but I knew damn well that I had to give them some small reasons to stick around. I had planned on arranging for Jessica to sneak out with us later; he seemed to like her. But now, because of his smart mouth, I had to be Mr. Fuckhead to him.

"So, what is it?" I asked stepping towards him. "Are you wanting to get knocked out, or are you fucking stupid? Because, if you want to feel my fist in your face, who am I to tell you no?" If he had been any one of the others, I would've already laid him out. I wondered what I was waiting for.

To my surprise, he didn't back down. He just stood there. I could see the fear in his eyes, but there was something else, something alive. He wanted me to fucking hit him. What kind of idiot just stood there waiting for someone to hit them? What the fuck kind of person was I, not jumping on the opportunity? I hesitated for about a millionth of a second, then put everything I had behind a punch I knew would knock him on his ass. He didn't even brace himself for it. I connected just how I wanted and watched him crumple to the floor.

"You done now?" I spat down at him, stepping away from him towards the window. "Leave this unlocked, would ya?"

Fuck, what was his problem? I'd been in a decent mood, and after leaving him on the floor I just wanted to hit something. How was I supposed to figure out what those goddamn eyes were hiding if he kept making me lose it on him?

I was too irritated to even go to the damn bar. I thought about finding Brett and starting something with him. He had a quick temper; it was easy to goad him into a fight. But that would take effort, and I was too fucking irritated to play games. Damn, all I'd wanted was to throw a bone to the little shit.

With a perfectly good night ruined, I headed home. I knew my father would be surprised by my early check-in since I typically pushed it right up until my 10:00 curfew, but I was pissed off and just wanted to call it a fucking night. I stuck to my usual routine, changing my clothes before entering the house.

"Hello." I checked my tone at the door.

"You're early," I heard from his room and made my way towards his voice. I knocked lightly and waited for his permission to enter.

"Come in." As soon as the door was open, he continued. "Why so early tonight?"

"Not a lot going on," I remarked.

"Keeping those grades up?" I almost rolled my eyes at his predictability but thought better of it. I knew he always checked my grades and attendance online. Thankfully, Christine had her study-period as an office aid, and after a few dates and make-out sessions, she gladly updated my absence record when I skipped class.

"Of course, sir. Things are going well." I turned and started to pull the door closed.

"I'm serious, Kevin. I raised you to succeed."

"Yes, sir, I know." When he didn't respond, I added, "May I be excused?"

"You're excused."

I never heard the end of his success stories. I knew my grandfather was a complete loser. I'd actually never met him, but I'd always heard about what a 'good for nothing' he was. My father grew up with nothing, working hard his whole life to have the nice house and respectable profession as a high-profile investment banker. Perception was everything to him. If I did anything that drew negative attention to our household, I was in for it.

I took the stairs two at a time. The clock on my nightstand read just after 9:30. Hell, it was too early to be indoors for the night. I knew it would be a restless one; thank god I had a stockpile of Wild Turkey to help me pass out. My last thought as I drifted off to nothingness was that it was time to throw a party.

The next morning I relayed my plans. "So, my father's going to be out of town again next week. Party time." Light snowflakes landed on my lit cigarette, dampening the paper slightly. First fucking snow of the season. I hated the goddamn cold. Made it harder to stay outdoors. I shifted the smoke in my hand to shield it from the snow.

That night at Dirk's, I had two goals in mind: get party favors for the get-together and then hook up—both goals I was confident of completing. After I had enough cash to treat the guys to a killer party, and a little extra to put aside for a rainy day, I headed to Normandy and found the table in the back where Jake hung out. I walked up, put my arm around him and whispered in his ear.

"Can you hook me up tonight?" He nodded slightly and I explained to him what I wanted.

"Gimme a minute," he said, getting up from the table. I watched as his lean, muscular body glided away from me. He was all man, and it always surprised me when I saw him in drag because even then he was fine as hell, the RuPaul of Utah for sure. I went to the bar and ordered a shot and a beer from the tall, too-skinny-from-coke bartender, Franko. I slammed the shot and made my way back to Jake's table, all the while keeping a close eye on a potential hookup for the evening. Several minutes later Jake brushed past me.

"Meet me in the john in a few," he said as he walked by without looking at me. I leaned against the wall and watched him disappear into the front of the bar, then took a few swigs and noticed a guy watching me. He was probably in his mid-twenties, and had one of the hardest bodies I had seen in Normandy in some time. I played it cool and acted a bit disinterested, but kept returning my gaze to him. When I finally stood to go meet Jake, I made sure to walk past him. I brushed up against his body, slowly, made an obvious point of checking him out, and simply smiled my half smirk. He was clearly interested.

Jake was able to meet all my needs, and shared a bump with me before he left the john. I followed him out shortly after, and went to find the man I knew I'd be going home with.

Rick

"Why don't you ever talk to me?" I asked my dad, interrupting his conversation with Sylvia and Emma during one of our rare family dinners. Sylvia and Emma stopped talking and looked at me, but I was tired of his coldness, of letting him ignore me. I didn't care if he yelled or screamed. I needed something. I needed a reaction from him. "Dad! I'm talking to you!" I said more forcefully, aware I was causing a scene in front of Emma but unable to stop myself. He finally glanced over at me as if he'd just realized I was sitting at the same table. "Do you even know I'm here?"

"I really don't care if you're here," he said, looking back to Sylvia.

I slammed my fork down and it cracked the plate. I stared at it for a moment, surprised.

"Rick, control your temper in front of your sister," Sylvia said bitingly, at the same time my dad said angrily, "What'd you go an' do that for?"

"To get your attention." I snapped back at him, ignoring Sylvia.

"Well, now you have it. What's your problem?"

"You! You're my problem. Ever since Jason died..."

"Don't you dare speak his name," he interrupted, "not

to me."

"He was my brother. I can say his name if I want to."

He stood up abruptly, his chair falling backward onto the floor. I heard Emma let out a little cry but I didn't look at her as my dad's words sliced through me. "You killed him. You have no right." He came towards me and slammed his palms down on the table. My eyes darted fleetingly to Emma, and I saw her tears welling up. "You'll never mention him to me again or so help me god!" he roared at me.

"Whatever," I said, getting up from the table. I had to stop Emma from seeing any more. He grabbed my arm and shook me.

"I'm serious, Rick. So help me. Don't you ever speak his name in this house. Do you understand?"

I yanked my arm from him. "Whatever," I mumbled again, not daring to look at him. It was the only word I could muster. I turned quickly and tried to walk casually towards the front door. I didn't want him to see how upset I was, but he was following close behind.

"Don't you dare leave! I'm not done!" he called after me. I picked up my pace and yanked the door open. It stuck a little and I worried he'd grab me again. My heart was racing, and I could feel the adrenaline course through me as I slammed the door and bolted into a run. I heard him pull it open again, his screams fading as I took off.

He was right, but to hear those words out loud was too much. I went to the only place I could think of — Zarahemla. I didn't expect anyone to be there and was glad to find the place empty. I found a pack of smokes and lit up. Dang, it was cold. I hated this city and the stupid winter, I hated not having Jason around, and I hated that my dad was right.

I threw my fist into a wall and the rotted wood broke easily under my anger. My knuckles cracked a little and burned as tiny slivers of soreness traveled up my arm. I looked for anything I could find to break or throw, trashing whatever I could get my hands on. I picked up a large board, and as I hurled it against the wall I lost my balance and fell. Too exhausted to stand back up, the emotion behind my anger washed over me. I knew he was right. It was my fault. I had killed him.

Kevin

Not a lot escaped me. I found Rick's tirade at Zarahemla fascinating. I'd ducked out the back when I heard someone coming. He was not quiet. This guy had some serious shit going on to freak the fuck out like he did. As I observed his breakdown, it made me all that much more curious about his story. None of the others had been nearly as interesting.

It was kinda hot seeing his anger explode. He was usually so collected. I scoffed at the idea of giving him the time of day, but pure testosterone always turned me on. Even more, I now had excellent ammo that would serve my needs perfectly. If I could only pinpoint his weakness, this would be the fuel I needed to keep him in line.

As I pulled my coat tight against me, I thought of him with no coat, throwing his fist through the wall. I considered whistling on my way home; he was going to be fun to break.

I was impressed the next day at school when I asked about his cut-up hand. He admitted without hesitation that he'd thrown it through a wall. When Mike asked why, he casually said because he felt like it. He was almost as good as me at hiding his shit. The only difference was that I could tell there was shit he was hiding, but no one had any clue about my life.

When the night of my party finally came, I had the guys over a bit early. My father was headed out of town, and I wanted him to see just the five of us. I'd let them know none of them better smell anything like smoke when they walked in or I'd kick their ass.

"You boy's going to watch some movies or something tonight?" he asked us.

"Yes, sticking close to home." I played the part of the good son well; after all, it was what he expected of me.

"Come on. A bunch of juniors? Don't you want to have some girls over?" He was goading us, trying to play cool and find out what my plans were. I knew he hated me having friends over, but I also knew that his desire to be perceived as a 'cool' dad made him grant me this small freedom.

"I know the rules. No girls when you're out of town and friends gone by ten," I replied automatically.

"Good. What are you watching?"

I nodded to Mike, who'd picked out the movies. He quickly recited the titles. I knew exactly what my father would want to know.

"Don't make a mess now," he said with a smile. "I don't want to come home and find popcorn everywhere."

"No, sir, we won't," Brett replied.

After he left, Brett commented on how awesome my father was.

"He's okay," I mumbled.

Granted, I was throwing a party, but I wasn't stupid enough to throw a party at my own house. I knew damn well my father would have the neighbors on strict lookout for any suspicious behavior. As soon as he left, I picked up the house phone and forwarded it to my personal cell, just in case he called while we were gone. Then, leaving the lights on and the TV going, we quickly slipped out the side door and headed to Kari's, which happened to be kitty-corner to Rick's house.

People started showing up around eight o'clock. I had a reputation for good parties, but people also knew I was an ass, and they certainly realized they better be respectful. There were never any fights (unless I started them), spilled alcohol, or broken shit.

I handed out the party favors to those who wanted them, and after taking my dose of E, I began to roll myself. None of them had asked for coke, so I kept that for my own pleasure. I kept the lights dim and candles lit, knowing this was the best atmosphere for a good roll. I had an excellent music mix going and watched as people started losing themselves.

I didn't allow myself to check out, but I did relax. I settled in the corner on a window seat and sipped my beer, keeping an eye out for any trouble. I watched the snow fall, blanketing everything in a clean white puff, and also found myself keeping an eye on Rick. I didn't trust him; he was too much of an unknown. He was with

Jessica, something I had expertly arranged. Of course, as planned, they seemed to be hitting it off. I knew girls could distract my boys, but I allowed it only if they remained loyal to me first. He was all over her and I was okay with this, for now.

In addition to being a willing host to my parties, Kari was also an amazing tool to keep up appearances. She was good for me because she liked to play and didn't want to be all committed and shit. We'd hook up if things were right for both of us, but I could screw around with other girls if I had to make a show of something. And I didn't give a fuck what she did. I was good to her in bed and that's what she stuck around for. We both knew it. I was damn proud of the world I'd crafted for myself.

"Hey, baby!" She came and wrapped her arms around me, draping her scantily clad body all over mine. As long as I guided her hands where I wanted them, I could tolerate her touching me. I had to admit, because of the E she felt good.

"Where have you been?" I asked, a little annoyed.

"Around, but I have a surprise for you."

"Yeah, what's that?" I grumbled, pushing her hands away as they tried to travel under my shirt.

"You'll find out soon enough."

"You know I don't like surprises," I said with irritation. It amazed me how some girls were so attracted to this asshole they wanted me to be.

"Honey, it's not bad, I promise. I'll give you a hint." She purred at me as she pulled the bottom of her skirt up just enough to show me some red lacy shit. This did nothing for me, but I knew I had to pretend, and getting off was getting off when it came down to it.

"Careful, might have to take you to the bedroom right now. Better go mingle while I still have the sense to behave." I gently spun her around and smacked her on the ass as she pranced off to gossip with her friends. God, I was so not in the mood for women. I wanted nothing more than to be tangled up with some hot, hard body from Normandy. Fucking appearances.

Mike was all over the place like a big, dumb, muscular animal, pouncing from one chick to another. Brett seemed totally lost in the music, and Jeremy was completely zoned out on the couch. Rick was getting it on with Jessica, and I was bored as fuck. The shit I did to keep them coming back.

By the end of my glorious party, I was fucking Kari in her bedroom. She screamed, I got off and left. It was an uneventful ending to a pathetic party.

Five...

Rick

Several days after the party, I came home to my dad pacing in the front room. It was well after dinnertime and it was too quiet in the house.

"Where are Sylvia and Emma?" I asked, straining to hear Emma's laughter from her upstairs room.

"Christmas shopping. What is this?" I looked at him for a split second before my gaze wandered to the worn guitar case sitting in the middle of the room. I bit down on my lip, not trusting myself to keep my mouth shut. "I found this in your closet."

I wanted to ask what he was doing in my room but simply stared at him. My instincts told me not to push him.

"We went through all this in California. You're not to play this. Get rid of it."

There was no way I was going to get rid of it but still

didn't trust my words.

"Did you hear me? I said get rid of it," he nodded towards the case as if he expected me to pick it up and throw it out myself.

"No." I took a deep breath.

"Excuse me?" he asked quietly.

"I'm not playing anymore, but I'm not getting rid of it."

"It's a distraction. I won't have you out there wasting time and money on some childish dream to be a rock star. If you won't get rid of it, I will." As he reached for it, I lunged and grabbed it.

"It reminds me of him," I said without thinking.

"Of who? Of him? Oh no, he had nothing to do with this."

"Yeah, he did. He believed in me. I don't care what you say. Jason loved me. He gave this to me, and it's all I have left of him."

"I told you never to say his name to me."

I ignored him, wanting to hurt him like I was hurting. "He always helped me hide it from you. I may not play now, but one day I will, and I won't let you take that from me."

"What do you mean he helped you?"

"I mean he helped me get to guitar lessons, and he hid my guitar in his room."

"Liar! He did not. Stop talking about him that way."

"Jason loved me and supported me, and he lied to you to protect me."

"He'd never lie to me!" he screamed.

"It was all his idea to keep it hidden from you. Yeah, your poster-child of a son came up with the idea to lie to you to help me. He chose me over you."

"The hell he did!" he yelled.

"He loved me—"

"You just don't get it, do you?" he screamed at me. "It should've been you!" He took several steps towards me, and panic screamed at me to run, but he was too quick. The back of his hand slammed against my face, and I stumbled, falling into the Christmas tree. Pain spiraled from the point of contact, and my vision swirled as the tree crashed to the floor. I tried to scramble away from him, but got tangled in the tree limbs and lights. I felt the glass of an ornament slice into my hand as I crushed it into the carpet. My stomach tightened in knots as he reached for me and yanked me to a standing position, instantly ripping me from the prison of the tree.

Struggling to get away from him, I somehow managed to fight my way out of his grasp and ran towards the stairs. I made it halfway up before he caught up to me, and I felt the carpet burn my knees as we crashed to the floor. I was able to kick free and half crawled, half ran the rest of the way to my room. He was right behind me and pushed me just as I tried to shut the door. His fists were flying at my face as I stumbled into my room. I saw blood fly from my mouth and was fixated as it spotted my carpet, but I lost my focus when his knuckles caught under my chin, cranking my neck backwards.

I landed hard on my back and rolled over to my side, curling into a ball and covering my head as he slammed his dress shoe into my stomach. I watched as the tiny white scuff marks flew towards my face. Then I felt his foot crack something in my body from behind and I wondered briefly how I'd ended up facing the other direction. At one point, I caught a glimpse of him and couldn't understand why he had tears falling wildly from his eyes. I thought I'd see anger or hate, but devastation just didn't fit with the agony my body was feeling at his hands.

He took several steps back when he saw me looking at him, then turned and ran from my room. I heard him leave the house, and I stared blankly at the door. The room spun around me. I could taste the blood running from my nose and the bleeding from at least one cut in my mouth. I tried to focus my eyes, but everything was so blurry from my tears that it made me sick to try. I wondered when I'd started crying. Hearing something behind me, I braced myself for another assault.

"Saint Ricky?" I heard a familiar voice. "What happened?"

It was Kevin. *This is so not what I need*, I thought.

"I came to tell you... I mean I forgot...I came in your window to tell you... fuck," he trailed off. I'd never heard him stammer for words before.

"Go away," I forced out in a breath, realizing at once that I had broken ribs. I didn't know how to explain things to him. I flinched as he placed a hand on my shoulder.

"Don't move," he commanded, not threatening but still Kevin. I heard him leave my room quietly. He returned moments later. "Now come here," he said, kneeling down next to me. I wanted to crawl under my bed and hide from him, from my dad. But his voice was hypnotic to me, and I found myself obeying his calm commands. I attempted to sit up and cried out before I could stop myself. Slowly, he took my arm and wrapped it around his neck. He waited for a second to let me get used to the position and then said, "Now try."

I took a deep breath and braced myself for the hurt as I used his body to lean against, gritted my teeth and slowly pulled myself into a sitting position. I leaned back against my bed, refusing to look at him. He reached up with a warm, damp towel and started to wipe blood from my face. He put a bag of ice against the right side of my cheek. He wasn't overly gentle or tender, pretty much like a doctor just doing what needed to be done.

"Here, hold this here," he commanded. I reached up and pressed the cold bag against my cheek, my fingers instantly chilling at its touch. He finished cleaning me up, then got a fresh shirt. "Put this one on." I looked down at my t-shirt and saw that it was splattered was blood. I stared at it, blinking, confused by the different shades of red. He stood back and waited patiently. "You need to change." I looked up at him, and he nodded slightly. With every breath and every move my ribs caught fire. My face felt like a balloon. I watched as he straightened up my room, spraying the blood spots on the carpet with a bottle of cleaner that had appeared out of nowhere. Finally, he sat next to me on the floor.

"You going to tell me what happened?"

What was I supposed to say to him? My dad hates me and freaked out on me because he wants me dead instead of my older brother?

"Your dad did this." It wasn't a question. "I saw him storm out of here." I couldn't find the words to admit to him what had happened. "How long's he been doing this to you?" he asked with a cutting edge. When I didn't answer he said more forcefully, "How long?"

"This is the first time," I admitted quietly. It had been a long time coming. I was surprised he'd held it together as long as he had after Jason died.

"Really?" He looked at me skeptically. He must have seen something in my face to make him believe me.

"He hit your sister or your mom?"

"Stepmom, and no."

He nodded, "Were they here?"

"No." I shuddered at the thought of Emma possibly witnessing the fight. There was no way I was going to let her find out what had happened.

"What set him off?"

"It's a long story."

"I have time."

"Not now," I said, shaking my head.

I expected him to push again, but he didn't ask any more questions. I got lost in the shock of what had happened. I ran through it over and over, going over everything I'd done wrong. If I'd only kept my mouth shut. I always had to learn things the hard way. I wondered what would happen when they all came home.

I didn't have to wait long until I heard Sylvia pull in and Emma's little feet running up the stairs. Kevin looked towards my door, then the window.

"Lock it," I whispered frantically, motioning towards the door, knowing the pain would keep me from moving fast enough to lock it myself. Seconds before Emma tried the door, Kevin flipped the lock into place.

"Rick?" I heard her tiny voice from the other side of the door.

"Not now, schmunchkin," I said hoarsely. "I have a big test in school tomorrow. Can we talk in the morning?"

"No, pleeeeeeeease!" I heard her beg and my heart broke. I hated denying her anything.

Just then I heard Sylvia holler upstairs for Emma to come back down and hang her coat up. I prayed she wouldn't try to come in again.

Eventually, Sylvia came to my door and asked what had happened to the Christmas tree and if I knew where my dad was. I told her I had no idea on either account, and she left to help get Emma ready for bed.

After the house quieted down, Kevin asked, "You okay to be alone tonight?"

I shot a startled look at him, having forgotten he was sitting next to me. I then looked at the clock and realized he'd been with me for over two hours without saying a word.

I thought about it, "Yeah, I'm fine."

"Text me if he comes after you again." He walked to the window. "I'm serious. If you need something, let me know!" He was harsh, but I knew I could text him if I had to.

"I will," I said hesitantly.

"Wear a long-sleeved shirt tomorrow to hide the bruises," he said, again with the commands. "You can't hide what's on your face. Tell people we got in a fight tonight with some guys. I'll back the story up."

"But you don't have any bruises," I said, feeling embarrassed. It would look like I got a total beat-down in a fight and he didn't.

"Don't worry about it. Just do it. K?"

"Fine," I said, still not liking the idea but thinking it was better than telling people my dad beat me up.

"Night, Rick." It was the first time he had called me Rick and not Ricky or Saint Ricky.

"Thanks," I answered uncomfortably. He jumped out my window without a reply.

Later, I tensed as my dad came home. When I heard him behind my locked door, I felt tears sting the cuts on my face.

"Rick?" he said, sounding drunk. I held my breath. "Rick?" he said again quietly. "I'm sorry."

The silver lining of being too terrified to sleep was the fact that, without sleep I wouldn't have any nightmares. On the flip side, it made me sick to hear him in the other room sobbing and Sylvia trying to comfort him. I was equally racked with guilt and hate as I tried to ignore the increasing pain that was screaming for my attention. I got up as the sky began to lighten, almost an hour before my dad's alarm was set to go off. However, I hadn't planned on running into Sylvia in the hallway. She stopped abruptly, looking at the bruises on my face.

"Does your dad know you got in a fight?" she asked distantly. I considered the irony of her statement before slowly answering her.

"Yeah, I think so."

"Did he ground you? I would've. You've brought nothing but pain to that man. It's a wonder he hasn't sent you off to boarding school just to be rid of you. Don't you dare let Emma see you like that," she said, narrowing her eyes at me as she turned sideways to squeeze down the hallway, afraid to touch me in any way.

Sylvia and I had never loved each other, but we at least used to treat each other with some level of respect. However, after the accident, all she saw in me was the person who'd taken the favorite son from the man she loved. I tried to shrug her off as I finished getting ready for the day. I'd hoped the new start would work out for us, but apparently I'd been wrong.

It was freezing out, and it was way too early to wait at the corner. It shouldn't have surprised me, but as cars drove by, I wondered how the world could go on like nothing had changed when everything in my life was out of control. Zarahemla at least provided a little shelter from the bitter weather and the sight of people living normal lives. I wasn't there ten minutes before Kevin walked in.

"Thought you'd be here," he said, smiling, a rare thing to see him do.

"What happened to you?" I asked, surprised.

"Told you, got in a fight."

"But you didn't."

"Didn't I?"

"Well, obviously. But…"

"I messed with the wrong chick. I knew it was coming, and that's why I knew the excuse would work."

"Looks like it hurt."

"Yeah, but you should've seen them," he smirked. "I got the better end of the deal, that's for sure. So how are ya hangin' in there this morning?" He was being way too nice.

"I need a drink." He reached in his bag and handed me a flask. *Well, that was easy,* I thought. *Should I ask for a million bucks next?*

"Did he come back last night?"

"Yeah, came to my room and apologized." I twisted the cap off.

"What the fuck?"

"Yeah, I know." I took a swig and winced as the alcohol stung the open cuts in my mouth.

"Whiskey, it's a bitch going down but it'll help with the pain," he said, taking the bottle back and helping himself to several swallows like he was drinking a glass of water.

"What about stepmom and sister? Any more run-ins?"

"Yeah, ran into Sylvia this morning. She assumed I got in a fight."

"Let her."

"Huh?"

"Let her assume that. It's our story right?"

"Yeah, I guess."

"So, you feel like going to school today?"

"Not so much."

"Wanna hang at my house? My father's at work."

I hesitated. This was Kevin; he was crazy. I wasn't entirely sure I wanted to spend the day alone with him. He obviously picked up on my reservations.

"I promise I won't bite."

Kevin

What the fuck was I doing? This was so not how I played my game. He'd gotten his ass kicked by his dad. So what? I should feel sorry for him? *Well,* I told myself, it was another thing I could use to break him. It would be a low blow, but I didn't get where I was by showing mercy. I also didn't get where I was by lying to myself. I felt sorry for the fucker, and I had to fucking stop if I was going to stay on top of his shit.

I had invited him over so I had time to deal with whatever it was that was fucking up my focus. If I got him alone, maybe I could figure out what was driving him. I needed to get a handle on shit before it was too late.

We didn't talk anymore about what had happened to him. We sat and watched TV. Well, he watched TV, I watched him. I didn't like feeling sorry for anyone. Feeling anything, other than in control, was not a safe place for me to be. Fucking irritation bit at my nerves, but I didn't let him see it. I had to figure out what was driving him so I could manage it.

"I need another fucking drink. Want one?"

"Yeah, why not? Helps with the pain, right?"

"Yes, so do these," I said returning with a beer and a few pain pills.

"What are those?" he asked.

"Lortabs. They'll knock you on your ass, but you won't feel shit once they kick in."

"Are they safe to be mixing with alcohol?"

"You seriously just asked me that?" I shot back, cracking a thin smile. "Take 'em," I said, sitting back down on the couch.

"Are you going to take any?"

"Already did," I said, focusing on the TV.

I glanced over and watched as he rolled the pills around in his hand for a few seconds, took a swig of beer, dropped the pills in his mouth, swallowed, and chased them down with more beer. I smiled to myself. They would help, but one pill would've been sufficient. Two, mixed with the booze, would literally knock him on his ass. I knew I had a short window between the pills kicking in and him passing out, so I waited about twenty minutes before I started with the questions.

"So, Jessica. You guys totally got it on the other night."

"Yeah, she's pretty hot," he said, and I could tell he was definitely faded.

"Did you have a girl before you moved here?"

"Nah, nothin' like her."

"What 'bout friends? Stay in touch with any of 'em?"

"Not so much."

My plan was turning out to be harder than I thought. Once people started to fade they usually loved to talk about themselves, not these short, dead-end answers he was giving me.

"Did you like your old school?"

"It was school."

"Why'd you move here?"

"Sylvia got a new job."

"Is your real mom in the picture?"

"Nah."

"Where is she?"

"Not around." Well, that was something we had in common. "So, what set your dad off last night?"

He hesitated before responding. "He's a jerk."

Fuck! He wasn't going to make things easy. "You said this was the first time he...lost it?"

"Yeah. Why all the interest in me, Kevin? Wanna

date?" he laughed. The pills had certainly loosened him up, too much.

"Shut the fuck up," I snapped at him, and he glanced worriedly at me.

"Sorry, man," he mumbled, and I knew my window had closed. Within ten minutes he was passed clean out on my couch. My plan to invite him over to figure him out had been a colossal waste of time.

Six...

Rick

My dad didn't come near me again for a while. He fixed the Christmas tree and even added some additional presents under it for me. He acted like it'd never happened, but it was there, the unspoken words of what he'd done. The bruises on my face, the ache in my ribs, they made me hate him even more.

Christmas day actually went surprisingly well. I think my dad and Sylvia were on their best behavior for Emma. It almost felt like it had before the accident; however, in this new life of mine, easy didn't last. On New Year's Day he struck again. I'd worked up the nerve to ask him about the guitar Jason had given me, while Sylvia and Emma had gone to exchange some Christmas presents. I should've known better. This time I tripped over a chair in the kitchen as I tried to get away from him. I crashed into the corner of the counter and it caught me right above my left ear. We both found out that head wounds bleed a lot, enough to make him back off. It became routine that he expected me to clean up the evidence of our fights so Emma and Sylvia wouldn't find out.

I flinched more when he was around and that irritated him. One time he actually asked me if he should just hit me and get it over with.

He apologized every time. He usually thought I was asleep, though I never was. Apology or not, I couldn't help feeling that I deserved what he was doing.

Emma certainly picked up on the tension between us, and I caught her watching us cautiously more than once. Sylvia pulled me aside several times, advising me in her cool tone that my dad was having a hard time adjusting to his new job, and that I should try harder to do what he asked of me.

Kevin had tried to find out what had sent my dad over the edge, but I wasn't about to give anything to him. He wasn't much of a threat anymore. He could hit me if he wanted; I couldn't imagine it being worse than what my dad was doing. But he watched me, waiting for me to slip up.

On the nights Kevin didn't have plans for us, I found myself avoiding my house by spending time at Jessica's. Things were moving quickly on the physical playground with her, and I wasn't complaining. She was completely out of my league. Anyone with two eyes could see that. But it was more than the making out. We'd stay up late watching old Quentin Tarantino flicks and eating sunflower seeds. Our conversation never seemed to get stale.

But Kevin wouldn't allow too much of a good thing.

And while I wasn't as scared of him, he still held my popularity in his hands. I had the feeling he could crush any social life I had if I pushed back too much. And I had to admit, any excuse to get away from my dad was a welcome one. Sometimes I felt bad about not spending more time with Emma, but I knew dad and Sylvia paid her enough attention to fill in for my absence. When it came down to it, things were probably better for her when I wasn't at home upsetting my dad.

Zarahemla, while insanely cold during the winter, offered shelter from the wind and my dad's rage, so I never turned down an invitation to join the guys. Thankfully, a makeshift fire and some serious alcohol kept us warm as we huddled close to the flame.

Kevin

The way he held his own with the guys surprised me. Now that I knew about his dad, I'd begun to realize just how smart he really was. If I hadn't stumbled on to what was going on, I was pretty sure I'd have no clue. This pissed me off. I was usually really fucking good at picking up on things I could use against people, but he hid shit so well that it was just dumb luck I knew what I knew. Luck was bullshit and unpredictable. When I pushed, he pushed back. But he had an uncanny sense to know when he should and shouldn't test me.

I didn't like how he was able to cover and improvise on the spot either. I felt something close to admiration for it, but it still irritated the fuck out of me. It wasn't easy keeping things buried so others wouldn't figure out who you were. I should know. I was surprised to see someone else keeping things so close. Most people wanted to bare their hearts, and this was good because it helped me figure out weaknesses easier. But Rick, he never spilled what was going on in his life.

What surprised me most was his ability to manipulate the situation around him. I was sure he had no idea what he was doing. It was an instinctual talent that I envied. I had to work hard at my manipulations. I was so careful, and it was like he was playing fast and loose with his talent. There were so many times I just wanted to punch him, but then he'd say something that would bring me up short, or flatout surprise me and the moment would be lost.

Rick

One night as we walked home from Zarahemla the knot in my stomach grew with intensity. Something was not right.

"Night, guys," I said as we approached my house. I hoped they couldn't hear the fear that was rising in my voice. I caught Kevin watching me, and it made me even more nervous. What was he thinking? Did he know I was scared? Was I scared to go home or scared of him? I felt I couldn't hide much from him. He nodded slightly towards me, then turned and walked away with the group.

As I approached the side of the house I noticed a light on inside. I stopped, frozen, not sure what to do. *Had I left the light on? Had he woken up?* I knew immediately that I didn't want to find out, at least not right at that moment. Zarahemla would have to do.

Once there, I found the water bottle filled with alcohol and took several swigs. It burned going down, threatening to come back up. I coughed for a moment, then took another swig, my throat still burning. I still didn't know how they stomached this concoction so easily, but if I was going to be busted, then I was going to be numb when it happened. Hopefully I wouldn't remember most of the confrontation, and I for sure didn't want to feel the pain that would go with it. The thing that bothered me most was being unsure if I'd be able to keep quiet enough to not wake Emma. It killed me to think of her finding out what our dad was capable of. He loved her, even if he didn't love me. I couldn't take her hero away from her.

The more I drank in the silence of my solitude, the closer my unguarded thoughts of Jason haunted me with their intensity.

"Now push in the clutch and shift into second," he said. The car made an awful grinding noise and stalled out. He started to laugh, "You almost got it buddy."

I hit the steering wheel with the palms of my hands in frustration. "Why can't I get this?"

"You're doing better than I did my first time. Be patient. Try again."

"I'm never going to get it," I said, frustrated.

"Don't you talk like that. No brother of mine talks like that. Now try it again," he said more sternly.

I worked the clutch with my left foot and the gas with my right, slowly starting the car. It rolled for a moment. Then I attempted to downshift it into second, concentrating on letting the clutch out and pushing the gas in. The car jerked a little but kept going.

"*Wahoo!*" *I sang out.*

"*Good, good! Now try to get it into third,*" *he said excitedly.*

With a few more jerks the car lurched forward but didn't stall out.

"*Look Jas, I'm driving! Look, I can do it!*"

"*Look at you, fourteen and already driving. Dad didn't teach me until I was almost sixteen. You'll be giving Emma rides in no time. See, all you have to do is believe in yourself and you can do anything.*" *He started to laugh with excitement as he patted me on the back.* "*Way to go little bro…*"

"I figured I'd find you here." A voice cut into my memories, and I startled with surprise to see Kevin walking in. I turned away from him and roughly wiped the tears from my face.

"Why are you here? Did you forget something?" I asked, pretending I was busy picking something up off the ground so he couldn't see my face.

"Nope, I figured you'd be here." I glanced up at him and he smirked, obviously noticing my tears.

"And?"

"And, I didn't want to go home either. What's it to you?" He sat heavily in his spot and pulled out a pack of smokes. "Do you have a problem with me being here?"

"Guess not," I said, backing down.

"Here, you want one?" he asked, offering the smokes.

"Sure." As I reached for the cigarette I almost fell off the log I was sitting on. I hadn't realized just how much I'd had to drink.

"You had a few too many?" Kevin mocked.

"I'm fine," I said, lighting up. We both took a few drags,

and I was left wondering what he wanted. I didn't know if I'd ever get used to being alone with him; it always seemed to be so tense.

"So why'd you guys move here?" he finally said. I glanced at him uneasily. I thought we'd been over this.

"Sylvia's job," I replied simply.

"And?" he asked raising his eyebrows slightly. He was pushing and I knew I'd have to give him more than the line about Sylvia's work at the hospital. There were several moments of silence. I hoped he'd give up and change the subject, but I shouldn't have been surprised when he didn't. For whatever reason, he had decided he wanted to know, which meant I was going to have to tell him something. I couldn't bear the thought of telling him about Jason.

"My mom's dead," I finally said. This had nothing to do with why we'd moved, but I had to give him some bit of information so he'd back off. I took another swig of alcohol and took a few drags of the smoke. He was waiting for me to go on. "She died when I was born." I was surprised when tears came to my eyes. I didn't often cry for her; it had been so long ago. I took several deep breaths and focused in on a broken two-by-four at my feet. "We moved here because of Sylvia but also to get out of California. There were a lot of memories in our house, and Sylvia didn't love competing with a dead woman for my dad's affection." I tried not to look at him, afraid he'd see I was lying. But hopefully the small truth about leaving town because of the memories of a dead loved one would hold true enough for him to buy it. I kept my focus on the broken board. He waited quietly.

"She's dead because of me," I added, an additional truth. I had the blood of two family members on my hands. No wonder my dad hated me. I hated myself. There it was. He knew about one death, the only one he'd ever know about. He could do with it whatever he wanted.

"That sucks," he said gently.

I couldn't help but look at him. I searched for a sign of sarcasm or mockery in his face, but he either hid it well or it wasn't there. After several moments he reached for the bottle of alcohol.

"My mom's not around either."

"Really? Where is she?"

"Not important." He took several swigs. "So, does anyone have any idea yet what your dad's doing to you?"

"No. God no! Just you. Not sure how long I'll be able to keep it from Emma, though." He nodded his head. It made me even more uneasy as the time passed and he didn't say anything mean or condescending.

"So what's going on with you and Kari?" I asked, trying to change the subject. He smiled, knowing exactly what I was doing. He let the fact that he was aware of it linger before moving on. Finally accepting the change in conversation, he laughed and became once again the Kevin I was more accustomed to.

"She's hot, a good fuck. What else is there to say? You tapped Jessica yet?" he asked with an arrogant smile.

"On my way," I said, trying to give him what he wanted to hear.

The conversation moved away from Jessica and stayed light and easy the rest of the night. The more alcohol we drank the more relaxed I was. We must have polished off an entire pack of smokes at the rate we were smoking.

By the time I got home that night, the beating that awaited me seemed surreal and dreamlike. Within moments of stumbling through the front door — too drunk to climb the tree outside my window — my dad's hand clamped around my mouth, forcing my silence, and the TV in the front room covered the noise of his furiously whispered warning for quiet. He had obviously planned my punishment for sneaking out. He dragged me to the basement, closing several doors along the way to minimize any noise I might make.

As the blows rained down, I focused in on the fact that Emma had been spared the truth one more time.

That would be sweet icing, indeed.

Seven...

Rick

Once my dad got a taste for his new form of punishment, he wasn't shy about delivering it when Emma and Sylvia weren't around. On one particular morning a couple of weeks later I was surprised to find him at the breakfast table. I fixed myself some toast and orange juice and sat silently as he read his paper. I took larger-than-normal bites of my toast, wanting to get going before he had a chance to get upset with me. Halfway through my second piece, he spoke.

"I got a call from your school yesterday," he said, his eyes still on his paper as he put his cigarette out in the ashtray on the table.

"And?"

"And," he said carefully, folding up the pages in front of him, "it seems you've been missing a lot."

"I haven't," I said, feeling my chest tighten.

"Don't lie to me," he said, standing abruptly. In

seconds, he had hit me, and I fell backwards with the chair, crashing to the kitchen floor.

"They're wrong," I stammered, trying to get up before he got to me, but I wasn't fast enough. He unbuckled his belt and in one amazingly fluid motion, tore it off, grabbed my bicep and threw me against the wall just as the first lash of the belt sliced into my skin. The sound of it alone, even without the searing pain that accompanied it, was shocking. I felt the length of the belt first as it cut into my back and then the tip of it as it wrapped around my side, finishing out like the whip of a snake tail. My back felt like I'd just been thrown on a scalding stove, and my legs dissolved underneath me. The leather bit into my flesh and I cried out. My body jerked involuntarily as my muscles fought to ward off the onslaught. The tears crashed out of my eyes, falling into small circles on the tile floor beneath me.

I couldn't tell where each lash hit, and my whole body screamed out in misery. One wild swing connected across the side of my face and the ringing in my ears drowned out the sound of the cracking leather. Somehow, my own sobs grew louder as I cried out again and tried to crumple to the floor, but this only seemed to spur him on. He picked me up and held me against the wall while he yelled about school and lying. For a moment, he discarded his belt in a heap like a coiled snake as he used his fists to pound my body, then threw me against the kitchen table and warned me to stay upright as he started in with the belt again. I held on to the sides of the table, trying to hold my weight. My legs would no longer support me. The remainder of my toast lay next to my head, and I could smell the butter on it. After several devastating thrashings, my muscles finally gave way, and I sank to the floor again.

He got off a few more good blows, then left, mumbling something about me getting ready and he'd better not get a call saying I wasn't in school. I wanted to laugh at the thought of me trying to make it to class.

I couldn't say how long it was between my cell phone going off and the knock at the front door. I prayed it wasn't the guys. Angry that I was being forced to move at all, I held my breath, grimaced through the pain and the tears, and pushed myself into a sitting position against the wall. If they came in, I couldn't let them see me curled up like a baby. I'd never be able to explain it.

"Rick?" I heard Kevin call from my bedroom. The front door must have been locked. "Rick, you still here?"

Please don't let the guys be with him, I thought.

"Rick, we were supposed to meet at Zarahemla this morning. Going downtown, remember?" I heard him calling through the house. "You can't get out of it. You better not be sleeping somewhere or I'll kick your ass. And I know you didn't go to school." He rounded the corner into the kitchen, alone. In moments he took in the scene—the chairs toppled over, my shirt in pieces, the blood and then me.

"It's not as bad as it looks," I whispered hoarsely. I hated the way he was staring at me.

"Jesus, Rick. What'd he do to you?" he asked, kneeling beside me. "Come on. Get to the couch." He helped me as I settled heavily but painfully onto my stomach. Most of the lacerations were on my back, and my stomach was the least agonizing position to be in. Similar to the first time he'd found me wrecked after my dad had gotten hold of me, he started to clean me up. Of all the people to see me beat up, it had to be him.

"What set him off this time?" he asked angrily.

"Skipping school. He got a call about me not being in class." I winced as he pressed a damp rag against my back.

"Shit, I should've seen that one coming. I'll make sure it doesn't happen again."

"And just how do you plan on stopping him?"

"Not him, the school. I can make sure he doesn't get any more calls."

"How?"

"I have my ways."

Kevin

What the fuck? Why couldn't he keep his ass out of trouble? If he'd stop getting his ass kicked, I could stop taking it easy on him.

As if reading my mind, Rick said, "I wish I could just figure out what would keep him away from me."

Contradicting my own thoughts, I murmured, "It's not your fucking fault." And I actually believed what I was telling him. It wasn't his fault his dad was such a dickhead.

"But there must be something I can do to make him stop. I know I deserve it but…"

"Knock it off. Just fucking deal with what he's doing for a few more years until you can move out. Until then, suck it up." I didn't like the way I felt inside. I was actually worried about him.

"I wish he was more like your dad."

I wanted to laugh out loud. "My father's an ass. We put on a good front." More than once it'd occurred to me that my father somehow knew I was gay. Maybe that was why he rode my ass so hard, but there was no way in hell I was going to tell Rick my thoughts on the topic.

"He always seems so nice to me."

"He's really strict."

"I just wish it all would stop."

"Things are the way they are, and you just have to deal with it."

"Why do you always help me when he goes off on me? Why not just walk away?"

I was surprised by his bluntness but shouldn't have been.

"You treat me different than you treat the others...."

"I don't," I said indifferently, but he was right and would've been an idiot not to pick up on it.

"You don't think so?"

"No, but if you do, I can try harder to treat you the way I treat everyone else." Helping him with his dad was one thing, but letting him get too close to me and my life was not an option. When he didn't reply, I finished cleaning him up without further comment. Again, I spouted off some things he could do for the pain and helped him to his room before disappearing out his window.

Needless to say, I never made it downtown with the guys. And try as I might, I couldn't shake the image of his dad railing on him. By the time the sun had set, my thoughts had turned dark. I hated it, but there wasn't a refuge from it. There were times when the control, alcohol, drugs and sex simply weren't enough to block out the night that swallowed my thoughts. Shot after shot of the whiskey only intensified the despair. I stumbled through the black streets, seeking out the company of the dark night. The hurt was a blur but was still sharp enough to cut holes in my stomach. I wanted to drink until my body couldn't function and I slipped into blackness. This was Rick's fault. His weakness was becoming my own. The darkness I held at bay was clawing its way back to consciousness.

I had enough sense to make it to Zarahemla and start a fire in the fire pit. Here I could slip into oblivion and not be disturbed. Drink more, stop the knife, stop the darkness, more alcohol, less thought. I fell clumsily to the dirt and stared at the ceiling, which slipped into doubles and triples. The booze made the coldness of the night disappear. Dark, so dark! I curled into a ball. My world spun and my stomach churned. Drunken sleep crawled over my body.

I woke because it was so damn cold. I was fucking freezing and sick. I rolled over and the last of the alcohol from the night before came up. I threw up for several minutes before I could even bring myself to open my eyes. I reached for my flask and found it empty, so I searched Zarahemla for the water bottle of alcohol and found it hidden beneath some floorboards. Fuck this cold. I popped open the top and grimaced as I shot several squirts down my throat.

Sitting against the wall, I lit a smoke and waited for the

hangover to numb. The dark memories of the night before seemed like a distant nightmare. The knife in my stomach was gone. My body ached, but I knew I had to get home and get into a hot shower. Passing out in a fucking barn in the middle of February was a stupid-ass thing to do.

"Where were you this morning?" Jeremy asked at lunch.

"None of your business," I said irritably, and he dropped the subject.

As we headed to the catwalk for our after-lunch smoke, my patience grew thin. I had no desire to put up with their incessant chattering. I let them walk ahead of me a bit, then quietly ducked away. I wasn't in the mood for explanations.

I walked home. After changing out of my clothes and swapping coats, I let myself in the front door. I stretched out on my couch and flipped the TV on. With any luck I'd be able to catch a quick nap and sleep off the remains of the bad night before my father got home. I was pissed that my emotions had gotten to me so much. It wasn't very often I lost control, but when I did, it took no prisoners. Hell, if I couldn't control my own emotions, how was I supposed to stay in control of everything else? It was exhausting.

"What's going on with you?" My eyes shot open to find Rick standing in my front room. I restrained the urge to jump up and slam my fist into him. It was fucking stupid to surprise me. Not only had he been able to follow me, but he'd been able to walk into my house and sneak up on me. I was dangerously off my game, but I strangled these emotions and barely twitched a muscle as he walked towards me.

"What's it to you?" I asked with a warning tone.

He hesitated but continued, "Well, something's obviously wrong with you." He came and sat at the other end of the couch. "I mean, you're not the nicest guy in the world, but today you're just being an ass."

"Again, what's it to you?" He was obviously weighing the risk of proceeding. He'd become increasingly bold with me when we were alone, and I wanted to see how far he dared push me.

"You've helped me out a lot with my dad. Just figured if there was something I could help you out with, I kinda owe ya."

I admired him for his guts. Flat out calling me 'not a nice guy' was pretty ballsy. I watched him weigh his words carefully. He was becoming more like me, and I hated to punish him for that.

"I'm fine, just hung over."

"You're always hung over, so why is today so different?" Damn, he wasn't letting up very easily. I felt like giving him a left hook because he was half the problem, but again, I felt bad for him after seeing what his dad had done to him the day before, so I tried to go easy on him.

"Just had a long night. It's really not a big deal. Have a lot going on."

"Like?"

"Don't want to talk about it."

Rick waited. Now that he'd seen I wasn't going to push back very hard, he was going to take as much as he could get.

"There's a lot you'll never know about, Rick."

"Why is that? Because you don't trust anyone?"

I stared at him for a moment. "And what makes you think that?"

He became uneasy, debating how much he should say. He absentmindedly tore at one of his fingernails. Not looking at me he said, "I'm not stupid. I'm not like the others. It's not hard to figure out, Kevin."

I wondered exactly what he'd figured out. Had he guessed about my other life? He couldn't have. I was too careful.

"And what have you figured out, Mr. Smart Guy?" I asked, masking the tension I felt with sarcasm.

"Nothing really," he said quickly, "just that there's a lot more to you than you let others see, that's all."

He wouldn't look at me. I watched his face and his body language to see if he was lying to me, to see how much he really had figured out. He leaned back on the couch, watching TV. He was done. He'd said his part, and now he was going to drop it, but I wondered if I really wanted him to drop it. He was the first one to ever really challenge me. I appreciated the game, but he had been getting too close. It was smart for him to back off before I had to make him.

Eight...

Rick

I woke up screaming his name over and over, thrashing so hard that I fell out of bed, tangled up in my sheets. A cold sweat had plastered my t-shirt to my body and I tore at its suffocating pressure, throwing it across the room. Focusing my breathing, I curled up in a ball on the floor as I glared at the clock on my nightstand. It was hours before I had to be up. I was only aware that I'd fallen asleep again when I jolted awake with images of Jason's disfigured body tormenting my mind.

I stood, angrily throwing my disheveled blankets on the bed. I strangled the urge to start throwing anything I could get my hands on. Instead, as my anger and frustration fought for release, I hurled fists into my pillows and blankets. Collapsing on my bed, grief overtook the anger as I clenched and coiled myself into the blankets, attempting to control the anguished sobbing as it ripped through my body.

I tossed and turned relentlessly, fading in and out of sleep. I wasn't sure if I was awake, or if I was lost in despairing nightmares as Sylvia and Emma got ready and left for the day. Exhausted and emotionally drained, I barely had the energy to turn off my alarm clock when it finally alerted me to the coming day. In a haze of sadness, I went through the motions of showering and getting dressed, successfully avoiding my dad and escaping the morning without running into him.

I got to the corner before the rest of them and lit up. I thought about calling Jessica, but knew she'd be in the dance class she took most mornings before school. Again, Jason ruthlessly overtook my thoughts.

"What's it about the guitar that you like so much?" he asked me.

"Not sure really. I think it's 'cause I don't have to be here when I'm playing."

"What do ya mean?"

"Well, when I'm lost in the music, I don't really remember all that I hate about this life."

"Come on, Rick, this life isn't all that bad."

"Yeah, not for you. You're the all-American son, star quarterback, hot girlfriend, dad's hero." He looked hurt at my assessment. "You're also my big brother and my hero, and I couldn't imagine my life without you. But to dad, I'm the one who killed mom."

"Now stop that, you didn't kill mom! You were born and that's the best thing that ever happened to me. I remember mom, and she'd be proud of you. She'd be even more proud if you would embrace your talent. Stop using her as an excuse."

"Whatever!" I shrugged indifferently.

"I'm serious. What happens when my football days are over? You're the smart one, the one with an actual future. I'm gonna blow my knee out at twenty, and then I'm done. I'll have nothing."

"If that were at all true, then why can't dad just accept me and be proud of what I can do?"

"To hell with dad, Rick! I'm tired of you making excuses. This is what you were born to do. This's what you want to do with your life. I'm tired of hearing that you don't want to do it. Quit using mom or dad as an excuse. Now, we're going to figure out how to make this happen for you."

"Yeah, like he'd ever let that happen. He won't let me do anything even closely related to my music."

"No, but I would."

"I know that, but still there's dad to deal with."

"What if I helped you? Between the two of us we could get around dad and Sylvia."

"What do you mean?"

"Like signing up for guitar lessons or something like that."

"I don't know Jas. If dad ever found out he'd disown me."

"Well, if that happens, then I'll tell him it was my idea."

"Yeah, and he'd believe that," I said sarcastically.

"So what? He won't have a choice, and it really is my idea. He won't get mad at me. You know that. I'll take the heat."

"I know he'll just turn it around and figure out a way to take it out on me."

"What do you have to lose? If he finds out, then he'll be mad. And if he doesn't, he'll still be mad, and he'll just find something else to get on your case for. At least this way you'll get something good out of it."

He had a point. "And you think we can pull it off?"

"You find the class you want to take and I'll do the rest. Don't worry, Rick. Things will turn out just fine." He *wrapped his arm around my shoulder. With him in charge, I knew things would be fine.*

"Hello?" I spun to find Kevin walking up, the completely burnt out smoke dropping from my hand. "Where the fuck were you just then?" I was surprised to see him because he'd been gone on one of his binges for the last three days. He usually up and disappeared for at least four or five days.

"Oh hey, sorry. Just spacing out." He slowed in front of me.

"Got a smoke?" he asked. I handed him my pack, and he tossed me one, then put the pack in his pocket. I slid it behind my ear as he rolled his between his fingers. I'd have to bum smokes until he saw fit to get me another pack.

"You look like shit."

"Thanks, so do you."

"Fuck you. What's with the eyes?" I knew my eyes were always a dead giveaway. No amount of eye drops and ice packs could hide the evidence. Still, he rarely called me out on it. I wondered why he wanted to be such a jerk. I guess I should've been thankful he hadn't said something in front of the guys.

"Didn't sleep well."

"I got that. Why?" He could be ruthless when he wanted to. I was never good at lying, especially to him. So I opted for the truth.

"It's none of your business," I said, meeting his stare and not backing down.

"Excuse me?" he said as he stepped menacingly towards me.

"I mean it." He could do what he wanted. I wasn't going to tell him about Jason.

"Who the fuck do you think you are?"

I watched, mesmerized, as the muscles in his face tightened one by one, then moved to his neck, down his arms, his hands finally clenching into fists. He was so controlled, even in his anger. I waited, thinking about the first time he'd climbed through my window. He'd had a point to make then, and I'd always left my window unlocked after his visit. Now all I could think about was how, after he'd left me lying on the floor that night, I'd thought about that pain, not about Jason. I didn't want to think about Jason anymore.

"Do it," I breathed when he didn't take a swing.

"What the fuck's wrong with you?" he asked after a moment of hesitation, stepping back instead.

"Do it," I said more forcefully and took a step towards him. His body tensed, and he was ready to hit me when Jeremy's voice broke through the tension.

"Hey guys," he said casually. Kevin shot a look at him and quickly turned his back on both of us. I shifted uncomfortably and tried my best to smile.

"Uh, everything ok?" Jeremy asked. We obviously hadn't fooled him.

"Fine," I said, smiling again. "Just tired."

"Yeah?" He looked from my red eyes to Kevin's shoulders hunched around his cigarette as he fought with his lighter. As usual, Mike and Brett arrived on Jeremy's heels.

"Whoa, what's up here?" Brett asked, picking up on the tension immediately.

"Fuck this bullshit!" Kevin said as he threw his lighter, which was obviously still giving him trouble. He held out his hand to me. "Give me your fucking fire."

I fumbled in my pocket and pulled mine out, which he anxiously grabbed from me before I could hand it to him. I noticed that his hand was shaking. He turned his back again and tried to light the smoke but still couldn't. I pulled out the one from behind my ear and lit it with Mike's lighter as we started walking. Within seconds he'd grabbed the smoke out of my hand and walked ahead of us.

Mike always had the ability to be goofy and lighten a mood, and he worked his magic. By the time we reached the catwalk, I was feeling better, and we were all ignoring Kevin. He pulled himself up and sat on one of the railings, his legs stretched across the walkway and his boots balanced on the other railing.

None of us noticed the teacher enter the catwalk until it was too late. I was standing between Kevin and Mike and was shocked when Kevin reached in his pocket, pulled out his smokes—which had been mine earlier—and a bag of weed, slamming them into Mike's hand.

"They're yours," he said, his chilling tone threatening Mike without looking at him. I watched the dread register on Mike's face as he looked down at what he held. He glanced nervously between the teacher who was still descending on us and Kevin, then to me. It was a no-brainer for me. One look at Kevin and I would've taken my chances with the teacher.

I shouldn't have been surprised, but I was. Kevin had been showing such a different side to me when the guys weren't around, but I couldn't let myself forget what he was capable of.

"Messed up," I mumbled under my breath, and for the second time that day I saw his controlled anger fall into place.

They got busted. Kevin and I didn't because we didn't have anything on us. For once, I was thankful he'd been a jerk and had taken my smokes. Mike was suspended and grounded for a month because of the pot, but Brett and Jeremy got off easier because they only had smokes. Kevin explained to Mike later that he'd already been busted with weed twice, and that the third time meant juvie. I didn't buy it. I didn't think Kevin was ever stupid enough to get caught once, let alone twice. While Mike was locked away in his house, Kevin kept the flow of smokes, alcohol, and weed in full supply. By the time Mike had served his time, he wasn't holding any grudges.

***

The end-of-school party was at Kari's house, and Kevin didn't bother to show up. Everyone was so much more laid back without him around. Brett and I were even getting along okay. The best part of the night was having Jessica at my side.

Talk of being seniors and ruling the school dominated the conversations. At one point, Brett and Mike got into it about escargot. Brett swore up and down that people in France actually ate snails. Mike, of course, dared Brett to eat one and Brett went out in the backyard and actually found a handful of snails. He brought them back in and boiled the things. Then to everyone's disgust he plopped two on a cold piece of pizza and ate them, shell and all. It was completely disgusting, and he had everyone rolling with laughter.

The beers went down smoothly, and Jessica and I smoked a joint together. It was such an easy night, no tension, no walking around afraid of pissing Kevin off. At the same time, I knew I wouldn't have any of this without him. He could have just as easily cast me out, since he'd made me part of this group in the first place.

"What's wrong, sweetie?" Jessica asked, lacing her fingers around my neck.

"Nothing." I smiled for emphasis. "Just thinking about next year. It's gonna be great."

"Hey, I was thinking," she began, then hesitated. "Don't take this the wrong way, but I think I want to see other people." My heart stopped in my chest.

"What? Why?"

"No, I mean, I still want to see you but, you know, we're young. I'm not really the 'settle down' kinda girl. I'd like to be open to dating other people."

"Is there someone else?"

"No, silly, but you know me. Free love and all that. Life's so beautiful and there're so many people we can share our hearts with. I just don't want to limit either of us to only each other. I'm completely into you…"

"You mean, like an open relationship or something?"

"Yeah, exactly."

"Wow!" I laughed. I never thought I'd be having this

conversation with a girl. Wasn't it always the guy who wanted to do that kind of thing?

"I've been upfront with you all along," Jessica continued. "I don't want to ever settle down with one person. It's just not me. I still want to see you, but I just want to make sure you know that I'm going to keep seeing other people as well. I'm going to let my heart be open to everyone, not just you."

"I get it. I guess I'm cool with it," I said, surprising myself. I'd always been attracted to her open spirit. She was kind and loving towards everyone, and I liked that. Who was I to try to take that away from her?

"Good!" she said, smiling broadly. "Then I say we disappear for a while." She tugged at my hands, pulling me up off the couch. Leading me into a spare bedroom, she kissed me lightly as we fell onto the bed together, but when she tugged at my shirt, I threaded my hands through hers, guiding them away.

"Why won't you ever take your shirt off?"

"I've told you, self-conscious."

"But, it's me. Are you going to leave it on the whole time?" The way she said it made me think she was talking about going all the way. I wondered if she meant she wanted to. I couldn't take my shirt off, not with what my dad had left.

"Is that a condition?" I asked, scared of what she'd say.

"No, of course not. I won't make you, but maybe one day?" She smiled shyly and I kissed her again, my mouth tasting hers. I took things slowly, simply kissing her until she started to pull herself closer to me, curving her body into mine. I slid myself on top of her, gently resting my weight on my arms while my hands slowly pulled at her shirt, making sure she was really okay with what I wanted. She sat up a little, letting me take her shirt off for her. She really was beautiful. I tried not to be nervous, paying attention to what she seemed to like. I pulled up short when a random thought about confiding this moment to Jason crowded into my mind, but Jessica started on my pants, and as soon as her hands found me, I was lost in her touch.

Nine...

Rick

My phone lit up with a text message. *Happy 4th of fucking July. I'm waiting out front.*

I groaned. I'd told them all I wasn't feeling well. I stared at my bedroom door, wondering what would happen if I threw my phone at it. I imagined my cell exploding with the force of impact, spraying dozens of pieces around my room. I could tell Kevin I hadn't seen his text, but that daydream lasted about a second; he'd know I was lying.

Now! My phone lit up again. Barefooted, wearing only boxers and a t-shirt, I yanked open my door and went out front where Kevin was waiting in his dad's car. He was alone. I leaned down, resting my elbows on the passenger-side door.

"Get in."

"I'm sick."

He tapped his fingers on the steering wheel impatiently.

"The hell you are. Go get your fucking shoes."

"Kevin."

"Not taking no."

"Really?" I asked irritably.

"Your dad's on one. I could tell when I was over the other day. You gotta get outta there. And aren't Sylvia and Emma at her mom's? You shouldn't be alone with him."

"Seriously, today's not good."

He looked out the driver's window. I noticed that his fingers had stopped tapping and now his knuckles were turning white as he wrapped them around the steering wheel. He wasn't taking no for an answer. I stood up and looked up to the sky. Maybe he could help me. If I went with him, I wouldn't be alone and that had its advantages. But I didn't know if I could really pull things off. I leaned back down.

"Fine! But no questions."

He stared at me for several seconds before nodding. I ran back to the house and got dressed, not bothering to let my dad know I was leaving. He wasn't around, and I doubted he'd show his face on this of all days. I wasn't surprised that his levels of avoidance had been increasing for the last few weeks.

"You now have plans for tonight," Kevin said as I got into the car.

"Fine. Whatever it is, we're getting messed up."

"Really?" he smiled. "I had a friend text me the other day and I may just be able to get what you need."

"Yeah, and what's that?" I asked, still pissed he'd made me come along.

"It's a surprise. All I'll say is that you'll be one happy motherfucker if things work out." He pushed a speed-dial number on his phone and brought it to his ear. I listened to his side of the conversation, trying to figure out what he had in mind. "It's me. Yeah, about that text the other day...enough for two will do. Okay, when? See you then." He hung up the call. "Looks like you're in luck."

"What're you getting?"

"I told you, it's a surprise."

"Whatever."

"Anxious much?" he asked, glancing at me as he sped through a yellow light.

"No questions."

He shook his head. "Fine."

About twenty minutes later, we arrived at an apartment complex. He turned in and wound his way through the cramped streets, backing his car into a spot.

"Wait here."

"Why?"

"Don't have to tell ya, do I?" He hated questions as much as I did. "The guy's paranoid. So stay," he offered.

"Just don't take forever," I said, not wanting to be left alone with my thoughts for long.

"So, what if I do?" he said, slamming the door shut without waiting for my reply. I wouldn't put it past him to take longer just to piss me off.

I was immediately overcome with thoughts of Jason again. I couldn't believe it had already been two years! *Knock it off*, I told myself. Just get whatever Kevin brings back and forget about things. I opened the car door and stepped outside to smoke, telling myself to hold it together.

I watched the clock impatiently, walking in circles around the car, checking the clock at each pass. Twenty-three minutes later he emerged from the complex with a smile, strolling to the car like he had all the time in the world. I took a deep breath and resisted starting something with him.

"So?" I asked a little too anxiously as he slid into the car. He tossed me a plastic bag of what looked like a bunch of dead sticks and leaves. "What's this?" I asked, annoyed. Was this some kind of joke?

"Shrooms. You'll like 'em."

"Fine."

"You're on one today."

"I warned you."

"That you did."

"There's not a lot here." I said, playing with the bag.

"Enough for two."

"Not going to call the guys over?"

"Not tonight. Not really in the mood to deal with them. Are you?"

"No. How long do they take to kick in?" I asked while examining the bag.

"Thirty minutes or so, maybe forty-five."

"Should we get started?"

He laughed. "Be my guest. Just have to warn you, though. They literally taste like shit. We should stop and grab some beer for a chaser."

"And how do you plan on buying it?"

"The same way I always do, my fake ID."

"What? Since when?"

"Since always." He smiled again. He was doing that more and more when the others weren't around, the smiling thing. I was glad he was in a good mood. I couldn't really handle jerk Kevin on top of what I was dealing with.

As soon as we left the gas station, I cracked open the beer and asked, "So what? Just eat 'em?"

"Yeah, eat half the bag. Really chew it until it dissolves in your mouth. I'll eat the rest."

I reached in and pulled out a piece. "It looks just like a dead stick. Are you sure this is part of 'em?"

He laughed again, "Yeah, I'm sure. Now eat."

I expected it to taste like dirt, but it didn't. It literally tasted like dried-up cow dung. Not that I'd had cow dung before, but I was sure that if it had a taste, it would be that of shrooms. "This is awful," I gagged. "You weren't kidding!"

"I told you so. Now make sure to chew it until there's nothing left."

"Seriously? This is brutal. I don't think I can take half this bag."

"Yes, you can," he said simply.

I closed my eyes and focused on chewing. It took a lot of concentration to get the stuff down. My mouth felt like a sandbox, but it tasted much worse than sand ever could. By the time I finished my portion of the bag, I'd gone through three beers just to get it all down. I had a nice little buzz going, which I was sure would only help the effects of the shrooms.

"So, is your dad going to be around tonight? I'd rather party at your place. My father is in town," Kevin said as he turned into our neighborhood.

"I'm not sure. Most likely not. If he shows, we could always bolt and go someplace else." If last year was any indicator, I knew my dad would be out drinking somewhere. Sylvia knew this too, and had decided to give him his space by going to her parents' house for the holiday. She didn't want Emma's 4th of July ruined by the memories she knew would be haunting me and my dad.

By the time we'd settled in front of my TV with the video games, I'd begun to get impatient waiting for the shrooms to kick in.

"Are you feeling anything yet?" Kevin asked me.

"Nope," I replied. "So, how will I know?"

"It's mellow. You'll know"

The first signs that they were working were the fuzzy lines spreading off the objects on the TV. Eventually, everything got fuzzy and colorful around the edges. I'd heard people talking about seeing energy and auras, and I was sure this was what I was seeing; however, a low level of anxiety settled over my body as the intensity of the high eased into my mind, and the force of Jason's absence grew stronger. This was not good. Shrooms weren't supposed to make me feel more. They were supposed to erase the pain.

"So how you feeling?" Kevin asked.

"This is so cool! I love these," I lied, then laughed, trying to sound more sincere. I hoped it didn't sound as forced to him as it felt to me. Every so often he'd ask me something or say something. I prayed he'd shut up because it became increasingly difficult to push Jason from my head. The more Kevin talked, the more my mind started to fracture and allow Jason in.

"How long do these last?" I finally asked after an hour or so. Was I going to be able to pretend all night?

"I don't know, four to six hours maybe. Depends on how good they are. These ones seem pretty good, so I'd say closer to six."

There was no way I was going to last six hours. I thought of going to the bathroom to make myself throw up, wanting to get rid of anything left in my stomach before my body absorbed it. The more I thought about it the more it seemed like a good idea, and I was about ready to do it when I realized I'd actually eaten the shrooms nearly two hours ago, so I was pretty sure they'd all been digested. Instead, I focused on the game. *I can do this*, I told myself. I'd been through much worse and been fine.

I'd heard that freaking out could send another person on a bad trip, and the last thing I needed was an unpredictable Kevin flying into a rage. Tears kept threatening as the night of Jason's death flashed through my mind.

Knock it off! It's the drugs, I thought. I knew I just had to get through the next few hours and everything would be fine. Once the drugs wore off, I could go to bed and sleep it off. Meanwhile I needed to hold it together. Thousands of people had bad trips. They all got through it, and so could I. I told myself that my body was just reacting to the chemicals, that it wasn't permanent.

I gripped the game controller and focused as things grew more intense, fading in and out on the game while I battled with the memories of Jason that filled my mind. I couldn't let Kevin see that this was killing me. As we came up on the third hour of my nightmare, he rose to reset a frozen system and I panicked as a picture of Jason drew his attention to the top of the entertainment center. *Ignore it*, I silently pleaded with him, but he picked it up and I stopped breathing.

"Who's this? I've never seen this before," he said.

"No one. Can we start the game?" I asked desperately.

"You have a picture of a stranger displayed in your living room? Who is it? He kinda looks like you. A cousin?"

"No. My brother."

His head snapped in my direction. "What? Your brother? I had no idea you had a brother. Where is he?"

"It's not a big deal. Let's just play the game," I said. Kevin had no idea what he was doing.

"Why are you acting all sketchy?" he asked, sitting down next to me.

"I'm not acting like anything. I just don't want to talk about it. Okay? You promised, no questions."

"I never said I promise."

"Kevin, just drop it." I said as tears pooled in my eyes. "I don't want to talk about it."

"Hey, what's wrong with you?" he asked gently. His kindness opened the floodgate, and images of that night rushed into my head as the tears started to pour down my face. I ran towards the bathroom, my stomach clenching and cramping. I lost it right before the toilet and everything came up in the middle of the floor as I collapsed, crying hysterically. It was too much.

My cell phone was ringing on the nightstand and the insistent tone brought me out of my sleep. I tried to ignore it, but whoever was calling kept calling back. Fumbling around in the darkness, I knocked the phone to the floor. I pried open my eyes so I could see the light from the display and grabbed for it.

"Hello," I said, disoriented.

"Hey, buddy, it's me."

"Jason?"

"I'm so drunk," he half laughed and half slurred.

"What?" Why would he be calling me at — I opened my eyes and squinted at the clock — four in the morning?

"I'm drunk," he repeated, sounding as if he was relaying the punch line of a joke.

"I can tell. Umm, it's four in the morning. Is there something you need?" I asked in confusion.

"Yeah, silly, Too drunk to drive. Come get me."

"Jas, you know I can't. I don't have my license. You know that."

"It's okay. I taught you. You can do it." I had heard him drunk before, but I had never heard him like this.

"Jas, I don't know — "

"Shhh!" he said loudly over the phone. "On the phone with little bro." He was obviously talking to the people at the party. "Wait, Rick? Going outside. Hold on, don't let me go." Several moments later, he came on the line again. I'd almost fallen back to sleep. I'd gone to bed after one, and three hours of sleep just wasn't cutting it. "You can come get me, right?"

"You're serious, aren't you? You really need me to come?" I asked, dreading the idea.

"Duh, I wouldn't call..." He trailed off, distracted by something.

I sat up, turning on the lamp by my bed and squeezing my eyes shut at the harshness of the light. "Jason?" No answer.

"Jason?" I said more firmly.

"Yeah, yeah, I'm here. You should see this girl. She's dancing. Wow! Hey, can you come get me?"

"Jason," I paused, trying to figure out what to say. I really didn't want to go get him. But on the other hand he'd never called me for a ride, so he must really need one. I sighed, "Fine, where are you?"

"Take dad's car. I think his keys are — "

"I know where his keys are Jas. Can you tell me where you are?"

"Hmmm," he started to laugh. "You know I really don't know. That's funny. Should be something I know, huh little bro?"

"Can you find out?"

"High school maybe, maybe by your guitar lesson place. Gosh, I think I'm lost!" he giggled. "Guitar! How's that going anyway?"

"What? My classes? They're fine, Jas. You know that. Is there someone sober I can talk to?"

"Why? Why can't you speak to me? You know you love you right? I mean, I love you, right?"

"I know Jason, just let me talk to someone who knows where you are so I can come get you."

"Right. Right. Yeah, okay. Hold on."

Several minutes later I realized the phone line was dead, so I called him back.

"Where'd you go?" he slurred.

"Did you find someone?" I asked.

"Someone what? Are you coming for me?"

"Jason," I said patiently. "Let me talk to someone who knows where you are." I laughed at how funny he was being.

"Oh, yeah, right." I heard him asking around for someone who could give me directions, and he finally located a nice girl who politely told me how to get there. I jotted the directions down and asked to talk with Jason again. It seemed he had wandered off, and it took her some time to find him. Finally, he returned to the phone.

"Hey, little bro. What you doin'?"

"I'm on my way, Jas. I should be there in about twenty-five minutes. You good until then?"

"Sure! I'm happy right now."

I hung up and slipped into the jeans I'd worn the day before, grabbed one of my t-shirts, which actually used to be Jason's, and threw it on. Within a few minutes, I was on my way. He'd been right about being close to my guitar classes, so I wasn't too worried about finding my way.

The party was still in full swing when I got there. I guessed this was what happened when a bunch of high school kids got together on the 4th of July without any supervision. I had to park more than a block away because there were so many cars there.

As I approached the house, I noticed he was out on the front lawn wrestling with some of his buddies. It didn't surprise me that even in his drunken state he was still able to stay on top of them. I stopped and watched him, overcome with what could best be described as pride, seeing him as others saw him. Even drunk, he was kind and considerate to everyone there. He was obviously the life of the party. Being surrounded with good-looking guys and gorgeous girls didn't seem to even faze him. I couldn't imagine his life. I wasn't jealous of him; I just wondered what it'd be like. Girls there seemed to adore him, and he treated each of them as if they were special to him. He truly cared for everyone he came into contact with.

He spotted me and half jogged, half stumbled in my direction. "Hey, Rick. What you doin' here?"

I laughed as he wrapped his arms around me in a big hug. He was never scared to show people that he loved me. "I came to get you, you fool. Are you ready?"

"Sure." Without looking behind him he raised his arm, waved and shouted. "Later everyone, brother's here to carry me home."

"Jas, shh," I laughed. "It's after 4:30 in the morning. People are sleeping."

"Right." He laughed with me. He raised his arm again and whispered very quietly, "Later, guys."

"Come on, you drunk." I said wrapping my arm around his waist to help balance and guide him to the car."

After much conversation I could barely understand, I settled him into the car. Once we were on the road he said, "Think I might be sick, better close my eyes."

"Go ahead."

"You are the greatest brother in the world. I'm so lucky. I love you!"

"I'm lucky, too, Jason. And I love you as well. Now close your eyes," I said, smiling at him.

He patted me on my arm and leaned towards the window with his eyes closed. I marveled at how amazing he was, but concerns of him going off to college and leaving me alone with my dad and Sylvia troubled my mind. I watched the road carefully, paying attention to the other cars and the freeway exits flying by. Finally arriving at our exit, I pulled onto the stretch of road leading to our neighborhood. As I gained speed I glanced in the rearview mirror for any cops. The last thing I wanted was to be pulled over without a license. As I brought my eyes back to the main road a brown flash flooded the headlights. My mind grasped that it was some type of animal just as I gripped the steering wheel and yanked it to the left, bracing myself by slamming my foot down, which hit the gas and the car sped up. I cranked the wheel to the right, trying to gain control.

I heard Jason say, "What the hell...?" just as the car spun and flipped.

I was screaming.

"Rick! Rick! Relax," someone was commanding me. I twisted, turned, and yanked away from the hands gripping me.

"Jason! Jason!" I screamed.

"Rick, it's Kevin. Relax."

"Where is he? Where is he?"

"Shhh, open your eyes."

"No! He's not dead! No!" I yelled as I squeezed my eyes shut. I couldn't open them and see Jason's bloody body lying on the street.

"Rick, open your eyes. Come back to me. It's Kevin. You're okay. Rick!"

His tone was harsh and the fear in it startled me. I blinked several times, and Kevin came into focus. I was lying on my bathroom floor and he was straddling me, gripping my wrists. I pushed him off and curled up on my side. The tears wouldn't stop.

"He's dead. I killed him," I sobbed. Kevin moved closer, and I felt him tentatively lay a hand on my back. He remained silent as I cried, unable to control the wrenching waves of pain.

Ten...

Kevin

What the holy fuck was that? A brother? A goddamn brother? It explained everything, but how the hell had I missed it?

Shit, one second I'd been completely shrooming, and the next Rick was lying in a pile of vomit, screaming. I had no idea what the fuck I was supposed to do. I'd climbed on top of him, and was just about to punch him to try to get him to snap out of it when he came back.

Between his sobs, I pieced together the events leading to Jason's death. I now understood what had prompted the move to Utah. The idea that Sylvia was jealous of Rick's mom had never set well with me and this made more sense, but when he started talking about how his dad blamed him for Jason's death and how he felt it really was his fault, I had to stop him.

"That's some pretty heavy shit, Rick, but it's not your fucking fault. It was a goddamn accident!" I snarled at him, angrier than intended. I felt murderous rage towards his dad but not him. Somehow, I'd gotten him in the shower and cleaned up. For the first time in my life, I wasn't thinking about sex when I was with a naked guy. Then, against my better fucking judgment, I actually laid down with him and held him as he cried. As soon as he passed out, I was up and out of his bed like a goddamn cheetah.

Needing to get shitfaced, I did one of the most fucked up things I'd ever done in my life—I left Rick alone. Any normal person would've considered the fact that his dad was sure to come home drunk, looking to take out his pain on the person he held responsible for the death of his favorite son. But the tugging at my heart and the foreign feelings of compassion and concern made me want to get away from Rick as fast as fucking possible. There was no way in hell I was going to spare a second thought on him, although every cell in my body screamed that he was the only thing I should be considering.

After checking in with my father, I nursed a bottle of whiskey while I waited for him to go to bed. As soon as he was out for the night I called a cab. The ride to Normandy was annoyingly long since I was itching to get fucked up. Every muscle in my body tensed as I fought the images of Rick screaming in a crumpled heap on his bathroom floor. The animalistic suffering that had escaped from him rattled the fuck out of me. What fucked with me the most was the fact that I hadn't seen it coming, and that was a goddamn problem.

Franko sent a shot my way the moment I walked in the door, and it must have been written all over me because he ordered up two more without asking.

"Be careful tonight," he cautioned as I went on the prowl.

The club party eventually moved to the house of a guy named Danny, where I ended up dancing with some little twink named Charlie. It took under five minutes to get him into a bedroom where I fucked him with more anger than I'd had in years. I took it slow at first, gauging his reactions, but the more violent I got the more he seemed to get into things. I had picked the right guy for the kind of night I needed. I got him off several times for every one time I got off, but I wasn't there to get off. I was there to fucking hurt someone, and Charlie was more than happy to play the part for me.

Rick

"Time to wake up, you worthless piece of shit," my dad slurred, tearing me abruptly out of my restless sleep. I rolled away from him, instantly covering my head for protection. As my knee slammed into the wall I had time to briefly consider the fact that Kevin was no longer lying next to me. Then, I felt my dad's hands grasp at my body, hauling the blankets and me out of my bed. He dragged me out of my room, and I was thankful I hadn't realized his intention to throw me down the stairs or I might have braced myself and broken several bones. I landed and skidded to a halt at the bottom as he stumbled down after me, clearly not done.

He picked me up and spun me around, slamming a backhand across my face. He didn't release my arm, and the full force of it propelled my head back. Blow after brutal blow followed. *He must be getting tired. He must be close to stopping*, I thought. I tried to focus my mind on something other than the torture. Kevin wasn't scared of anything. He wouldn't let anyone do this to him. How would he handle it? I had to learn to take it, to not let it bother me. I had to be stronger than my dad's fists. It was temporary and would be over soon.

At the same time, my mind fought to embrace the torture. I'd killed Jason. I deserved this—the taste of blood in my mouth, the smell of my dad's cologne (the smell was nice; I think Jason had worn it), the smell of alcohol, the same way Jason had smelled when I'd picked him up at the party. It all kept coming back to Jason. I was in a ball on the floor, trying to disappear, and he kept picking me up to give himself a larger target to hit. He held all my weight since my legs couldn't manage the task. *This isn't happening to me*, I thought. Things were spinning and I was brought back to the suffering. My mouth was watering. I could taste the blood but didn't know if it was coming from inside my mouth or from some cut on my face. Everything was out of focus. I felt like I was about to throw up. He shook me hard, and I focused again, misery screaming from my throbbing body.

He slammed me against the wall. "You deserve to die for what you did."

I couldn't argue with him.

"I should kill you!"

And I wished he would. He raged at me, then shoved me into the wall again. My head exploded with agony and little lights immediately flashed throughout the room. Then the anguish slowly started to disappear. I wondered if Jason had seen little lights as he died.

My dad was gone and I was on the floor in the kitchen. One of my eyes wouldn't open and the other was swollen shut. The taste of blood was still in my mouth, salty and metallic like a penny. He must have cooked something to eat because the air in the kitchen smelled greasy. I couldn't move, and for a moment I wondered if I'd been paralyzed by his brutality, but then I realized my body simply didn't want to embrace the fire raging through my limbs. I gritted my teeth and let the tears come, as I forced myself to crawl to my phone. It was lying on the coffee table where I'd left it while playing video games with Kevin. It was hard to believe that had only been a few hours ago. I had to get out of the house. I stretched my arm as far as I could, trying to reach the phone, but the pain wouldn't allow it. I had to sit up more. Finally, I was able to clench my fist around it and I gasped for breath, waiting for my body to handle the daggers it was sending out. Through one squinted eye I dialed Kevin's number.

"Yeah?" he answered, sounding tired.

"It's me," I forced out.

"Yeah?" he said again.

I swallowed hard, but the words wouldn't come.

"Rick? You there?"

"Help," I breathed out, unsure if the word actually made it out of my mouth.

"You okay? Rick?"

I was getting dizzy again and I felt myself starting to fall, my body screaming as I hit the floor.

Someone shook my shoulder lightly and I recoiled

before I heard Kevin's mumbled, "Fuck." I opened my eyes and closed them again. Lights flashed and faded.

"Get me out of here." Again, I wasn't sure if I was actually talking or just thinking the words. Things began to spin again and I felt myself slipping. I heard him calling my name from far away as I struggled to stay with him. But he was gone.

It still hurt. I woke to a dull ache, but the pain was not as bad as I'd expected. Where was I? I focused my eyes in the darkness and saw Kevin in a chair next to wherever it was I was lying. His arms were folded across his chest and his head was bowed, his dark hair covering his face from my sight. From the soft snores escaping his mouth, I knew he was asleep. I realized I was in his room and it was dark. I searched for a clock and found one; it was 11:17 PM. I shifted in the bed, trying to sit upright, and my movement startled Kevin. His eyes shot open, and he immediately looked at his door, then to me. He quickly looked around the room, gathering his bearings, then relaxed back into his chair.

"How ya feelin'?" he asked, wiping the sleep from his eyes.

"Better than I thought I would."

"Yeah, I've kept you pretty drugged up."

"How'd we get here?"

"You don't remember?"

"No," I said, trying to piece together my last memories. "I think I remember calling you. Did I?"

"Yeah, you did."

"When was that?"

"In the middle of the fucking night."

I looked at the clock again, "It's only eleven."

"Last night."

"I've been here all day?"

"Yeah."

"Your dad?" I asked.

"Left town this afternoon. He'll be back day after tomorrow."

"How'd I get here?" I repeated.

"I came and got you. Brought you back," he said shortly.

"My dad?"

"Passed the fuck out when I got to your house. Good thing. I didn't want to have to fuck him up to get you out of there."

"But how? How did we get here? I don't remember anything."

"You were pretty out of it, but we managed. Wasn't easy, but," he paused, "well, I had to get you away from him."

"Did you have help?"

"No."

"You got me up here by yourself?" I couldn't seem to concentrate on any of the real issues, focusing instead on how I had gotten to his house.

"It's not that big of a deal. You hungry?" he asked, getting up from his chair.

"No, not so much."

"I'm gonna make me something. You sure?"

"Yeah, I'm fine."

When he came back he had two grilled cheese sandwiches.

"Figured you might want this anyway," he said, putting the plate down on the nightstand.

"Thanks," I said, still not much interested in eating. "I could use a smoke."

"Think you can manage getting outside? Here, take a few shots first. It'll help numb ya up a bit." After tipping his flask back a couple of times, I hesitated as he reached down for my elbow. "Let me help you," he commanded at my resistance. I felt a flash of anger at having to depend on him. However, my legs weakened and the room spun as soon as I stood and he reached out to steady me with both hands. "Sure you can make it?"

"Yeah, I'll be fine. Just go slow." He led me down the hallway and through the basement living room.

"Hold on to the couch," he said as he unlocked the door leading outside. He pushed open the attached screen door and propped it open before returning to help me.

"So, why is it that you always seem to be coming to my rescue?" I asked once he had me settled in a patio chair. My lips were both swollen, and dragging on the smoke made me conscious of just how much my dad had messed me up.

I noticed, not for the first time, how Kevin made sure to hold the cigarette far from his body, letting the slight breeze blow the smoke away from him. I figured this was a trick he used to minimize the smell of smoke on his clothes. The crickets chirped in chorus around us as I stared at the stars, waiting for him to answer.

"No rescue would've been needed this time, if I hadn't left you there in the first place," he said slowly. "I should've known your dad would be gunning for you after the shit you told me."

"Not your fault."

"Still."

"And what would you've done? Finding you in my room in the middle of the night would've only made it worse."

"I should've gotten you out of there," he mumbled.

"Knock it off," I said irritably.

"What?"

"I mean, I can't quite figure out what you're after. Don't take this wrong, but you're an ass."

His eyes narrowed a little as he glanced sideways at me. A warning? I had a feeling he wouldn't nail me in my condition, so I proceeded. "I mean, you're not one to really care much about others."

"And who says I care about you?"

"Then why get all bent about leaving me alone?"

"I'm not all bad."

"But you're not....good." I stammered.

"Well, Rick," he took a long drag on his smoke, "I know a thing or two about keeping secrets."

"Yeah, and what are you hiding?"

"They wouldn't be secrets if I told you, now would they?" he said, his voice calm, not betraying anything.

"Well, you know mine."

"And you won't know mine." He flicked his smoke and reached out for my arm again to help me back inside.

"I'm fine," I said, pulling away from him.

He turned and walked away with a shrug, leaving me to regret my insistence on independence. Slowly and painfully, I eventually made it into his room. He sprayed some cologne on me as I walked in, masking the smell of smoke on me almost completely. I was thankful my dad drank and smoked because I didn't have to work as hard keeping it from him. "You're staying here for a few days," he commanded.

"Thanks, but I can't."

"You can and you will."

"Your dad—"

"Doesn't have to know. Drop it. I need sleep."

And with that the conversation was over. He settled back in his chair, leaving the bed for me, and closed his eyes.

He left me alone a lot; I slept and took whatever pills he threw at me. Kevin had had the sense to grab my phone and charger, but my dad never called.

On the next night, he came in with some weed. "Feeling up to getting high?"

"Sure."

He lit up the joint and some incense to mask the smell of the pot, which was much easier to disguise than cigarette smoke. I figured that's why it was okay in his mind to smoke weed in his house but he insisted we smoke normal cigarettes outside.

"Feeling better?"

"Yeah, think I can go home now. Still sore, but nothing I can't handle."

"What if he comes at you again?"

"I don't think he will. I think he'll lay off for a while."

"That's stupid thinking. It could get you killed," he said irritably.

"Well, if I don't think that way then I'll be too scared to ever go home, and we can't have that."

"Kevin?" I heard his dad holler from upstairs, followed by footsteps.

"Fuck, he's home early." Kevin threw the joint out the window, slamming it shut as he did. He then turned and shoved me towards his closet while he sprayed some air freshener. We heard footsteps on the stairs.

"Get in here and shut up."

His dad threw open the door of his bedroom just as the closet door swung towards me but didn't latch. Kevin whirled around. Through the open crack I could see the back of Kevin's dark shirt as he stepped away from the closet.

"Shit!" I heard him say quietly.

"I asked you to mow the lawn while I was gone."

"Sir, I didn't expect you until tomorrow."

"So you wait until the last minute? That is not very smart."

"I will do better." Kevin backed up closer to the closet door.

"Empty promises do not mean anything in this house. You screw up, you deal with the consequences." He took a deep breath and his voice came out low and controlled. "Move!"

I heard Kevin's sharp intake of breath.

"Sir, please. I'm sorry. I'll go do it right now."

"Excuse me?" his dad asked. I couldn't see him as Kevin was still standing with his back to the closet, but I could hear his voice getting closer. "I said move. Do not make me say it again!"

"Sir, please." Kevin repeated, his voice pleading. It unnerved me to hear his tone so out of character for him, so close to begging. Suddenly, he was yanked away from the closet and I saw his dad throw him against the wall. I grasped my hands over my mouth, not breathing as I stumbled backwards into his clothes, desperately trying to still myself so not to alert Kevin's dad to my presence.

"Why do you insist on making this harder?"

His dad laughed and it scared me more than any of his words had. It also frightened me that I'd seen this side of Kevin often, and I thought I knew what followed.

His dad pushed him against the wall face first. It reminded me of a scene in a movie where some guy's getting arrested and has to put his hands on the wall. Kevin separated his feet and bowed his head. From where I was I could see how he carefully spread each one of his fingers.

"Good boy."

His dad took his time unbuckling his belt and pulled it loose from his pant loops. He wrapped the end around his palm twice, tugging at it for a good grip and letting the buckle end go so it swung and settled heavily on the floor next to his shoes. He stood there for several moments, and I could see Kevin's shoulders rising and falling slowly. As his dad pulled his arm up, I pressed myself hard against the back of the closet and closed my eyes. This couldn't be happening, not to Kevin. I expected screaming, but all I heard was the belt hitting him and the whistle of his breath as he pulled it in through gritted teeth. The sound of it slicing through the air sent terrible images of my dad beating me ripping through my head. My dad held onto the buckle end, which made sharp, cracking noises, but Kevin's dad slammed the heavy buckle into his body, replacing the crack with a dull thump. I opened my tear-filled eyes just as Kevin collapsed and fell to the floor on one knee. His dad didn't stop.

"Next time, get it done," his dad finally said coldly. He was putting his belt back on as he walked out the door and shut it behind him. I waited until I heard the TV turn on upstairs. Wiping the tears from my face I took a deep breath and pushed the door slowly open, moving cautiously towards him. He was still kneeling on the floor by the wall as I came up behind him.

"Give me a minute." His voice was harsh and strained. He looked at me, and I was surprised to see that there weren't any tears on his face, only the struggle for control.

"Fine, umm," I said, thinking of what he'd done for me the first time my dad hit me. "I'm going to get a damp towel in the bathroom."

He started to pull himself up. Again I was surprised at how quickly he was recovering from everything. It'd taken hours for me just to get myself moving that first night.

"Do you need help?"

"Please, no. Just go."

"I'll be in the bathroom."

The light flickered slightly as I walked into the bathroom attached to his room. I found a towel and ran some water on it. I knew how Kevin felt. The first time my dad hit me had rocked my world. The first had been the worst, so unexpected. I wondered what had finally pushed his dad to the breaking point. I knew I had to find a way to be there for Kevin the way he'd been there for me; however, there seemed to be something different with Kevin. I couldn't put my finger on it, but the idea flirted at the edge of my mind. What had happened just didn't feel the same as what my dad had done to me.

I turned as I heard him in the doorway, and the towel slipped from my hands. Having removed his shirt, Kevin stood stiffly, staring unapologetically at me. My eyes wandered over his bare arms and chest, taking in the images that refused to make sense. There were so many bruises, I couldn't tell where one began and another ended. His left shoulder was nearly black, while a giant bruise under his ribcage was yellowing around the edges. There were red circles and streaks appearing around his sides from the belt hitting him moments before. Then there were the scars—hundreds of little hair-like white wisps and bigger red, screaming ones, jagged and raw. At first I was confused what I saw before me, but then realization clenched down and solidified immediately. I'd assumed the beating had been his first, but the multitude of scars and bruises told a different story. How'd I miss the signs when I knew them so well myself? What could I possibly do or say to him? I noted the tears silently falling from his unwavering eyes. Kevin? Crying?

As soon as I met his eyes, he took a few steps towards me, grabbed my face roughly, and smashed his lips into mine. The first thing I felt was pain from the remnants of my own beating, then the realization of what he was doing. I shoved him away instantly, appalled by what he'd done. He fell against the wall and grimaced. With his head bowed, he slowly raised his eyes to mine. They were unlike anything I'd ever seen. There was such depth and openness that my heart started racing in my chest, and after several beats, I reached for him and returned his kiss. He desperately grabbed the back of my neck with both hands and pulled me into a more demanding embrace. I didn't think. I just reacted, moving my lips frantically against his. I pulled at his body, only thinking for a split second about his bruises as my hands ran across his rough and textured skin. My mind shut off and instinct took over, adrenaline and desire driving me towards him. He stopped abruptly and pulled slightly away from me, holding me firmly several inches from him as my body continued to gravitate to his. I saw in his eyes what I felt but couldn't explain. My breath hitched in rhythm with his. I wanted him to kiss me again, and I was equally repulsed by the idea. He dropped his hands to his sides, took a few slow steps backwards and turned away from me.

My first lucid thought was that I wanted to run away, to leave this room with the flickering light. In a daze, I instead took several steps into the steady light of his room just in time to see him pull his shirt carefully back over his head. As it fell around his shoulders and then to his waist, I watched as the colors of his pain disappeared. When I looked back up at his face, I didn't recognize the person looking back at me. What else didn't I know about him?

"Well?" he said shortly.

I honestly didn't know what to say to him. "Well what?"

"Fuck, Rick!" he said as his shoulders heaved. "Maybe you should leave." He turned and shoved open his bedroom window, clearly showing me my exit route.

For some reason, it was the last thing I expected him to do. It felt cold—like a rejection, even though I didn't know what he was rejecting me from.

"Why?"

"Unless you want to talk about my father beating the shit out of me or the fact that I just fucking kissed you and you liked it, then I think we should just call it a fucking night." He glared over at me and I felt my defenses kicking into place.

"What's your problem?" I shot, not able to comprehend what was happening.

"Jesus, Rick. This really isn't the fucking time to be challenging me!" he spat at me as he walked towards his bathroom. "I think you should leave now."

I was feeling angry and hurt all of a sudden.

"No!" I said, trailing after him.

He turned and cut his eyes at me as they darkened into several shades of cold.

"Out," he dismissed me.

Kevin

I shut the bathroom door behind me and locked it, half expecting him to follow. I gripped onto the sink, staring at myself in the mirror. My mind was reeling. I could feel my heart racing in my chest, and I felt like things might actually fucking explode. My fingers flexed around the edges of the sink, and I forced air into my lungs, counting, only half listening for Rick to make his exit. When I was sure he'd left, I went back into my room, found my stash of coke and laid out two lines, which I immediately chased with several shots of Wild Turkey. I counted, pushing any memory of the last few days away until I felt the effects. As soon as there was enough padding in my mind, I allowed myself to calmly sort through the facts.

There had been close calls in the past—nosey teachers, school counselors, even a few church leaders asking questions about the bruises. My father was smart. He'd only overdone it once and had to take me to the hospital, but that was after the first beating. Since then, he'd hidden things well, making sure to avoid my face and visible areas. What he did leave behind, I made sure to cover with clothes. Fucking long pants and shirts were a bitch in the summer, but not even close to the beatings I got after some fuckhead came around asking questions. People didn't want to believe what they suspected. A united front and a well-placed story from both of us did the trick with surprising ease. A few forged doctor's notes to keep me out of gym, and an unspoken agreement between the two of us to keep shit hidden had kept my secret safe, until now.

Rick knowing about my father was about the last thing in the world I'd wanted to have happen. I knew the second I'd seen his eyes after my father left that Rick thought this was the first time for me. I should've seen that as an opportunity and run with it. Instead, my stupid ass pride got in the fucking way. I couldn't stand the thought of him pitying me. I'd torn off my shirt and planned on playing it cool. I was going to march into the bathroom and prove to him that I could handle a few easy lashings of the belt, wanting him to see that it wasn't a big deal.

How the fuck I went from proving a point to fucking kissing him, I don't know. One minute he was trying to comprehend what he was seeing and the next he was looking at me like he fucking gave a shit. I hadn't even realized I'd started crying. I didn't cry. Even during the harshest of beatings, I rarely shed a tear. I especially never cried in front of another person. The second I felt the tears, I panicked and kissed him before I fucking thought it through. In that moment everything changed. I wanted him. I'd never seen it coming, but the second his lips sought mine, I felt my control beginning to slip. Stopping the heat between us had taken an amazing amount of self-restraint. Even after I ended the kiss, walking out of the bathroom was a desperate attempt to put some distance between us. I would've taken him to my bed right then if I hadn't walked away.

The point was that he knew the two biggest secrets of my life. Rick having that kind of power and control over me was nothing short of terrifying. I paced in my bedroom, knowing I had to figure out how the hell everything had gone to fucking shit. I laid out another line as I started to plan damage control.

Rick

My dad avoided me and I avoided Kevin. I'd come home after being gone for days, and my dad had glanced at me long enough to see the remnants of the thrashing he'd given me. I'd stood there staring at him, letting him see exactly what he'd done. I'd even thought of taking off my shirt like Kevin had to give further evidence, but after several moments he'd averted his eyes and taken great care to avoid any contact as he escaped from the kitchen.

Unfortunately, Kevin didn't give up as easily. I was disgusted with what had happened between the two of us, and I blamed my response to his kiss on everything leading up to it. I hadn't been in my right mind. Just the thought of it made my stomach turn, bringing on a bout of nausea.

There was a part of me that felt guilty for not reaching out to him. He'd been around for me so often after run-ins with my dad, and a small part of me felt like I should be there for him. But every time I thought about what his dad was doing, I ended up thinking about what Kevin had done. How he'd kissed me.

There was a part of me that knew it was dangerous to ignore him, and I knew him well enough to know that my house was no safe haven from him. It'd take Kevin very little effort to track me down and corner me. When he did, I wasn't sure what I expected him to do, but whatever it was, I didn't want any part of it.

Only hours after I'd returned home, I called Jessica.

"Hey, stranger, where you been?" she asked cheerfully.

"Yeah, I know. I've kinda been lame about keeping in touch."

"No biggie, it's who you are. You know it's cool by me. Remember, no strings." My heart hurt a little when she said this. I felt like I was taking advantage of her sometimes—just hooking up when it worked out. But then the thought of Kevin's lips on mine pushed into my memory, and I glowered at the ceiling over my bed.

We did the small-talk thing. I asked her how her summer was going and she told me about a new deck of tarot cards she'd gotten. As usual, she didn't ask a lot about what I was up to. It'd always been that way. I think she knew that if I wanted to share, I would. Finally, the real reason I called couldn't be avoided.

"So hey, I need a favor, and feel free to say no, but it would help me out a ton," I said, carefully avoiding the need to lie. "You see, I kinda messed with the wrong guy and I'm worried he's gonna come looking for me." I knew the bruises my dad left would lead her in the direction I wanted without actually lying. "I know your parents are in Cape Cod right now. Would you mind if I crashed at your place for a few days?" I didn't have to hold my breath for long.

"Sure, no problem. When will you be here?"

"Jessica, this is kinda a big deal. Are you sure?"

"You've never asked me for anything, Rick. If you need this, it must be serious."

"It is. But what about your parents? Will they find out?"

"I'll think of something. Don't worry 'bout them."

I was stunned into silence, not quite believing she would've granted my request so easily.

"Rick, you there?"

"Yeah," I said, biting back my emotions.

"Listen, it's no biggie. Just come on up when you're ready. I'll see you soon."

I heard the line go dead, and I sat there holding my phone for several seconds before slipping it into my pocket.

I'd just finished packing my bag for Jessica's when I heard Sylvia return home with Emma. As usual, Emma came barreling into my room with excitement, coming up short when she saw the bruises and cuts on my face.

"Hey schmunchkin!" I said, swooping her up in a hug while ignoring the soreness the best I could. She resisted only a little, pulling back to look into my eyes.

"What happened?" she asked with concern.

"Nothing, honey, I'm okay. Just got in a little car accident." The lie came so much easier than I'd expected. "I'm going to be just fine." She eyed me cautiously, not sure if she wanted to believe me. I smiled at her, trying to reassure her that things were going to be okay. "Tell me how Grandma and Grandpa's was," I said, changing the subject as I dropped her down gently onto my bed.

"I missed you," she sighed, accepting my reassurances.

"I missed you too, but I bet you got to watch some fun fireworks."

After a fairly lengthy description of her weeklong adventure and a bout of tickle torture accompanied by wild giggles, I broke the news to her that I was going to stay with a friend for a few days. At her look of sadness I promised I'd call her every night before bedtime. Sylvia interrupted us moments later, asking Emma to go say hello to our dad.

After Emma left, Sylvia paused for a moment at the sight of me before asking, "Another fight?" with a slight edge to her tone.

"No, a car accident." I said flatly.

"Uh huh," she commented as if she didn't believe me—and she shouldn't have. "Anyway, I'm not sure what's going on with you and your dad, but you really need to try harder not to upset him." She continued on without showing any concern about my make-believe car accident. "The last thing he needs right now is you going off on one of your rebellions."

"What are you even talking about?" I asked, barely holding back my anger. Even if she was stupid enough not to see what was going on, how could she launch right into a lecture after seeing the condition I was in?

"He's drinking more and I know you're not helping the situation. Just stay out of his way, okay? Just let him be. You've done enough."

"Yeah, not a problem." I said, grabbing my overnight bag. "I'll stay out of his way. Let him know I'll be home when I'm home." I stepped around her and took the stairs two at a time, not able to get out of my house fast enough.

Although I went out the front door, I immediately went around the side of the house to the backyard. I had to be incredibly careful to avoid being seen by Kevin, which meant I stayed off the street and went through all the backyards on the way to Jessica's. I was counting on the fact that Kevin wouldn't think I'd be stupid enough to move in with his next-door neighbor while trying to avoid him. Also, asking my somewhat girlfriend to crash at her place while her parents were out of town took more balls than I think he gave me credit for.

The next several days were some of the easiest and most relaxed days I'd had in years. We stayed up late talking about the most random things and never seemed to run out of stuff to say. She asked me only once if I wanted to go out to her hot tub or look at the stars on her roof, but she backed off when she realized I didn't want to leave her house. We did talk about the bruises, and she seemed skeptical when I laid out a different story for her. She asked if the guy I told her about was the same one I always seemed to have problems with. Part of me wished she would just ask if it was my dad. I wondered if she even considered it as a possibility, but even if she had asked, I would probably have denied it.

Despite my soreness, I was determined to show her a good time in bed. That's what boyfriends — or whatever I was — did when parents were out of town. I even convinced myself that I wasn't thinking about Kevin's kiss while we were having sex.

The night Jessica's parents came home, I made myself scarce and snuck out the back door. I figured it was early enough for the guys to not be out at Zarahemla yet, and decided to swing by and smoke a quick joint before facing my dad. I sat in the seat Kevin had pretty much assigned me that first night and pulled out a joint. My mind numbed a bit, and I felt the anxiety of the past week drift away as I exhaled each stream of smoke.

When I was almost done with my joint, I noticed a slight movement in my peripheral vision and spun to find Kevin sitting against a sidewall, staring at me. I took in the long hair falling loosely around his face and wondered if I'd I ever really noticed how his dark hair cast shadows across his set jaw. His arm rested carelessly on the black jeans of his upraised knee. His shirt clung tightly to his body and I remembered what it was hiding. Even in one-hundred-degree July weather, the long-sleeved shirt made sense now. A half-smoked cigarette dangled from his fingers. He had a slight smile on his face and my stomach lurched at the sight of him.

"I figured you'd show up here sooner or later," he said as he stood and casually walked towards me. He reminded me of a black cat, stalking its prey.

"How long have you been here?" I asked, standing and glancing towards the door, my exit.

"Since before you."

I jerked my head back to look at him. "Why didn't you say anything?"

"Because I enjoyed watching you."

"Well, I hope you enjoyed the show because it's over now." With exit plan in place, I headed for the door.

"Why are you avoiding me?" he asked, and I heard him making his way towards me.

"I'm not avoiding you. I just don't wanna be around you right now."

"Isn't that what avoidance is?"

I kept walking. He grabbed my arm and spun me around. "Don't touch me," I said angrily as I yanked my arm away from him. "What's your problem?"

"What's yours?" he spat back at me.

"Kevin, the other night..." I hadn't meant to bring it up, but he had to know how grossed out I was.

He laughed. "Is that what this is all about, Saint Ricky?" Although he was laughing, his eyes were dead. He was being cruel like his father.

"I'm not playing your games," I said, turning to walk away again and making it almost to the entrance before he grabbed me and shoved me into the wall, using his body weight to restrain me. One hand held my arms above my head while the other closed around my neck.

"Tell me about the games I'm playing," he hissed, glaring at me.

"Whatever that was the other night, it was disgusting!" I said, pushing out as his fingers tightened.

"That's not what your actions told me," he whispered as he moved his mouth close to mine. I didn't breathe, though I still struggled against his hold. In an instant I was both scared he'd kiss me and terrified he wouldn't.

"What kind of game are you playing with me?" I asked as anger coursed through my veins and I looked away.

He used his hand under my neck to force my face towards his, but I refused to meet his eyes. I was afraid of what my body might do if I did. "Rick, look at me," he said coldly as his grip on my neck tightened. "Look at me."

He sounded like his father, and my gaze shifted to his. He smiled, but the smile didn't reach his eyes as I felt his lips on mine again. At first they were both soft and cold, but within seconds they turned hard and demanding. I struggled to pull away from him, fighting him as much as I fought my own body, but at his persistence my weakness caved to his power and my mouth started to move with his. He let go of my hands above my head but still used his weight and his hand around my neck to keep me in place. I felt my arms circle his neck, surprised that they were drawing him even closer to me. His free arm slipped behind my back and he pulled me tightly against him as I gasped at his strength.

"It seems your body tells a much different story than your words, Saint Ricky," he gloated as he abruptly ended the kiss and reality crashed over me.

With everything I had, I balled up my fist and slammed it against his face. He stumbled back and brought his hand up to his cheek.

"I didn't know you had it in you," he smirked.

"You have no idea what I'm capable of," I threw at him as I shook off the tingling pain I felt in my hand and wrist.

"I wasn't talking about the punch," he said, then winked and turned away with a smile.

Eleven...

Kevin

Sweet Jesus, Holy Mother of God! These were the first thoughts that flew through my head as I walked out of the barn, followed by the realization that I was hard as a fucking rock! As soon as I was hidden from Zarahemla, I leaned against a nearby tree with my hands on my knees, trying to control my damn body. I'd planned on doing a lot more than just a little kiss, but holy fuck, the second he'd caved and stopped fighting, I'd completely lost it. I had no idea what the fuck had happened. I slammed my fist into a tree, distracting myself from the body that'd just betrayed me. How the fuck was I supposed to control Saint Ricky if I couldn't even control myself?

I had a plan for how to play my game with him. Rick's greatest weakness was his damn heart. He fucking cared. So all I had to do was get him to care about me as more than a friend and I'd seal his fate with mine. If he outed me, he outed himself. And it went without saying that if he fell in love with me, I could string him along until next summer, until I was safely out of my father's reach. As long as he cared, he'd keep my secrets; however, the whole damn thing hinged on me being in fucking control. I was completely losing it, and it scared the shit outta me. I knew that being off my game could get me killed. I'd survived my father's punishments as long as I had because I was able to shut out what my body felt. I could snap my mind into a place where the pain was dulled — never extinguished but controlled. If I couldn't control a lousy hard-on, how the fuck was I supposed to handle a beating with a broom handle?

I knew this was completely un-fucking-acceptable! I had to pull it together. What I needed was to talk some sense into myself. I needed more than just an end goal. I needed action steps to get me there. Step one would be to tease him. I had to keep him thinking about me, giving him just enough but always leaving him wanting more, but he also had to feel safe. He had to be able to trust that I wouldn't push him too far. Finally, he had to want me, trust me, and care for me enough to let me fuck him. That was the crown jewel. I had to get him in bed. Once he submitted to me, I owned him.

I ran my fingers through my hair, knowing it'd be hell. He never reacted how I wanted him to. I could get him almost where I wanted, and then he'd go and do something that would fuck it up. And now the most unpredictable shit of the whole mess was my own goddamn body. I was just going to have to deal with that.

I'd dealt with much worse than blue balls.

I knew he didn't trust me, but I was also aware that he wanted me enough to respond to me physically. My plan was to go back to the basics. I had to flirt with him. I was sure I could handle it as I'd been charming men into bed for years. I just never thought I'd have to use my talents on a classmate; that's where my fists usually came in. But Saint Ricky had managed to cross into the world where my sex appeal was stronger than any violence I might use to keep him in line. I steadied myself. Rick would be no match for the magnetism I was about to turn on just for him.

I walked back into Zarahemla. I hadn't heard him leave, which didn't mean much these days, but I was hoping he'd still be there. I had to be patient. I would begin small.

"Hey, forgot my smokes," I said, barely glancing at him. I made a show of picking up an empty pack of smokes and shoving them into my pocket. As I was about to walk out the front entrance, I hesitated, turned slightly towards him, shook my head and kept walking, knowing he was watching every step I made. "Fuck it," I mumbled loud enough for him to hear and turned to him. He averted his eyes immediately. "Listen, I'm sorry. That was outta line." I was well aware he'd never heard me apologize to anyone. Fuck, I didn't apologize to anyone but my father, and this thought brought a flash of me apologizing to him while Rick was hiding in the closet. Cursing, I shoved that memory back where it belonged. I hated how he was wrapped up in all three of my worlds. No one had ever crossed a single boundary, let alone all of them.

When he didn't respond to my apology, I took a well-thought-out, tentative step in his direction. The best lies and manipulations were built on truth, I reminded myself. "I was kinda freaked out, you know? I mean no one knows that shit about me." I wanted to crawl out of my skin as I acknowledged what he knew about me. I didn't want to talk about this shit to anyone. It wasn't right. When he looked like he was about to say something, I spoke first. "So anyway, gotta run. Just sorry, you know?" God, I sounded pathetic. I turned and hurried out before he could reply.

I left him alone. I had to be patient. It wasn't easy, but it was part of my plan, so after taking off, I pushed the motherfucker far from my mind. Every instinct told me to act fast, to rip off the band-aid all at once, but I didn't trust my instincts with him. True to form, he kept his distance over the next few days, and I allowed it. I still wondered where the fuck he'd disappeared to that night after leaving my house but knew one day I'd figure it out.

I began small. I'd let him catch me watching him and I'd look away. After a handful of these lingering glances, I stopped looking away and tried to lose myself in his eyes. It wasn't as hard as I thought it'd be. Every now and then, I'd actually find a smile tugging at my lips when he didn't look away either. At the beginning, I could tell he was still repulsed by the idea, and I had to admit it fucked with my pride, but as the exchanged glances happened more often, the awkwardness started to fade right on schedule.

On the walk to Zarahemla one day, I let my hand

brush against his as we walked next to each other. He flinched from the contact, but pulling my hand back wasn't staged. There was heat, and it surprised me just as much as it did him. When I found myself sitting next to him at someone's house, I'd use his thigh to help myself stand up. Whenever I walked behind him, I'd trace my fingers along the small of his back. Again, he avoided my touch whenever he could, but the more he resisted me, the more I knew I had to have him.

I was addicted. It was a challenge for me to find different ways to touch him and not be noticed by the others. With every gaze and every stare, I knew I was getting myself into trouble, but I also knew I had to stick with my plan if things were ever going to be in my control again. One could only win big by risking big, and I was risking it all.

I was still an ass in my own right. I had to be. I couldn't lose my standing with the others, and this also meant putting Rick into place when he stepped out of line in front of them. But I began enjoying it less and less. It seemed so damn counter-productive to cut him down when I was trying to get him to trust me.

Rick

My mind exploded and my heart stopped the second I felt the heat from his fingers. The movie continued to play and the guys were engrossed in it while I had no clue what movie was even on. I sat on the floor in front of him, and he was lying on the couch behind me. When his hand casually fell to his side, the brush of his fingers against the base of my neck sent chills down my arms.

My body fought to lean into his hand, to feel more of his touch, but my mind paralyzed me.

I hated him. I hated the way he made me feel and the way he'd started to haunt my dreams. He was playing at some sort of game, and it was messing with my head, making me feel things that were wrong and could destroy my life. I wasn't gay, and considering how many girls I'd seen him with, I knew he wasn't either. I had to ask myself why he insisted on tormenting me with his twisted ploy.

I wondered if he even knew he was touching me. There was no way he could not know what he was doing to my resolve. My mind whirled around and around as I tried to focus on anything but his fingers. Then I felt it. It wasn't much, but it was deliberate. One finger moved excruciatingly slowly, hair by single hair. He couldn't have moved his finger more than a half an inch up, then back down my neck when he stopped, still in full contact but not moving. I felt every cell in his finger where it connected with the back of my neck. The fire that seemed to radiate from his touch swirled and centered only where his skin touched mine, followed by the anxious and dreaded feeling in my gut, screaming at my body to ignore him.

Minute after minute, I fought the urge to run from his house. I wanted to get away from him and what I was feeling, but with a single finger he had bound me to the spot. Just when I thought I must have imagined his movement, he made another play, tracing two fingers of fire across my skin. Slowly. I held my breath. Deliberately. As chills screamed to the surface of my body, I knew he saw what his touch was doing to me, and I was completely helpless to stop him.

Every time he did something along these lines, I was convinced he was setting the trap. He was going to do something or say something to the guys and they would all know. He'd convince them that I wanted him, and my life would be over. At first, I was sure it was all in my head — the looks, the accidental touches — but with his fingers tracing fire on my skin, causing my stomach to clench and tighten, it was most definitely not in my head. I couldn't bear the thought of him touching me any longer. I was disgusted with the way my body was reacting to what he was doing. In slow motion, I shifted away from his touch, tucking my legs under me to assist in standing up. I had to get away from him, and a temporary escape to the bathroom seemed my only choice.

I felt his eyes tracing every inch of my retreating body. His front room was impossibly long, every step taking an endless amount of time. I could still feel his burning eyes as I closed the bathroom door. Even though it was around the corner and down the hall, if anyone had x-ray vision, it was Kevin.

Kevin

I was impressed. He didn't even seem rattled, but if I was, then he had to be. I knew he was still fighting himself, what he wanted, or, should I say, who he wanted! I reached in my pocket and slowly pulled out my phone. Without drawing attention to myself, I pushed several buttons until my ringtone interrupted the movie. I flipped it up to my ear.

"Yeah," I said, standing up and leaving the room. I looped through the kitchen, my voice trailing behind me in a one-sided conversation. As soon as I was out of the living room, I slipped the phone onto silent and back into my pocket. The last thing I needed was it actually ringing and fucking up my plan. I could hear the water running in the bathroom and prayed he'd left the door unlocked. Of course, he hadn't.

I waited patiently outside the door. I could hear the water splashing in the sink and imagined him flushing it over his face. It was what I'd do. The water turned off and I poised myself, hand on doorknob. The second I heard the lock click, I turned the knob, pushed my way in and closed the door quietly behind me, locking it again. He stumbled back a few steps, obviously confused. I waited. The confusion faded, followed by questioning, doubt, and then realization. I smiled.

"Hi," I said simply.

"What...?"

I took a slow step forward, and he snapped his mouth shut and took a step back. Another step.

"Umm..." He looked towards the door, panicked. I didn't want panic.

"The door's locked," I said, pleased to see a little bit of relief. He wasn't as scared of me as he was of the guys walking in, which told me he wanted me. He couldn't turn off the desire I saw in his eyes, even if it was mixed with fear. He took another step back. He was not on board yet. Two more steps and he'd be out of room to back up. I liked the perspective the mirror gave me. He had a nice ass. I could see the mischief in my black eyes—seductive and charming. It was a look I had perfected, and it'd never let me down.

"Kevin?" he strangled out.

"Yeah," I answered as I took another casual step, relaxing my body. I didn't want to threaten or scare him.

Silence, and he was out of steps. He glanced at the counter behind him and I took advantage of his distraction to move my body in line with his, my hands pressing gently on the edge of the counter to either side of him. He made a noise, a startled intake of breath, almost a question lacing through the wisps of air as he exhaled. Cinnamon? When had he started chewing gum? A smattering of thoughts raced through my head. *Fuck! Control! Goal! Focus!* Failing could literally cost me my life at the hands of my father. I'd never had anything so big on the line.

His eyes hazed over like thin clouds over the sun on a hot day. I felt my desire and knew I had to allow him to see it, to believe in the reality. I relaxed my body into his. He leaned back further but didn't bolt. I saw his chest muscles tighten under his shirt as he tensed for a fight. I took a deep breath, inhaling him—cinnamon, smoke, sweet and sexy. I felt my own lust dawn in my eyes and saw his reaction as it happened, his body coming forward, not fighting the inevitable. I moved towards his neck, wanting more of his smell, trying to breathe in more, my lips resting near the base of his ear, softly kissing, wanting to taste his skin. I wondered if he would taste like his smell or like his mouth. The last time I'd kissed him, his mouth was rich and deep like hickory.

Would it be spicy with cinnamon now? Another deep breath and I pressed into him harder.

A small voice in the back of my head warned me to hold onto the counter, to keep my hands firmly in place. Fuck, I didn't want to. I wanted to feel my fingers dig into the skin that smelled so delicious. My mouth opened and my tongue slowly touched his neck, assaulted with salt and a hint of bitterness. I wanted to claim his body, to mark him and leave my own taste behind. As my lips descended, he strangled out a ragged, "Shit!" His hands were on my chest, pushing me away, and before I knew what he was doing, he was out of the bathroom. Dazed, I stared at the open door, confused by the emptiness I felt.

"Ahh, fuck me," I breathed out. *Way to fucking seduce yourself*, you hot piece of shit. Even my self-scolding sounded pathetic. Things couldn't have gone any worse.

I heard the front door open and close and knew he was gone. Damn, how the hell was I supposed to explain his disappearing act to the guys? Then I heard the garage door opening. Really? I cursed again. Couldn't God give me one second to sort out one fuckup before he threw my father into the mix? Grabbing my phone, I brought it back up to my ear and re-entered the kitchen the way I'd left.

"Sure, I completely get it, babe," I said into the phone. "Okay, gotta run, I'll see you tomorrow. Good?" I acted like I was ending the call and returned the phone to my pocket before my father walked in. I glanced at him and then quickly to the guys on the couch, making sure he was aware of the situation before he said a word. He nodded slightly and walked into the kitchen. Without thinking much about it, I took a step out of the kitchen in the opposite direction.

Slipping into my 'life-is-perfect-in-the-Vincent-home' role, I asked about my father's day at work. He smiled. He knew his part and I knew mine. We chatted back and forth about his day, both making up lies to convince our audience of the truth we wanted them to believe. He asked what I wanted for dinner and if my friends would be joining us. I'd never invite them for a meal, and we all knew that. He actually started preparing the food as well. This was not a good sign. I knew his rhythms. I could almost always tell the kind of night it was going to be within moments of him walking in the door. In most cases, I saw it coming days in advance, and I should've seen this one coming. These were always the easiest to peg. The nicer he got, the more creative he was becoming.

The normal beatings, with a belt or whatever, were the ones that happened on a regular basis. They moved in and out of our lives like steady ocean waves. Roughly once a week, they came crashing into things, slowly subsiding and then returning. It was as natural as breathing—in and out, in and out. Sometimes I mouthed off just to get it out of the way. Other times I knew that nothing I said or did would lessen what was coming, so I kept my mouth shut.

But routine was boring and he had to mix it up. As he got closer to his creative punishments, he became nicer, smoothing out the edges of our dysfunction so he could tear it apart with calculated ease.

His emptiness was what I really needed to be scared of. It was deadly and it terrified me. But he was in his creative mode. I quickly scanned back to his last creative session, nearly two months ago. This was good. The longer the stretch between meant the more time he had to come up with new methods. Two months would be bad but not life-threatening. Nonetheless, if I hadn't been so focused on Rick, I would've seen it coming days ago and would've had more time to prepare. Now I was going to have to fucking take what he gave me with little time to get myself into the right frame of mind.

As the guys left and the front door shut, he was quick to command.

"Bedroom, now," he said from the kitchen. I wondered if he was turning the heat off the half-cooked ground turkey. Centering myself, I counted the stairs to the basement, trying to clear my mind. The anticipation was sometimes worse than the actual punishment. He was right behind me, itching to get things going. When I reached the bottom of the stairs, I started over, counting how many steps it took to get from the last stair to the center of my bedroom. I knew how many; I'd counted hundreds of times: twenty-four.

He threw a broom handle on the carpet near my bed. "Kneel," he ordered.

I hesitated for a split second, knowing it was going to be a painful one.

"Kneel!" He grabbed my shoulder and pressed me down towards the broom as I positioned my knees on the handle. The sharpness of the pain immediately sent shooting spears up my thighs and a dull ache towards my feet. I sat down on my ankles, hoping to alleviate some of the pressure, but his belt immediately lashed across my back.

"No! Up!" I quickly straightened, returning all the pressure to my knees, and began my internal countdown: one, shut down thoughts of school; two, shut down thoughts of hard, hot bodies; three, shut down thoughts of the guys; four, relax the muscles in the neck; five, relax the shoulders, and so on.

"What did I do wrong?" I asked, trying to give myself more time to get into my head. The belt lashed again, but he said nothing as the buckle cut into my back. He was good. He rarely hit my face, usually only when I pushed.

"You will kneel here until I am satisfied you have learned your lesson." Fuck, I knew there was no lesson. This was a creative session. But I needed more time.

"What lesson?" I asked, and the belt lashed again. I lost my balance and fell forward.

"Five times for every time you move off the handle." I struggled to position myself as the belt rained down on my back again and again. Okay, maybe there was a lesson. That was something to focus on. My mind started to search the possible lessons he thought I should learn. Had he found out about the clubs? No, it would be much worse if he had. It couldn't be the cleaning. I'd mastered that years ago. *Fuck, my knees!* Hell, I had to figure things out. The longer I kneeled, the more distracting the pain became and the more difficult it was to hold on to any thoughts or logic.

"Ten minutes and still nothing?" The belt crashed against my back again, surprising me and making me lose my balance. As I hurried to center myself back on the broom, five more lashes crashed against my skin. I gasped, throwing my head back. I squeezed my eyes shut, trying to focus my thoughts. *Goddamnit, focus, you fucker*, I thought to myself harshly. The agony in my legs started screaming at me, the muscles in my back constricting from the onslaught. It was impossible to figure out what he wanted; my mind could only find the pain.

"Twenty minutes." The lash came, but I braced as I heard it swing through the air and didn't lose my balance. There, I had the focus within my reach. It was coming. *I can do this*, I told myself. Shutting down thoughts of Rick, shutting down thoughts of pain, shutting it all out was part of the process.

During the next four hours, every ten minutes the belt would fly through the air and crash into my back. I grasped onto my focus and fucking held it for all I was worth. It wasn't easy. I lost my balance seven more times, four of them in the last hour as my body gave out on me. He never told me what lesson I was supposed to learn. As I lay on the floor, trying to pull myself together, I reminded myself that there was no fucking lesson.

Twelve...

Rick

"So, yeah. The Homecoming dance is tomorrow. I know it's crazy short notice and kinda lame, but...," I drifted off. I hadn't planned on asking Jessica to the dance. I hadn't planned on going to the dance at all. But after the week I'd had with Kevin, I had to prove to him that I wasn't interested in what he was pushing. I prayed she hadn't already been asked. As perfect as she was, I was sure she had, but at the same time I hoped people assumed she was going with me and stayed away. It wasn't fair to wish this for her, and guilt coursed through me.

"Are you asking me on a date, Rick St. James?" she said, smiling up at me through her eyelashes.

God, she is so beautiful, I thought.

"I guess."

"You guess?"

"Well, I mean...of course I am. I'd be insane not to ask you to Homecoming. What better way to start our senior year together?" I asked, believing every word I said to her.

"Why the short notice? You ask someone else and get turned down?" she teased.

"There's no one else," I said, feeling the lie as it came out. Stepping in front of her to stop her from continuing down the hall, and bringing my hands to both of her cheeks, I gently brought my lips to hers and kissed her. *Come on*, I told myself. *Let this feel right!* Her body melted into mine and it seemed that she'd break. I deepened my kiss, searching for more, needing more.

"Gosh, you've sure turned up the heat the last few weeks. Okay, okay, I'll go." I let out a sigh of relief as she ducked out of my arms and said, "You're rather convincing, Mr. St. James." She smiled brightly and my heart caved in on itself. The blush in her cheeks was evidence that my kiss had done to her exactly what I'd wanted it to do to me. She was turned on and I was empty. There was something wrong with me. "I'm gonna be late to class," she said, skipping down the hall. "We'll talk details later." She disappeared into the crowd, and I sighed as I turned and ran right into Kevin, with Mike and Brett on his heels.

"Details of what?"

I knew it was safer to have this conversation with Brett and Mike nearby.

"Details for the dance tomorrow. I'm taking Jessica," I said and held my breath.

"You fucked 'er yet?"

"Jesus, Kevin," I said, walking away from him, not wanting him to see in my eyes what I really wanted.

"Are we done here?" His hint of coolness didn't escape me.

"I'm gonna to be late to class," I said, picking up my pace.

"Your class is in the other direction," he called after me. He paused as I slowed to a stop. "Same way we're headed. We'll walk with you." His face didn't betray any emotion as I turned and started walking with them, but I noticed that he didn't move as smoothly as he normally did. I watched him closely, aware now that he hid just as much as I did. He was definitely in pain. I was distracted from the nightmare of my life as I watched him weave, almost gracefully, down the crowded hallway without ever coming into contact with another body.

We hadn't talked about anything that had taken place over the last few months. There was no mention of my brother or his dad, and other than the moments he was intentionally tormenting me with his game, he acted as if nothing had changed. In the meantime, I felt like my world was spinning out of control. When Jason died, my world had stopped. Now Kevin had turned it upside down, and I didn't recognize anything anymore.

Thankfully, Brett and Mike ran with the conversation, asking how far I'd gotten with Jessica. I answered them without ever really telling them anything. Kevin said he'd asked Kari to the dance, but I knew he was lying. I'd talked to her that morning and she was going with someone else. I was not stupid enough to call him on it though. And now, because Kevin was going, it seemed all of us were going to the dance together. So much for trying to get away from him.

With flasks loaded in Jeremy's dad's van and Mike's brother's car, we picked up our dates and headed to dinner the next night. Kevin had managed to sucker Kari into going with him. She'd ditched her other date as soon as Kevin turned on his best behavior. It made me sick to witness. I'd somehow managed to get stuck in Jeremy's van with Brett, but it was better than being with Kevin and Kari.

As soon as we got to the dance, I pulled Jessica behind me and disappeared into the throngs of people, wondering why I'd ever thought coming to the dance with these guys would be a good idea. Then I remembered I *hadn't* thought it was a good idea; it was all Kevin's doing.

I tugged on Jessica, heading for the dance floor.

"You must really love to dance."

"What?" I asked, glancing at her behind me.

"Dancing. You must love it. I've never seen you so focused, you know?"

"Oh yeah, that. Umm, dancing's okay. I just want to get you alone, away from them," I said, turning and pulling her into my arms. My eyes scanned the crowd behind her, immediately finding Kevin. He was staring right at me. I spun her around so my back was facing him. I wasn't going to pay him any attention. Out of sight, out of mind. I smiled down at her. "You don't mind, do you?"

"That you stole me away? Not at all." She smiled. I pulled her slender body into mine, feeling the way it curved around me. I knew this should be what I wanted.

I tried to tell myself that this had to be what I wanted.

"Hey, sorry I missed your birthday a few weeks ago," she said, looking up at me.

"Wait, how'd you know it was my birthday?" I hadn't told anyone and had intentionally tried to forget about it.

"Ahh, so I'm right. An August baby." She smiled innocently. "I knew it had to be over the summer, but you wouldn't tell me so I had to try to narrow it down somehow. Kevin's in August as well. Both of you are such young babies. Seniors and just barely seventeen. I don't get why you guys are all shy about it."

I couldn't really tell her that my dad avoided my birthday since it also marked the anniversary of my mom's death, but I found it weird that Kevin hadn't mentioned his either. And there he was again, invading my mind.

"So, why did you agree to come with me? I bet there're a dozen guys who asked you," I said, hoping she'd drop the birthday conversation.

"Why wouldn't I go with you?"

"Why would you?"

"You are so fishing for a compliment."

"Maybe." I used my hands to move her hips with mine, swaying with her to a song that wasn't quite slow enough to wrap her in my arms, but not fast enough to pull away from her. I turned on my best smile and cocked my head to the side. I'd seen Kevin do it with all his girls and I wondered if it'd work for me. And there he was in my head again. I flexed my fingers in frustration and must have gripped onto Jessica harder than I thought.

"That's why," her lowered voice purred at me, "'cause I'm never sure what I'm gonna get with you—hot, cold, totally into me, then just friends, sweet and innocent, or bad and sexy."

I barked out a laugh. "What are you talking about?" I spun her around and my eyes landed on Kevin again, still staring at me. I focused in on Jessica.

"Just that. See, now you're being all normal and light, and a second ago I saw a darkness across your eyes and you got all broody and sexy."

"Me, sexy?"

"Yes, silly. You so have that bad-boy-with-a-heart-of-gold act working for you."

Again, I couldn't help but laugh.

"Jessica, I'm so far from a bad boy."

"You drink, you smoke, you're a player and you hang out with Kevin Vincent. You're the perfect bad boy."

"And you are so nuts. I'm not a player."

"Yeah, then how many girls have you kissed since you moved here?"

"Easy—one."

"What?" Now it was her turn to be caught off guard.

"You heard me."

"Bull!"

"It's true."

She lightly smacked me on the arm. "And that just proves my point. Heart of gold. How's any girl supposed to resist that?"

"Why would one want to resist?" I asked, teasing her.

"Oh no, I'm not. I just never know what I'm going to get from you."

"I don't know half the time either." I bent in and found her lips. Kissing her was easy. Jessica was so laid back and the banter came naturally. I really liked her, and she was so honest. I always knew exactly what I was getting with her. I didn't need to worry about any games or hidden agendas. I immediately felt guilty because all she got from me were lies and hidden agendas. I made myself get lost in the kiss with her, trying to make her feel good, to feel what I wanted to feel. She broke off the kiss, breathless.

"And with talent like that," she whispered, "you're going to break my heart one of these days."

My stomach tightened into a knot. "No, I think you're much more likely to break mine. I mean, how can I compete with all that free love?" I teased her. She was right. If I couldn't make myself want her, I'd end up hurting her. I didn't want that. I reached for my flask to take a quick nip, but groaned out of frustration when I couldn't find it, and she immediately took it wrong.

"I know," she sighed. "I feel the same way." She tucked herself into my arms as the music slowed. I closed my eyes and tried to imagine actually dating her and not just fooling around with her — taking her to the movies and calling her to tell her goodnight and that I loved her. I could picture it all.

As the song ended, I led her off the dance floor. I told her I'd left my flask in the car, and that I was going to run and get it. She seemed fine to hang out with some of her friends, so I hit Jeremy up for the keys to his van and kept an eye out for Kevin. Luckily, since I'd left the dance floor, I hadn't seen him.

Flask in hand and several shots later, I stopped dead in my tracks as I passed Mike's car. There in the window was Kevin, and from the looks of it, even though I couldn't see her, I knew he was in the middle of nailing Kari. She must've been lying down and he was leaning over her, and almost as if he'd planned it, he looked up at me within moments of my stopping.

I should've looked away. My mind screeched at me, warning me against the inevitable place it would go. I should've run, but I stood and stared at him. He smiled and winked at me, and I stopped breathing. His body moved and rolled while strands of his black hair stuck to his forehead with sweat. He kept his rhythm as his gaze traveled down my body, and I knew what he was thinking. I was thinking the same horrible thoughts. I wondered what it would feel like to have him move like that with me, to feel his sweat drip on me, to see his muscles clench and move under his shirt like they were. His pace quickened and he threw his head back, finally breaking the stare that held me in place. As his body tightened and thrust, I watched with total focus, unable to break away from his power. When he was done, he fell out of view, not looking at me again, and I felt heat flush my body.

I turned, feeling anger rise as I went back towards the school. I tried to tell myself that I wasn't mad, that I didn't want to feel his skin against mine. I was just pissed because he was playing games with me, and I didn't like being toyed with. By the time I entered the gym I was itching to leave again, to go find a quiet place and smoke a joint. As I searched the crowd for Jessica, I was surprised to find her and Brett off to the side of the dance floor. He leaned towards her and — I swear to god — he kissed her, and that's all it took to send me through the roof. I saw her try to pull away, but he stepped towards her again. She obviously wasn't welcoming his advances. I nearly sprinted towards them and slammed both of my palms against him, watching him fly to the side and stumble with surprise. "Get your hands off her!" I roared as I pictured Kevin's hands on Kari.

"What the hell, St. James? What's your problem?" Brett said as he turned, ready for a fight. He took several steps and swung at me. I ducked, my fights with my dad having prepared me more than I'd expected. Any fear I may have had disappeared because I knew that nothing Brett handed me would compare with what my dad dealt.

"Come on, Brett, you've been itching for this for a long time. Let's have it." I threw a punch and connected, the shock from the force sending tingling daggers through my arm. He shook it off and threw his fist up under my chin. My head snapped back.

"What the fuck?" Kevin's voice sliced through the music. Without thinking, I turned and directed all my anger at the real source. All the rage I had in me flew through my body and was looking for one way out. Seconds before I connected, he reached out, gripped my flying fist in his hand and spun me around with my arm locked securely behind my back. "Rick! Outside now!" His voice was cold enough that it put out my temper instantly. "Brett. The rest of you, stay the fuck here!" he commanded, shoving me towards a nearby exit. As he slammed me through the door, he ordered, "the catwalk, and don't say a fucking word or I swear to god I'll lose my motherfucking temper." I could tell by the strain in his voice that he was actually trying to control himself. I obeyed. While I wasn't scared of Brett, I'd seen what Kevin's dad was capable of, and I was positive Kevin could do the same.

"What the fuck was that?" he asked when we were hidden away from everyone at the catwalk. I wasn't sure if it was a rhetorical question, so I played it safe and kept my mouth shut. "Answer me," he said tightly.

"He's been gunning for me all night, and then he kissed Jessica."

"Are you kidding? You caused all that attention. Shit, you're gonna get us all expelled because he kissed the piece of ass you're trying to make me jealous with?"

I blanched. "What? Make you jealous? This has nothing to do with you."

"The fuck it doesn't. It has everything to do with me."

"What world do you live in? 'Cause in my world, things don't revolve around you."

"The one where even though you can barely tolerate the thought, all you think about is this," he said as he grabbed me and kissed me. There was no hint of gentleness, just heat. He pushed me against the handrail and roughly took my lips into his mouth, biting down. I could taste blood and kissed him back, caving into my nightmares. My body pressed into him, picturing the way he came in the car. And then I pictured Kari underneath him and shoved him away, quickly backing out of the catwalk so he couldn't corner me.

"Seriously? You think I'm going to go for that? I just watched you nail Kari in the backseat of your friend's ride. I know you're not gay! I know you have something up your sleeve. I'm not someone you can screw with or use as a pawn in your game. Find some other guy or girl or whatever your flavor of the minute is. Because you aren't getting anything from me." I turned my back on him and steadily walked away. My ears became sensitive to every little sound, expecting him to tackle me from behind. With every step, I tensed, waiting for the fight that never came.

I avoided the gym entrance, not wanting to deal with the crowds, Brett or Jessica. I found a side entrance, and as I reached for the door I noticed my hand shaking, the adrenalin starting to fade as the aftershock of what had happened settled in. As soon as I was in the doors of the school, I sank to the ground. After several attempts to open the lid of my flask, I was able to get it off and downed all of the remaining vodka. The flask slipped and clattered to the floor.

I tried to push the feel of his body against mine from my head, the way his lips had taken control and forced a reaction out of me. I fisted my hands in my hair, yanking as I fought the images. I hated how he was making me feel simply for his own perverted game. I never even heard the footsteps.

"Is this yours?"

I looked up at the tight, striped shirt and too-short slacks belonging to Dr. Mortensen, the school's principal. I'd barely heard what he'd said, let alone understood it.

"Huh?" was all I could manage.

He looked down and I followed his stare. He tapped my flask with the toe of his worn brown loafers.

"The flask. I assume it's yours."

This couldn't be happening. I couldn't even think fast enough to respond adequately.

"No, sir," I stammered as I tried to stand up, shaking now for an entirely different reason. I'd never been in any serious trouble. "It's not mine."

"No? Then whose is it?" he asked, looking up and down the hall, tilting his head a little so he could look through the top half of his bifocals. I looked around as well, in search of anything or anyone who could help me. He bent and picked it up. "Well, I suppose we should go call your parents."

My legs nearly gave out on me again, and I stumbled back towards the locker. He looked at me and I could see he assumed I was drunk.

"Sir, it's not mine, but I'll take detention. I'll do anything, but please, don't call my dad." I didn't want to imagine the way he'd react if he got a call from the principal of my school. Him busting me was one thing. Me getting in real trouble was new and I was willing to bet it came with a much worse punishment. I tried to take a step towards him and was mortified when my legs actually wouldn't hold me and I stumbled to my knees. "Please," was all I could get out before I fell.

"It's mine."

My head jerked in the direction of the voice, and I saw Kevin appear out of nowhere.

"Excuse me?" Dr. Mortensen asked with some confusion.

"The flask," Kevin nodded towards the principal's

hand. "It's mine. Rick here was trying to get me to get rid of it. Something about the dangers of underage drinking, if you believe that shit."

I stared at him, incredulous, wondering if I'd finally lost my mind.

"Language."

"You're lecturing me about saying 'shit' when you're holding my flask of vodka in your hand. Don't you think we have more serious matters to discuss?" Kevin turned and started walking towards his office. Dr. Mortensen looked at me, still kneeling on the floor, and then toward Kevin. After several seconds, he shrugged, obviously deciding that a confession from the notorious Kevin Vincent was better than the denial I was offering.

He hadn't even looked at me. Kevin had stepped in and taken the blame without a glance at me. He'd prevented Dr. Mortensen from calling my dad, and they were on the way to call Kevin's dad instead. He took more than just the blame; he was taking a beating that should've been mine, and all I could think about was the taste of his lips.

Thirteen...

Kevin

"Seriously. Shut the fuck up!" If he said he was sorry one more fucking time I'd have to make him sorry.

"I'm sor...I mean, I just don't get why you did it." Apparently, my little stunt with Dr. Mortensen had helped him get over his general disgust for me as of late, and now he wouldn't shut his fucking trap!

"We are so not talking about this anymore. We've been over it a billion times. Drop it."

"But your dad..."

I turned and slammed him into a row of lockers. Shit, I was losing my cool, and in the middle of the hall no less. I told myself to take a deep breath before speaking.

"A: We don't ever talk about him in earshot of anyone else. B: I told you, Mortensen has been looking for a reason to bust me for a while. At least with this, I got to decide when it happened. C: It had nothing to do with you, so just fucking leave it. Don't push me." I released him and stepped back. If there was a god, I prayed that Rick would believe every word I said. Maybe if he started to believe it, I would too. I watched his face carefully. He backed off, for the moment.

"Fine, whatever," he said, ducking past me.

I was still pissed that he'd started something with Brett at the dance, but I wasn't as mad as I'd led them all to believe. I really had just wanted to get Rick alone. But Brett had been growing increasingly annoying, and I was proud that Rick was learning to stand up for himself.

Some guy named Jeff from my Earth Science class walked past and gave me a hard slap on the back.

"Way to go with Kari. I heard you scored with her at the dance last weekend."

Fuck me! I gritted my teeth. My father hadn't been easy on me and the slap on the back nearly buckled me, but I plastered a smirk on my face and shrugged.

"Don't fucking touch me!" I growled. I wondered if people would ever get it through their heads to keep their hands off me.

He started laughing with his friends as they continued down the hall, paying more attention to my smirk than to my warning.

"You okay?" Rick asked.

"Fine." I said automatically.

"Liar."

I cut my eyes at him sideways. "Fuck off."

He stiffened a little. "It's my fault."

"Jesus Mary mother of fucking hell. You're like a goddamn broken record. It's been like twenty fucking seconds." I veered off down another hallway, making it clear that he wasn't invited to join me.

I'd made my decision and hell if I wasn't in pain for it. I didn't need him being all weepy and shit. I didn't have the fucking energy to make him feel better about my goddamn father. I made my way to a locked door that I, of course, had a key to. It led to the roof and it was the one place in the world I could go that nobody else knew about. The halls emptied, and it was easy to slip in unnoticed.

If positioned right, I could look out over the city at the football field. It was ideal. While I didn't fuck guys my age, there was something hot as hell about watching a bunch of guys in tight-ass pants ram their bodies against each other. I sat down, carefully avoiding leaning against anything, and lit up a joint.

My mind still raced with questions as to why the hell I'd stopped Mortensen from busting Rick. I hoped the weed would quiet the buzzing. He'd looked so scared, on his knees, pleading. It really was quite pathetic, but at the time all I could think about was keeping him out of his dad's hands. I hadn't thought it through. When the fuck had I stopped thinking things through? I'd been bad. Cardinal rule, don't fucking get caught. Perception was everything to my father.

The weekend was fast approaching. With my father on edge, I was anxious to stay out of his way, so I readily agreed to go to a party hosted by Beth. It was kinda nice just to show up for something and not worry about planning all the details.

The party was a few houses down from Rick's house. Beth's parents were Mormon, and she was a good girl, but I wasn't as interested in the party as I was at having a chance to get Rick alone. I'd ignored him pretty much all week, so I figured he'd keep his fucking mouth shut and not make me think about my moment of stupidity. Beth's house was a perfect setting because her backyard was big enough for anyone to disappear in. The yard consisted of several levels, each level surrounded with and hidden by pine trees and brush oak. It provided many secluded private spots, which was perfect for those of us who didn't want to be found. Shortly after arriving, the guys found an area closed off from the party where we could knock a few back.

When Beth spotted us coming back to the main group, I waved at her and she immediately looked away. I couldn't blame her for not liking me after I'd used her to bait Rick when he first started hanging out with us. I was pleased with the look of disapproval on her face. Even more so, I loved how she was too intimidated by me to stop me from doing what I wanted. We didn't fit in well with her friends, but we were able to plant ourselves on the outskirts of her party and got along just fine with our own kind.

Rick, however, found himself happily in Jessica's company. Jessica and Rick had always meant something to each other, thanks to me. But since I'd turned up the heat, I'd noticed that he was certainly working harder at their relationship. Interestingly enough, as busy as he seemed to be flirting with her, he made himself just as occupied watching me and making sure he knew where I was at all times. This was the sign I'd been waiting for. I'd made him sweat things long enough to make my next move. He probably wasn't ready mentally, but physically he couldn't stand it anymore. I watched him enter the back of the house, and I could see him through the sliding glass door, talking with her. The guys seemed buzzed and wrapped up in their own flirtations with other girls. I knew I'd not be missed.

"Hi, Jessica," I said with exaggerated charm and a slight bow. She smiled warmly at me, her eyes bright and a little too knowing for my taste.

"I suppose you've come to fetch Rick from under my spell," she laughed.

"You suppose right my dear. May I borrow him for a smoke?"

She reached up on her toes and wrapped her arms around his neck. "Only if you promise to bring him back."

"Now, you know I don't make promises to anyone." Jessica was one of the few people I could actually see myself being friends with, if I had friends. However, the way she was draping herself all over Rick had me fighting my instincts to grab him away from her.

I turned to Rick and forced a calm breath. "Let's go."

"Yeah, sure," he remarked coolly. He turned, pulled her tighter into his arms, bent slowly, and found her lips. I watched as she melted into him, and I realized my hands had tightened into fists. Then I noticed how careful and gentle he was being and immediately knew he wasn't one bit interested in her. My anger gave way to curiosity. I knew damn well how he liked to be kissed and what made his body respond, and this was not it. This so-called kiss was nothing more than a message to me and maybe to himself.

"Be back in a bit, okay?" he whispered softly to her. When he turned, a triumphant look on his face, I wanted to burst out laughing, but for the sake of not causing a scene, I reigned in my amusement and made for a fast exit.

He followed me out the door and up a small hill to the side of the yard. I then circled around some trees to a secluded area I felt would give us the privacy I needed. Away from the lights of the party, it took several moments for our eyes to adjust.

"So, where're the guys?" Rick asked when he realized no one was around.

I smiled into the darkness, taking a step towards him. I slid my arm quickly around his waist and pulled his body against mine. With my other hand, I thrust my fingers through his hair and forced my lips to his, giving him the complete opposite experience he'd just given Jessica. I expected a struggle and got one. And damn if his kiss didn't get me instantly hard; it was fucking distracting. He shoved against me and broke free.

"Don't..." was all he was able to get out before I was kissing him again, pushing him towards a big tree that I knew would keep him in my grasp. I moved my hand up under his shirt, partly to touch his skin, partly to absorb and protect him against the shock of the tree that was about to come into contact with his back. Even with my arm there, he winced and I paused briefly, allowing him to center himself. When I saw the pain leave his face, I wasted no time securing him tightly against my body. He pushed against my chest again, but I noticed that he took care to avoid hurting me as well. His struggle moved almost seamlessly between shoving me away and pulling me towards him, alternating every few seconds as his mind and body fought it out. I went with his indecision, doing everything I could to avoid thinking about how fucking impossible my body was behaving. When I finally noticed him arching towards me more than fighting against me, I gripped him firmly and, with two calculated steps backwards, tipped us into a hammock, him coming down hard on top of me.

The hammock started swinging wildly, threatening to throw us off at any moment. I found his lips again and deepened my kiss, immediately losing myself in his taste, his heat and his continued struggle, though it got weaker and weaker. *So help me fucking god, let me get through this,* I thought. I wrapped my hand around the back of his neck, holding him to me and trying to balance out the swaying world around us.

He struggled only a few more moments before giving in completely and grasping onto me, his fingers digging into my back. In his abandon, he forgot about being careful. Pain from recent wounds immediately coursed through me but seemed not to matter next to the pleasure he was giving me. It felt as if he was holding on to me so he wouldn't lose himself. Hell, I knew that if he was drowning then I was going with him. When I couldn't stand it any longer, I rocked my hips into him, needing friction, and he violently jerked back from me.

"Rick, knock it off!" I clenched my teeth into his shoulder in frustration. "You know you want this as much as I do."

"I don't," he said, pushing harder and struggling again

with near madness. I reached down between the two of us and grabbed him. My head screamed for control as I felt him in my hand. He was just as hard as I was.

"You lie. You want me." I took possession of his mouth again and the struggle continued. I left my hand where it was and used the gravity of the swaying hammock and the fact that I was simply stronger than him to keep him on top of me. I lowered my voice and spoke with real anger. Whether the anger was at him for not giving in, or at myself for not being able to control my own damn body was anybody's question.

"Stop your struggling," I commanded. He relaxed a little when he heard my anger but still strained against me.

"Let me go, Kevin."

"I will not. Not until you admit you want me." I had to hear him say it. It hadn't been part of the plan, but I needed him to admit that he wanted me just as much as I wanted him.

"Never. I don't want this."

"Hold the fuck still," I whispered desperately. He was pushing his luck. The hell he didn't, and I was going to make him admit what he really needed, what we both needed. I gathered every ounce of control I had left and slowed my pace. I wanted nothing more than to take him right then, but he wasn't ready. I slid my hand up his shirt again and was pleased when he calmed down and shuddered under my touch. I demanded with my lips that he open his mouth to me. I lessened my restraint and his arms found their way around me. "Say you want me." I kissed his neck right below his ear, taking my time exploring his taste. I trailed my mouth down the side of his neck, finding the hollow near his collarbone. "Say you want me," I whispered as I traced my tongue back up to his mouth. I pretended like I was about to kiss him but just brushed his lips gently with mine. "You know what I want," I said breathlessly. He needed me to kiss him; I could feel the electric current pulling me towards him. Again, I barely touched my lips to his but refused to give him more.

"Jesus, Kevin, I want you!"

His words sounded almost like a sob of defeat, but the moment his voice mixed with his exhaled breath I took possession of him again. It wasn't long before his lips started to explore my neck and my body went into overdrive. *Shit! Fuck! Shit! Fuck!* I threw my hands behind my head, jamming my fingers in my hair and pulling as hard as I could. He paused, wondering why I'd stopped holding onto him.

"Keep going, don't stop," I forced out. If I allowed myself to touch him, I'd tear off his clothes without question. I needed some motherfucking control. His lips were covering my neck again, and I clenched my teeth as I allowed him to explore. I'd never experienced such agony in my whole life.

I wanted to fuck the hell out of him, but my need to keep him from sharing my secrets was much more critical. Forcing thoughts of completely consuming him out of my mind, I decided to let him do whatever he wanted without moving my fucking hands from their tenuous grasp in my hair. The goal was to get him to trust me so he wouldn't betray me. I'd let him set the pace and challenge him, making him want me until he couldn't resist. Then I'd have him—body and mind alike.

When he stopped, I welcomed it because my control was wearing dangerously thin. He didn't pull away from me. He simply laid his head on my chest and said nothing, breathing heavily.

After some time, I came back to reality and found my control. Still without moving my hands from behind my head, I asked, "Wanna get outta here?" He shifted his weight slightly, and I easily rolled out of the hammock and stood up. I knew I needed to put some distance between us. It crossed my mind to actually extend my hand to him to help him up, but I didn't.

"Where we goin'?" he asked as he pulled himself out behind me, not looking at me.

"Zarahemla." He hesitated and I knew he wasn't ready for another round of resisting me alone. "I promise I won't try that again," I said, nodding toward the hammock. He grimaced a little. He obviously didn't even like talking about it. "Unless of course you make the first move," I said, just to be an ass.

"Shut-up," he mumbled but followed me.

As we left the party, I noticed he kept his eyes glued to the ground. I was sure he was ashamed of what he'd just done with me, and was worried others would see it written on his face. He didn't even think about saying goodbye to Jessica. I wasn't about to mention that shit. The last thing I wanted was him trying to prove to himself that he didn't want me by messing around with her. So I kept my mouth shut.

"Can I ask you something?" I said when we were out

on the street. Using this question made it seem like he could say no if he wanted to. It gave the appearance of control on his part. I found that people responded much better if they thought they were controlling the situation, when in all reality they were only responding to what I helped them think.

"I guess."

"Why don't you trust me?" I asked him, playing my first card.

He started laughing almost uncontrollably. Admittedly, this unnerved me. I didn't understand what he thought was so damned funny. "You have to be kidding," he got out between bouts of laughter.

"What's your problem? It wasn't meant to be funny," I spat out at him as I restrained the need to punch him.

"Why do you care if I trust you or not? You have me where you want me. Well... most of the time anyway."

I practically stopped walking. If I had him where I wanted, he'd be in my bed.

"What the fuck's that supposed to mean?"

"Kevin," he said, still laughing, "nobody in their right mind trusts you. Isn't that how you want it?" He was acting like he knew me, like he was some kind of friend of mine. Well, he could fuck himself because he didn't know a goddamn thing about me. Before I could get my anger reined in, he slid his hands in his pockets and asked, "Do you want me to trust you?"

My breath caught. My answer should've been an immediate yes. But when he said it, it sounded different than what I really wanted. I didn't dare open my mouth, unsure what would actually come out, so I just nodded my head.

"Why?"

"Why what?" I asked irritably.

"Why do you want me to trust you?"

"Why not?"

Rick shook his head, glancing down as he kicked a rock with the toe of his tennis shoe. "Yeah, that's the way to do it," he mumbled.

"What the fuck is that supposed to mean?"

"You make it really hard for anyone to get to know you."

"Fine. Ask me anything you want and I'll answer," I said. He wanted to know me. What the fuck did I have to lose?

"Whatever."

"Whatever what? Ask."

"Seriously, you think I'm gonna open myself up like that?"

"What the fuck are you talking about?" I asked. "I'd be the one opening up."

"I ask one wrong question and you'll lay into me. Sorry, not looking for a beating tonight. 'Sides, like you'd be honest."

I wondered why the hell I always felt I was trying to control my anger around him. Most of the time, when someone pissed me off, they got the full wrath of my temper without me even sparing a second thought about it.

"Fine. Three questions," I grumbled. "Any question you'd like, and I swear I won't kick your ass. And I promise I'll tell the truth." I doubted he could cause any harm. He already knew my two biggest secrets, and I was willing to do whatever it took to make sure he kept his mouth shut.

"And what do you get out of it?" he asked. He wasn't stupid. I couldn't very well tell him the full truth though.

"After you're done, it's my turn," I said.

He considered this for a moment. "To ask three questions? Okay," he said hesitantly. I'd bet his instincts were sending up red flags, but thankfully he wasn't listening to them.

"First question," I said, pushing forward.

We walked several steps before he took a deep breath.

"The night I found out about your dad, why did you react the way you did?"

"Not going to start with my favorite color or something a little easier?" I asked, trying to stall. I knew he'd go for the gold, but I still didn't like it.

"Don't care what your favorite color is."

"I'm hurt."

"No, you're stalling."

He could be such a fucker. I knew I had to get him to trust me, and he was obviously smart enough to call me on my bullshit. That left being honest. Damn it, I'd walked myself right into a fucked up situation. On second thought, I knew I didn't have to tell the whole truth. I could leave shit out and not tell him everything. With this in mind, I carefully spoke my answer.

"So, when you ask why I reacted the way I did, what exact reaction are you talking about?" Hell, if I was going to suffer, so was he. He was going to have to fucking say it out loud.

"You know."

"I don't, for sure."

He glared over at me, finally saying, "Fine. Why'd you kiss me?"

I laughed because he actually choked on the word kiss. But then I had to think about my answer, and the humor left me altogether.

"I was scared," I said simply. He was patient with the silence, but I was better at waiting him out.

"Why were you scared?" he finally asked.

"Second question?" I pushed.

"Fine, second question. Why were you scared?" he asked angrily. I knew I had to keep things based in truth. I considered each word, not wanting to give away more than I had to but enough to let him see I was trying.

"No one knows what my father does to me. It was just a lot for you to see, to know about me."

"So you did what you did?" I noticed he still avoided using the word kiss.

"Question three?"

"Kevin, this is not going to work if you play games with me. This was your idea, remember?"

He was right. I had to play nice. I couldn't make everything so painful—well, painful for him. I saw no way to escape the unease that had settled in on me.

"So, yes, I kissed you," I forged on.

"That doesn't make any sense to me. That's what I don't get. I find out what your dad does to you, and you know that my dad does pretty much the same thing to me, and it scares you, so you kiss me? Help me connect the dots here, Kevin."

I reached for my flask and took several swigs before offering him some. He shook his head, and I took a few more drinks before putting it back into my pocket. With my goal in mind, I proceeded.

"I didn't expect your reaction. I expected pity or some other bullshit like that, but when I walked into the bathroom, I didn't see pity in your eyes."

"What'd you see?"

I took a deep breath and blew it out slowly. "I saw someone who cared."

"And that scared you?" he said, trying to fit the pieces together.

"Fuck yes."

"Why?"

I ran my hand over my eyes and into my hair. This was a stupid idea.

"Because it's been a very long time since someone looked at me that way."

"Like they care what happens to you?"

"Yes."

"I still don't understand why that led to what it did."

I marveled at his ability to dance around the subject while still avoiding the word 'kiss' whenever possible. At this thought, an idea entered my mind. I'd been responding to him from my point of view, and to this day I still didn't fully understand why I'd kissed him. I looked at him curiously and asked slowly, "Rick, are you asking if I'm gay?"

Without looking at me, he replied, "I know you're not."

"And just how do you know that?" I'd actually never

really come out to anyone, and it surprised me that I felt nervous.

"You have more girlfriends than anyone I know."

"So?"

"So, you like girls too much. You're screwing with me. I know that."

"What if you're wrong?"

He looked at me, and I swear to god I saw hope in his eyes. I didn't even want to think about what the fuck that meant.

"Wrong about what? Are you?"

"Just screwing with you? Or gay?"

"Either. Both. I don't know!" he said in frustration, and I enjoyed watching him grasping for answers instead of me.

"No and yes," I said simply and watched as he processed my reply.

"So you are…" When he didn't finish, I helped him out.

"Gay, yes. Screwing with you, no." In any other situation I would've denied the shit out of being gay, but I fucking knew he needed to believe I wasn't just toying with him if he was ever going to end up in my bed.

He fell silent for the rest of the walk to Zarahemla, and I didn't like it much. It's not every day you come out for the first time, and his lack of response pissed me off. I wasn't entirely sure he actually believed me. Once we got there, I considered taking a seat on his same level, but I couldn't bring myself to do it. I automatically pulled myself into my spot on the broken wall that positioned me higher than him. He sat back and lit up a smoke, his eyes darting around the ceiling, not focusing on anything. It was like watching him search his own head for words.

"Out of questions?" I finally asked.

"No, too many to pick from. I don't want to waste the third."

By my count, he was well over three, but I resisted the urge to point that shit out to him.

"Am I ever going to have this chance again?" he asked.

I thought for a moment. If I was able to get something in return, I could always use these to get what I wanted. However uncomfortable they were, they weren't as bad as him turning on me. It was a risk I was going to have to take.

"I suppose. Another day, another time, we could try again."

He nodded, still putting a lot of thought into his final question.

"Why did you pick me?"

"What?" I asked, sincerely confused.

"That first day, you offered me a smoke. Why me?"

"I was trying to be nice." The lie came automatically and he didn't justify it with a response. God, he was a shithead. He knew what fucking buttons I didn't want pushed. Half-truths based in reality, I reminded myself. "You looked like you needed a friend."

"And you're so friendly and all," he said with biting sarcasm, and I knew his patience was running thin.

"I was that day."

"Look, again, this was your idea. What was your reason?"

"Okay, you looked like you needed a friend, which made you an easy target." He flinched, and I felt the stirring of something—guilt maybe? I pushed on. "I need people around me who are easy to keep in line." He looked away from me, and I didn't like what I was seeing on his face. "People not like you. I was wrong about you; you're not an easy target." His eyes shifted back, looking skeptically at me for any hint of a lie.

I wanted to get rid of the look on his face so I plowed ahead without thinking. "Just look at this goddamn situation. Do you think we'd be here if you were just like the others? You're different. You push all the wrong fucking buttons, and you know too goddamn much. Do you think that's what I planned? I picked you because I thought you were weak. I was wrong. I'm never wrong. Okay, fuck. You're not the easy target I thought you'd be. Happy now?" I jumped off my seat, clamping my mouth shut. I thought that might have been the most words I'd said in one breath to anyone. I slammed around the floorboards, looking for a stash of weed.

"What are you looking for?" he asked quietly.

"A fucking joint," I blurted out, my irritation boiling over.

"I've got one." I spun around and watched as he pulled one from his pocket. He held it out to me. "Want mine?" he asked.

Motherfucker if my head didn't fly back to the first day we met, with him on the ground and me holding my smokes out to him. What was I agreeing to if I gave in to him? Did I have a choice? Had he had a choice? If I said no, did I shatter the trust I had just built? The questions assaulted my brain too quickly for me to defend myself against them. Just as I had, he started to pull back, pushing me to make my decision. Was he playing the same game? Fuck if I had time to find out.

"Give the fucker to me," I growled as I ripped it from his hand. I watched his face for a sign of a battle won. He didn't look smug or proud, just reached in his front pocket and pulled out a light, tossing it to me—like I had that day. I snatched it out of the air and turned my back to him while I lit the joint, slipped his lighter into my pocket, and walked out back. I needed to cool the fuck down.

After several minutes, he stood beside me. I passed the joint to him and he took a few deep hits before passing it back.

"Your turn," he finally said. "What do you want to know?"

I forced myself to relax. For my plan to work, he couldn't be intimidated by me, and I knew I sent shock waves of tension out to those around me. He noticed.

"I don't want to know anything."

"But you said after I was done it was your turn to ask questions."

I brought my voice down a few notches, lacing it with some breath. "I said it was my turn, and you assumed that I wanted to ask questions. I never said that."

"Then what do you want?" he asked, and I could hear the anxiety in his voice. I waited several beats before turning on all my charm.

"I want you to kiss me."

"What? No," he said without even thinking about it. He took several steps back, turned and walked into Zarahemla. I let him go, giving him a few minutes to mull it over. Hell, I had to give myself several minutes to consider it. I was still fighting the aftereffects of the hammock where his lips had pressed into mine. I thought briefly about taking care of myself before going back in, just to get control of my body. While the thought was nice, I didn't have the time to execute it. I worried that if I gave him too much time on his own, he'd run away from me. The blunt was pretty much done, so I smashed it out with the tip of my boot and went to find him.

"We had a deal," I said, walking in. I was glad he hadn't decided to leave. That meant I had a chance.

"No, we didn't. I didn't agree to that."

"Fine. You're right," I consented. "I might have let you think something else, but this is what I want in return."

"You tricked me, and I don't have to do it."

I was ready to play my cards. "Again, you're right. You don't have to." He looked at me with mistrust. "I agree that I was not upfront with my intentions." To level the playing field, I sat down next to him and he stiffened only slightly. "Here's the deal. I won't force it, but in return, I'm not going to answer any more questions." I was giving him the choice. If he really wanted to get to know me, we weren't going to argue semantics.

"Why do you want this?"

I pulled myself off the seat and kneeled in front of him so I could look into his eyes. I was not loving being lower than him. This was not a position I ever put myself in. He immediately crossed his arms, guarding himself from me. "Rick, I've kissed you four, well kinda five times if you count the time in my bathroom. And every single time you've fought me, pushed me away, even hit me." I laughed a little. God it took nerve to hit me. "I want you to kiss me, just this once. No forcing, no fighting and no running." I noticed how he stopped breathing, and I also recognized the lust boiling up in his eyes. "I want you to want this. It doesn't make you gay. It just is what it is."

"And if I don't, you won't ever answer my questions again?" he asked raggedly. I knew I had to give him something to blame his desire on. I wasn't blind; he was disgusted by the idea of being attracted to me. I'd go so far as to say that at times it made him physically sick. I'd been around enough newly 'out' guys to recognize the signs. It would take him time, and I had to try not to take it personally.

"That's right."

"Why do you always have to get something?"

"Trust me. You will get a lot out of it too." I let myself smile. It was the truth and we both knew it. I stood and waited. His eyes scanned my body, traveling from my dark hair and clouded eyes to the black shirt that fit well but left some to the imagination. His eyes paused at my belt line, shifted away, then back and down to my black boots. He then made the journey back up to my eyes. I could see he was fighting himself. I wanted nothing more than to reach down and thread my fingers through his short hair, take his face into my hands and kiss him myself. But, like him, I fought my own body and stayed perfectly still, letting him take the time he needed. He stood slowly, shuffling his feet but not looking at me. I could swear I felt the heat from his body attack mine though we were still inches apart.

"I've never..." he began quietly.

"I know," I finished. I reached out for him, placing my hands on his hips, gently guiding him towards me. I knew I had to let him kiss me, but I couldn't resist touching him any longer. Our bodies didn't connect, but I was ready to come anyway. Just having him look at me the way he was had me searching for willpower. I ran my fingertips up his sides, onto his shoulders and then down his arms until I was holding onto his hands. Slowly bringing them up to my face, I closed my eyes and cradled my cheek into his palm, inhaling his scent.

I felt myself relax into his touch. I felt his body move closer to mine, starting to connect and touch—first his thigh as it brushed against my own, then his elbow as it bent softly against my chest. I tilted my head into one of his hands, losing myself in his touch. His other hand pulled from mine and I felt his thumb trace the outline of my cheekbone. I slid my hand down his arm again, disconnecting only for a second at his elbow before weaving around his back and pulling him into me. The palm cradling my cheek tilted my head a little and I felt his lips, chilled with the fall night air, touch mine—so gentle at first that I thought I'd imagined the contact, and then he kissed me again, tentatively and experimentally. I tried to match his pace, feeling like I was pulling against some invisible rope that wanted to bind me to him. He was holding back too. I could feel it in his body, but he had to allow himself to give in. I couldn't push.

I let go of what I needed and tried to focus on what he wanted. It was the only way I'd be able to make it through without taking control of him. I tightened my arm around him again, running my hands under his shirt and across his skin, careful not to hurt him. I listened to his body. If he tensed, I knew I was near a painful place and I avoided it. He became more demanding with his mouth, wanting entrance into mine. He didn't have to push hard. I was ready to give him whatever he needed.

We relaxed into a rhythm of kissing. The world slipped from my consciousness minute by minute as everything I knew faded into the oblivion that was left behind. I could live in his embrace for eternity and be content. As he pulled away slightly, it felt like someone had lifted a warm blanket from me and exposed my skin to the cold. Goose bumps immediately broke the surface of my skin. He noticed them and ran his hands up and down my arms, looking only at my chills and never my eyes.

I knew I should say something, anything to let him know how I was feeling, but I couldn't bring myself to break the mood that seemed to hang precariously around us.

"Speechless," he smiled. "That's rare." He finally looked at me.

"How do you know I'm speechless? Maybe I'm just not impressed," I teased.

"From the sound in your voice and this," he said, indicating the chills on my arms, "I'm going to call your bluff. I think you're impressed."

I let out a small laugh. "So, you're all sorts of confident all of a sudden?"

"Well, it's easy to be confident when I render Kevin Vincent speechless with a kiss."

Fourteen...

Rick

I'd made the choice to kiss him. I could list all the excuses in the world for why I'd done it, but it didn't change the fact that I had kissed him, and I couldn't think of anything but that stupid kiss. I wondered if the guys would notice a difference in me or us. I was terrified that just by looking at me they would be able to see what I'd done. I knew what I was feeling was wrong; it was wrong for me. I wasn't gay, even if he claimed to be. I was normal.

Going home that night, I was sure my dad would take one look at my trembling hands and try to beat the experience out of me. But he hadn't, and the guys acted the same. Even when I showed up at Jessica's, desperate to lose myself with her, she didn't treat me differently.

In the moment, I had found myself in him, experiencing a rush of feelings that were so foreign and overpowering that I hadn't been able to stop myself.

Now, I knew better. I knew that even if he was gay, he was still playing games, and I knew that I wanted a girlfriend, not Kevin. Which meant I went back to Jessica and started avoiding him, and it surprised and unsettled me when he allowed it.

When Jason's birthday arrived, I stayed as far away as possible from my dad and pretty much did everything I could just to hold it together throughout the day. By the time I slipped into the house late that night, my dad was clearly passed out on the couch. The stench of alcohol was so heavy that I knew he wouldn't be waking up and coming after me anytime soon.

After a few beers and a joint to take the edge off, I slid into the blankets of my bed but soon found myself kicking out of them because of the suffocating heat, although it didn't take long for me to get cold and pull the covers tight around me again. Even with my earphones in and my face buried in my pillow, the sound of sirens whirled around in my mind as I remembered the police telling me we'd rolled eight times — five side-to-side and three head-over-end. I fluctuated between trying to block everything out, and trying desperately to remember the car flying a hundred and thirty-four feet in the air.

The car had landed upside down, and the memory of crawling out the driver's side window onto the pavement littered with shattered glass tore at my nerves. I rolled over in my bed again, squeezing my eyes shut at the recollection of that night's events. I desperately wanted to escape the pictures flashing through my brain, and the memories that began to cripple my breathing. In my mind's eye, I could see a mass dozens of feet away. In slow motion I walked towards the debris as the blood and wreckage became vivid in my tortured thoughts. As always in my half-awake nightmare, the silhouette of a woman stepped in front of me and steered me in the opposite direction, shielding me from the picture of what was left of my brother, but leaving me to my own imaginations.

As that horrific night's events continued to stream through my semiconscious delirium, I recalled collapsing and screaming for Jason. They'd told me that despite people trying to keep me at a distance, I'd run back to him and tried to pick him up, that he had been dead before he ever hit the pavement, and that he'd broken his neck when he was thrown from the car. They'd told me a lot of things, but even in my nightmares, I seemed to block out most of the bloody details.

Staring at the clock, I watched as it turned 2:22 AM. I made up my mind that I couldn't lay in my bed thinking about him anymore. I rolled out of the tangled sheets and got dressed. There was no point tossing and turning. *Maybe if I walk it out*, I thought, *I'll get tired enough to sleep.* I slipped out of my window and used the tree to swing down like I normally did. As I landed, I spun around, catching a form sitting against my house. I jumped back, expecting my dad's fists, but the small red flame on the cigarette lit up Kevin's face as he took a drag.

I stared at him, not really sure if I was glad he was there or unnerved by it.

"Three questions?" he asked, standing, handing me his flask and walking towards the street. The shot of whiskey burned going down. I followed him, still trying to determine what he was doing at my house. He began walking in the direction of Zarahemla, and I trailed after him absentmindedly. I wasn't in the mood for his games, but realized that in the last few moments the tortured thoughts of Jason had subsided, so I debated playing my part. I wasn't about to give him something in return though.

"It's a freebie tonight, no favors in return," he said annoyingly as if reading my mind.

After some time I submitted. "Do you remember your mom?"

"A little. She left a long time ago."

"Why'd she leave?" I asked, rolling my shoulders back a few times, trying to release the tension I felt.

"Probably because my father was an ass."

I really didn't have the energy to pull information out of him, so I fell silent. I thought about how nice it would've been to know my mom. Jason had been so good about relaying the stories my dad had told him so I could feel like I knew her. My dad had always blamed me for her death, while Jason did everything he could to assure me that my mom would've loved me like he did. I tried to believe him, but with him gone I just couldn't quite trust it anymore. And the fact that Sylvia had never shown either of us any real motherly affection made it that much harder for me to believe in a mother's love. After a few minutes, Kevin cracked his neck side-to-side and continued.

"He didn't start in on me until after she left. I mean, he laid into her while she was around, so it was reasonable to assume he'd eventually turn on me, but when she left, he'd never ever hit me so I think she told herself it'd be okay to leave me behind." He paused for the distance of several houses, lost in his own haunted memories. When he picked back up, the sound of his voice calmed me. "She left when I was six, so I don't remember a lot, but I remember her singing me to sleep at night. And this one time, I remember going to Taco Time with her, and as we drove home," I noticed a small, unguarded smile on his face as he continued, "I tried one of the tater-tots and it was really hot. So she rolled down my window and told me to hold it out the window to cool it down. I thought it was the funniest thing in the world. I remember laughing and laughing. I still hold the fuckers out the window to cool 'em down." He laughed a little.

I tried to picture Kevin as a little boy, giggling and carefree with his mother as they held tater-tots out the window. It was like watching a dream or a movie in my head. I couldn't find any reality in the imagery.

"Got anything else for me?" he asked.

"No, not really." It just felt too exhausting to think. "I don't really wanna talk."

"Sure. Here, take this. It's a downer. It won't do a lot, but it should shut off your head for a while." He handed me a round white pill about the size of a miniature M&M. I swallowed it with several more shots, not caring what it was. I had to give him credit. He didn't say anything, just laid down in the dirt outside of Zarahemla and clasped his hands behind his head. This struck me as an intimidatingly relaxed position for Kevin. I couldn't relax, so I took to pacing around the place, checking out the vandalism on the walls, picking up garbage, throwing it into the fire-pit, and eventually leaning against the back of the building to smoke a joint. I'm not sure what it was — maybe the pill, maybe knowing he was close by — but my head eventually calmed down. Instead of a raging mass of intensity, it was just a dull ache of painful memories. I don't know how long it was before he came looking for me.

"You ready to go?"

"Yeah, better be getting home."

"It's been awhile since your dad came after you too hard. Just a little here and there, right?" Kevin asked. I didn't ask how he knew.

"Sure."

"Well, from what I've seen, he's probably getting pretty close to boiling over."

"Sure."

"And Sylvia and Emma are at Sylvia's parent's house again?"

"Yep."

The tone of his voice turned cold and I could hear his anger. It was a welcomed distraction from the pain swirling around in my head. "What I'm trying to say is that you should watch yourself. He tends not to hold back when they're gone."

"Sure," I said, knowing it would piss him off.

"Knock that shit off."

"What?" I replied evenly.

"The 'sure' shit. This is serious."

"What, you're mad at me now?"

"Yes, you're being careless, and that's fucking stupid and dangerous."

"And you care so much," I threw at him, knowing it was the wrong thing to say, but the anger rising in me felt better than the ache that was currently there. He flinched and his jaw tightened.

"I know where this is coming from. I'm kinda the master of this bullshit. It won't work with me."

"Just 'cause you know a little bit about my life doesn't make you the expert here. I can take care of myself, and I don't need you warning me about my dad or waiting for me under my window. It's creepy!" A knot of dread replaced the pain as I considered the fact that he might actually stop acting like he cared.

I watched as his face went carefully blank, but I could see the anger in his eyes rising to a level I was all too aware I should be avoiding.

"I'm not doing this with you tonight. You're fucked up," he said.

"So, it's okay for you to go all psycho angry violent on people, but I can't?"

"No, you cannot. Because this is not you, and you will regret it."

"It seems I'm doing a lot of things lately that aren't me and that I regret," I spat at him.

"Rick," he said coldly. "I am not going to fight you. I know that is what you want, but I do not want to hurt you. Do you understand me?"

I recognized the coldness in his tone, but I also recognized something new. I'd never heard such a strain in his voice. It brought me out of my rage.

"Do you know you do that?"

"What?" he asked tightly, still wary.

"When you get really mad or cold, you don't swear as much and you don't use contractions."

"I don't?" he asked slowly.

"Nope, no contractions."

"Never?"

"Just when you get all scary."

He smiled a little. "All scary? You sound like you're ten, talking about the boogie man."

"Nope, you're way scarier than he ever was." I returned his smile. He was right. He was not the person I was mad at. My hatred was all on me.

I watched the tension slip out of him as my anger dissipated as well. When it came down to it, he was right about my dad, whose hands clamped around me as I climbed into my window, pulling me through and tossing me like a doll against the wall.

Kevin

I turned as I heard the crash above and was about to pull myself up the tree when I heard his dad yelling. I let myself back down to the ground silently. I knew intervening would only make it worse. I clenched my teeth and tightened my fists, straining against my desire to go and tear his dad apart. I knew the violence I was capable of would put him to shame, but still, I also knew this was not the time or the place.

I pushed against the vinyl siding, trying to glue myself to the house. I could hear Rick's cries, and I found myself fighting back tears. This fact alone scared the shit out of me. I didn't fucking cry. Shit, even the worst of beatings rarely brought me to tears. My instinct was to get the fuck away from whatever I was feeling, but I couldn't seem to get my feet to move. I knew he'd watched my beating, but it would've never crossed his mind to help me. He was trained to respect authority. I didn't give a fuck about authority, and hearing his pain made me crazy. I knew I should leave, but just as strong was my instinct to stop what was happening.

I slammed my fist into the tree and my hand started burning immediately, diverting my attention for a few seconds. I tried to focus myself, to block out his wails, but each time he screamed in misery, it broke through my concentration. Just the sound of his agony seemed more powerful than the blows my father dealt. As the minutes dragged on, my tears of complete frustration and helplessness broke through. I sank against the side of his house, barely able to keep my sobbing silent. Even though I'd been weak and let a few tears escape the night Rick witnessed my thrashing, it was nothing like this wracking, uncontrollable despair that escaped from my soul. It felt like there were years of tears tearing me apart. With each new cry of agony above, I felt the torment rip from my gut.

Eventually he quieted to a whimper, and I knew his father had left him shattered, but my tears didn't stop. I couldn't bring myself to go see the destruction I'd just heard. My mind couldn't add the blood to the sounds without breaking me. I pictured him torn and bleeding on his floor. It wasn't hard to imagine. I'd found him so many times before. But now, things were different. Then I had cared but not really for him. Now, he obviously meant something to me, and I knew I couldn't take seeing him broken. Hating myself for my loss of control, I sat beneath his window, pulling my jacket against the cold. I heard his sobs above, and marveled at the tears that still flowed for him below.

Fifteen...

Kevin

I tried to hide my irritation from the guys the next morning at the corner when Rick lied to me in a text message. He actually thought I was stupid enough to believe his lame-ass excuse for not showing up. I'd expected the no-show, but I hadn't thought he'd feed me some line about not being ready for a test. It just added to how pissed off I was at myself for letting my emotions get so wrapped up in him. I'd even pushed back a little, but he'd stuck to his story, and I ended up laying into Jeremy for no reason. When Rick pulled the same shit the next morning it took a fuck load of self-control not to storm over to his house and call him out on his bullshit lies. By the time he showed up at lunch on the third day I'd been damn near ready to fuck him up. I kept telling myself that I wanted to kick his ass for lying to me, and I did. But I also knew damn well that the real reason I was pissed was because I gave a damn about the fuckhead.

Rick

"Three questions," I suggested as Kevin took a long hit on his bong. He held it in, then blew it in my face with a smile. He'd been so tense the last few days that the smile was a welcome change.

"Okay."

I hesitated, looking out the window of my bedroom. I'd been turning over the same questions all week but hadn't been sure how to approach him. He wasn't going to like what I had to ask. I started out with the easiest one, not ready to jump into the hard stuff.

"How do you sneak out without getting caught?"

"Years of practice," he replied shortly. As always it took him a bit to respond to my questions with more than his habitual short answers. "My father has locks on all the doors and windows. They have to be opened with a key."

I looked at him with surprise. "So what, you're like locked inside your house like a prisoner?"

"Pretty much. It used to be even harder. Whenever he used to go out of town, when I was younger, he'd always have someone from church come and stay at the house. One time, someone noticed the locks and asked him if it was safe. After that, he didn't like the idea of people snooping around. So, when I was fourteen he started leaving me alone, of course asking the neighbors to check in on me from time to time, but at least they're not always up my ass."

"Wow, that's pretty messed up." I was amazed at the lengths his father had gone through to maintain control over him.

"Anyway, long story short, one night he left his keys home when a co-worker picked him up for a late-night dinner with a client. I knew it might be my only chance, so, while he was gone, I called a cab and went to a hardware store to make several copies of his master keys. Since then, I come and go as I like. He sometimes locks me in my room at night as well. That just makes it easier because once he locks the door, it doesn't cross his mind that I could leave through one of my windows."

"Man, your dad is insane."

"Literally, I think," he replied evenly.

I closed my eyes so I couldn't see his reaction and forced out the words of my next question. "When's the first time he hit you?"

I could hear his deep intake of breath and the whistle as he blew it out. I heard him inhale again like he was about to say something, but didn't. I opened my eyes just in time to see him shake his head. "You sure like to go in for the kill, don't you?" He exhaled again as he laid back on my bed, staring up at my ceiling.

I shifted from the view of my window, picking up a yellow ball and throwing it against my door, bouncing it back into my hands. I kept throwing the ball as I remembered seeing Kevin take a pretty severe belt lashing without much more than a wince. Yet when my dad took to pounding on me I seemed to crumble in his hands.

"I was seven," he finally broke through the silence, and I stopped the ball. "My mom had already taken off. Bounce the fucking ball would ya?"

I looked up at him quickly, then back to the ball held

firmly in my hands. When he didn't say anything else, I obeyed his command and began to throw it against the door again.

"It was really stupid. I'd been eating lunch on a bar stool, and as I went to get off, the stool tipped over. He lost it; I ended up in the emergency room. See, I think he was used to hitting my mom. She could take a lot more than my seven-year-old body could. He learned quickly what he could and couldn't do, what would leave the least amount of evidence and still cause the most pain. I mean, he still likes to see the blood sometimes, but he's careful."

"And how did you learn to handle it?" I knew it was always better just to let him talk, but I needed to know how he was able to withstand the beatings like he did.

He rolled over on his side so he could see me bouncing the ball and narrowed his eyes. "Is that what this is about?" I sensed something in his voice, a return of the anger he'd been holding on to all week. The ball bounced out of my reach, and I watched it roll across the floor. I couldn't bring myself to look at him.

"I'm so weak, Kev. I need to learn to do what you do."

"What are we talking about here, Rick? Did something happen?"

I debated telling him how bad things had gotten the other night, but couldn't bring myself to do it. I was so scared my dad would let loose on me with Sylvia and Emma home, and I knew I had to keep it from them. I just didn't know how to control it like Kevin did.

"Nothing really, it's just, I need to know."

His voice was hard when he responded, but at least he

kept going. "I've had ten years of practice. You haven't even had a year yet. Not to mention, your dad hits out of emotion, not for fun like mine. There's a difference."

I knew I should pay attention to the tension in the room but didn't know if I'd ever have the chance again. "I need you to teach me."

"What do you mean?" he asked, and I could hear the astonishment in his voice. "Teach you what?"

"To take it like you do. The tricks you use to deal with it, like how to keep quiet. I mean from the first night when you got me to change out of my shirt and came up with a cover story for me, to warning me the other night that he'd come after me soon."

"And did he?" his words came quickly and were sharp, like a slap to my face. I immediately looked at him. His eyes were dark but not as angry as I'd expected from his tone. They were more like the sky before a summer storm rather than the emptiness of night I sometimes saw. It caught me off guard how incredibly attractive he was at that moment.

When I didn't answer, he sighed and rolled back over on my bed.

"You've got the basics down," he grumbled. I tried to reel in my thoughts, forcing the look in his eyes out of my head and listening to the words as they came out of his mouth. "As you know, come up with a story to cover your ass. You don't want people to ask questions. Where's that goddamn ball?" I looked around in the direction I last remembered it rolling off to, and found it nestled between a clothes basket and my desk. I scurried over to it, but before I could start bouncing it again he said, "Give the fucker here." Once he got in a rhythm of bouncing it against my ceiling, he resumed. "Turn your body during the beating, and keep the blows in places you can cover with clothes." He paused as he threw the ball over and over. "You've already figured out that it always hurts worse the second day, but be careful with that. If you feel okay the first day, don't overdo it or you'll be that much worse on day two and watch out for possible concussions." I heard him mutter a few swear words before he went on. "Get to know his rhythm." Here he stopped throwing the ball. "It's pretty easy to sense. I mean, I've already picked it up. I told you the other night he was going to come after you." It was obvious from the bruises that he had, but I didn't have any plans to talk to him about it. The ball picked back up, this time a little harder. "Just plan on it every four or five weeks."

As the ball bounced again and again without further comment, I finally ventured, "Anything else?"

The bouncing continued as he considered his thoughts. "Sometimes, when he starts getting edgy, you may be able to push him and get him to snap early." His tone changed, and I could hear the warning in his voice. "You have to be careful with this. Sometimes it causes the fuse to burn quick and then, boom, it's done and over. Other times, it can just make it worse because he has a lot more energy and he can keep going without ever exploding. This is a dangerous spot to be in."

"How can I tell when to push?" I asked nervously.

"Practice. You just have to try it out through trial and error. It's not fun, but if you can get it down, it can help."

He looked over at me and said, "I noticed a bruise he left on your arm from last weekend." I automatically pulled at the cuff of my sleeve to hide the evidence. "If you get a brush, you can comb it out. I'm not sure what it does, breaks up the blood or something, but it will help it heal faster." I was surprised at how much information he was giving me. I usually never got him to speak in more than one or two clipped sentences, and he was giving me a book of rules.

"How do you take it without breaking down?" I finally ventured.

I saw the muscles in his arms tighten and his hands clamp tightly around the ball. He was fighting some serious anger, and I figured I'd pushed too far.

"Again, practice," he said slowly. "For me, I found that my father got harder when I cried, so I learned to hold it in." He took a ragged breath. "I count. With each number I try to wash all thoughts of a certain area out of my head." I wondered if that's what he'd been doing with the ball as he bounced it repeatedly against my ceiling. "It's not easy, and it took me years to master it. Sometimes the pain is still too much though, and you just can't turn it off."

"What do you do then?"

He let the ball fall and rolled over to look at me, "Pray the fuck you don't die." I rocked backwards at his words, and I knew he meant what he was saying. At my visual reaction he spoke a little softer but still with an edge. "Relax," he said, his eyes fixated on mine. "When he goes to hit you, let your muscles go as limp as possible. The more you tense, the more your muscles contract and the force of the blow will be worse." He let that sink in before rolling onto his back again, and resuming his cold stare-off with the ceiling. "It's not going to get much better between now and when you get out of here," he said after several minutes of silence. "The best you can hope for is to roll with the punches, literally. Then we'll leave and won't have to deal with any of this shit anymore."

My heart stopped at the word "we'll." I wondered if he'd meant to say it, and reminded myself that Kevin rarely said anything he didn't mean. Did he mean that we'd leave together or just that he knew we'd both be taking off at some point? My mind raced through the possibilities, momentarily forgetting what we were talking about.

When he broke through my daze, he asked, "Any other questions?"

Knowing he'd answered more than his fair share, I felt I was pushing my luck, but I needed to know what he'd meant. As I started to speak, I heard myself ask him the first thing that came to mind, rather than what I really wanted to know.

"Why are you answering so much for me today?" It seemed like a simple question to me, much safer than the one I was thinking, but he waited so long to answer that I'd pretty much decided he wasn't going to tell me.

"Because I knew you needed to hear them," he said shortly.

Something in the way he said it made me suspect there was more that he wasn't telling me. "Why today?" I pushed.

"Because you asked today."

"You're not telling me something."

"I gave you the information without a fight. What more do you want?"

"I want you to be honest."

"Fuck, Rick, you've got room to talk."

"What's that supposed to mean?"

"Okay, why don't you talk to me about what happened between you and your dad the other night?" he asked, sitting up and swinging his legs off my bed, glaring down at me on the floor. I was startled by his sudden question.

"We got in a fight," I stammered. He knew this. The evidence was visible.

"Yeah. And?"

"And nothing."

"How bad was it?" His words felt like darts, stabbing at my defenses.

"Not bad," I said, standing up and looking for the ball, trying to play things off. The last thing I wanted was to go down this road with him again.

"Exactly!"

"Exactly what?" I asked, snagging the ball off the end of the bed where he'd left it.

"You just lied to me," he said bitterly, and I couldn't help but look at him.

"Why do you care? You lie all the time."

"That's different."

"Explain that one to me."

"I've been trying all week to get you to tell me what the fuck happened between you and your dad."

"So?"

"So, why the hell didn't you tell me?"

"Tell you what?"

"Fuck, Rick, how bad the fucking fight was."

"But it wasn't," I stammered, sticking to my story, and knowing the second I did that it was the wrong thing to do. I took a few steps back, recognizing the boiling anger that flashed across his eyes.

"Goddamn it, I fucking heard the fight."

I dropped the ball. "What?"

"And I know it wasn't a typical fight. I know it was harder than your usual. I sat right outside this window." He spun and grabbed onto the sill. I could see the tension in the muscles of his arms and back as he tried to control his temper. "And I heard you cry out for god knows how long. And then you lie to me all fucking week about it. That's why I told you what you needed to hear. I know it's getting worse."

I stood there, too stunned to say anything at his outburst. He finally continued in a quieter voice. "I need you to not lie to me. You can't leave shit out, though god knows I do it all the fucking time. But when I ask you pointblank about something, don't fucking lie to me." I saw his shoulders heave a few times. He turned suddenly and sat back on the windowsill, looked up and said. "My turn. I want another kiss." The change in him happened so fast that I just stared at him, my mind not fully comprehending. "You knew what I wanted walking into this one. You can't back out," he said, taking several long steps towards me.

Like before, his hands found my hips, but he was more urgent this time, more impatient. His thumb brushed against my lips. "Kiss me," he whispered, leaning in towards me, his breath hot on my mouth, but he didn't close the gap. Before I realized what I was doing, our lips connected. He set the pace this time. He wanted more and wasn't willing to wait for me. He steered me towards my bed and pulled me down on top of him. My mind screamed out for me to stop, but it was like there was a complete disconnect with my body—it refused to listen.

It amazed me how his hands moved heatedly without hurting me, causing my stomach to tighten and warmth to flush my face. There were so many painful areas from my dad, but he seemed to know how to avoid them all.

He tugged at the button of my jeans, but didn't unfasten it, giving me a chance to stop him. Again, my mind battered me with horrible thoughts as I felt my hips press into his body in reply. In response, he gently maneuvered himself so he was on top. As he slowly kissed his way down my chest I knew what he was planning on doing and was shocked at the look of desire in his eyes as they locked onto mine. I'd gone down this road with Jessica, but she'd never looked like he did. With a smile, and not breaking our eye contact, he pulled my jeans down. It was me who threw my head back and broke our stare when I felt his mouth on me.

Kevin

Not surprisingly, I got him off. What did surprise me was my ability to stop once I did. It was damned hard, and thoughts of taking him closed like clamps around my brain. After seeing him wither under my touch, I knew he was as good as mine, but I had to ease him into it.

Something in his head kept resisting me even though his desire rivaled my own. I was still pissed as fuck at him for lying to me, but knew the real reason I was so mad was because my damned emotions were getting involved. My end goal was to get him to care for me and get him into bed. I was beginning to realize that how I felt about things may just end up lending a level of sincerity, but that came with a fair amount of risk as well. In the end, it didn't matter if I cared about him. All that mattered was that he kept his mouth shut.

"Listen, I gotta go. We've got that stupid Halloween party at what's her name's tonight, and we both need to get ready," I drawled out as I untangled myself from his limbs.

"Yeah, what time are the guys expecting us?" he asked, and I could tell he was still affected by my talents.

"'Bout an hour. They're coming to my house first. You'll be there?" I asked the question, knowing I wasn't giving him much of a choice.

He hummed his confirmation before adding, "Your dad?"

"He'll be there, but I figure if we're in and out pretty quick, it should be fine."

"Yeah, okay."

I didn't trust myself to stick around much longer, so I quickly swung out his window and made my way home.

The guys all showed up on time. I had to work hard not to place myself next to Rick. He was like a fucking magnet.

"Where you been?" Jeremy asked innocently. I didn't like the sideways glances from the others, anticipating my reaction.

"Does it fucking matter to you?" I snapped.

"No, I mean," he stammered, while nodding towards Rick. "It's just both of you haven't been around much." He was trying to shift attention from me to Rick without knowing this would get him into more trouble. Rick paled, and I saw his fear.

"And I'm his keeper all of a sudden? What the fuck do I care if he's not around? And what the fuck do you care if I'm not?" I took a menacing step towards him, blocking his view of Rick, hoping Rick had enough sense to pull it together. I knew we'd been disappearing too much. When it came down to it, I hoped they were scared enough of me not to give me much shit about being gay, but if word got out and my father found out, I'd be dead.

As we were walking out the door, my father turned the hall corner.

"You going out tonight?" he asked with a smile that I knew all too well.

My stomach dropped as his hand came down on my shoulder. From the guys' perspective I knew it would look fatherly, but as his claws dug into my skin, I forced my control into place and responded. "Yes, sir, I told you about it on Tuesday. Halloween party." I was proud of my light and even tone.

"Kevin, may I have a word with you alone?" He looked at the guys with a smile. "You guys don't mind, right?" I avoided looking at Rick as they started to leave my house.

"I'll be out in a minute," I said, as the door shut behind them. "They're right outside." I said, my heartbeat racing. My father's fist flexed around my shoulder as he turned and thrust me towards the kitchen. I moved quickly, putting as much distance as possible between the front door and the attack that was coming. I knew I had to stall, get to the kitchen and turn the radio on so they didn't hear anything.

"I don't really care where they are." He slowly moved towards me. Rounding the corner I reached for the radio with my left hand, but he grabbed my wrist before I could hit the button.

"Sir, the noise..." I tried to pull towards the radio as he yanked my arm and roughly backed me into the wall.

"You will not make any," he threatened calmly. He wrapped his hand around my small finger and I stared at him in dismay. His eyes, calculating and cold, betrayed nothing. I tried to pull away, but his grip tightened even more. His stare bore into mine as I slowly felt the tension on my hand increase, and then the searing pressure finally gave and my finger snapped back. I slammed my head into the wall and bit my lip to keep from crying out.

He enclosed my ring finger in his hand and repeated the slow, painful process of breaking it. My free fist flew to my mouth and I bit down to keep from screaming. My mind started scrambling for focus. He smiled but didn't release me. He wrapped his fingers around my middle finger. "Next time I will break every one of your fingers," he said gently before he released my hand and walked away.

I sank to the floor and took several deep breaths, trying to push out the throbbing. With my good hand I pulled out the cell phone my father didn't know I had. I knew I needed to set my fingers before I could leave. It was humiliating asking Rick, but I didn't see any other choice if I wanted to make it out of the house without another incident. I could do it on my own, but that would take twice the time. I debated for moment. Would it be better to take my chances that my father would come back for more, or ask Rick for help? I typed, *Come in — JUST you, my bathroom,* and sent it to him. I slowly pulled myself to my feet and silently made my way downstairs to find some bandages. I'd long ago purchased popsicle sticks for broken fingers.

I didn't hear him until he was right outside my door, which was good. The quieter he was, the more likely my father hadn't heard him come in. "You okay?" he asked.

"Fine." I said irritably. "Help me wrap these." I turned and thrust the first aid shit at him. To his credit, he took one look at my hand, nodded and started to work. "What'd you tell the guys?"

"Forgot my wallet. What're you going to tell 'em?"

"Smashed 'em in the door."

"They're not stupid."

"Yes, they are." At his raised eyebrows, I added, "You never knew."

"True."

"Go now. I'll be out in a minute."

"You sure?" he asked, glancing around, looking for my father.

"Yes."

I sat on my bed and threw back several shots of Wild Turkey. I focused, counting to a hundred. Pushing the pain down as far as it would go, and plastering on the best normal-looking Kevin mask I could muster, I ran up the stairs and slipped out the front door, ready for a party.

Sixteen...

Kevin

People in lame-ass costumes carried on the usual conversations in the kitchen, and I was bored out of my fucking mind. Rick had disappeared over an hour ago, and I thought I had been pretty fucking patient not to go knock him on his ass for his stunt. The throbbing in my hand had started to spread up my arm, and I thought this was as good an excuse as any.

"I'm gonna go find something harder for the pain," I mumbled as I lifted my arm. It fucking irritated me that I was even making an excuse. Things were definitely becoming a lot harder to balance.

I knew I'd find him with Jessica. She was decked out in a damn hippie outfit. How fucking predicable was that? It shouldn't have bothered me, but it sure as hell did. I'd always liked Jessica, but seeing her with Rick now made me hate her just a little.

"Smoke, outside, now!" I said, walking past but not looking in his direction. I got outside and lit up. I could see him through the windows, but he made no attempt to follow me, even though he glanced at me several times. Fuck! Pushing me when we were alone was one thing. Pushing me in public was just plain stupid on his part. I calmed myself more and more with each drag. By the time I was done with my smoke, I was ready to put him in his place. I hated what I had to do, but between Jeremy's comment and Rick's complete lack of respect, I had to do something. I'd put on a show for the world—one that was aimed to hurt Rick. If he wanted to play the straight role, I'd show him how it was really done.

I sauntered back in and wrapped my arms around a girl named Liz. She'd been watching me for weeks, so I knew she'd be easy, and with Kari nowhere to be found I had to find the next best thing. I pulled her tight against my body.

"Well hello, beautiful," I said huskily, laying it on as thick as I could. "Been watching you for a while. Wanna dance?"

She melted into my arms at the unexpected attention. After several minutes of whispered nonsense, she threw her head back and laughed. I knew exactly what she wanted. I pressed my lips to her neck and kissed her, drawing out the response I expected. She stiffened slightly with pleasure and then wrapped her arms tightly around me. I spun her around to the music, getting her to giggle, all the while drawing attention to the obvious sexual tension I was creating.

I saw Rick out of the corner of my eye. He was watching

us intently, barely paying attention to Jessica now. I found her lips and backed her softly into the wall. Women like it soft, I reminded myself. I kissed her gently; I could taste the stale smoke of weed on her tongue. Mixing a little pressure into the kiss, I intentionally made it feel like I was struggling to hold back. Going through the motions, I pulled her tight to me, then backed off as if I realized what I was doing. Each step, each move, I carefully calculated and executed. She responded like they always did. Still kissing, I tugged at her and made my way to a bedroom. She smiled as she realized where we were going, making a perfect show of everything. God, I was good at this fucking shit. I found Rick in the same spot, still staring at us. I winked at him as I closed the door behind me.

We fell onto the bed together. I knew she wasn't down for sex, which was why I'd picked her. *Let Rick's imagination go where it wants*, I thought. It was all about the show. All I had to do was make out with her and convince her I was feeling what she was. This was the easy part—match what she was doing, take it one step further until she started to pull away, then stay at that level and finally put a stop to it. Do it nicely. Rick had to see us leave the room with a smile. Like baking a fucking cake using step-by-step instructions.

"I gotta stop," I said, abruptly pulling away from her.

"What, why?" she asked with alarm, a flash of insecurity in her eyes.

"I'm going nuts here. I want you so bad it hurts." I paused until realization flashed across her face. "I don't think I can do this any longer without..." I paused again, pretending to search for the words. "You know," I said, waiting until she caught on.

"Oh, oh, it's all good, don't worry about it," she said, trying to act frustrated herself, but I saw the relief on her face. I didn't want to come on too strong. I had to make her feel like it was her decision and that I really wanted to fuck her.

"I mean, we can, if you have protection."

"No, no, I don't," she said quickly, and I could tell I'd played this one successfully.

I acted frustrated but cool with things, making sure to carry out the game to the end. I stalled, talking to her, pretending to want to get to know her. All the while I was just making sure the timeline fit. I knew that leaving the room with her would cause talk, and that talk would make it upstairs to the rest of the guys in a matter of minutes.

After enough time had passed for a climactic moment to have occurred, I asked her to go back out to the party and dance with me. We ran right into Rick as I flung open the bedroom door. He had his hand raised like he was about to knock, and flushed when he saw me. I smiled at him, making a point to straighten out my pants, like I'd just put them on. He shook his head without saying anything and walked away. I turned to Liz.

"Thanks!" I said lightly, giving her a small kiss on the cheek just to rub it in as Rick kept walking. "I'll catch up with you later for that dance, alright?" She smiled, and I turned to follow Rick out before she could say anything. I caught up with him in the front yard as he lit up.

"You have something to say to me?" I smirked.

"Nope," he said shortly, taking a deep drag. Without a glance at me, he started walking towards the street.

"Liar," I baited him

He snorted, "You really gonna go there again? After what I just saw in there?"

I paced myself to catch up to him. He walked for the length of several houses, then turned abruptly and kissed me. I stumbled slightly backwards, not expecting the kiss or the force with which he'd grabbed me. He'd never kissed me on his own. My mind raced, but my body dominated my thoughts. I responded immediately and pulled him hard against me, working around the worst of our bruises. I felt his hand slide beneath my shirt as he struggled to pull me closer to him. The heat from his hand sent shock waves through me. I lost my mind completely.

"Jesus, Rick, I want you," I whispered, burying my head into his neck. As I said this, the full weight of my surfacing emotions came crashing into my body, and my legs considered giving way under the intensity. I'd started this game as a way to control him and keep him quiet, but with his arms around me and his lips coercing mine apart, I knew I'd never felt anything close to the passion that was consuming me. Now, with his body pressed against mine, the feelings I'd been so terrified of seemed welcome and comforting.

"I want you too, Kevin," he said, pausing. "But, I can't be with you." I felt his tears on his face before I saw them. He pulled out of my arms and said, "I can't be what you want me to be. I'm sorry, but I just can't."

I stared at him, watching his mouth move but not

hearing what he was saying. The words that came out of his mouth didn't fit or make sense with what I was feeling inside.

"What are you talking about?" I stammered. I reached for him and tried to kiss him again, trying to stop whatever he was saying from being said.

"Kevin, no!" He pushed back from me. "I can't trust you. All your games and lies. Not to mention, this is just wrong."

"What?" I interrupted. I felt the warmth of my previous emotions draining out of me and a coldness starting to replace those feelings. "You don't understand," I said. Again, I reached for him, trying to get his warmth back. With every step he took away from me, I felt the fury in my soul creep back in.

"I understand," he said with a hint of anger. "I understand that not ten minutes ago you were in that room with Liz doing god knows what. Probably telling her the same things you're telling me. I'm not going to turn my back on everything I know is right just for you."

"No, Rick. It's not like that. It's different with you," I said desperately.

"Kevin, I don't think you understand how close you came tonight. I was ready to try things with you. I was ready to damn myself to hell and give up on a normal life. But the second you got all over that girl I realized this is not what I want it to be. I was ready to give up everything for you, and it's all just a game. I knew it all along, but you just proved it."

"Fuck that!" I said, my nerves suddenly exploding. "You were all over Jessica and then you had the fucking balls to completely disrespect me. You have no room to fucking talk."

"What are you talking about?"

"Jessica! Disappear for a goddamn hour and make me come find you. You know damn well how that looks in front of the guys—me letting you get away with shit I never let them get away with. Then, I flat out demand you go with me to smoke, and you have the balls to fucking ignore me and make me look like a complete ass."

"What? I have no idea what you're talking about. Go out for a smoke? When?"

"Downstairs! Don't fucking pretend you didn't see me. You kept looking at me while I was out there smoking."

"Jesus, Kevin. How was I supposed to know you wanted me out there? Did you consider asking me?"

"Ask? Fuck no. I demanded, and you just sat there all up in Jessica's business."

"Seriously? I didn't even hear you!" he spat out angrily. "I saw you once you were out there smoking, but I didn't see you walk past me, let alone hear you with the music so loud. Don't you think I know better than to push you like that in front of others?"

I stammered, "Well, that still doesn't explain you being all over her."

He groaned loudly and threw his hands up in the air.

"Kevin! I'd just spent the last hour telling her I couldn't sleep with her anymore because I wanted to try things exclusively with someone else."

"What? Who?" Again, rage coursed through me at the thought of competing with yet another girl for his attention.

"You're an idiot!" he spat at me furiously. "Kevin, I never know why you do what you do—maybe to get to me, maybe to feel powerful and smart, maybe just to show off what a stud you are. Whatever the reason, tonight you made me see that I don't want to be with someone like that."

"Then why did you just kiss me?" I asked, my anger deflating as I realized I was losing this fight. He started to walk again and I cut him off. "Why, goddamn it?"

"Because, I'd wanted to all night and then you were standing there, and I couldn't help myself. And when I did, I saw just how poisonous you are for me because the image of you with Liz disappeared the second you touched me. Everything disappeared."

"What's wrong with that?" I asked, smiling slightly, trying to play it cool even though all I wanted to do was wrap my arms around him and keep him from walking away.

"Because, Kevin," he said, tears once again forming in his eyes, "you'll never feel that way about me. You couldn't if you wanted to. It's too much to give up just so you can win whatever game you're playing."

His words cut through my bravado. "But I do care...it's the same..." I tried to interrupt, but he kept going.

"You don't care, Kevin. Caring would imply you have a heart, and yours is as dead as your father's!"

Despite his words, I felt my so-called dead heart boil with rage as my temper flared. I was not about to stand back and let him tell me I couldn't feel, when I felt more than I'd ever felt in my life.

"Fuck off, you bastard!" I shouted as I threw a punch, wanting to break his jaw but stopping just short of any real damage. As he stumbled backwards, instant regret took over, and I almost crumbled myself as I saw the hurt tear across his features. Instead, I stormed off with every intention of finding my way to Club Normandy.

Rick

I watched him hurry away, astonished that he'd actually hit me. He hadn't done it for show or to set boundaries. There was no one around, no one to make a point for, and he'd hit me. I thought of going after him, but I hadn't done anything wrong so I let him go.

I went back to the party to find a bottle of alcohol. I didn't care what it was, I just knew I wanted to drink to forget. Jessica found me taking several big mouthfuls of Goldschlager.

"You okay, sweetie?" she asked with gentle concern.

"Afraid so," I replied bitterly, realizing I'd just gotten what I'd asked for. She reached up and thumbed away some drying blood from my lip.

"Looks like you got in a fight."

"Yeah, hanging out with Kevin Vincent tends to get you in a lot of trouble."

"Is it just the likes of Kevin who does all the damage?" she asked, running her thumb across a bruise near my wrist where my dad had grabbed me several days before. I narrowed my eyes at her. Did she know?

"Pretty much," I said vaguely, pulling my wrist from her gentle touch.

She nodded. "Looks like it might not be such a good

idea for you to be alone tonight."

"Thanks Jessica, but like I said earlier…"

"Oh no, not like that," she said, raising her hands. "I only meant that I could be a friend if you need one. We're still friends aren't we?"

"You really are an amazing person," I said, smiling, knowing she truly meant what she'd said.

"I keep trying to tell you that," she replied, and the twinkle in her eye made me forget Kevin for a minute. I wondered if I ever could make it work with someone like Jessica. For a moment, I wanted to kiss her, but I knew it wouldn't be fair to her, so I just smiled.

"Yes, I could use a friend about now."

She kept the conversation light and easy, which allowed my mind to wander to what had happened between me and Kevin. I'd been so sure he was playing games with me, but when he'd hit me I'd seen the real reason in his eyes. He was scared, and that changed everything. If he was scared, then I knew at least some of what he was feeling towards me was real. And I had to face the fact that even though it was wrong, I wanted to be with him.

Having no idea what to do with this information, I drank and flirted with Jessica. When I woke up in a guest room with her next to me in the bed, my first thought was relief that she'd stayed with me, immediately followed by dread. I hoped I hadn't had sex with her again, but after a quick inventory it appeared we were both still fully dressed. Sensing my worry, she assured me that nothing had happened. I prayed that my dad had been too drunk the night before to realize I hadn't come home.

I skipped meeting the guys at the corner, and arrived to the class I had with Kevin a little late, surprised to actually find him there. He nodded at me, which completely threw all my warning bells into overdrive. But after class ended, he simply gathered his stuff and told me he'd see me around. After school, he continued to act like nothing had happened. He went back to the cold, detached Kevin I'd met when I first moved to Salt Lake. I didn't know if I was thankful or terrified of this change.

His indifference went on for weeks. I was once again just one of his minions. He rarely looked at me, and when he did it was usually to slam me for something. I pushed him a few times, and he cut me down with his words but never came close to touching me physically. I knew this was what I'd wanted, but I didn't think we'd stop being friends. He'd given up so easily, like I never even mattered to him.

If I'd never seen the other side of him, I wouldn't have cared. But I had. I'd felt his lips on mine. I'd seen the fear in his eyes that last night, and I began to see my mistake in assuming he didn't care at all. He'd seen me shattered after a beating and had taken care of me. Why hadn't I thought about these other things before I'd flown off the handle? And now he was simply there, not speaking to me—no sidelong glances when the others weren't looking, no soft touches as he brushed past me. And even though I had tried to find reasons to be close to him, he always managed to stay clear of me. As much as the thought of wanting him still made me sick at times, not having him in my life was worse. He wasn't angry or even all that cold towards me. He simply didn't care anymore, but once the idea of giving up everything for him had entered my mind, I couldn't seem to shake it, even if he didn't care about me anymore. I did the only thing I could do: I kept pushing for any sort of reaction.

Kevin

The room felt claustrophobic. I knew my father had turned in for the night so I got out of bed, pulled on my coat and threw my backpack over my shoulder. With my flask full and ready to go, I unlocked my bedroom window and pulled myself out quietly. I'd been trying for weeks to shut Rick out, and it wasn't becoming any easier with time. That last night had shown me just how dangerous he could be for me. I still had to get him into bed, but I had to make sure I had control over myself first.

As I walked down the dark and abandoned street, I wondered if the people in my neighborhood had any idea what went on behind the closed doors of my house. Most of them saw us every week at church, and they considered my father a respectable member of their congregation, a leader in the community, and a strong example of what a man should be to his family. His reputation had only been enhanced by the story he'd spun about my mom, addicted to pills and running off with another man, leaving him to raise me alone. As I walked past house after house, I realized I knew most of the people who sat behind these closed doors, and I wondered if they had secrets as deep and dark as my family did. Or did they all just go along in life pretending that evil didn't walk among them?

Could they really be that naïve? Honestly? Sure, there had been a few people who had questioned along the way, especially when I had to miss school, but they were so easily convinced that all was well. It didn't hurt that we had money, not to mention my father's good looks and charm. (Thankfully, I had inherited those helpful traits from him.) At least one person along the way had actually reported the suspected abuse, and an inadequate caseworker had shown up at the house. The beating that followed after she left was one that would go down in the history books. She never came back.

My father hated the idea of people thinking I was anything other than perfect. On the rare occasion when he broke his own rule of avoiding my face, I think people saw the bruises and assumed I'd been in a fight at school, which my father hated, but not as much as he would've hated the truth coming out. No one had ever come right out and asked me what was going on, even though people rarely saw me get into any sort of actual fistfight. Of course, the church members didn't think it was my father. He was doing the best he could and it was understandable that I occasionally acted out, knowing the history with my mom. It was helpful when it came to the guys because they assumed I was a fighter, and that kept them in their place. Well, it kept all of them in place except Rick.

I was not beyond using violence as a means to an end. But what I'd done to Rick had been a completely emotional response. It was never good to fight from fear.

It was dangerous and I knew better.

I hate the fucking cold, I thought pulling my coat tighter, *and I hate being locked in the house with my father*. I lived in the wrong state with all the fucking snow and freezing temperatures.

My plan to shut Rick out was going perfectly. When the right opportunity presented itself, I was ready to let him back in. I knew if I cut him out, he'd be begging for my forgiveness. And, as planned, he wasn't happy with his demotion back to my groupie. I had to be careful since he knew the truth about me, and I wondered how long it would take him to betray me—only a matter of time, I was sure. But if I could hold him off at least until the end of the school year, I might have a chance to escape the consequences of his betrayal. The only way to do that was for me to remain in control. As long as I kept him coming to me, I had the power to make sure he stayed.

By the time I got home from my walk I was beyond cold. Once inside the house, I took several shots of Wild Turkey to warm up. Rick was in my head. I'd considered going over to his house just to make sure he was in his place, but I knew I had to play my cards right. I had to wait until he was ready, and then he'd be mine for good. I could only imagine the sweet satisfaction it would bring to finally have him. I pictured his body moving with mine as I took care of my own needs before passing out.

I welcomed the next morning. It meant one more night I'd been able to get through without facing my father, and the hangover that always accompanied my mornings was pretty much unnoticeable. Regardless, I took a shot to ease the headache. Starting the day off with a slight buzz made things so much more tolerable. When I got to the corner, Rick was already waiting. He was so predictable.

"You're here early," I said, glaring at him. I wasn't ready to play nice yet.

"You have a problem with that?"

"Don't fucking push me."

"Wouldn't dream of it."

As usual, people started to walk past us, making their way to school. A group of three girls walked by, and I could tell they were trying hard not to look at us.

"Hey there, Beth!" Rick said, strolling out to her. She smiled weakly at him but didn't respond. He held his smoke out to her. "Wanna try?" I think my mouth literally fell open. What the fuck was he doing?

She kept walking, faster than before, and focused in on the conversation with her friends. Rick fell into stride with them. "Hey, Beth, seriously, it's not that bad." He took a long drag of his smoke and blew it at her. She was visibly upset and was trying hard to pretend he wasn't there. I didn't like where things were going. This behavior was so out of character for him. He kept up the act past several more houses while I followed slowly behind him as he danced around them. I noticed, however, that he was getting angry and kept looking at me. Then it hit me—he was desperately trying to get a fucking rise out of me. This was not going to end well. He didn't know how to play this game.

He swung his hand back and landed a hard slap on Beth's ass. She yelped out in surprise, turned and slapped him. I felt like doing the same thing. I don't think he realized what he was doing when he grabbed her wrist and spun her around so her arm was pinned behind her back. Then he wrapped his other arm across her neck from behind. My mind went blank with shock and the only thing I could think was Fuck! Fuck! Fuck! Her body was pulled tight against his and I found myself reacting. Fuck!

I stopped and several people around us did the same thing. I know I should've stepped in and knocked his head off, but I couldn't get myself to move. We all watched Rick, uncertain of what he'd do. He realized suddenly that people were staring at him, and I saw a flash of doubt cross his face before he looked at me. He whispered in her ear and then roughly pushed her away. She stumbled to the ground. Again, rage coursed through me at his behavior, but I couldn't tear my eyes from the unfolding scene.

He knelt down next to Beth, and I was shaken to see he was using one of my tricks on her. He brushed the back of his hand against her face and looked at me as he whispered something else into her ear. This time he was ready for her hand as it flew at him. He caught her wrist and laughed, never taking his eyes from mine.

My stomached lurched. I wanted to walk away, to pretend I wasn't interested, but he knew he had me. I couldn't move as he slowly came towards me. Leaving Beth behind without a second glance, he walked right past me.

"Got your attention now, don't I?" he said arrogantly. My confusion and shock quickly evaporated as his smugness broke through my dismay. I had to gain control of the situation.

"You think?" I retorted, turning quickly to follow him. "You think your little performance was all that?"

"By the look in your eyes, I know it was all that," he said smugly. I hated him because he was right and because he had forced my hand. Now I had no choice but to play his game.

"So what, you think I fucking care?" I laughed, hoping I sounded sincere.

"I know you do."

"Fuck off."

"Where you going?"

"Away from here." I was headed back home to my territory where I could get him alone. He may have forced my move, but I still had the upper hand.

"Am I invited?" he asked, smiling at me.

"Don't really care," I said, picking up my pace, trying to act like I didn't care. When we got to my house, we hadn't said a word to each other, which gave me plenty of time to lay out a game plan in my head. I stormed into my room and took another shot of Wild Turkey.

"Let's have at it, Rick," I said, spinning on him, ready to play my cards. "Why is it you're so fucking wrapped up with the idea that your little scene with Beth got under my skin?" I took a deliberate step towards him. "Is it possible that even though you claim you don't want anything to do with me, you actually long for my attention?" I paused for a heartbeat and took another step. "And me?" I let my words sink in. As he clamored for a response, I continued, "Does it make you feel better to get a rise out of me? Does it make you hot when you look at me the way you did? Well, you know what, it makes me hot too! It makes me ache to feel your body against mine! It makes me...."

"That's not what this is about," he finally managed to interrupt me.

"Oh no, then why don't you tell me what your little act of voyeurism was all about," I said, closing even more distance.

He started to back up. "Don't you realize what you're doing to me?" he blurted out.

With a quick step, I was inches from him. I smiled and ran my fingers down his cheek, just as he'd done to Beth. He'd obviously not shaved before school and I could feel the roughness of his skin. He shoved my hand away.

"If you pull stunts like that with me, Rick, you may get more than you bargained for," I said, moving in to kiss him, but he turned his back to me. I pressed my body against his and placed my hands gently on his shoulders. "Why do you keep resisting me?" I whispered in his ear as I gently traced his earlobe with my tongue. I felt his body stiffen against mine and knew he'd been longing for contact again. "Rick, I want you!" I moved my hands slowly down his arms, gripped his biceps and pulled him tight against my chest, "And I know you want me." I pressed my hand against him, and his body confirmed his desire.

"Kevin...oh god!" he exhaled as his head tipped back to rest on my shoulder. I seized my opening and started to kiss his neck. My teeth expertly nipped at his skin. With my years of experience, he didn't stand a chance.

He turned suddenly and grabbed my face. The weeks of separation had obviously done the trick. His resolve had finally abandoned him, and his passion nearly crushed my control. I checked my emotions though, careful not to let my feelings get in the way like they had the last time, but I let my body completely react to his hunger.

"Wait!" he said, pulling away breathlessly.

"Fuck, what now?" I mumbled in frustration.

"You'll never hit me again," he said firmly. "Promise me, on everything you claim to feel for me, you'll never do that again."

I took a step back. He was right, and goddamn it if I hadn't regretted the punch the second it had happened. "I am sorry." As the words crossed my lips, I realized it was the only sincere apology I'd ever given. "I promise, it will never happen again."

He nodded, taking my face into his hands and kissing me, his passion quickly turning to near desperation.

"Slow down, Rick," I said, smiling as I reminded myself to stay focused and in control. I drew him into my arms and returned his kiss with the same passion he showed and then some. I, after all, was the expert, and I was going to make sure he'd beg for a repeat performance.

Finally, Rick St. James was going to be mine.

Rick

It was hours before our naked, sweaty bodies separated and I came back to reality. The way I'd responded to him amazed me. I couldn't even call what Jessica and I had done together sex. He took his time with me, allowing my body to open up to him, to submit and become his. I could still feel his lips on every inch of my skin. I couldn't believe I'd resisted him for so long. At the same time, I tried to ignore the voice in the back of my head screaming at me in disgust. No matter how much I'd wanted to be with Kevin, being gay was still not something that set well with me.

"Do me a favor," he said, breaking the silence.

"Mmmm." I hummed into his chest, trying to quiet the noise in my head.

"Don't ever pull a stunt like the one you did with Beth again."

"What?" I asked stupidly, knowing exactly what he had said and what he meant by it.

"You heard me."

I curled tighter into his body, trying to play off what I was feeling. "It wasn't that big of a deal. Got your attention, didn't it?" In truth, I hadn't planned on doing what I did, but I couldn't stand his coldness anymore. In a split second, I'd decided to cross his line, become the alpha and challenge him to his territory. I knew he wouldn't be okay with me taking control. It wasn't until I was halfway through my stupid plan that I realized what I was doing. It wasn't just about him and me; I was hurting Beth. But when I saw him and the emotion burning in his eyes, I knew I couldn't back off. I had what I wanted and, like chasing a high, I wasn't going to stop until I got more.

The night he hit me I'd made a mistake. As I watched him the following weeks, I began to realize I needed him in my life. I didn't care if it was wrong. I was addicted to him. I couldn't help it.

"I'm not fucking kidding. Don't go there again, got it?"

"What's your problem? I've seen you do a lot worse," I said, trying to deflect the guilt I felt. Kevin did do a lot worse, but I couldn't help thinking of how disappointed Jason would be, and I knew I was going to have to figure out a way to apologize to Beth. He tensed beneath me, and I noticed his hand twist and clench the blanket.

"That's the point. That wasn't you out there. That was me. You're better than that. Don't fucking sink to my level."

I looked at him evenly and saw that his face was tight with control. He actually meant what he said.

"Hey, okay. I'm sorry. I know it was wrong. I promise I won't do it again." I hesitated, wondering if I dared continue. "Can you promise me the same?" At his look of shock, I laughed. "I know you've got your rep to protect, but if I can't be a jerk then neither can you."

His tension started to waver. He flipped me on my back as his lips began to kiss their way up my abdomen and my body shivered.

"Quit making deals. You made me wait far too long for this, so be quiet and let me play," he whispered before finding my lips and deepening his kiss while my back arched up to connect with his body. His hand gently moved down my chest and then stopped abruptly as he rolled off the bed, smiled and pulled on a pair of jeans. My body immediately protested.

"You've got to be kidding!" I blurted out before I realized just how desperate I sounded.

He got his self-satisfied grin. "Afraid not. Now get ready to go. If we hurry, we might actually be able to make it to school before lunch ends. Don't want to be accused of disappearing again, do we?"

Seventeen...

Kevin

The boy could fuck. His appetite was insatiable, and what they say about the quiet ones being wild in bed wasn't far off. Once he got a taste of what I could give him, there wasn't any location, time or place that was off limits. From sneaking away to the bathrooms at school to risky rendezvous at Zarahemla, we couldn't keep our hands off each other. Even though I could feel there was a part of him that still hated himself, he didn't deny his body what it longed for.

We settled into a routine more quickly than either of us expected. I was surprised at how easy it was to be with him. I'd always assumed that once my goal was met, it would take work to keep him coming back, but he seemed to genuinely want to spend time with me, even when we weren't fucking. For the first time since I could remember, I actually slept at night. I didn't pace, go check on the guys, or venture to the clubs.

My father was out of town, and since the weather was so damn cold I'd snuck the guys in the side entrance of my house to avoid the neighbors noticing. When Rick got a call from Jessica and went out back to talk, we were all stoned, listening to music and playing video games. When he didn't come back in for a while, I went to check on him and found him smoking on the patio. Living up on the benches of the Wasatch Mountains provided my house with a killer view of the entire city. Glancing to the left, I could just barely make out his roof several houses away, shielded by the trees and the nighttime. Directly below my backyard was Jeremy's. Our hill, overgrown with scrub oak, sloped down 'til it met the fence that separated our properties. I followed his yard with my eyes until I found his room. Jeremy had texted me, letting me know he wasn't going to be able to make it. I wondered what was going on in his little world below mine that had kept him from being where he was supposed to be.

"Everything okay?" I asked as I wrapped my arms around Rick from behind, gently pulling him to the opposite side of the house with me.

"Fine," he said, smashing out his smoke as we went. "She just wanted to say hi." My lips descended on his, listening carefully for any noise that might disturb us. "I was hoping you'd come find me," he whispered as I bit down gently on his neck. Being around the side of the house would allow me the chance to disengage from any compromising position we might get ourselves into before anyone would find us.

"Is that why you stayed out here in the cold so long?"

"I figured you could warm me up."

"I'll do more than warm you up." Knowing time was precious, I aggressively pulled at his pants, wanting immediate access. He wasted no time helping with mine; however, my instincts were finely tuned, and at a slight sound I pushed him gently back against the wall and raised my finger to my lips to keep him quiet. As I yanked up my pants and buttoned them with one hand, I found a smoke, snapped it three-quarters of the way down and lit it just as I stepped around the corner to find Mike lighting up his smoke.

I leaned quietly against the wall, noting that he hadn't seen me appear. When he finally caught site of me in his peripheral vision, he did a double take and a startled breath clued me that he was indeed surprised to see me.

"I wondered where you went to," he said smoothly. "Is Rick out here?"

"Haven't seen him," I said, blowing the smoke out of my nostrils.

"Didn't he come out here to talk to Jessica?"

"I guess."

"Bet he decided to go next door and bang her. Bet'cha we don't see him again tonight," he laughed knowingly.

I didn't respond, letting him take his story where he wanted. It had been a close call, but I was the master of avoiding close calls with my father. I hoped Rick overheard what Mike had said and would take off. It was as good an alibi as any, and I knew damn well he'd be back in my bed as soon as the guys left. This was our new normal.

Rick

I surprised myself. I knew I was doing something wrong,

but I'd become addicted to what Kevin did to me, and I was actually beginning to think it wasn't all a game for him either. He was still Kevin, and I wasn't stupid, but it was crazy how easy it was to see through his façade as each day went by.

After a particularly cold January night, he'd called it quits early and sent the guys on their way. Afterwards, we sat on the couch in his front room, all the lights off, looking out his big picture window at a raging storm. The snow blanketed everything and gave a false sense of peace. We both knew the world was anything but peaceful. But, alone with the snowstorm, we could almost pretend. I brushed my finger against his jaw line and whispered, "This one's new."

He reached up and held my fingers gently against the purpling bruise. "Yeah, right before you guys got here." He left his hand on top of mine.

"He usually avoids your face."

"Guess he forgot," he replied distractedly.

"What happened?"

He narrowed his eyes thoughtfully. "You know, I'm not sure what set him off this time. Probably just wanted to get in a good one before leaving town."

I nodded slightly, knowing that his dad laid into him far more than mine did me, and often without any reason.

He asked me quietly, "Have you ever thought of getting outta here?"

"What'd you mean? Like out of Utah?"

He nodded as he tipped a beer into his mouth. The way his lips wrapped around the head of the bottle caused me to flush immediately. He noticed and winked.

"Well, yeah, all the time," I answered, though the thought of leaving Emma behind sent a stab of pain to my stomach.

"Where do you wanna go?" he asked, staring into the darkness like he was searching for a road that would take him away.

"I don't know, California, New York. What about you? Do you wanna leave?"

"Fuck, yes," he said shortly. After a moment of thought he added, "I think I could do New York, maybe even California. I guess anywhere would be better than here." He took another drink. "I might even try to find my mom."

"Wow! Do you know where she is?" I asked.

"No. Pretty sure she went off the grid so he couldn't find her."

"And you haven't seen her since she left?"

"Nope," he said, and I could feel his body tense.

"Why do you want to find her if she abandoned you like that?"

I could hear the defensiveness in his voice when he replied, "Because I know what it feels like to be willing to do damn near anything to get away from him." He paused again. "Why do you want to go to New York? California, I get. But New York?"

Without much hesitation, I replied, "Guitar." It was only after it came out of my mouth that the thought of him giving me a hard time occurred to me.

"Guitar?" he asked, surprised.

"Yeah, I play. They have a good scene in both places," I said, watching nervously for his reaction.

"Really? Since when do you play?" he asked with a genuine smile that eased my nervousness.

"Since forever."

"How do I not know this?"

"You don't know everything."

"Sure I do." He flashed a smirk that caused butterflies in my stomach. "But seriously, you play?"

"I used to, but my dad put a stop to it that first time he hit me."

"Uh-huh."

"He found the guitar Jason bought for me. I haven't seen it since."

"So, that's what set him off. You think he tossed it?"

"I'm sure. I asked about it once and got pounded on. Been too scared to ask since."

"What a fucker."

"I hate him," I said bitterly. "Losing that guitar hurt more than any of my beatings."

"Really?" he asked, surprised at my anger.

"Yeah, it meant a lot to me." Immediately my thoughts became crowded with Jason, and I shifted on the couch, feeling anxious. For the most part, I had become able to think of Jason without crippling side effects, but there were moments when it still felt like my heart was being crushed.

Kevin reached out and gently placed a hand on my back. "You should get a new one, get back into it."

"Yeah? And how do you think that will go over with my dad?"

"You can practice here, leave it in my closet and write me some cheesy bullshit song."

"Yeah maybe." I could almost hear Jason saying the same words to me. The similarities were too much to handle. "What do you want to do?"

"What do you mean?"

"Like college or a job."

"Don't really know." He took his hand from my back and sipped on his beer. "Haven't thought about it much."

"Why not?"

"I've always just focused on getting through each day."

"Why not think about being a shrink?"

"Excuse me?"

"Well, you're pretty good at the head-game thing," I said. He glanced at me, and when he saw my smile, he laughed.

"Yeah, I'm kinda good at that, aren't I?"

"Well, you seem to be able to read people fairly well. You should use that," I said more seriously.

"I don't know, seems like too much work. I'd have to go to college and all that."

"You don't want to go to college?" I asked, surprised. I'd been brought up that the next step after high school was college. That was all there was to it.

"No, don't really think it's something I wanna do. That's what my father wants, not me. You thinking about college?"

"Well, yeah."

"Why?"

"Never really thought about it much, just what I know is supposed to happen next."

"Don't know the next step for me. Traveling maybe. I wouldn't mind seeing the world. Maybe someplace like

Japan. That'd be cool. I just don't see myself staying in one place for very long."

"That's something I like about music. I can see it taking me to a lot of new places."

We stopped talking, the mood suddenly changed as our eyes settled into each other.

"I want..." but didn't finish. He smiled, his eyes traveling to my lips. He didn't move, knowing what I wanted but making me go after it.

"Yeah?" he smirked at me. He knew I still found it hard to initiate things. I moved in cautiously, slowly. My lips brushed against his, and I saw him grip the beer bottle tighter, but other than that, his body barely moved. I kissed him slowly, tasting the tobacco and beer on his lips. It only lasted a few moments, but it took my breath away. As I pulled back, he smiled.

"Nice," he said quietly. I settled in against him, both of us staring into the storm. "I wonder if there's a place for us? You know, where we could just...." he trailed off.

I didn't respond; it was rare to hear Kevin talk about us. "I mean, think about it, where we could kiss and hold hands without caring." He leaned in, bending his head and kissing me again. He shifted his weight and wrapped his arm around me. "A world where these feelings aren't wrong," he continued, his mouth taking more control of mine. "A place where people aren't scared of what this means." He smiled and his lips gently coerced mine apart. I wrapped my arms around him and let my body surrender to his. "What we have is too good for this world."

I gasped against him. He'd never spoken about what

we did together with such gentleness and I longed to believe what he was saying. Usually things were so intense and almost desperate. As he brushed his lips against mine, they felt like feathers lightly dancing across my skin.

He put his beer bottle down, reaching out to pull the blinds shut. His body covered mine like a blanket of snow, completely smothering out anything other than the peace and passion I felt with him.

Between the memories of Jason and Kevin's unexpected gentleness, I cried as he made me come, overtaken with powerful emotions. At first I was mortified, but he immediately took me into his arms and tightly held me against his body as the tears fell.

Kevin

I didn't know the first thing about buying a fucking guitar, but there I was at Riverton Music trying to pick out something he'd like. I tried my damnedest to ignore the fact that I was planning on giving him this shit, lessons and all, for Valentine's. I wondered when I'd become such a fucking sap. But hell, the way he'd looked when he talked about playing, I knew I had to do everything I could to keep him looking like that. I tried to tell myself that it was all part of my plan to keep him quiet, but I knew damn well he wasn't ever going to tell anyone.

I packed the shit into my car after telling the clerk to give me the best acoustic in my price range, the case and all the other shit he'd need.

Rick had made it clear that he wanted me to leave him

alone for a few days—which pissed me the fuck off—so he could work on college applications. More than once I'd considered dropping by to say hi but knew it would just lead to us in bed, and he really needed to get that shit done. At the insistence of my father I'd submitted my applications early. By the time my father realized I wasn't actually going, I'd be eighteen, and he wouldn't have a say anymore.

Rick's absence was annoying but good. It gave me time to check in with the guys. Since it was senior year, they didn't seem to mind their newfound freedom. With me wrapped up in all things Rick, they'd done pretty well keeping themselves entertained, but I still had to assert my power. They were my only exercise for staying focused and they appreciated the doors I opened for them. I knew my control was wearing thin, and I needed them to sharpen my skills.

I stopped by Brett's house on the way home from the music store, invited myself in, and threw myself into a recliner in his front room, kicking my feet up. He didn't put up with me as much as he used to, but I only had to keep him around for another six months, so I wasn't worried. Providing drugs while playing on some of his lingering fears, it'd be easy.

I suggested that we all go to a hockey game the next night—okay, not so much suggested as indicated that we were going to do it. I also advised that I wanted to go downtown the following weekend and chill at a new coffee shop. He laughed at the mention of a coffee shop, then quickly changed his attitude when I nearly jumped out of the recliner to pound him. Rick was one thing, but

I was not about to start tolerating bullshit from Brett of all people.

Rick

"What was that all about?" I asked, my head resting on his bare chest, my fingers lightly tracing the multitude of scars. The smattering of colors—reds, purples, greens, yellows and blues—mesmerized me. Who knew bruises could be so artful? It was weeks after Valentine's, and I still couldn't believe he'd given me a guitar and lessons. I hadn't told him yet, but I was working on a song for him, just like he'd suggested.

"What, the phone call?" he asked as he placed his cell phone back on the nightstand next to his bed.

"Yeah."

"Just my father checking in."

"Why didn't he just call the house?"

"He did. I always forward the home phone to my personal cell when he's out of town."

"You do? Does he know you do that?"

"God, no! That would defeat the whole purpose. I have two phones. The one he pays for and monitors like a hawk and my personal cell that I pay for."

"Does he check in often? I haven't noticed you taking calls."

"Fuck yes he does. I'm good about it. He'd kill me if he ever heard anyone else, so I always duck off."

"I can't believe I haven't noticed."

"Because I didn't want you to." I could hear the smile in his voice, the confidence in his ability to keep people from knowing what was going on with him. "You know,

I never know when he or one of the neighbors will call to check in on me. It would be just my luck for him to call while I was out smoking or, you know, off doing whatever. So I got in the habit early of always forwarding the house phone to my cell. That way, I never miss a call and he thinks I never leave the house without his permission when he's gone."

"Man, he thinks of everything doesn't he?"

"Yeah, but so do I."

We laid there in silence for a while longer as I contemplated the lengths his father went to. I couldn't imagine how Kevin had survived for as long as he had. With as much control as his father expended, I knew Kevin had to be brilliant to keep him from finding out about everything he got himself into. I marveled at his ability to hide so much from his dad. But I guessed that when life depended on it, anyone would make it happen. The more I thought about Kevin and what he had to do just to survive, the more I felt the urge never to leave his side. Of course, that immediately led to the fact that sometimes things just felt so wrong despite my growing feelings for him.

"Why do people hate us?"

"What do you mean?" he asked with a bit of an edge.

"I mean, not us so much as, you know...what we do."

"Oh," he said, and I could feel the grin of comprehension, then a sigh. "The world is not a nice place," he said absentmindedly as he ran his fingers over my back. I closed my eyes and reveled in his touch. I was tired of angry Kevin. He had changed so much in the last few months, and I wished I never had to deal with that other side of him.

"When did you first know you were gay?" I asked.

"Forever ago."

"What, like when you were five?"

"Well, it's kinda like the stories you hear. I knew I was different when I was little. Eventually I realized I was attracted to guys."

"Did you ever struggle with it?"

"No, not really. It's just who I am."

"But if you're so okay with it, why not come out?"

"Not really about me, it's about my father. How do you think he'd take it if people found out his precious son was a raging homo?" He continued to tickle my back. "Besides, I've created two worlds for myself. They both serve a function. One is to play, the other is to survive."

"And where do I fit in? Which world?"

"You've presented a bit of a problem for me," he teased.

"I'm serious. I know nothing of this other life you talk about. God, I don't even know if that's what I am." I couldn't quite bring myself to say it yet.

"Trust me, you are," he said, pulling me tight against him.

"Have you ever slept with another guy?" I asked. His body stiffened and his hand stopped tickling my back. "What is it?" I looked up at him. "How many?"

"Why is it important?"

"Why wouldn't it be? How many?" I asked, sitting up. I could tell by his body language that I wasn't going to like his answer.

He shrugged his shoulders. "I'm really not sure."

"How can you not be sure? It's not a hard question.

Five? Ten? Twenty? Fifty?"

"Probably more than that." A strand of his black hair fell into his face and he impatiently shook his head.

"More than fifty? What, like a hundred?" I accused. I pulled away as he reached out for me.

"Like I said, I don't really know. Come back here."

"How? How could you possibly be with that many guys? Did you care for any of them?" I asked, pulling even further out of his reach.

"I met most at the clubs. I didn't care about any of them, not like you. Most were from when I was tricking," he said without looking at me as he rested back into the bed.

"Tricking?" I forced the word out of my lungs and past my heart, which had lodged itself firmly in my throat.

"What's the problem, Saint Ricky?" His old nickname for me felt poisonous rolling off his tongue.

"Don't you dare do that now," I cut him off.

"Do what?" A small smile tugged at his lips. He knew exactly what he was doing.

"Don't you start to play your games with me. I'm not about to let you try to control this situation. We're past that." He laid naked on the bed, with a simple sheet draped over him, his arms resting behind his head like he didn't have a care in the world. His eyes were empty, the flat stone I hated. I knew he was weighing his choices. He was scared and trying to protect himself. "I know you better than you think, Kevin. You're trying to figure out how to play this game with me to your advantage so you don't get all those bottled-up feelings involved. You stay right here, checked in with me and without your games, or I'll walk out of here and I won't come back." His eyes flashed with anger as he struggled to control his emotions, and then they became empty again. At last he resigned, and his soft, dark eyes returned.

"Well then, let's have it," he said rolling out of the bed and fishing for his clothes on the floor.

"When's the last time you tricked?"

"Long before I slept with you."

"And all these guys you've been with, were you at least safe with them?"

"Sometimes."

"God, Kevin, how could you and not tell me?"

"I've been tested."

"So."

"Several times, as recently as last week. I'm fine."

"Still."

"Still what? I'm fine and I've always been safe with you, so you're fine." He had his back to me, and I could see his scars screaming at me.

"You should've told me."

"Why? So you could get all self-righteous like you are right now and judge me? Excuse me for wanting to put this off for as long as possible. I'm not that person anymore, Rick."

"So you haven't tricked since before we slept together? What about just plain old screwing. Have there been other guys?"

"Yes."

My heart left my throat and descended rapidly to the pit of my stomach, feeling like he had just sucker punched me. I wished he had. "When? How many?"

"Just one, the night you left, after I hit you."

"How could you? You know what I've given up for you? How could you throw that away?" Outrage at opening myself up to him blinded me.

"What?" he asked bitingly. I could tell he was trying to control his anger, and I worried he might snap on me. "Are you fucking kidding? All that you've given up for me?" He stood up, his voice becoming more controlled. "You can't be serious! How many fucking times did you run to Jessica after I kissed you?" he mocked me. "And you were the one who called it off that night. What did you expect me to do? Come running after you and beg you to stay with me? I don't chase guys, Rick. I don't need to. Do you see this shit?" He motioned to his finely sculpted chest that was somehow even sexier with the scars. "Why in god's name would I chase after any guy with all I have to offer? I am so much better than that!"

"Better than that, are you?" I threw back at him, my face flushed with heat like someone had just opened an oven and all the hot air rushed at me. "So, I should consider myself lucky to be with you?"

He shook his head and glared at me. "Knock it off. Quit being like that. You know that's not what I said. Don't try to twist my fucking words on me."

"What'd you mean by it then?" I demanded, shoving my legs roughly into my jeans and grabbing my shirt.

"Whatever! And how many people have you fucked? I know for a fact you were with Jessica. Anyone else I should know about?"

"That's different."

"What?" He let out a short laugh. "Explain that one to

me."

"She's a girl."

"And?"

"And..." I stammered. "And, it's different."

"How?" he asked, his voice chillingly calm. "How is it different, Rick?"

"I'm not...!"

"Not what, Rick? You can't even say it! You're not what? Gay? Queer? A faggot? You don't even know who you are!"

I reeled at his words, taking several steps back at the hate he threw with them.

"I know I'm not like you!" I spat at him.

"Fuck, yes you are! My cock was in your ass. You're a fag, just like me. Own it already."

"I am not!" I shouted, only half believing my own words, terrified he was right. I started to grab my stuff to leave.

He was in my face, screaming, and my instincts were warning me to get out of his way. "Fag or not, do you have any fucking clue what you mean to me?" he shouted at me as his face darkened with several shades of red, and I turned to put some distance between us. He grabbed my arm and spun me around to face him. "Damnit, Rick! I gave up that whole other life for you. I used to sleep around with hundreds of men. I could fuck any guy I fucking wanted. And now look at me. I'm sitting here practically begging you not to go. You've made me fucking weak." He slammed his palms into my chest and shoved me against the wall, but his anger turned to desperation. "You've made me lose control!

You claim to know me, so tell me, what does that fucking mean?" Tears built up in his eyes and gradually started to run down his face, while I stared at him in disbelief. His voice came out in a harsh whisper, "Tell me what it means." He stopped, backed up, spun around and punched a hole in the wall. Grabbing his fist, he glared at me. "Get out!" Unable to move or say anything, I stood there until he took several steps towards me again. "So help me fucking god, don't make me break my promise. Get the fuck out of this house!"

Kevin

Within seconds of Rick running up the stairs, I knew I was going to fucking chase him. As I roughly wiped the goddamn tears from my cheeks, I thought, *Me, Kevin Vincent, is crying and is going to chase after a goddamn guy. I might as well start using clichés like my life has gone to hell in a handbasket or I made my bed, now I should sleep in it.*

I wasted another thirty seconds trying to talk myself out of going.

"Fuck, you know you're going to do it. Just get it over with," I mumbled to myself as I grabbed my jacket and went after him.

The last thing in the world I expected to see was Rick in front of my house talking to Brett, Mike and Jeremy. I pretty much ran right into them, thinking I was in for a chase. All four just stared at me.

"What the fuck?" was all I managed.

"Just wondering what happened," Jeremy said quietly.

"We were supposed to meet up at Zarahemla an hour ago," Brett said with an edge.

"Did you forget?" Mike asked, more to Rick than me.

My mind was completely blank. I looked over at Rick who was looking at his feet, waiting, as expected, for me to answer. I couldn't grasp what the fuck was going on. All I knew was that I was chasing Rick down. I had no idea what the guys were talking about, not to mention the fact that my nerves were screaming at me to get the five of us away from my front yard so my neighbors didn't see us and report back to my father. After several more uncomfortable beats of silence, Rick spoke up.

"Did we forget? I distinctly remember Kevin telling us to meet here, not at Zarahemla." He was fucking covering for me.

"No, it *was* Zarahemla," Brett pushed.

"It was Zarahemla, but if you remember, he changed his mind. Oh, that's right. Maybe you were too busy checking out that new girl to pay attention."

"And all three of us heard wrong?"

"You calling Kevin a liar?" Rick spat.

That shut them up, and as usual I marveled at how quick he could be on his feet. I shouldered past them, trying to act like the whole thing irritated me enough that it didn't justify my attention, but in reality I was horrified to realize how much I'd fucked up. I knew they'd follow, so I headed to Zarahemla, hands jammed in my pockets, head down, hair shielding my eyes. Fucking up and forgetting to show up was one thing—not showing up was not out of the norm for me—but having Rick in my bed where the guys may very well have come looking for me? That could have been a colossal disaster. Five minutes earlier, and they would've found us naked. And then being caught so off guard that I couldn't get my head on straight, and Rick having to cover for me? I was no longer just off my game; I might as well be on a fucking suicide mission. *Un-fucking-believable*, I thought.

I didn't say a word over the next three hours as they went on about the shit they normally talked about. Rick did a good job keeping their attention from me, knowing I could snap if one of them said one wrong thing. I stared at the fire Jeremy had lit to keep the bite of spring weather at bay. All I could think about was Rick. From fucking up with the guys, to the tears, to the goddamn chasing, I had to figure out how to stop everything from spinning even more out of control. Walking home, we dropped Rick off like normal and I continued on to my house. Before my door closed I had my phone out and was calling him.

"I don't think I'm ready to talk yet," he said, answering the phone.

"Then why'd you answer?" I spat out at him, still on edge. "Fuck, I didn't mean that. Don't talk, just listen. Come back out. I'm on my way back down." I hung up, hoping he'd at least come out and tell me off face to face.

When I got to his house, he was sitting on the curb, smoking.

I didn't say anything and kept walking. He followed my lead.

"So talk," he said after a few minutes.

"I'm off my game."

"I know."

"I mean, bad." I tried to emphasize how big of a deal this was.

"And you want to blame me," he said shortly.

"No. This is all on me."

Rick glanced sideways at me, and I noted the look of irritation fade slightly from his blue-gray eyes.

"So, you're off your game, and that's bad. I get it. But how does this have anything to do with you and all your boyfriends?"

"That's just it. I'm not on my game anymore." I took a deep breath and forged on. "I'm not in control of shit anywhere. Not with the guys, not at home. For sure not the fuck with you. I don't even know what I'm saying right now, rambling like this. Since when do I fucking ramble? I don't go to the clubs anymore, I don't fuck anyone but you, and you have me spinning so far out of control, I don't know which way is up. I mean, I fucking chased you tonight, and then when we ran into the guys, I couldn't think about anything but making sure you didn't walk away from me."

"Okay," he said, and I could hear the lack of trust lacing his one word.

"Fuck, I don't know how to say it. That guy you're pissed at, that was before you. I don't know who I am anymore, but it's not that person."

"So you stopped sleeping around because of me?"

"Yes!" I said, pausing a beat and not wanting to continue, but I had to. "Wait, no! Fuck. I don't want you to get the wrong idea. I'm not all noble and shit. Yes, I stopped fucking around because of you, but it's not like that." I ran my fingers through my hair, knowing I wasn't making any sense. "Sit," I said, stopping and pointing to a curb. He looked at me carefully.

"It's really cold out here," he said.

"I need to get this out and I can't fucking concentrate and walk at the same time, alright? Fucking sit, would ya?"

"Fine," he said, slowly sitting on the curb. He pulled his flask and smokes out and put them to use. Grabbing my own flask and taking several long swallows, I started to pace in front of him.

"Okay, I know that for this," I said, motioning between the two of us, "to ever work, I gotta lay this shit on the line." I took several deep drags on my smoke, trying to figure out the best way to say what I needed to say, like I knew what the fuck I was doing. "That time you asked me why I kissed you?" He nodded. "I told you I was scared, which was the truth. But what you really should've asked is why I kissed you the second time." I took a deep breath and started rambling again.

"After you found out about my father and the whole 'me kissing you' thing, I got scared. You know I think he'll literally kill me if people find out. I knew I had to keep you quiet. You're a good person, so I knew if I got you to care for me, you would keep quiet about my father." I took another deep breath and steadied myself. He was not going to like what I had to tell him. "And I knew that if you cared for me, you'd let me fuck you. And once I fucked you, you wouldn't tell anyone because it would out you at the same time." I waited, expecting him to walk off, blow up, or hit me — god knows I deserved it.

"Jesus," I heard him breathe, but I didn't look at him.

Not being able to stand the silence, I continued. "I stopped fucking other guys because I was so focused on keeping you quiet. But I should've known better. You were never just one of the guys, and even though I started out all wrong, I ended up here, with everything right. Fuck, everything's not right, but you are."

I sank down and knelt in front of him. "Don't you see? Everything's wrong now, everything's out of control. You know what that does to me. All I see is you! I don't party, I don't play, I'm nothing like the person I was when you first met me. And that's just it. I'm not that guy anymore. Yes, I'm still an ass, and I'm still going to fucking blow up and do all the wrong things. Shit, here I am laying everything out for you, rambling like a complete asshole, and I know you're not even okay with the whole gay thing. But we're more than that. We have something and you can't deny it. For the first time in my life, I fucking care about something. I care about you, and no matter what I did in the past, I promise that's not who I am when I'm with you. You're all that's good..." My voice cracked and I felt the tears start to burn my eyes again. *Goddamnit*, I thought, *when had I become such a fucking mess?* There was so much more I wanted to say, but I shut my mouth, scared to go on.

"It was all a game," he said simply, and I heard the distance in his voice that I didn't want to hear. He pulled away from me and stood up. My heart crashed, and I ducked my head, ashamed to look at him. I could hear him taking drags on his smoke. I fell back and sat on the concrete, knees raised and my head cradled in my arms. I couldn't bear to watch him walk away. "It's probably best if you give me some space," he said as his footsteps faded into the darkness.

Eighteen...

Rick

When I got home, I headed straight to the shower, hoping I wouldn't wake anyone up but not caring too much if I did. I knew there was no way I'd be able to lay down and relax with the multitudes of thoughts tearing through my mind. I hoped the water from the shower would ease the tension in my muscles and take the edge off my overwhelming emotions. The water slowly heated up, and the initial sting faded quickly. I felt so exhausted. I'd never seen Kevin so unhinged, and it took its toll on me. I couldn't help but hear what he was saying; he was out of control, it was dangerous, and I was the center of the whole thing. Not to mention the idea that everything I felt for him had been based on a game to keep me quiet. I always suspected he was playing at something, I just didn't expect to be at the center of his ploy. I didn't even want to be this way, and here I was dealing with all the drama that went along with it. I was so tired and overwhelmed that I could barely stand. I cradled my head in my arm against the shower wall and ran my palm against my short hair, brushing the water out of my eyes. I just wanted to lie down and sleep off the crushing feelings. I flipped the lever to start a bath and turned off the showerhead. It splashed into the empty tub, immediately beginning to puddle. I waited several seconds until it began to cover my feet, then slowly sank to the tile, my shoulders slumping as the warmth began to envelope my body. I turned the knob to make it hotter and felt the heat begin to spread at my feet.

I didn't want to think. I couldn't anymore. I felt and saw only the water that pooled and rippled around my bruised body. I turned the knob again, adding even more heat. As it reached my torso, I let myself slide further in. It slowly crept and wrapped itself around my aching limbs. As the heat stung my skin, the mental tension and physical pain began to fade away. My ears sank beneath the water level. I closed my eyes and the world became muted. My breathing became even and steady, inhaling the steam that billowed above deep into my lungs. I could hear the water pounding into the bathtub, but the world outside was distant. My body floated and swayed with the movements of the splashing. I reached up with my foot and pushed the knob to off. The roar was gone and it was silent. My thoughts remained as weightless as my body. My sense of gravity, pain, light, and noise were all muted. Heat wrapped around me, and the soft swaying suppressed my anxiety, dissolving my broken life while my body remained behind, floating weightlessly.

To his credit, at school the next day he let me have my space. He watched me cautiously but kept his edge clear. He focused in on Mike, who was talking about his brother who had joined the Army awhile back. Apparently, Mike had let his parents know that he also wanted to join, and they were giving him just as much crap as they had his brother.

Towards the end of the day, I ran right into Jessica in the hall.

"Howdy, stranger," she beamed up at me.

"Hey." Putting on my best smile, I leaned in and gave her a hug.

"What's wrong with you?" *Leave it to Jessica to zero right in on my mood*, I thought.

"Nothing."

"I call BS."

"Really, I'm fine."

"And I'm not an idiot. Hate to break it to you, but you're a horrible liar." If she only knew all the lies I'd told her. "Plans with Kevin tonight?"

I narrowed my eyes at her. Why did I always feel she knew more about what was going on than she admitted? "No. Why?" I ventured cautiously.

"Good, you're coming over for dinner. My parents are making manicotti at six. Don't be late."

I called after her as she sailed down the hall, trying to get out of her plans, but she didn't slow down. Sometimes I wondered if she was even more stubborn than Kevin.

After dinner with her amazingly normal mom, dad and little brother, she tried to get me to go out on her back porch, but knowing how close her house was to Kevin's, I talked her into hanging out in her basement. I hoped we'd watch TV or a movie or something, but the second I sat down she turned to me and said, "Okay, dish."

I tried to laugh good-naturedly at her. "About?"

"Whatever has you in such a funky mood."

"Jessica, like I told you—"

She interrupted me, "Rick, come on, it's me." She scooted closer to me on the couch and took my hand in hers. "I know better than that."

I fell back into the cushions of her couch. As much as I didn't want to talk about anything, I knew she was just trying to be there for me.

"Is this about your new exclusive dating friend?"

"Huh?" I asked distractedly, still thinking about Kevin being next door.

"The person you want to be all exclusive with?"

"I can't talk to you about all this. It's weird."

"Only if you make it."

"Me talking about the person I'm sleeping with now, with the girl I used to sleep with? It's weird!"

"Hi, remember me?" she said, waving her hand in front of my face. "The free love hippie chick. You don't think I can handle it?"

I wished I could tell her everything—about my dad, Kevin, Kevin's dad, and, most of all, my feelings for him and what he'd done. *What a joke*, I thought.

"Melissa." The name came out of nowhere. I hadn't planned on talking about Kevin, but making up an imaginary name for him suddenly made it seem possible.

"Is that her name? We're making progress. Now tell me what's going on with her."

I closed my eyes so I didn't have to look at her. "I don't really know. It's such a crazy relationship." She hummed in response, letting me ramble. "I never thought I'd fall for her. I didn't want to—that's for sure. In fact, I didn't really like her when we first met, but now, I just don't know. She's..." I searched for the best way to describe Kevin, "screwed up."

Jessica laughed, and I looked over at her. I hadn't meant to be funny. "Aren't we all?"

"Not like this."

"What do you mean?" she asked, smiling gently.

"She has this really intense past and doesn't trust anyone, but she claims to trust me. If I believe her, then I'm like the only one who really knows her. But on the other hand, she could be totally full of it and just playing me. And to top it all off, it's just not an easy idea," I paused, "being with her."

"Why would she play you like that?"

"Power, control—I have no idea, but she admitted to me the other night that, when we first met, I was simply a game to her."

"Ouch!"

"I know, right? But now, she says it's something different, but that was only when she thought I was leaving her. I don't know what to do. There are times I'm still scared to be with her. She comes from such a crazy place, and part of me knows it's not right. It's hard to tell what's real. It's all just so complicated."

"Well, what's your heart telling you?"

I laughed a little. Of course, it was that easy for Jessica. Just listen to my heart. I thought about it for a second. "I don't know. That I like her? But so much of it still feels so wrong."

"Well, that was convincing. Like her or love her, Rick?" I blinked at her. The question pierced into every fear I had. I'd never allowed myself to even think about him that way. I sat silently. Was it possible? Had I fallen in love with him?

"Oh, Jessica," I sighed. "I don't know. How did this happen? Why did this happen?"

"Is that a yes?"

"I don't know what it is." I sat up impatiently, wringing my hands together. "It's just not that simple!"

"Is being in love so bad? Love is a beautiful thing. Why are you resisting it so much?"

"You don't understand. Things are so complicated."

"Well, help me understand then."

I leaned back again and thought about it. Would she understand my feelings for a guy? How could she? I barely understood myself. Added to that, I had feelings for a jerk like Kevin. But he wasn't the person most people thought he was. He tried to take such good care of me. Ever since my first run-in with my dad he'd been taking care of me.

"God, Jessica, I think I'm in love!"

"That's what I thought."

"But this is so not right."

"You can't pick who you love," she said softly, almost sadly.

"Should I tell her how I feel?"

"That's up to you."

"I don't even know how she'd react if I did."

"And you won't know unless you tell her."

"This is so not how I pictured my whole first love

thing going down."

"I don't think it happens like any of us thinks it will."

"Sometimes I just wish it'd been you," I said regretfully.

"It would've been nice, but it just wasn't right. That doesn't mean I don't love you."

"I love you too, Jessica."

As she walked me to the door that night, she gave me a giant hug, reassuring me that if I trusted in love I wouldn't regret it. Sadly, I didn't feel as confident about the idea as she seemed to be.

Several days passed, and I still hadn't come to terms with everything he'd done, or my newly realized feelings for him. I felt that on some level he must have been telling the truth, but I kept going back to the idea that I was all part of his game, that what he said he felt for me was just a pretense to keep me from telling anyone what I knew, as if I'd do that anyway. And if what he'd said was the truth? Then it just made me even madder that he had actually thought I'd tell someone in the first place. I always thought he understood me better than anyone else, and if he really thought that about me, then he didn't know me at all. Finally, there was a part of me that wanted it all just to be a game for him. That way, I could walk away and not look back. I'd have a reason to shut out how I felt, and then maybe try things with Jessica again.

In my efforts to avoid Kevin, I found myself spending more time with Emma. After returning from the park with her one evening, we settled down to watch a movie when my dad walked into the front room.

"Emma honey, would you mind going to your room

for a bit? I need to talk to Rick," he said, looking at her but not at me.

"But daddy, we're watching a movie."

"I know sweetie. The movie will be here later. I need to talk to your brother. Can you be a big girl and go to your room?" As he said this, I knew whatever conversation was to follow would not be a good one.

"Come on," I said, taking a deep breath and turning to her. "Listen to dad. We'll watch the movie later, ok?" I nudged her gently and she huffed in my direction.

"Fine!" she pouted as she slid off the couch.

"Thanks, honey, and please close your door," my dad called after her.

"Basement. Now," he said still not looking in my direction.

"Why?" I asked in defiance. If I was going to get it, I wasn't going to make it easy for him.

"Excuse me?" he said, turning to me.

"Listen, whatever you have to say, say it. We don't have to get into it with Emma home."

"I said get your ass downstairs!"

"What's this about?"

"Like hell you don't know." His anger was rising and I knew it was stupid to argue with him, but I honestly didn't know what he was mad about. And like Kevin had recommended, I sensed it might just be easier to get it over with by pushing him until he blew.

"I don't know! That's why I asked," I threw back at him.

I flinched when he reached out and wrapped his fingers around my arm. Yanking hard, he pulled me up and off the couch, shoving me towards the basement.

"This is about the fact that you have no respect for this house anymore. You come and go as you wish." As I started through the door to the stairs, he pushed me and I stumbled down several before catching the railing for balance. "Think you can keep whatever hours you want? You don't think I notice when you don't come home at night, or when you sneak in at five in the morning?"

"I thought you liked it that way," I snarled at him as I made my way to the furthest room in the basement, hearing him shutting each door behind him. "I know you can't stand me. Figured I'd make it easy and stay out of your life as much as possible."

The sting from his hand against the side of my head surprised me, because I'd expected him to wait until we were barricaded as far away from Emma as possible.

"You still live here, and as long as you do you will show me respect." I nearly ran to the room that had become my torture chamber, concerned only with keeping the noise from Emma. And again, just like Kevin had taught me, I began to count as soon as the belt met my skin, hoping I'd be able to restrain my cries enough not to be heard. In the end, I think the pillow I grabbed and buried my face in helped more than anything.

I'd known my blatant disregard for his curfew would eventually catch up to me, but I had no plans to change my habits. Plain and simple, when I wasn't at the house, he had less of an opportunity to come after me, and that alone was worth the risk of an occasional punishment. I knew one of the main reasons I got it this time, was because I'd been home more in the last week and, frankly, my dad couldn't stand my presence.

As I hoped, when he finished with me, it wasn't as bad as it could have been. Pushing him did make him blow faster and harder, but he burned out quickly. I quietly made my way to the bottom of the stairs and heard him asking Emma if she wanted to go out for ice cream. He gently told her I was busy when she asked if I could come. As soon as they left, I began the painful process of cleaning up. It rattled me how easy it was becoming to pick up the pieces after his attacks.

When Kevin didn't show up the next morning, I assumed he was off on one of his party binges and was relieved not to have to deal with his irritable aggression, on top of the pain I was already battling. I never liked the idea of him disappearing like he did, but it wasn't until this incident that it crossed my mind he might be off screwing around with a bunch of guys. I was completely zoned out in my own world when I heard Jeremy ask Mike if Kevin was going to be okay.

"What?" I snapped at him, and he looked at me with a confused expression. When he didn't respond, I felt the heat rush to my face and heard myself demand, "What did you just say?"

"What about Kevin?"

"Yeah. What about him? Did something happen?"

In the few seconds it took him to answer, I thought only of what his dad was capable of doing.

"Yeah, he was in a car accident last night with his dad. Didn't you hear?"

I stared hard at him, not wanting to hear what he said next. Jason came crashing into my world and my knees gave way, sending me to the ground.

"Holy fuck man, you okay?" Jeremy asked, kneeling next to me.

I couldn't find words but searched their faces for any sign that Kevin was alive. They didn't look torn up, but they didn't really like him all that much, so maybe they weren't upset.

"Is he okay?" I stammered.

"Is who okay?" Jeremy asked, and I blinked several times before I saw realization dawn. "Who, Kevin? Yeah, he's fine," he said, rushing the words out, and I felt my world start to right itself, my pounding heart no longer threatening an attack. "It was just a fender bender. He has some whiplash, no big deal. Are you alright?"

I immediately started to regain my composure. "Sure," I said standing up. My legs were still shaking, and I could hear a tremor in my voice but hoped I could pass it off. "I drank too much last night, been throwing up all morning. Thought I might toss it again. Sorry." I started walking again as the guys exchanged confused glances.

"You sure, man?" Mike asked.

"Totally, just had too much fun is all. With Kevin out of commission, you guys still want to head to Old Dogs tonight?"

Jeremy took the bait, "Honestly, I'd rather not. I have a shitload of homework I'm behind on and if I let my grades drop, my parents will kick my ass." I briefly wondered if he really meant they'd literally kick his ass or if it was just a figure of speech for him. I narrowed my eyes curiously at him, trying to detect the physical signs of violence. Even though I didn't see any, I knew well enough that no visible signs didn't mean anything.

"Fuck, I'd much rather be seeing my woman. I say we call it good," Brett offered. While Kevin was around, we all pretty much did what he wanted, but when he disappeared, we had started to split up over the last few months.

The second we got to school, I found an opportunity to duck out and text Kevin. *I'm coming over.*

Kevin

The light from my phone alerted me to a new message. I stared blankly at the screen for a few minutes before responding. *Fine.* I took a deep breath and started to count backwards from a hundred. By the time I reached one, I felt I was ready for whatever Rick was going to hand me. I was positive he was going to tell me to fuck off after everything I'd told him. Within a few minutes of focusing myself, I felt my anxiety start to build again. I fumbled in my jacket pocket for the joint I knew was there, and went downstairs to take a few hits, hoping to pull the edge out of my nerves. By the time he showed up, I had to work real fucking hard to keep the bite out of my tone. If he let me have it, then I deserved it. I couldn't blame him for hating me after what I'd done to him.

"Hey," I said flatly.

"You okay?"

"Fine." I felt short answers were better, less of a chance for me to be an asshole.

"Seriously?"

"Yes."

He shuffled his feet nervously. "You're not acting fine."

"How the fuck is fine supposed to act?" I shook my

head at myself. *Goddamn nerves*, I thought.

"Why you being like this?"

"Like what?" Again, I knew I was being a prick, but I couldn't help it. I was waiting for the words that would take him from me, and I just couldn't seem to find any way to be okay with what I knew he'd say.

"When I heard, I was so worried —"

I cut him off, "Heard what?" I asked, confused.

"About the accident."

My mind shifted gears. "What accident?"

"Last night?"

"How the fuck did you hear about that?" I hadn't talked to anyone about it. A fucking fender bender was hardly something to be upset about.

"The guys."

"How the fuck do they know?" My mind started racing. People knowing shit about me without my knowledge pissed me right the fuck off. He stammered, seeing my anxiety turn into full-fledged anger. Before he could get a response out, the pieces started to fall into place in my head. One of the cops on scene was a friend of my father's from church. I'd lay odds that Jim Taylor had told his wife, and once she found out, the whole goddamn congregation was bound to know. It was only a matter of time before word got to Mike's parents, who in turn probably mentioned something to him. And with a deep release of breath, I focused again on Rick. "Never mind. Is that why you're here?" I felt my defenses slipping back into place. "To make sure poor Kevin didn't get hurt in the car accident?" He hadn't come over to even talk about what the hell was going on with us, only to play good old Saint Ricky and check on me.

His eyes started to gloss over, and I immediately recognized the emotion playing across his face.

"It's just..." he stammered. "When I heard about the car accident..." the tears slipped down his cheeks. "The last time..."

"Oh, god!" Realization slammed into me. "Oh no! Fuck, Rick, I'm okay." I rushed and caught him as he started to crumble with his memories. I felt him flinch and knew he must have taken a beating from his dad recently.

"I just thought... I mean, they said you were okay, but I had to make sure," he sobbed into my arms.

"Fuck, I'm such an idiot. I'm sorry! I didn't think. I'm okay, Rick." I pulled away from him a little, placing his face in the palms of my hands. "See, I'm okay." I tried to get him to look at me.

He caved into my arms again, crying harder. "I know. It's just.... for a minute there I thought I'd lost you."

I found myself holding onto him tighter though still careful of his pain, whispering my apologies. "Rick, I am so sorry. Please forgive me." My words rushed out in a breath of emotion, begging forgiveness for everything I'd done to him. I kissed his wet cheeks, tasting the saltiness of his tears. My lips searched out his mouth, trying to connect our bodies so he could feel what was in my heart.

As he calmed down I finally dared to ask what I dreaded. "Are we going to be okay?" I held my breath as I waited for him to answer.

"Yeah, I think so." He pulled in closer to me, his tears still falling lightly into my damp shirt. I let out a long sigh.

"You think so?" I needed more than a half-assed answer.

"As long as you're telling me the truth now…"

"I am," I interrupted him.

"I hope so." I knew it would take him time to trust me again, but as long as he was willing to try, I knew I could prove to him that what I felt was real. I just needed time.

Rick

While there was still a part of me that was wary, I wanted to trust him. I let him take the lead and watched as he tried to prove himself to me. At times, it was funny. He'd get so tongue-tied trying to say the right things. I had to admit I enjoyed watching him squirm, and would intentionally let him try to talk himself out of a hole just for my own enjoyment. Without the lies between us anymore, things were easier, as long as I didn't let myself get into my head too much. When I did, I couldn't help but wonder if he was my savior or the demon that would drag me to hell. He seemed to sense when I was having a hard time with things and would become gentle, giving me space to battle my doubts.

"I can't believe we're graduating in just under two months," I said one day while sitting with him at a pizza joint.

"Where the fuck has this year gone? Shit, I feel like I just got you in my bed and here we are making plans to get the hell out of here in August, like we're married or some crazy shit like that."

We talked about leaving all the time, but I was still

unsure if a life with him was what I wanted. He picked up on my mood.

"Listen, you don't have to make up your mind today. You don't even have to commit to being with me, but we both need to get out of here. It's too dangerous to stay." I could feel the wounded pride behind his words, and knew he was hurt but trying to put on a brave mask for me.

We sat waiting for our food to come. Thankfully, in an effort to appear like the cool father, Kevin's dad let him borrow the car occasionally, though he kept tabs on the mileage to make sure Kevin didn't abuse the privilege. Thus, Kevin had taken up the responsibility of getting me to my guitar lessons each week, and we usually grabbed a bite to eat before heading home. I positioned my elbow on the table in an arm-wrestling stance and smirked at him, trying to change the subject. His eyes lit up.

"I don't know why I always try this," I laughed. "You always slaughter me anyway."

"Cause you like it when I show you how tough I am," he teased, patting his muscles, which admittedly turned me on. Then he wrapped his fingers around mine and placed his elbow firmly on the table. "Are you ready?"

"Go," I said, smiling. We struggled for a few seconds. I knew he wasn't trying very hard because he could usually take me down pretty quick. After another second or so, he slammed my arm back onto the table. I challenged him again, even though I knew he'd win, but I liked to see how long I could keep him from winning. Sometimes it was only a second, but sometimes I felt I put up a decent struggle. I'd even been known to beat him a few times. Granted, it was usually after he'd been drinking quite a bit. We went a few more times until he insisted we stop. He won every time, with ease.

"Seriously, I don't wanna hurt ya," he laughed.

"Oh come on, just one more time," I reached out for his arm just as our food was brought to the table. We sat talking easily about the rest of the school year and where we thought the guys would end up five years after graduation. About halfway through our pizza, a family came in and sat at a table behind us. Before even sitting down the dad looked as us and rolled his eyes. Apparently deciding he didn't like the way we looked, he murmured under his breath, "Punks." A familiar anger flushed Kevin's face and he started to push off the table. I grabbed his arm and felt him tense under my restraint.

"Please don't," I pleaded. He looked at me and back at the family. They weren't even paying attention to us anymore.

"And why the hell not?" he spat at me as he sat back down.

"Because, he has his kids here."

"What's it to me?"

"They're kids, Kevin!"

"Whatever," he said, standing up again, but this time he stormed out of the restaurant, putting distance between himself and the man. I threw enough money on the table to cover our meal and walked after him. Granted, we didn't fight as much, but he was still as big of a hothead as always.

"Where to?" he grumbled as he slid into the car. I shrugged my shoulders. I hated it when he copped an attitude with me, and I found it easier to keep my mouth shut. "Fine!" he said, slamming the car into gear and taking off.

I rolled down my window. It was warmer than usual for this time of year, and I loved it. I felt like my bones were finally beginning to thaw after all the snow.

"You're gonna get a ticket," I said after he ran his third red light.

"Fuck off."

"You first," I snapped back at him, and he actually started laughing.

"When did you grow a pair?"

"When you lost yours," I sparred, glad of the lightening mood.

"Why don't you swear?" His question came out of nowhere, and I considered my response for a second.

"Why do you?" I finally said.

"Cause I fucking like it."

"Well, I don't."

"Like swearing or like me swearing?"

"Like to swear. With you, it's sexy."

"Really? What else to you find sexy?"

"Like your head needs to be any bigger!"

"So I've been told."

"Knock it off," I said, smacking him on the arm. "Where we goin'?"

"Fuck if I know," he laughed. We drove in silence for a while. I leaned my head against the seat and closed my eyes, opening them again when I felt him pull the car to the right and slow to a stop.

"What are we doing?"

"Hiking."

"What? You don't hike."

"Says who?"

"Says I have never seen you do anything athletic, except fight, in the year and a half I've known you."

He got out of the car and started walking towards a trail. I let myself out and looked around. It was beautiful. I couldn't believe I'd never been up the canyons when I pretty much lived within walking distance of two of them.

"You think this is a good idea?" I called after him.

"Why wouldn't it be?"

"Well, in my Wilderness Survival class they told us —"

"Unbelievable."

"What?"

"I don't know how I ended up with such a nerd."

"Hey, I'm not," I said, pouting.

"Yeah, you are. But I don't fucking care. You're still hot," he said, turning back to me and winking.

I stopped talking. He had a point; I did worry too much. After some time on the deserted trail, we came into a clearing. It was breathtaking. There was a massive area of just green. It looked like it may once have been a giant riverbed, overgrown and surrounded on all sides by ledges that were just as green. In the middle of it all, a gigantic tree had fallen across a cliff high above the ground, making a natural bridge.

"This is it."

"You've been here?"

"Nope."

He grabbed my hand and hiked up one of the sides,

weaving and making his own trail in order to reach one edge of the fallen tree. He pulled me along after him. Even though the tree was massive, we were still careful to balance as we made our way out and sat down right in the middle.

Kevin

"What the fuck are you doing?" I asked irritably. We'd been on the damn tree an hour and, par for the course, I wasn't a patient person. It'd been my brilliant idea to go on a fucking hike, but then Rick started his little project and lost interest in me, and I was ready to take off.

"Just gimme a second."

"You've been at that damn log for like twenty fucking minutes. How many more fucking seconds do you need?"

"Seriously, Kevin," he looked up, head still bent, hand shielding whatever he was doing. Shit, he was just asking to be fucked, looking at me the way he was. "Stop trying to peek."

"Peek? You really just accused me of trying to peek? What are we, like five?" A glint entered his eyes. He knew damn well I'd been trying to see what he was up to. "Fine!" I mumbled in annoyance and laid back on the log, my feet dangling off each side. "Three questions?"

"We're still playing that game? Aren't we past that?"

"Yeah, but I need a fucking distraction, so shoot."

"And what will you be requiring in return?"

"Well, after you get your answers, I get to see what the fuck you're doing to that log."

I heard him laugh a little. "That hardly seems fair. I

already plan on showing you when I'm done."

"So, you're walking out of this ahead either way, and you're arguing with me about it? What the hell's wrong with you?"

"Granted. Okay, let me think."

"Well, make it quick. These trees are hardly enough to distract me."

"Really? I thought you liked it here." He knew he was pushing buttons, but judging by the way his tone changed, I could tell he was talking to himself more than me. "I find the trees distracting. It's so quiet up here! It's peaceful, you know? No one to worry about," he trailed off. Whatever he was doing, he stopped, the silence of the trees descending on us.

"Yeah, I get it," I said, bringing my smoke to my lips. I could hear the crackling of the paper as the fire lit it with my inhaled breath. It was silent, but the more I listened, the more ambient noise started to seep into my head. I heard the sounds of undisturbed nature. I didn't have to look at Rick to know he was craning his head back, looking up to the tips of all the treetops. I heard the crack of branches breaking after years of bearing the weight of snow, a slight breeze being the push that finally caused the break. I could see a bird in flight, heard the scurry of a nearby creature darting for cover. On the surface, everything was so silent and serene, but when I listened, everything was fighting for survival just as much as I was.

"Other than your dad," Rick's voice broke through, "what scares you more than anything else in this world?"

Fuck this honest, no-filter shit that always happened

around him. I closed my eyes and draped my arm across my face. I didn't want to be tempted to look at him. I wondered why it was that every single time he knew exactly which questions he shouldn't ask. "You," I said shortly.

"Why?" he asked after several minutes of silence.

"Question two?" I replied.

"Fine."

"You have to be working on that shit. The whole point is to distract me until you're done. If you stop working, it defeats the fucking purpose," I grumbled. I heard him resume what he was doing. "Fuck! You should know why," I said, trying the easy route. He didn't respond. "Son-of-a-bitch, fine." I pushed out my breath. Could I really tell him this shit? "You scare me." I heard him stop working again. "Don't fucking stop or I'll stop talking," I snapped at him. The scraping started up again.

I took a long haul on the smoke, then flicked it off the side of the tree, watching it tumble end over end until it disappeared into the overgrowth dozens of feet below us. I forced my eyes back to the treetops and thought about counting them to focus myself.

"You already know this shit, but what the hell." Again, I paused and hoped he'd let me off the hook. "I'm not in control when you're around." I finally said. "That's really dangerous for me. Like, life-threatening dangerous." He kept busy. "I think about you when I should be thinking about the next blow or the next punishment. But even more, you scare me because I can't seem to filter this shit." And the real truth came out. "I sure as hell can't control my fucking body either. I don't know what the fuck's wrong with me." I took a deep breath, fished another smoke out and found my flask. I poured several shots down my throat, then lit up. He kept working, not saying a word. He was probably waiting me out, hoping I'd give him more. I wasn't planning on it.

"K, I'm done," he said quietly.

"Huh?"

"I'm done. Wanna see what I was working on?"

I sat up. He had his hands still shielding what he'd been doing.

"Promise you won't laugh."

"No."

He actually looked a little shy. I let my lips curve into a small smile, a promise of no laughter, and I felt his eyes searching for my reaction as he removed his hands. My breath caught. Goddamnit. Something so silly, but so Rick. A simple, jagged and uneven heart carved into the trunk of the tree with our initials RSJ + KV carved in the middle. I knew how hard on himself he was about the way he felt, and his innocent gesture spoke volumes to me. He cared, even if he couldn't always admit it to himself.

"Question number three, what are you thinking right now?" he whispered.

I couldn't look at him. I couldn't tear my eyes off his carving. After all the shit we'd been through, this is what fucking got me, a goddamn heart carved on a tree. My emotions had been barricaded behind a dam for so long, and he'd managed to find the one spot that was the weakest. He moved towards me, covering the heart with his body. I glued my eyes to the spot it had been. I knew if I looked at him, I'd lose it. I started counting, trying to shut out the flood of reactions I was feeling. His fingers found my face and then threaded into my hair.

"Come back to me, Kev. It's safe here. You don't need to go there." His voice weaved through my head, cradling the thoughts that wanted to break apart and shatter. I looked into his eyes and felt the truth of his words. I suddenly felt like I was falling and I grasped onto the wrist of the hand threaded in my hair. He flinched slightly, and I knew I hadn't hurt him, but I also knew better than to move that quickly. Reflexes were instinctual.

"Don't let me go," I cried as he moved closer to me and wrapped his other arm around my waist, pulling my body into his, my face resting on his chest. Desperately, I grabbed onto him, feeling the hot tears burn my eyes. My chest hitched, trying to find air.

"Shhh. I've got you," he whispered.

My hands fisted into his t-shirt, clenching and unclenching. My muscles coiled, wanting to run, then released as I caved into him. My hand brushed against the heat of his skin, and I immediately tore at his shirt, needing to feel his body.

"Shhh," he said again, pulling away a little. But his eyes held the same need as mine. "Come," he said, pushing himself up and holding his hand out to me. He pulled me up and backed slowly off the log, keeping his eyes locked onto mine. I wondered if he thought I'd fall to pieces if he turned his back on me. As usual, his instincts were right on. His eyes were the only thing that kept me from breaking apart.

Once off the precipice of the fallen tree, he led me towards a huge boulder, flat on its surface, and pulled me into him. I came willingly, falling into his embrace. He took me in his arms and kissed me, pulling at my shirt, then his. His hands traveled my body, knowing the areas that were still sensitive. He knew me.

I reached for the button on his jeans. "No," he said softly and I stopped, confused. "Let me," he said, pulling at my jeans.

"Sure?" I asked, my voice unsteady and throaty, asking him as much as asking myself. I topped; I'd never let someone else take the lead.

"Please?" he responded, knowing my question had been more for myself than him. I moved my body so I was the one backed up to the rock. A fleeting thought of being cornered and trapped assaulted me. He must've seen it in my eyes. "Hey," he said. "It's just me. We don't have to."

"No, I want to. It's just..."

"I know. It's okay. Take your time," he said gently.

I found his hands and moved them again to my jeans. It was Rick. I was safe with him, I repeated to myself. Up here in the middle of this silent world, my father was far away. I could let my control go. I could let go for him, for us.

Rick

His body was beautiful, and to see him let go of his control and let me bring him pleasure was more than I ever thought it could be. As he cried out in desire and pure abandonment, it brought me to a new high. I'd almost told him I loved him as we came together, but I found myself still in doubt.

After he gave his body to me, I finally believed he cared for me deeply, but as the days went on there was still a small part of me that didn't trust him. And while I didn't really believe in God, in the off chance He was out there, I was pretty sure He hated gay people, and I wasn't loving the idea of going to hell. Add to that the thought of what my dad would do to me if he found out, and it all seemed a pretty high price to pay. These torments tore and wedged their way into my daily thoughts so often that, one day after guitar lessons, Kevin picked up on my distraction.

He looked cautiously at me as I slid into his car. "What's wrong?"

"Nothing," I mumbled. There was still a lot both of us held close, things we weren't ready to be really open about but didn't want to lie about either. My doubts were one of those items, something I wasn't about to share with him. I knew it drove him crazy. He liked to know everything, but he tried hard to respect me. I watched as his hands tensed slightly on the steering wheel, but he didn't say anything.

"I was thinking," he paused for a few moments. "Want to grab something to eat, then maybe catch a movie?"

"Did you just ask me on a date?" I asked, trying to hide my smile. I loved the idea, but I had to give him a hard time. It seemed that when we were with each other, I could see no other future for us but one in which we were together.

"Fuck no. I mean, well yeah, I guess. That's if you want to go and shit."

"You are quite the romantic, aren't you?"

"I just asked you on a fucking date, didn't I? Like I know what I'm doing here." He shifted in his seat several times and I enjoyed his discomfort immensely. "Well?" he said impatiently.

"Yes, Kevin, I'd like to go on a date with you. But first, I really must go home and freshen up," I teased.

"What the fuck?" He looked over at me with shock until he realized I was kidding.

"Seriously though, I do have to shower. I just rolled out of bed this morning and didn't do much."

"Fine, but I'm not going home. I'll wait."

"I figured."

I wiped off after the hot shower and pulled my blue jeans and t-shirt on, finding Kevin waiting in my room. He slowly rose off my bed and came to me. "You smell good," he mumbled into my neck.

"Showers do that."

"I know, I like." He laced his arms around me and pulled me into him.

"Do you now?"

"Sure do." He brought his lips to mine and kissed me slowly. "Among other things."

"Yeah, what else do you like about me?" I wondered out loud, sincerely, but he teased me in return.

"Ahh, fishing for compliments, are we?" he laughed, but continued. "I like how your hair is getting longer, so I can pull on it like this." His fingers twisted and fisted in my hair. He pulled my head back and his lips found my neck. "I like how your skin tastes," he said as his teeth scraped against my shoulder, "damp and clean." He bit down at the base of my neck. The slight pain and pleasure traveled through my body, and I pushed him towards my bed. I straddled him, positioning myself in the exact spot I knew would drive him crazy. "I like when you're aggressive and try to top me." He easily flipped me over, and I found myself in the opposite position with him on top. "But I like to top you even more." His fingers went under my shirt and slowly traveled up my chest, pushing my shirt to my neck, "I like your body, tight and hard." He pulled my shirt off, throwing it on the floor, and in the same moment flung his aside as well. "And, I like how your skin feels against mine," he said, stretching out on top of me and finding my lips again. My hands ran across his back, the scarred texture again reminding me of his strength. He tensed a little but continued his assault on my mouth.

I heard the back door open and close and my dad's keys being tossed on the table. In an instant, we both shot off the bed.

"Shit," he breathed. I looked at both of us with our shirts off and then heard my dad moving through the downstairs.

"You need to hide," I said, my panic level rising. "Here, in there," I said, motioning towards the closet. Kevin looked at the closet, then at me.

"No way."

"Are you kidding? He's coming up the stairs," I said, terrified, moving towards him, trying to get him to budge.

"Not no, but hell no." He braced against me as I pushed at him.

"Kevin, please, he'll kill me if he finds you here...us here...like this. You know what he's capable of."

"I'll go out the window." I heard strain in his voice, but I didn't have time to worry about it. He tried to go for the window.

"There's no time!" I grabbed the closet doorknob with one hand and his arm in the other, desperately trying to move him in.

"Fine, fine," he growled at me. "Just don't fucking push me." He yanked his arm away from me and something strange crossed his face as he moved around me and into the open closet. I literally shut the door as my dad burst into my room.

"We need to talk."

"Uh, okay."

"Sit," he commanded, pointing at my bed and I flinched away from his pointing hand. He grimaced and took a deep breath. He didn't appear angry. I told myself to keep my cool. I sat quickly, grabbing a pillow and putting it on my lap to hide the effects Kevin had on me.

"What is it?" I asked, a little worried. We didn't talk much unless I was in trouble.

"I've been thinking. Things have been a bit tense around here lately." I almost laughed. Whipping me with a belt was much more than a bit tense, in my mind. "I know things haven't been easy, for either of us. I know I haven't been the best dad." He was pacing back and forth in front of my closet, and it took everything I had to listen to what he was saying and not freak out. "Things with work are stressful, you know? And ever since Jas…I mean, since… hell. Work, work is hard. See, I have this boss…" And he started rambling. He was seriously complaining to me about his job. Something about a project he was working on and didn't have time to finish, and his boss getting more credit than she deserved. Then he was talking about some co-worker. He sounded like he'd had eighteen cups of coffee too many with how amped up he was.

"Anyway, Sylvia and I were talking last night and we think it would be a good idea to go on a family vacation, you know, all four of us." I stared at him. My mind was blank of any thought. I noticed his light hair cut in typical businessman fashion and the eyes that looked exactly like mine. "Like back to California, well maybe not there. Maybe Disneyworld, Hawaii or something. We need to change things up. Maybe go as soon as next week or right after graduation. Just get out of here for a while."

"Seriously?" was all I could say. Was he really asking me to Disneyworld, after all that'd happened between us? I searched his face for another message, something I was clearly missing.

"Yeah, why not?"

"Sure," I said cautiously.

"You don't sound sure. Is something wrong? What's going on with you?"

"No dad, it's cool," I said, trying to convey excitement. "Sounds like a great idea." I smiled, but I was sure he was seeing right through me.

"What, you don't think it's a good idea?"

"It's a great idea," I repeated. "I bet Emma will be thrilled." I saw the change in his eyes just before his fist caught me under the chin, throwing me backwards off the bed.

"You ungrateful little shit! I told Sylvia you'd hate the

idea. I don't know why I bother," he mumbled as he slammed my door behind him. I laid there on the floor for a second, trying to figure out what had just happened and what had gotten into him. As I pulled myself up, rubbing my jaw, I heard the TV flip on down in the living room.

"I'm sure it's safe," I said to Kevin, examining my face in the mirror for a potential bruise. When he didn't respond, I said louder, "Kevin, you're okay to come out. I don't think he'll come back up." When he didn't say anything, I continued, "Listen, I know you're pissed, but get over it." When I was only met with silence from the closet, I walked over and yanked open the door. "Kevin…" I stopped.

He was sitting on the floor with his legs pulled up to his chest. His hands were over his ears and his eyes were squeezed shut. He was rocking back and forth. "Kevin?" I dropped to my knees and laid a hand on his bare shoulder. His eyes flew open, and he pushed himself into the corner of the closet, sheer terror flooding his face. I fell backwards, surprised by his reaction.

"Kevin, whoa, Kevin…it's just me, Rick." He didn't seem to recognize me. He was staring through me. "Look, it's okay. I'm not going to hurt you. It's just me." I reached out to him again and his body stiffened, his eyes darting from my face to my hands and then to nothing. "Okay, okay, I won't touch you." I said, staying where I was. "But you're scaring me. Do you know who I am?" He didn't say anything, just pulled himself tighter into the corner. I had no idea what was going on with him.

I sat for several minutes, debating. "Did you take something? Are you tripping?" I asked, but he didn't respond. How would I explain him in my closet without a shirt on? I tried to reach out for him again but he flinched and shuttered as he turned his face away from me. "Kevin, should I call an ambulance?" I finally asked after 15 minutes, seeing no other choice.

"No, don't." His voice sounded so small. "I'm okay. I'm back. Just give me a second," he said as he raised his head.

I looked closer at him and realized that he did recognize me, that his eyes were no longer those of a terrified stranger.

"Okay, are you sure?"

"Yeah, a second," he said quietly. He pulled himself just outside the closet door and leaned against the wall, closing his eyes. I cautiously watched him gain control, piece by piece, Kevin coming back. First, his breathing returned to normal, not the short, quick intakes he'd been doing. Then his shoulders stiffened and he sat up a little straighter, and his head followed, no longer hanging down but pressed firmly against the wall. His eyes opened, and they were full of stone again.

"Sorry," he said shortly.

"Umm, it's fine." When he didn't move, I asked, "Do I get to know what that was about?"

"Nothing. I'm fine."

"That was not nothing."

He looked at me briefly. "I didn't mean to scare you," he said, again looking away. I waited. "I don't do well with closets. I'm sorry."

"You don't need to apologize." When he didn't continue, I filled in the missing information. "I assume it has something to do with your dad?"

His chest stopped moving, not breathing, straining to

hold onto his control.

"Yes," he finally whispered. I watched as his struggle continued. His breathing quickened again and then steadied. "It's one of his favorite punishments." He paused for a minute or so. I sat and waited. "It's the only one that really gets to me. I don't think he's aware how much it gets to me. If he knew, it'd be the one he used exclusively." He wrapped his arms around his legs, pulling them tighter to his chest. "Can I have my shirt?" he asked.

"Sure, sure. Here you go," I offered, handing him the previously discarded black shirt. He pulled it over his battered chest and quickly drew his legs in again.

"I suppose if he saw me the way you just did, he'd know. When it's done, he just opens the door, doesn't ever really look at me. I don't know why it's the hardest. It's certainly not the most painful." He stopped again. "The first time was right after I was released from the emergency room, after that first beating. They had asked questions, and he was furious. He hit me, of course, but then he locked me in my closet. I was still little and the dark scared me." He took several steadying breaths. "Every few hours, he'd pull me out and beat me, then throw me back in. I think that's why he doesn't realize how bad it is, too busy worrying about the beating, doesn't see what the closet does to me." I could see the muscles in his neck strain as he pushed his head against the wall. His eyes were empty as he remembered the punishment. "I guess I should be thankful for small favors, right? Anyway, it went on for days. Honestly, I thought I was going to die in there."

"There were other times?"

He let out a small laugh. "Fuck yeah, there've been other times."

"When's the last time? I mean, was it recently? Or, often?"

He shrugged, "My disappearing acts."

I thought of all the times he just disappeared for days. "The binges? I just assumed—"

"Assumed what I wanted you to assume. What was I supposed to say? Hey, sorry, couldn't answer the phone, was locked in the closet and beaten for the last four days." The resentment dripped out of his voice like poison, but I knew he wasn't mad at me.

I shook my head, "I just don't get how he can be so cruel."

"I literally think he's a sociopath, Rick. I had a psychology class last year and the book outlined different personality disorders. Sociopath was on the list and he met pretty much every characteristic. I remember reading it over and over, something finally explaining the monster I live with."

"But how? How does he do that to you for years without anyone finding out?"

"Just like the bruises, people only see what they wanna see. And if they see more, they would much rather hear a sugar-coated lie than the ugly truth that's staring at 'em."

"I just don't get it."

"How many people have questioned the evidence left on your face, or arms or wherever?"

I thought about it. Other than Jessica—and I wasn't even sure with her—I didn't think anyone had put two and two together.

"You see, people don't want to believe there are monsters living next door, that there are innocent kids screaming for help. They want to believe the story of the dashing businessman rising to the occasion after the drug-addicted mother runs away. Even to the fuckers who work in the system, it's just one more case to add to their already overworked asses. They don't fucking care. Nobody does." I could hear the emotion in his voice and see the gleam of tears in his eyes.

"But I do. I care, Kevin, and you care about what happens to me."

"I know, but we're on our own. It's just me and you, and that's why we gotta stick together and get the fuck out of this place."

I couldn't think of anything to say. It wasn't the first time he'd talked about all the people who had had a chance to help him but didn't. It was clear why he stood on his own, not trusting or depending on anyone but himself. His being in control was the difference between life and death in his world.

"I had no idea about the closet. I'm sorry I made you get in there."

"I didn't love the idea, but I didn't think it would hit me that hard." Another long pause. "I don't know why this one gets to me. With the shit he puts me through, I don't know why this one makes me lose it. But I guess now I know I can't do any closet. I should've guessed—I hear us homos have a hard time with closets," he joked, smiling weakly.

Nineteen...

Rick

Sylvia and my dad never mentioned the trip again, and Kevin and I never made it on our date. He promised he'd ask me again, and I teased him relentlessly about being a romantic, which I know he loved. After the trip to the mountains, he opened up more and more, telling me stories of his past. He didn't have a lot of happy memories to share, but he tried. Most of the time he recounted the nightmares of living with his dad, and then begged me to tell him of happier times I had with Jason. Jason would've really liked the Kevin I was beginning to know.

We counted down the days to graduation. As soon as school was over we planned on ditching the guys and making ourselves scarce until August. He turned eighteen just a few weeks before me, and would go to New York first. He'd saved enough money over the years to get things going for himself, and now he included me in his plans. As soon as I turned eighteen, I'd leave my nightmare behind. We often talked about taking off early, just disappearing one day. I knew my dad wouldn't come looking for me but we were sure his dad would use every available resource to help him search for his missing minor son. Being eighteen took one more tool out of his dad's hands. One less option he had at his disposal to hunt us down. Kevin was working on changing our names so our dads couldn't find us. We planned on disappearing into the city and never looking back. I couldn't deny our future together any longer. Even if I still struggled with the idea that I might be gay, one thing was for sure—I was in it for the long haul with him. I felt that powers stronger than us were lining up the pieces. It was only a matter of time.

Even though the conversation with the guys was the same as always, the change of scenery was nice. Downtown Salt Lake during spring break was not happening by any standard, but it beat a trashed old barn any day.

"Seriously man, my mom took my phone and everything. I can't believe her," Mike complained.

"Well, you did get caught, so it's kinda your fault. If you're dumb enough to get busted, then I don't feel sorry for ya." Brett elbowed Mike.

"It's not like I meant to, dumb ass. How was I supposed to know she'd be waiting up for me?"

Towards the end of the guys' light-hearted banter, I noticed Kevin stiffen slightly, not anything anyone else would've noticed, but I knew his body well. I glanced around, seeing a guy walking towards us with a very pronounced swish in his hips. I watched as he noticed Kevin, and a smile spread across his lips. A pang of jealousy shot through me.

"Hey, honey!" he said, obviously talking to Kevin.

"Fuck off, not interested." Kevin spat, his fists clenched as he jammed them into his jacket.

"Whoa, sweetie, don't ya remember me?" he asked, then paused. "Charlie, from Danny's?"

"The likes of you? No." Kevin said as he pushed past the guy, ramming his shoulder into him.

"Dude's got a crush on you, Kevin," Brett blurted out and I choked as I inhaled my smoke. Kevin barely looked at Brett, but he shut up real fast. I prayed Kevin would keep his cool.

"Whatever, bitch," the Charlie guy said as he continued to walk away.

"Fucking faggot." Kevin gritted through his teeth, and my stomach clenched at the slur.

"Excuse me?" Charlie said. "Last time we met, Kevin, you weren't so shy."

As his name escaped out of this guy's mouth, Kevin turned, took three steps and curled his fist into Charlie's stomach. When he doubled over, Kevin slammed his knee into his face, and he stumbled back, falling to the ground.

"I don't know any goddamn cock-suckers," he sneered and kicked at him, narrowly missing his head and landing his boot squarely in his chest.

The out-of-control Kevin who stood before me now was nothing close to the person I'd gotten to know. I watched in shock as he delivered blow after blow. I thought I should do something, but with so much on the line, standing up to him in front of the guys could blow up in my face. I watched as he kicked the guy several more times, each kick punctuating a statement that broke my heart. With a final kick, he turned to walk away.

"I know you like it rough, but I don't remember you being this aggressive when you were fucking me in the ass, sweetheart," the guy sputtered from the ground.

"Oh fuck!" I breathed as Kevin pulled the guy up and slammed him into a nearby building. In one motion he had his knife out and was pressing it into the guy's throat.

"I'm going to kill your faggot ass," Kevin sneered. The sight of blood at the tip of the knife drove me to action. My smoke slipped from my fingers as I rushed at Kevin and grabbed the arm holding the knife. He flung me back and the knife again made contact with the guy's throat. Kevin was crazed, showing none of the calm, controlled violence he usually displayed. Again, I grabbed his arm. Desperate to stop him, I lowered my voice, praying only he'd hear me.

"This is not the part of you I fell in love with."

His head snapped to me, and I could barely hear him as he repeated one word.

"Love?"

The question was strangled and painful from his lips. I nodded slightly. A confused look crossed his eyes and he shook his head, his black hair loose and wild around his face. He looked to where Mike, Brett, and Jeremy stood, and I watched him pull into himself, straightening his spine and rolling his shoulders back. He took a deep breath, asserting his control, and looked back at the guy he'd pinned.

"Do it, Kevin. Kill the faggot freak," Brett said behind me, and I wanted to turn and rip out his tongue with my bare hands. I watched Kevin flinch. His grip on the knife tightened and the guy gasped as it pressed harder into his neck. I silently squeezed Kevin's arm again, pleading with him to stop. He looked at my hand and then at me, and I was amazed as the hate in his eyes disappeared, giving way to something I'd never seen in him. For several seconds he just stared at me. Then I watched as he crumpled in on himself, shoulders hunching over, eyes slipping to the ground. He pulled his hand back, and with a cry — not quite anger and not complete anguish — he slammed his knife into the brick wall, shattering the handle. He yanked his arm from my grasp as if my hand was burning him, then turned and ran. As he disappeared into the darkness, I knew I had broken him.

Kevin

I figured I was in shock. My life had completely imploded, and I stood there staring at a fucking water fountain shooting fifteen feet into the air. I needed to get high. I knew it wouldn't be long before the entire gay community found out what I'd done to Charlie, so I had to get to the club and get drugs before the word spread. Thank god no one knew my real last name, and if the police got involved they'd be looking for a 21-year-old who lived downtown, not a high school student from the suburbs.

I walked to the bar slowly, as though moving through

molasses. Flashes of Charlie with my knife at his throat tore at my goddamn nerves. I couldn't bring myself to think of what would've happened had Rick not stopped me. As I had beat the fuck out of him, all I could hear were his words, outing me, and with each punch I hoped the guys would believe less and less what they heard. If they believed him, or even suspected, the rumor was sure to make it to my father's ears, and that would be the end of it.

My dealer, Jake, was running low on my usual. He had crystal. I debated; I'd seen crystal fuck up so many lives. I knew it was a drug that robbed the soul, but with the realization that I didn't believe I had a soul to lose, I walked away with enough to make me numb for days.

The only place I could think of going that I wouldn't be found was the roof of the high school. Rick had heard me talk about it, but I doubted it would cross his mind as a place I'd go. With alcohol and a food supply, I asked the cab driver to drop me off at a house near the school. For three hours I'd kept myself busy making plans, getting drugs, alcohol, shelter and food, in that order. Now, I had to fucking deal with the suppressed emotions.

Moments after I had started running, I had thrown both of my phones. I knew myself and knew what was about to happen. I didn't need the distraction of the outside world while holding the pain suffocatingly close. I was prepared, and as I closed the door quietly on the roof, I set the bags down and shattered.

They were the darkest hours of my life, and at times I wasn't sure I'd come out of them alive. It was daylight when my tears dried long enough to take my first line of meth. My surroundings became sharp, and I counted the bricks on the roof over and over. Then my mind dulled, and as soon as I started coming down, feeling the edges of terror playing at my nerves, I took another line. The drip at the back of my throat caused by the meth became reassuring. As the rollercoaster of the high continued, I recognized the thoughts of my father and the knife at Charlie's throat as a sign that the drugs were wearing off, so I'd lay out another line and go soaring again. I didn't think of Rick.

I never touched the food I'd brought, but I drank to stay hydrated. I lined up rocks, counted the scars on my arms, unlaced and re-laced my boots, counted how many steps it took me to walk from one end of the roof to the other and then how many it took to walk the perimeter.

I prepared. Even if my father had not been told of my sexual deviance, I'd fallen off the grid for days. I debated if it'd be better to go home high or sober. If sober, I was more alert. High, I was numb and it wouldn't hurt as much. Self-preservation made up my mind for me and I decided sober was best. I was more likely to get out alive if I could play my cards right, and to do that, I knew I had to be on my game. Things were fuzzy, but I wasn't tired. I focused on the small things — big things were too much. I went back to the rocks, making designs, organizing by size, then color.

After nearly fifty hours of being high, I could feel the sleep deprivation kicking in. I pulled out the weed I'd bought and rolled a blunt that would knock me on my ass. I knew enough about crystal to know I had to come down. In my current state, I felt like I could keep going for a few more days, but I had the presence of mind to force a crash. As soon as I started coming down again, nerves tugging at the edges of my consciousness, I smoked the blunt as fast as I possibly could and polished off several shots. I needed to be fucked up to sleep off the effects of the crystal.

I fought coming back to reality as long as I could, tossing and turning on the hard pavement of the roof. I knew I didn't want to wake up, and my mind held the reason just out of my reach. Finally, a flash of my knife and Rick's pleading eyes had me doubled over, throwing up the little liquid I had in my body. I was dizzy and lightheaded, but forced myself to drink some Gatorade and gag down the energy bars I'd brought with me.

As I watched the sunrise on my third day, I could barely wrap my head around the disaster my life had become. I made a mental list of things I was going to have to fix. I had lost control of my rage and almost killed someone, and the fact that I was capable of killing someone was something that was going to take some time to work through. I had backed down from a fight at Rick's insistence, and I hadn't kicked his ass for stopping me. The guys would be itching to challenge me, but I didn't have the energy to defend my position. I had to focus on my father. The guys would probably put all the pieces together, and I was sure half the neighborhood knew I was gay by now. They may have even placed Rick into the mix already. Rick. Rick loved me. Had they heard him tell me that? I'd given up all control by running. And I knew I had to face my father. The list made my head hurt, and I longed to lay out some more meth, but I tucked it deep inside my jacket pocket.

I knew I had to get home and shower before my father came home from church. Cleanliness was next to godliness. I felt off, but I was sober—well, as sober as I ever was. I still wasn't ready to feel everything that had happened.

I walked home, planning time for a shower and some extra time to allow me to gain my focus and control. Unless I planned on giving away the fact that I had a spare key hidden outside for the side door, I knew my only choice was to use the key my father had given me for the front door. Thankfully, he wasn't waiting for me when I slipped inside. As I had hoped, he had kept up appearances and had gone to church.

After showering, I slipped into some boxers, not bothering with a shirt or pants, knowing he'd probably rip them off for easier access with the belt. I fixed myself some chicken and a protein shake, anticipating my need for the energy to deal with what was coming. When it neared time for him to get home, I sat on my bed and calmly waited. As expected, I heard him walk in the door right on schedule. I listened intently for him to come downstairs, but he didn't. From the sounds of it, he got busy making an early dinner, then turned on the TV. I could hear the beginning music from The Who on a CSI rerun.

He didn't come down, but I sure as hell couldn't sleep; every creak in the house made me shoot out of whatever rest I was about to fall into, sure he was going to burst into my room any second. I was wide awake, although exhausted, when his alarm clock went off the next morning. I rolled out of bed and ate two protein bars, again trying to give myself the energy needed. I heard him shower as usual, and then, at last, I heard him on the stairs.

"On your knees," he said as he walked into my bedroom.

"Sir?" He remained silent. After a few seconds of hesitation, I slowly pulled myself off the bed and bent to my knees.

"Hands behind your back." I felt the cold metal of handcuffs snap around my wrists, then the sound of tape as he bound my ankles together. I remained motionless. After several moments of silence, I felt something hard press against the back of my head.

"You were gone for three days. You will remain like this for three days. You will kneel during the day, and you may sleep lying down. However, your restraints are not to come off. If I come in and find you disobeying in any way, I will use the gun I am pointing at your head." I closed my eyes. *Does he know? Has he heard yet? Is this it?* My thoughts threatened my focus. "Understood?" I didn't know if I should talk or nod my head. I didn't want to set him off either way. Before I could make up my mind, I heard the safety on the gun being released. "Understood?"

"Yes, sir," I released in a gush of breath.

"Good. Remember, you are to kneel for fifteen hours, then you have my permission to sleep for nine. I will bring you water, you will have no food." I was glad I had had the presence of mind to shove down the damn energy bars. He remained behind me, safety off, for several more minutes. Finally, I heard it click back on and a few seconds later the door to my room shut. I wasn't sure when I'd started holding my breath and I doubled over, gasping for air. He'd never used a gun. What the fuck? He had to know.

I settled onto my heels and sat. Why hadn't he beaten me? He had to be up to something. Kneeling was uncomfortable, but it couldn't be worse than a beating, or for that matter, the closet. The only instances he'd made me kneel for any length of time was on a broom handle or a pile of rice. Kneeling on the floor with no threat of a belt was too easy. I knew immediately he was trying out a creative session, which meant he wasn't finished with me.

My father couldn't have known that half the punishment would be leaving me alone with my thoughts. With no alcohol or drugs to turn to, thoughts of Charlie and that night tried to fuck up my focus.

Several hours into the punishment, my arm muscles ached slightly and my hands were tingling from the awkward blood flow. I tried to roll my shoulders forward to stretch a little. My legs were a little better off because I could raise myself or settle on my heels, but a dull pain had begun forming in my knees. After a few hours, my muscles ached. At six hours, they burned. At eleven, they screeched with excruciating agony. When I did the math and realized I had sixty-six hours to go, my stomach clenched and I threw up, emptying what little sustenance remained.

As the agony increased, the panic did as well. My focus held fairly firm, and even though I was terrified, I managed to keep the images of Rick and Charlie at bay. I started to feel pain in muscles I didn't know I had. I wondered if my ankles and wrists were bleeding from the pressure of the restraints. It felt like every time I moved, the bindings cut into my flesh. My neck and then my head started to pound. Several times I almost said fuck it and stood up. The instinct to rid myself of the pain was increasingly difficult to ignore. Then I'd remember the feel of the muzzle at the back of my head, and I had no doubt my father would hold to his promise of using the gun.

I stared at the clock on my nightstand — thirteen hours in, only two left until I could stretch out and sleep. It wouldn't relieve my arms, but perhaps it would allow my legs and feet to get some circulation. My father hadn't checked on me yet and I wondered if he was trying to create a false sense of security. My head dropped down towards my chest, which made it hard to breathe, but I couldn't seem to hold it up any longer. I knew I was not well rested and my body was less capable of coping. The hunger pangs were barely noticeable next to the fire in my muscles. He must have researched torture tactics. A beating usually lasted minutes — hours at most. This torment was scheduled to go three days. And it didn't help that my mind was at war as well.

As 10:00 PM approached, I couldn't tear my eyes off the clock, counting down the minutes. At 9:59 I heard his footsteps on the stairs, pausing in front of my door. The second my clock switched to 10:00, he came in, gun in one hand, a glass of water with a straw in the other. I didn't move.

"You will not sleep in your bed. You will lie down where you are. You are to remain bound. I do not need to remind you of the consequences of disobedience." My eyes flicked to the gun. "Lie down," he commanded.

With relief, I started to stretch my legs from beneath me. The moment I moved, unexpected, searing pain shot through my body and I bit down on the side of my cheek, instantly tasting blood. The less he heard from me, the better. I stopped moving. Even if I had wanted to move, there was no way my body would willingly subject itself to the kind of agony I sensed was waiting. It would've been like asking someone to slowly cut off his or her finger by running it back and forth against a sharp blade. Most people simply would not be able to do it.

"Lie down," he commanded again. I hadn't let him see my tears in years. As they threatened to break through, I ducked my head and tried to stretch more. "Look at me." He knew what this was doing to my body and to my resolve. It was as if he somehow knew what I'd already been through and was choosing to break me. Keeping my head bowed, trying to control my emotions, I felt the coldness before I realized his intent. He placed the gun under my chin and pulled my head up with the muzzle so I was looking into his dead eyes, and the barrel was aimed right at my throat.

"I have asked you to do two things. You have yet to do either of them successfully. I want you to lay down and look at me, and I want you to do it now." The safety released, as did my tears. He smiled as he witnessed my resolve break. In one swift movement, he swept his foot out, catching my ankles and yanking them straight. My back coiled and my body convulsed as my vision blurred. I had the sense to bite down on both cheeks but I couldn't keep the tears back.

I focused in on his methods, distracting myself from the pain. I'd suffered many long and agonizing punishments at his hands. This punishment wasn't necessarily more unbearable than some of the worst. It was different, and with difference came the unexpected. When I didn't know what to expect, I didn't know how to prepare. I didn't know which muscles to relax before it was too late.

The pain, combined with my inability to keep my head straight, seemed to weaken my mind. Where I once would've been able to remain closed off to my father's cruelty, I succumbed to it and broke. As I landed on my arms, the pain ripped me open, and I felt the blackness quickly erase everything around me.

I awoke, every muscle screaming at me in outrage. I immediately realized I must have pissed myself. Between not being allowed to relieve myself all day and the obvious loss of control over my body, I wasn't terribly surprised, and I suspected it would happen again over the duration of the next two days. I glanced at my clock and realized my father had turned it around, intentionally not allowing me to know what time it was. The glass of water he'd brought lay tipped over beside me. Even though my body burned in every muscle possible, it was better while lying down. I didn't move as it only sent stabbing daggers through my body. My mind fought the battle of time. It was still dark outside, but how much longer I had before 7:00 AM was out of my grasp.

I must have dozed in and out all night. At one point, the door flung open, and I jolted upright, shocking my body into a near blackout again with the sudden movement.

"It's seven." He had the gun and another glass of water. "On your knees," he said as he set the water down, then turned and left without making sure I obeyed. I'm not sure how long it took me, but I managed to get myself back on my knees, feebly grasping onto my focus.

Twenty...

Rick

"I haven't heard from him. Have you?" Jeremy asked on the walk to school.

"No, but it's not unusual for him to disappear," I said. In truth, I'd left too many voicemails and sent too many text messages to count.

"What do you think of all that, you know, shit that guy was sayin?" Brett asked, lowering his voice a little, almost as if he were afraid Kevin would appear and lay into him. Days later and we were still talking about what had happened.

"What, that fag? Total setup, so obvious," Mike said.

"I don't know..." I said, trying to make it sound like I was doubting Kevin like Brett was. I had to keep them off his scent so it didn't get back to Kevin's dad. The only way I could think of doing that was keeping them away from our secret. If they thought I was doubting him, then maybe they wouldn't figure out what he really meant to me.

With every passing moment I feared the worst for him. We'd been downtown on Thursday night. When I hadn't heard from him the next day, I used the key I knew he had stashed in his shed and snuck into his house both Saturday and Sunday morning to look for him. I'd been worried I'd find him locked in his closet, but his room had been eerily silent. I couldn't wrap my head around how normal it had looked when so much had transpired since the last time I'd seen him.

By Tuesday afternoon I knew I had to go check on him again. The fact that I hadn't heard from him, that he seemed to have completely disappeared had me considering calling the cops. I knew he was scared his dad would kill him if he ever found out he was gay. And after Thursday, I feared that he might have.

On Tuesday I let myself into the side door of Kevin's house, like I had the previous times. When I opened the door to his room, the curtains were drawn and I was met with the same muted dimness as before. As my eyes focused, I tried to wrap my head around the figure kneeling in the middle of the room. He was unmoving, head bowed, and breathing in slow, deep breaths, but the forward tumble of black hair was a dead giveaway.

"Kevin?" I whispered.

His breathing became more shallow, and after a few seconds he slowly raised his head. As his eyes came into contact with mine, I saw the haze of distance and pain.

Closing his bedroom door behind me, I took several steps towards him.

"Stop," he said barely over a whisper. "Does he know?"

"What?" I asked, struggling to understand his question.

"My father? Does he know?" he asked quietly. I took a few more steps, trying to hear him better. As I got closer, I noticed first the handcuffs and then the black tape. His wrists and ankles had red marks that stretched with painful-looking swelling. "Stop," he said again, and I looked back to his eyes. The haze was fading, and I started to see his fear.

"Kevin, are you okay?"

"Does he know?"

His meaning finally hitting me, I stammered, "Umm, no. At least I don't think so." His shoulders fell as he let out a breath. "Let me help you." My mind scrambled, trying to figure out the best way to free him.

"No," he said, his head slowly rising back up. He closed his eyes for several moments. When he opened them again he seemed to look past me. "Leave."

"What?"

"Leave."

"I can't. I won't. I can't leave you here like this." I kneeled down and the terror returned to his voice.

"The pain," he said, struggling for words. "I have to focus. I can't focus with you here. It's too much."

"Kevin, let me help you," I pleaded with him.

"He'll kill me. Please." Tears came to his panic-filled eyes. He stammered weakly. "I can't focus with you here…he'll kill me."

I stood, taking several steps back, and his head dropped again. I kept backing out of his room, out of sight and into his attached bathroom until I ran into the wall, where I slid down to the floor. His words had burst open the fear that had been playing on the edge of my mind since he'd run from us, from me. I had broken him.

He couldn't focus with me near. He'd been telling me this for months. He'd tried so many times to warn me that losing his focus was dangerous for him. I hadn't heard him, thinking he was only scared of his feelings.

I replayed every time he'd told me that loss of control was bad for him, why he had to stay focused to survive. He'd been telling me all along that I distracted him, and in his world, distraction could be fatal. I was so lost in what I'd done that I didn't realize I'd been sitting in his bathroom for hours until I heard his dad come home from work and make his way downstairs.

"It's good that you're learning some focus again."

His dad's words echoed the thoughts tearing through my head. I scooted myself to the door to peer out. His dad squatted down in front of him, balancing on the heels of his perfectly polished shoes. I nearly cried out when I saw the gun held loosely in his hand. He pointed it carelessly at Kevin as he started talking again. Kevin's head was still bowed.

"You're out of control, Kevin. You need to get back into the swing of things." In a swift motion, he slammed the butt of his gun against the side of Kevin's head, standing up in the same amount of time it took for Kevin's head to snap to the side and his body to crumple to the floor.

The second the door shut, I scrambled over to Kevin, half crawling, half running. He was motionless, but I immediately noticed his chest rising and falling. I pushed the hair out of his face and looked at his closed eyes. I knew if he woke and found me, it would be too much for him. I bent to him and placed my lips softly on his. Even though he wouldn't see me again, I had no intention of leaving him alone. I made up my mind to stay in his bathroom for as long as his torture lasted.

I knew he had gained consciousness again when I heard his moaning from the bedroom. He cried out in agony as he pulled himself upright and moved his body into the kneeling position I'd first found him in. I watched silently from the bathroom doorway as he took in a deep breath, held it for three seconds and then slowly exhaled. He continued this routine, every now and then fighting a muscle spasm. His body was obviously warring with his mind. I settled quietly on the floor, leaning against the door jamb, watching. His breathing was hypnotic to me. When I heard his dad coming down the stairs, I sank back into the shadows.

"It's ten," he said as he opened the door. "Move," he said calmly.

I couldn't hear what Kevin said, but I knew he'd made some sort of noise.

"Pathetic," his dad said. The word seeped, with boredom, from his mouth and the cry that followed didn't sound human to me. I gritted my teeth together and fought back the urge to run. Curling up into a ball on the bathmat, I drifted in and out of sleep as the hours crept by.

On Wednesday morning, his father slammed open the door but left without saying a word. When I was sure he was gone, I peered out and saw a fresh glass of water, and Kevin fighting to get into his kneeling position again.

It took everything I had not to rush to help him.

The next twenty-four hours were excruciatingly long. I struggled not to interfere with his concentration, but kept a solid watch from his bathroom door. My heart broke and my fists clenched each time he cried out. In my mind, I kept telling him I was there, that he wasn't alone, that he was going to be okay, somehow hoping he'd sense this, that he'd feel my energy. I concentrated on the idea that my strength could somehow help him.

On his dad's final visit Thursday morning, I could hear him roughly removing Kevin's bindings. He howled out in exhaustion, which caused my eyes to sting with tears and frustration again. I heard his father dismiss Kevin's punishment, praising him mockingly for handling it like a man. I actually felt the bile rise in my throat but choked it back. When it was clear that he had gone for the day, I crept quietly to Kevin, now curled up next to the bed, his body in almost the same position the restraints had kept him in for days. I didn't want to frighten him, so I whispered his name quietly, but he didn't move. After several failed attempts, I reached out for him, not able to resist the urge to help him any longer. As my fingers came into contact with his scarred shoulder, he flinched, which sent his body into a spasm of pain, and he cried out in misery as his muscles fought the onslaught of agony. As he writhed and sobbed on the carpet, I felt desperate to stop his hurt. Without thinking, I knelt on one knee next to him and tried to pull him to me, bracing myself with my raised foot. I didn't know if I was doing more damage than good, but all I could think about was covering his injuries with my body, trying to get closer to him to somehow absorb what radiated from him. He resisted against me, crying out until his eyes flashed open briefly. In that second, I didn't see Kevin looking back at me — rather a stranger with two black empty holes. Then there was a flash of recognition in his face and he closed his eyes again, curling into me, still convulsing slightly, but he rocked with my arms instead of against them. After several more minutes, I was able to position myself behind him, my back to his bed and him fully in my arms, my legs straddling either side of him. I held him and tried to force every bit of love I felt for him through my arms and into his crumpled form, hoping it could somehow heal him.

Kevin

I woke in my bed. I couldn't remember moving off the floor, but then I didn't remember much past the first twenty-four hours of my father's punishment. There were moments of searing agony that I couldn't block out, but most of it just bled together. Flashes of Rick being in my room seeped in like a haze, but I wasn't sure if he was a dream or real. I took a deep breath and winced at the throbbing that coursed through me. Glancing at the nightstand, I noticed the clock had been turned back around, reading 11:13 PM, but I had no concept of what day it was. Behind the clock, barely visible, sat two pills that I immediately recognized as oxys. I knew I wasn't stupid enough to have left them there but didn't question it. I slowly turned my body, going with the hurt rather than trying to fight it. I swallowed the pills without any water and allowed them to overtake my consciousness.

The next time I surfaced briefly, there was a glass of water next to a new set of pills. As I faded in and out, I repeated the routine countless times. Eventually a grilled cheese sandwich was added to the nightstand, which made me certain it was Rick who was caring for me, but this left me questioning his absence. I wasn't hungry, but knew well enough that I had to get something in my body. In one of my half-awake hazes I saw a shadow walking away from me into my bathroom. Another time I woke feeling dampness on my skin, the smell of soap and clean clothes.

While I was sure I had vague memories of painfully stumbling to the bathroom a few times, I still fought against the urge to take a piss. My mind was becoming clearer and I felt reality start to ease back in, but, with reality, I recognized that my most recent dose of oxy hadn't muted the throbbing yet, and I dreaded moving. Finally, my need pushed me to move. I rolled off the bed, using the edge to slowly stand up and catch my balance. After several agonizing steps, I made it to the bathroom where I stumbled over something.

"What the fuck?" My voice came out hoarse as I fumbled for the lights. Rick sat up, pushing himself into a standing position quickly and blinking furiously at the light.

"Oh, I'm sorry." He looked at me and then to the door of the bathroom. "I didn't hear you get up. You should be in bed."

"What are you doing here?"

"You're right. I'm sorry, I'll leave."

"Wait, no. I didn't mean it like that."

"It's okay, I gotta go. My dad…"

I narrowed my eyes at him. "Does my father know?" I asked, the familiar sense of panic invading my body.

"No, I don't think so," he replied simply.

I leaned slightly against the door for balance as my anxiety eased and the pain continued. He took a step toward me, then thought better of it and stepped back.

"How long's it been?" I asked.

"Since?"

"Since Charlie."

I watched him count the days in his head. "Ten."

"Fuck," I said, feeling tired again. The room started to spin, and I closed my eyes.

"Easy," I heard him say as I felt his fingers gently touch my elbow. He started to guide me back towards the bed, and even though I still had to piss, I let him because I was afraid I'd pass out. As I drifted off into an aching haze again, I was sure I felt his lips brush my forehead. The next time I woke up, there wasn't a sandwich on my nightstand.

Rick

I could see the old Kevin in his eyes and felt he could take care of himself without my help. I knew the only way to make sure he stayed okay was to stay away from him.

When I walked in my front door that afternoon after leaving Kevin's house, I shouldn't have been surprised to find my dad waiting for me.

"What? You think you can just take off for five days without letting anyone know where you are?"

I was exhausted and honestly didn't care much what happened to me after seeing what Kevin had gone through, so I just stared at him. I really was shocked that he'd even realized how long I'd been gone.

"No excuse? No explanation? Give me your phone."

"What? No," I replied automatically.

"Well, we already shut the service off. We're not going to pay for it if we can't get a hold of you. You might as well hand it over."

"You have no right," I yelled at him.

"The hell I don't," he said as he stepped towards me, landing the back of his fist against my face. I stumbled into the couch and when my eyes focused, I saw Sylvia and Emma standing in the entryway, shopping bags in their arms, staring at us. In seconds, I was kneeling down in front of Emma.

"Hey schmunchkin! Did you see that? Wasn't that cool? Dad's showing me some blocking moves for football. Do you think that will keep those guys away from the ball?" I asked, smiling through the pain, seeing the fear in her eyes. When she didn't respond to me, I turned to my dad. "Right dad?" With his blank stare jumping from Emma and back to me, I repeated, "Right dad, you were just showing me some football moves?"

"Yeah, yeah sure honey," he managed, finally catching on. He walked over and mussed her hair just as I picked her up in my arms. She was getting almost too big to carry, but I couldn't think of anything else to do. With a slight smile, I saw that she was beginning to accept our lies. I wanted to whisk her away from what she'd seen, so once she was in my arms I said, "Let's go for a walk, shall we? I need to hear all about your week since I haven't been home." I glanced behind me, daring either of them to try to stop me as I walked out the front door with her.

Thankfully, my dad had been too rattled to follow through on any punishment he might have had planned for me, so in the following days I was able to try and figure out the best way to handle what I had to do with Kevin. On his first night back to Zarahemla, if I hadn't known better I would've had no idea what he'd been through. No one mentioned what had happened with Charlie or Kevin's subsequent disappearance. I marveled at the damage his dad had been able to do while leaving little-to-no physical evidence. His ankles and wrists were still bruised and swollen but easily hidden with a long-sleeved shirt and jeans. I wondered, not for the first time, if this had been one of the worst punishments for Kevin. I couldn't imagine it getting more deranged than what I'd seen. I firmly believed what Kevin had told me—his dad was a sociopath.

I ducked out the back of Zarahemla, dreading what I knew was coming. Tensions were high because Kevin was trying to reestablish his power within the group. He was pushing all the right buttons, just waiting for someone to snap. But after what the guys had seen him do to Charlie, no one was taking the bait easily. I took a long hit on my joint and fought the urge to cough. Kevin could fake being okay all he wanted, but I knew his body was still fighting to recover.

"Hey." I heard him walk up behind me. He brushed his hand against my back briefly as he stopped next to me. I didn't respond. "So, I told them I was coming out to find you. Mind looking all pissed off at me and shit when we go back in there? They're just not giving me what I need tonight," he said lightly.

"I think I need to make myself scarce," I blurted out, not intending to start this conversation but somehow being unable to contain it any longer.

He glanced sideways at me, his near-black eyes dancing a little as they took me in.

"Okay, I guess I can just tell 'em I sent you home. My father is out of town; maybe you can come over later?"

It'd been almost two weeks since we'd been together, and the way he was looking at me made me realize that what I was about to do was going to be harder than I'd originally thought.

"I mean, like permanently," I said into the darkness, looking away from him.

"What?"

"This is not working out. Things are a mess."

"Don't be a fucking idiot." I could hear the nerves in his voice. "Why would you even think that's a good idea?"

"It was your idea."

"Bullshit it was."

"You told me to leave."

"Fuck you, I didn't."

"At your house, when I first found you." I felt him flinch next to me. We hadn't talked about what I'd seen, and I wasn't sure he even remembered me being at his house. "You said it yourself. You're out of control when I'm around."

"Leave my house, not me you fucking idiot. You're

unexpected and aggravating as fuck, but you didn't point a gun at my head. That was all him."

It was my turn to flinch. He hadn't mentioned the gun, and he didn't know I'd seen his dad with it. I shut my eyes at the memory.

"But that wouldn't have happened if I wasn't here to make you lose your focus. You've pretty much said it yourself. Losing control could cost you your life."

"Since when do you listen to me?"

"Where'd you go after Charlie?"

"What?"

"You were MIA for three or four days, where'd you go?"

"I had to get my head on straight."

"Where'd you go?"

"The roof of the school."

"You sat on the roof for four days?"

"Yeah, so?"

"What were you on?"

"What the fuck does it matter?"

"It matters to me. What were you on, Kevin?"

"Fine. Meth," he said angrily.

"That's just what I'm talking about. You don't do that. You're losing it, out of control, and you know it. Have you even had time to crash through everything that's happened in the last two weeks? You've been so messed up that you haven't been able to pull it all together and deal with it."

"No—" he tried to cut me off me.

"No lies, no games, Kevin. You're dad even said it. You've lost your focus."

"How the fuck do you know what my father said?" he interrupted me.

I ignored him and kept going. "I know you've thought about it. Even today, as you strut around in there, you're walking a thin line. I'm destroying you." Part of me wished he'd grab me and shake me and tell me I was wrong, but he couldn't.

"You're out of your mind. This is not the answer. I won't let you go."

As I'd sat in his bathroom hour after hour, I'd known it would come to this.

"You don't have to let me go. I'm going to let you go." I glanced behind me to make sure no one was able to see us, and I kissed him, careful to keep a lookout for the guys. I felt the tears well up and my stomach turn to stone as I realized it would be the last time. I threaded my fingers into his hair, pulling his mouth against mine, wanting to savor his taste, to remember the feel of his rough skin against mine, to hold onto him. I knew I was about to break both our hearts, and I prayed we'd be strong enough to handle it. I hated what I had to do as I tore myself away from him and walked briskly into Zarahemla.

Kevin

"You can go to hell!" I heard Rick say behind me. I was still trying to compose myself after his kiss. I brought my fingers to my lips, touching the skin he'd just lit on fire. I turned at the sound of anger in his voice, curious who he was talking to. "I'm tired of you bossing me around." I followed after him. "Seriously, Kevin, I'm done with all of this." My stomach clenched as realization slammed into me.

"Knock it off, Rick." I said, pleading with him in my heart to stop what he was doing but clipping my voice for the guys to hear.

"Make me," he said, letting the words hang in the air. "After what I saw you do the other night, I don't want to be part of this little gang of yours."

"It's not really your choice." I said, throwing words I knew would've come easily if it were any of the others. Goddamnit. He knew I couldn't back down twice in front of them.

"What are you gonna do about it?" he challenged.

"Do not push me, Rick," I snarled at him, truly meaning every word I said.

"What are you gonna do Kevin, hit me?"

It was a fucking low blow, and he knew it. I felt my heart constrict, remembering my promise to him. He swore if I did, he'd leave. I threw him against the wall and growled at him.

"Fucking stop this bullshit."

"I'm sorry," he whispered. I barely heard him, just saw his lips move. He pushed me back. "You're pathetic. You ran away from a fight the other night and now you're scared to even throw a punch. What happened to you? Maybe you really are a sissy!"

"Goddamnit!" I cursed. I felt coldness clamp around my heart. *One*, I thought, shut out thoughts of the guys. *Two*, shut out thoughts of my father. *Three*, shut out thoughts of Rick. *Four*, shut out the pain. As I pulled my arm back, I knew I was about to destroy all that was good in my life. But good didn't keep me alive.

He relaxed, taking my own advice to absorb the hit rather than tense against it. He stumbled several feet. "That's all you got?" he flung at me, and I threw another punch. Fighting against everything my heart was screaming at me, I stepped into a swing that folded into his stomach as he curled over, coughing. Though I knew I hadn't landed it as hard as I could have, guilt racked me at the thought of worsening any injury left by his dad.

"You done?" I glared at him.

"Still a fairly weak punch there, Kev," he coughed.

I grabbed him and threw him on the ground, making a show of wrapping my fingers around his neck but applying no pressure. I leaned close to him and whispered frantically in his ear. "How far are you going to push me?"

"'Til they hear you tell me to leave and never come back," he said quietly.

I raised my voice and regretted the punch that followed. "Still think my punches are weak?" I lowered my voice and spat furiously at him, "I will not say that."

"You've already lost me. You broke your promise. Make it official." He knew damn well that if I threw him out in front of the guys, I'd have no fucking choice but to stand behind my words. Goddamn him!

"Never," I gritted through my teeth as I stood up, turning my back to him. There was no way I was going to do what he wanted.

In near slow motion, I tried to block out the sounds of him advancing on me. "I hate you," he cried at me. I felt his foot connect with the small of my back the same moment his words tore into my heart. My back arched from the onslaught, and I fell to my knees first, then down on all fours as my hands slid into the dirt. My muscles screamed at me and my wrists caught fire. I closed my fingers around the rocks in the sand to absorb some of the sting. I was completely shocked when his foot caught me again, this time in the stomach, my body flipping and landing flat on my back. It'd only been a few days since I'd gotten myself out of bed and my body was far from fucking healed. I pulled in my breath, fighting against the pain.

I was a fighter, and my adrenaline kicked in. As the blackness of the world descended into my vision, all I saw was Rick standing over me. Instinct took over, and I rolled to the side before he had the chance to strike again, springing to my feet. Rage blinded me, and I saw red. I used the shattered pieces of my heart like weapons of glass, letting them tear me up inside and give me the ammunition to take control. I took several steps towards him and alarm flooded his face. He knew he'd pushed too far. The image of Charlie pinned against the wall, my blade at his throat, tore to the surface. It brought with it the memory of Rick's confession of love. I stopped a moment before I laid into him, straining to find anything that would keep me from destroying him. Face to face, his fear of me was tangible.

"Come back and I will kill you," I said, not recognizing my own voice. He stood for a second before stumbling backwards. Walk the fuck out of here, I prayed. One more fucking word from him, and I was scared shitless of what I'd do.

Twenty-One...

Rick

My heart exploded at the sight of his anger. Praying I was making the right decision yet knowing I was saving his life, I told myself he could handle whatever I'd done. He'd handled worse. After all, he'd still be alive, and that was better than anything I could offer him.

Every step I took towards home grew heavier. The selfish part of me screamed to go to him and take back what I'd done, but it wasn't about me anymore. I couldn't risk his life just so I didn't have to think about the hurt I'd caused. It was about keeping him alive, and as long as I was around, he couldn't focus. And without his focus, his dad could kill him. I'd been stupid not to hear it all along.

I paused as I pulled myself into my window, waiting to see if I could hear movement within the house. After my recent disappearing act I wasn't looking for another run-in with my dad. As I shut the window behind me, my hand hesitated over the lock. It'd been over a year since I'd tried to keep him out. The moment it clicked into place I flicked it open again. *I can't do this*, I thought. I stood for several more minutes, hand on the clasp, finally making the decision to lock it and pull the blinds closed.

I curled up into a ball on the bed, dreading the nightmares that were sure to come. I fought off sleep for as long as I could, and it crossed my mind to be grateful to my dad for shutting off my phone. At least I didn't have to battle the added temptation to call Kevin if I didn't have my phone.

I rolled over and wasn't at all surprised when I heard scuffling at my window. I could hear him trying to pry it open and then silence. I stared at the blinds, ears straining to hear any sound from outside. I could almost sense him glaring at me on the other side. I knew he'd be furious at me for what I'd done. As sleep evaded me, my eyes stayed glued to the window, desperately listening for his presence. At some point, I must have drifted off.

The night air was chilled, but I couldn't feel it, and there was the crunching of glass beneath my shoes as I struggled to get free from the car and the smell of gasoline. I looked up and down the deserted road, spotting something lying in the distance.

"Jason?" I called as I staggered towards the unmoving form. As I got close, someone pulled me away, but I yanked myself free and sank to my knees as the blood-covered, mangled flesh and jet-black hair registered in my head.

"Kevin! Noooooo!" I wailed at the repulsive scene at my feet.

"He lost his focus," a voice said as a shadow appeared,

standing over the remains of Kevin's body. His dad, gun hanging loosely in his hand, began to laugh...then the sound of a gunshot.

I jerked, falling off my bed. Fighting the urge to scream out with the pain of Jason's death and with the sinking horror of what may lay in Kevin's future playing at the edges of my mind, I made no move to get back in bed. With tears streaming down my face, it felt like the first day of school all over again—no friends and a heartache that threatened to kill me.

When the time came to get ready I dressed in the same clothes as the night before. The sun was creeping in through the kitchen window, casting rays of dust particles through the room. I killed time by smoking in the backyard after everyone had left, then started towards the corner shortly after I knew he'd be walking with the guys to school. Hard as it was going to be, I knew the safest place for me would be near the guys. As long as they were within earshot, he'd have no choice but to treat me as the outcast he'd made me.

I held my breath as I approached, praying I'd timed it well. He leaned against the cement wall, and as he caught a glimpse of me, he pushed off the wall and started walking away. Nervously, the guys glanced at me and followed him. It was what I'd wanted to have happen, but the unexpected burning in my eyes had me drawing in a ragged breath. *It'll get easier*, I thought.

I talked to the counselor and my teacher at the school, convincing them that I needed to drop the class I had with Kevin. I told them I had a great job opportunity and that I needed to be released for work-study. I had a plan to finish the coursework independently. Overall, I'd always been a good student, and it wasn't hard to have all the right paperwork signed by my dad. Kevin had taught me a few things. At lunch, I made it a point to disappear into the drama hall, knowing Kevin wouldn't dream of venturing into that nobody-land.

After school, I walked behind him again, hoping my public humiliation might play on any feelings he had for me. If he saw how hard everything was for me, maybe he'd leave me alone. I knew I only had to avoid him for the last two weeks of school. After that, I'd have to figure out what to do with my life without him. I tried playing video games, but they reminded me of him—everything did. My dad was slamming things around the second he walked in with Emma, so I found refuge in my bedroom.

With nothing to keep me busy, I started to crumble. I crawled into my closet and shut the door. The darkness descended and I squeezed my eyes shut, trying to keep the tears from escaping. I thought about Kevin being locked in his closet for days, and I found it comforting being close to his suffering. It was morbid and horrible, but being close to any part of him was better than tossing and turning in my own nightmares.

Towards the end of the second day without Kevin in my life, Jessica caught up with me in the hall.

"You okay?" She asked.

"Fine."

"Really? You don't look fine."

"Thanks."

"I've been hearing things…" she wanted me to finish.

"There's nothing to hear."

"You're not hanging out with them anymore. There must be some truth."

"I'm sure there is, but I'm too tired to care what others are saying." I cringed at the word tired. It didn't even come close to explaining how I felt.

"I heard you two got in a fight."

"You heard right."

"That's huge. I hear the last guy he fought he almost killed."

"Is there a point to all this, Jessica?" I sighed.

"Yeah, I'm worried about you." I slowed my pace, aware of her concern.

"Really, I'm fine. He's a jerk, and I've had enough. We're not friends anymore."

"I'm sorry."

"It's not a big deal," I said as I bit my lip, trying to fight down the emotion that threatened to crack through my voice.

"Okay," she said hesitantly. "Well, in any case, why don't you come over this weekend? I'm having a few friends over."

I smiled. It sounded really nice. "I'll try." And I meant it when I said it.

That night I fixed a bowl of ramen for dinner and sat and watched it steam on the kitchen table, the smell of the fake Asian spices doing nothing for my appetite. As I stirred the soup, I tried to think of the last time I'd eaten; I couldn't remember, but I didn't care.

As the sun set, I found myself on the closet floor again. I'd heard Kevin try my window and it sounded like he had banged his palm on the pane in frustration. I sat frozen, pulled into myself, scared to move as I pictured him angry and slamming his fist through the glass. My mind raced with ideas of what I'd do if he broke into my room. Would he burst in and kiss me or hit me? The tears that swept me into sleep were much different than the tears that jolted me awake as Kevin's bloody body screamed into my dreams.

On the third day, I ran into him twice in the hallway at school. The first time, we stopped, staring. His eyes had narrowed at me, fists clenching, but I couldn't read his expression. It looked as if he were about to say something, then his eyes darted around, noticing the slowing of the crowds. We were definitely a source of gossip. He shoved past me, nearly knocking me down. The second time I saw him, he didn't slow his pace.

Kevin

It had been sixty-eight days since he'd walked out on me, fifty-five days since graduation, thirteen since my last serious punishment and only seventeen days until I turned eighteen and got the fuck out of this bullshit town. My plan was San Francisco. I wanted sex, and that was the best place I could think of where I could earn some quick money and fuck until my dick fell off.

I watched as the three guys walked out the front door of the bar. The big guy was perfect. I waited until they were away from the main entrance and the security cameras before I circled in front of them. I shoved my hands in my pockets, ducked my head and quickened my pace. Heading right towards them, I slammed my shoulder hard into the big one.

"Christ, watch where the fuck you're going!" I shouted, throwing my hands up, turning and taking a few steps backwards.

"What the hell's your problem?" the guy said, puffing up for his friends. It worked every time.

"Fucking drunk!" I flung at him.

As expected, he descended and my adrenaline soared. I allowed him to take the first punch. It was like gambling. If they didn't win a little, why the hell would they keep playing? After letting him get in a few good hits, I unleashed my rage, rushing at him again and again, connecting with my fists, elbows, even my head — the harder the better. I wanted to have to wrap my hands when I was through. I wanted to split my skin open, to throw my arm out of socket, to see red blood, to feel the pain and destruction leave me and enter into the loser who'd been stupid enough to take my bait.

It was one thing to pick a fight with a big guy in front of his friends — he'd always try to win first — but brotherly loyalty usually kicked in, and I wasn't looking for uneven odds. As soon as his friends entered the mix, I punched my way out and ran.

They gave chase for about a block, then fell back. I slowed, spat the blood from my mouth and tongued the cut on my lip. I tried to stay away from the headshots for the same reason I did with my father, but sometimes the fuckers got lucky. I started to fuck with my lip, and it felt good. The hurt was consuming. As I made my way home, I bit down gently, then harder, testing the limits of my own tolerance. Fucking pain was good.

Sleep hadn't been my friend for years, but in the last

few months, we were flat out enemies. The damn bitch wouldn't give it up for anything. By the time I finally felt some semblance of being tired, the sun was rising again and I had to endure another day. Even without school, my father expected me to be working. I went through the motions of going to work every day, but in reality I had enough money to get me through until I got to San Francisco. It wasn't hard to forge a paystub accounting for my hours. As long as the deposits I made into the bank account my father monitored matched up, he seemed convinced everything was happening as expected.

After showering and cleaning up my hands from the night before, I started upstairs, all too aware that my father was still home. Nervousness pricked at my skin. The balance in the house wasn't right, and I proceeded with caution to the kitchen where he was making himself some scrambled egg whites.

He looked up casually at me as I entered, then did a double take. I knew he was looking at my lip, well aware it hadn't come from his hand.

"That's the fourth time."

Silence was often the best response with him.

"People are going to start asking questions." He scraped the eggs onto a plate next to a piece of wholegrain toast. He leaned back against the counter and started eating. I knew I wasn't dismissed, so I gripped the edge of the kitchen table, waiting for him to continue. Going out and trying to fuck up the world helped, but it could get me in a lot of trouble with my father. Taking bites of the eggs and chewing slowly, he finished eating his entire breakfast, rinsed off the plate and put it in the dishwasher before speaking again.

"Against the wall," he finally said, tugging at his belt. My head dropped. Fuck. I pulled in my breath and started counting. As I walked towards the nearest open wall, I reached over my head, grabbed a handful of the back of my shirt and pulled it up and off in one motion. I tossed it into the corner and positioned myself, relaxing my back muscles first, then my neck, working my way through my upper arms and even reminding myself not to tighten my hands against the wall. The first lash was always the hardest, jarring my muscles to attention. As much as I tried to relax, the searing pain coursed through me. I had to focus more than usual on letting my shoulder muscles go. Instead of focusing on the throbbing, I focused on the marks I knew the belt would leave. I could picture the exact wound each lash seared onto my body based on the angle, how much of it I felt slice into my skin and the strength he put behind it. I could see the skin changing colors, welting and splitting as he crashed down on the same area over and over. I could feel my flesh start to tear and envisioned the wetness of the blood running in single raindrop lines from the angry mess. I closed my eyes tightly, thinking only of the imagery he was painting with his strokes.

"No more fighting," he said as I heard him slide his belt back on.

I still had my head bowed, hands pressed against the wall, when I heard the garage door shut behind him. I had to work on easing myself back into my body just as much as I had to work on getting out of it when the beatings started. Slowly I pulled myself into an upright position, adjusting to the soreness. With calculated breaths, I cleaned the drying blood and added bandages to the deeper lashes. After putting my previously discarded shirt back on, I left the house. I couldn't risk him finding me at home. I'd made plans to chill at Brett's house most of the day. I didn't drive. My father assumed I took the bus to the job I told him I had secured for the summer—even though there was no job. As much as I would've liked to take the spare car, I knew that leaning against the seat after a beating would be outrageously stupid. Not to mention the lack of explanation to my father for the additional mileage. As I walked past Rick's I saw him out of the corner of my eye, coming out his front door. I pulled up short and thought about turning back to my house but then felt like kicking myself in the ass for even considering running away from him. My anger flashed at the fact that he was up and going for the day. He never got up early unless he had a reason to, and I knew he hadn't found a job. The whole reason I was walking past his fucking house was because he wasn't supposed to be around. Again, I wanted to kick my own ass. It didn't matter what the fuck he was doing. I reminded myself that he was dead to me.

I felt him watching me as I kept my pace confident, easy and steady. My eyes burned with the need to glance at him, but I knew I'd end up wanting to knock his teeth out, and he wasn't worth it.

By the time I got to Brett's, I was still rattled. It had been less than an hour since my father had been raining blows onto my back with a taut leather belt. Then I had the fucking misfortune of running into Rick. And to top it off, I had to walk into Brett's house like I owned the goddamn place.

"Wow, what happened to you?" Brett asked, creating the distraction I needed, obviously commenting on the split lip and healthy bruise forming on my cheek from the night before.

"You should've seen the other guy."

"I've been the other guy," he quipped. I narrowed my eyes at his sudden show of courage.

"Yeah, you got off easy."

"What'd he do?"

"Pissed me off." I couldn't very well tell him that it was my thirteenth fight in the last few months and that I went out several times a week just looking for some asshole to fuck with.

"So, there's this party this weekend for the 24th..." Brett began.

"And."

"And," he hesitated. "Well, we were talking—"

I interrupted him. "We?" I asked, just 'cause I felt like being an ass.

"Yeah, Jeremy, Mike, you know." When I didn't say anything, he kept going. "So yeah, there's a party and we were thinking..." he stopped.

"Thinking what?" God, sometimes it was painful to watch him squirm. I knew I wasn't helping him spit it out, but, Jesus, he could be so ridiculous.

"It's at a guy's house from Olympus. Maybe we should go," he managed to say just as a good song came on his radio. Without responding, I turned up the music and ignored him. I sprawled out, stomach down on his couch, and buried my head in my arms, leaving him to wonder if I was pissed or just bored. I wasn't really either. Mostly I wanted to hit him, and I knew that probably wasn't the best answer.

By late afternoon, Jeremy and Mike had shown up at Brett's. Part of me wanted to go ballistic and just fuck them all up, but after Charlie it had taken me a long time to regain my footing with them. I'd dished out a lot of free booze and drugs in the weeks that followed, and I didn't want my investment to be wasted. Once I felt comfortable with my position again, my patience had started to return to that of a fucking two year old. I found it easier to keep myself from completely going off by clamping my mouth shut.

It wasn't until I was ready to go home that I brought up the party.

"So, I heard about a party this weekend," I said, narrowing my eyes at Brett. I waited to see if he'd step up and say something about the fact that it had been his idea. I wished he would. I really was itching for an excuse to pound him. "I was thinking we should go," I continued, smirking, trying to bait him.

"Sound's good," Mike said, looking at Brett. It would appear that Brett had drawn the short straw and had been sent to talk to me about the party. Their obvious confusion made me feel a little better. Just fucking with them kept my mind busy.

I knew I pushed all of them more than normal without Rick around, but I wasn't stupid. I kept the weed and beer in good supply. I personally made it through each day by taking downers or fucking pain pills, trying to keep my temper in check. When I didn't spend time at Zarahemla or one of their houses, I was out cruising the closing of the bars, looking for some hopped-up meathead to fuck up.

Rick

"I don't know how I ever let you talk me into this," I called out from the bathroom.

"Come on, Rick, you've been locked in this house for months. You need to get out. Besides, it's a state holiday for the Mormons. What better reason to go get trashed and light off some fireworks?"

I grabbed a comb out of my drawer and ran it several times over the bruises on my upper arm. I wasn't sure the trick actually worked, but it didn't hurt to try. "Yeah, but a party with a bunch of people I don't know?" I asked as I pulled the door open. Jessica leaned against the wall right outside.

"That's the point, you won't run into..." She stopped. We didn't talk about Kevin, not since she had asked me about him in the hallway at school. I wondered if she thought I might have stronger feelings for him, but she never pushed it. "I mean. It'll be a nice change of crowd."

"Yeah, I guess."

"Hey, did I tell you? I got my acceptance letter from ASU."

"Seriously? That's great, Jessica. Congratulations. Does Derek know yet?"

She looked absolutely beautiful when she laughed, "Of course he does. We'll both be attending."

"Wow, look at you settling down into monogamy," I

said, giving her a hug. She really did deserve such a great guy. He'd been chasing her for years, and she'd finally realized how amazing he was.

"I wouldn't go that far," she smiled, but her eyes saddened a little.

"Hey, what's wrong?" I asked.

"Nothing."

"Come on now. You can tell me," I insisted.

"It's you, Rick. I wish you were coming too. You're like my best friend, and I don't want to leave you here alone."

I almost blurted out that I wasn't alone, but I stopped myself. There was no point lying to her. "I'll be fine. If you haven't noticed, I'm kinda stubborn that way."

"Have you heard back from anyone yet?"

"No, not yet," I lied. I'd been accepted at NYU, IU and Berkeley, but part of me couldn't imagine leaving Kevin to deal with his dad on his own. In reality, I knew I couldn't actually do anything for him, yet I hadn't accepted admission at any of the schools. "So, whose party are we going to?" I asked as we headed out the door.

"Some guy named Mason."

Kevin

"Where the fuck is this guy's house? What's his name again?" I asked, tapping my fingers irritably on the steering wheel.

"Mason, and it's just around the corner," Mike said from the backseat of my car.

"What the fuck kind of name is that?"

"It's there." Mike's hand appeared from the back,

pointing out the front window to the left. The street was already lined with dozens of cars.

"Looks like a good one," Jeremy said when he got out of my car. As we headed to the house, we came alongside some girls dressed in next to nothing.

"Well, hello ladies," I drawled out, running my hand through my hair and flashing a half smile. They giggled, and I almost gagged. "Going to Mason's, I assume?" The name still sounded fucking idiotic to me. I held out my arm to the hottest girl of the group. "May I?" I asked her. She glanced excitedly towards her friends and laced her delicate hand, fake nails and all, through my arm. She told me her name, which I filed away for use if needed, but I didn't think I'd actually need to remember it. She was all for show. A few kisses, some dancing, wandering hands and people would be satisfied.

I noticed another car that looked familiar drive by and park down the street. It was too dark to make out all the details, but I made a note to pay attention to see if I knew anyone else at this lame-ass get-together.

My first goal was to find alcohol. The discarded beer bong on the table seemed to fit in perfectly with my plan.

"Hey, Jeremy, why don't you do the honors?" I said as I motioned towards the bong. It was a hell of way to start out, one of the quickest and cheapest ways to get fucked up, and I planned on all four of us getting hammered. At his hint of hesitation, I said, "Fuck, if you're not man enough, get that shit ready for me." I pulled the high-heeled, tight-ass-shirted blonde behind me. "Would you like to go first?" I asked with a smile. It was never a good idea to be a complete ass to a female.

"I'm okay."

"You sure?"

"Yeah, go ahead."

"Don't mind if I do. Put two in there," I said, turning back to Jeremy. As he poured, I got down on my knees and put the end of the hose in my mouth, thumb over the hole. As soon as the beers were loaded and bubbles tapped out, I released the pressure and felt it shoot down my throat. I had no problem swallowing. I'd long since rid myself of my gag reflex and the beers sailed down smoothly. The crowd around me cheered.

Rick

"Looks like they got the beer bong going," Jessica said as we walked past a crowd of cheering people. "Wanna try?"

"Nah, not tonight. You?" I asked, barely glancing at the group.

"No, not really. Got a joint? I could use a hit."

"Yeah, let's go out back," I said, spotting a patio door off the kitchen.

After several hits, she turned, grabbed my arm and put it around her, nestling into my chest. It wasn't the first time. She was a touchy person, but it always made me uncomfortable. She'd move or twist the wrong way, and I'd have to concentrate on not flinching as she hit a sore spot.

"Are you gay?" she asked, suddenly. I choked out the smoke I was holding in.

"What the...?" I coughed and stalled.

"I don't care if you are. I just want you to know that

I'm okay with it, you know, if you are."

"I'm not," I finally said, and she remained silent. Strangely, as my mind reeled with dread, I thought it weird that she'd ask about me being gay before she asked about the bruises. Going back to what Kevin had said once, it just confirmed that people didn't want to believe there was a monster living next door. After the shock of her question wore off, I considered answering her. It'd be nice to have someone to talk to about Kevin. But when it came down to it, I didn't even know if I was gay for sure. "I mean..." I stopped. She had shared so much with me and had never asked anything in return. "Why do you ask? I was with you."

After several moments, she offered, "I'm not sure, just a feeling."

"Do I act gay?" Fear settled in. God, if she suspected, then I wondered who else might have guessed.

"No, not at all," she said, wrapping her arms around me.

I continued tentatively, "I don't know," because I didn't have an answer for her. I didn't know if it was just Kevin or if it was me. I hadn't had those feelings before him, not like he described. And at one point I had been attracted to, and turned on by Jessica.

"Have you ever kissed a guy?" Again, I considered answering her, but I knew this was a loaded question, and Kevin's secret was not mine to share. I trusted her not to tell anyone, but I just couldn't risk her putting things together.

"No," I lied and she believed it. She was always far too trusting of me.

"Do you want to?"

"I've thought about it. Does that make me gay?" I replied honestly. "Have you ever wanted to kiss a girl?"

"Yeah, I guess. I'd be willing to try it."

"Does that make you gay?"

"Huh. Hadn't really thought about it that way."

"I think it's different for girls. I mean, it's hot to think about girls like that."

"Maybe you're not gay," she laughed, and I knew I'd effectively steered her clear of my secret and of Kevin.

With the joint done, I had no reason to hide outside anymore. Luckily, I was able to find a beer and a room of people playing video games. Hiding behind a game controller was almost as appealing as hiding behind a joint. I sent Jessica off to find Derek, and sat cross-legged in front of the couch, tuning out the people around me.

Kevin

I hated shitty-ass parties. Two beer bongs and I was barely feeling a buzz, but I was getting more and more anxious. I'd fucking left my flask in the car as well, and was too goddamn lazy to go get it. I started wandering the rooms, aimlessly looking for the blonde I'd walked in with. She'd be something to keep my hands busy. I heard cheering from a room towards the front of the house, and as I approached I could see the animation of a video game on the TV. I stopped for a second, watching the game, then started to scan the room for my blonde.

"Hey, sexy," I heard behind me and spun to see her gliding towards me. She came into my arms, and I backed up lightly against the wall, bracing myself in a comfortable position. As I kissed her, I closed my eyes, imagining a hard body beneath my hands.

Rick

"Hey Jessica, I'm gonna take off."

"We just got here. What happened to the game?"

"Not feeling it tonight," I said, glancing back over my shoulder at the room I'd just left. "Will you be okay if I head out? Derek's here, right?"

"Sure, but do you really have to go?"

"Yeah, I'm tired. I called a cab."

"Why don't you take my car?" she asked, fishing in her pocket for her keys.

"No. No thanks, a cab is good."

"Really, I don't mind. I'll just go home with Derek."

I wasn't sure how I could consider her my best friend when there was so much she didn't know about me. There was still no way in hell I was getting behind the wheel.

"I'm okay." I said, leaning in and giving her a quick kiss on the cheek. "Love ya. Tell Derek g'night for me."

Kevin

I threaded my fingers behind her neck, guiding the kiss.

"Someone call a cab?" I heard near the front door.

"Yeah, me," a voice said.

My heart stopped, my eyes shot open, and I shoved the girl away from me, searching for the voice. My defenses were down, which left me completely vulnerable to him. Why the fuck was he here? I caught a glimpse of his back as he slid out the front door. I slammed past several people, spilling beer everywhere. I wanted to call out to him, but I couldn't get my mouth to work. I was going to kick his ass. I reached the front yard as he shut the door of the cab. As it started to pull away, he looked up, and I was fucking sure he saw me.

Twenty-Two...

Kevin

"Goddamn him," I swore under my breath. "What fucking right did he have to crash my party?" I murmured as I paced the patio. Two smokes later and I hadn't been able to shake the mood he'd put me in.

"What the fuck you lookin' at?" I growled at some guy who'd stumbled out the door. I just needed one reason to let loose on him. I hoped he'd be stupid enough to give me one.

"Fuck you," he slurred at me. *Here we go*, I thought, lunging at him.

He straightened up quickly, tossing the red plastic cup he was holding. His left hook came out of nowhere, knocking me on my ass. My cheek hit the deck and slid, splinters tearing into my skin. I pushed off the ground, barreled my head into his stomach, and was surprised when he didn't fall to the ground as I'd expected. I'd severely miscalculated this guy's ability. He was obviously a fighter and knew exactly what he was fucking doing, but what was he going to do that was worse than my father? The splinters in my face would be proof of another fight. I figured I might as well take the scenic road to hell.

As my fist connected with his face, I thrilled at the sound of his nose breaking and the blood that immediately gushed out. He landed another punch under my jaw and then one right under my left eye. But the sight of his own blood had him freaked out, and he started to panic, which was his first mistake. His second mistake was letting me get him on the ground. As I jumped on top of him, my fists and elbows began to throw blows on his face, causing blood to run into his eyes.

Somebody tore me off him, and I came out swinging at the fucker who had gotten in my way. My fist connected several times before that person crumpled to the ground.

"Jesus Christ," I spat out as Rick looked up at me. "What the fuck are you doing here?"

Rick

He was out of control. Red drops trickled from a cut below his eye and his hair began to stick to his forehead in a mixture of sweat and blood. For months I'd been watching his fuse become shorter and shorter. I recognized his new bruises for what they were, and they weren't leftovers from his dad. The dead giveaway had been the cuts on his hands. They were obviously cuts from fighting, and he didn't fight back with his dad. As I stared into his hate-filled eyes, I cringed at myself for coming back to the party, wondering if the person I'd fallen in love with was in the body standing before me.

"What the fuck are you doing here?" he asked again, his voice beginning to chill. He took a step towards me, and I couldn't help but flinch. Then the guy on the ground behind him moaned. Kevin looked at him with a bored expression and turned back to me. "Goddamn you!" The words curled out of his mouth as he glared at me before walking away.

Jessica was suddenly next to me. "What happened? I thought you left," she said, looking closely at the blood from the cut over my eye.

"I forgot..." I managed. I forgot what? My head? My sanity? What had I been thinking, stopping him from fighting again? I was prepared to avoid him, to see him and pretend not to notice him. But when I saw him standing in the yard, I asked the taxi driver to come back to the party because I forgot what? My sense of self-preservation? "...my jacket," I supplied weakly.

Kevin

I left the guys at the party, slamming the gas pedal. If I wasn't careful I was going to have to fucking punch out any person who looked at me. I had to get home, away from people, or I was going to go all out on someone. As I burst through the front door the lights went on and my father stood there in the entryway. "You smell like cigarette smoke and alcohol." It was the first time I'd ever forgotten to change my clothes before entering the house when he was home. In that moment, I knew I was fucked. "And I told you, no more fights." His irritation was showing, and I took a few steps back. He reached for me and clamped down on my arm with enough pressure that I worried about a break. "It has been a while since you have seen the inside of the closet," he said, yanking me after him.

He threw me into my bedroom wall with just the right amount of force to knock me right back into his waiting hands, and his fists repeated the same calculated actions I'd delivered to so many in the last few months. He wrapped them up in tidy combos that had me flying from one end of the room to the other. I welcomed the distraction of the pain.

Four days later, he had to leave town. He hadn't wanted to end my punishment, but what fun was locking me in a closet if he couldn't be around to enjoy it? If he hadn't been called away, I wondered if this would've been the one that ended me. He knew my birthday was just over a week away, but I hoped I had played the obedient son well enough for him not to suspect my plans. The second I turned eighteen, he couldn't send the cops after me. Until I was safe in San Francisco, I wasn't about to pretend my life wasn't on the line. With him gone, I had a few days to recover and try to get things under control before dealing with what had happened at the fucking party.

I must have dozed off on the couch because I startled awake, jumping to my feet. I didn't know what had awakened me, but I sure as hell wasn't going to find out lying down. The last thing I expected to see was Rick standing across the room.

"What the fuck are you doing here?" I spat at him, my anger rising quickly. He stepped back at the sound of my voice. My blood boiled as I wondered if he really thought pretending he was scared would work with me. It wasn't hard to let him see the hate in my eyes.

"I was worried—"

"Bullshit," I spat, cutting him off. "Try again motherfucker."

He flinched. "I was."

"If you're going to lie, get the fuck out."

"I'm not…" he trailed off, ducking his head and taking a deep breath. "You're obviously okay?" he said, forming a question out of his statement.

"Okay is relative."

"You're angry with me."

"I don't care enough about you to be angry." Another flinch. *Overkill*, I thought. He raised his eyes briefly to glance at me, then looked away.

"I'll go."

"Why the fuck'd you come?"

"I was worr… it doesn't matter."

"The fuck it doesn't."

"Look at you, you're out of control." His words came out in a rush. "You've been in more fights the last two months than I can keep track of. Just look at your hands. They're raw from fighting. Do you think I can't see that, that I don't worry?"

"Did you come to finish what you started?"

"What does that even mean?" Rick asked, and I heard the defensiveness in his voice.

"Playing me for a fool a second time won't work."

"What are you talking about?"

"I'm not a fucking idiot, Rick. You may have played me once, but it won't fucking happen again."

"Played you?"

"I'm not falling for this innocent routine again. You're fucking brilliant, way better than I ever gave you credit for, but I'm not the village idiot."

"Kevin, I have no idea…"

"I underestimated you once. Never again. I know damn well you played your cards so you could walk away, so I'd have no choice but to let you walk. So fucking what? You hold all the cards and I know you're going to play them when the time is right, but if I have to go down, you're going with me."

"Kevin…" he said taking a step towards me. He must have seen my body tense, ready to rip his fucking head off, because he stopped. "Listen to yourself. You're out of your mind."

"Like I'm going to believe a word you say."

"Think about it," he said calmly. "You're smart enough to know that what you're saying doesn't add up. What would I gain by getting you to toss me out, by coming here today? Take a look at what my life has been the last few months. I returned to having no friends but Jessica the last two weeks of school. I was pretty much locked away in my house with my dad. You know how much he loves that. I suffered through graduating and the third anniversary of Jason's death by myself. Tell me again, what was in it for me?"

"A life away from me."

"And you think I want that?" he asked, letting out a sarcastic laugh. "Have you been so wrapped up in that delusional head of yours that you haven't even seen what all this has done to me? Look at me, Kevin. Do I seem happy to you?"

I fought against my desire to fucking notice him. I didn't want to see his deep, blue-gray eyes or his short hair cropped close to his forehead, but I focused my eyes anyway. I noticed the damn smattering of freckles on his cheeks and the cut above his eye from our fight the other night.

"Goddamnit, Kevin, look at me!" he demanded harshly. "Really see me."

Rick never talked to anyone that way, especially not me. I took a step back. It'd been months since I'd let my gaze linger on him. As I took in his slumped shoulders, pain threatened my heart. He appeared so fucking tired, deep shadows under bloodshot eyes. On closer examination, I could see that his hair was longer than usual. His face was different, and it took me a second to realize that his cheeks actually seemed sunken in.

"Do you fucking eat?" I spat out before I could stop myself. Again, pain stabbed my heart, and I tried to push the feeling away.

"No, I don't eat, and I don't sleep either. I don't do much of anything but worry about you spinning out of control. For someone who used to notice everything, you don't notice a damn thing anymore. You've been so caught up in fighting with everyone that you haven't noticed anything but your own anger."

At the hurt I felt in his words, I stumbled backwards and sat heavily on the couch. "I don't fucking believe you," I said weakly.

"Don't believe me then. Believe your own eyes. Do I look like I got what I wanted?"

"Then why?"

"Why what?"

"Why did you make me do that to you? Why take off like you did?"

"I told you. What were you on that night?"

I looked up at him blankly while he took several steps towards me.

"Can I sit?" he asked cautiously, as he took a few deep breaths to control his own anger. I didn't answer, which he took as a yes.

"Kevin, you made it very clear that you were out of control with me in your life. I saw firsthand what happened with your dad when you lost your focus."

"My father?" My mind raced. What was he talking about? "But you said you hated me."

"What? Jesus, that was for show. I had to make it look real, and I knew you wouldn't let me walk out that door without a fight."

"You hit me. In front of them!"

"Kevin," he pleaded. "I had to make it look real. I had to get you to toss me out."

"But I didn't want you to leave." As my filters began to crumble I wondered if there was a limit to how pathetic I could be with him.

"I think you did."

"Fuck you."

"You'd been telling me for months how dangerous I was for you."

"Yeah but—"

"But nothing," he cut me off, and my temper flared.

"Don't fucking interrupt me." I said, glaring over at

him, and he kept his mouth shut. "That was not what I fucking wanted. You backed me into a corner that night. You took all my control and threw it back at me."

"But it was to protect you."

"From what?"

"From your dad," Rick said with exasperation.

"What the fuck? That doesn't even make sense." My head began to throb as I tried to put together what he was saying.

"If I'd stayed in your life, eventually you'd have lost your focus with him and he'd..." He didn't finish.

"What? Kill me? You're fucking kidding me, right? You think you could stop him from doing that if he wanted to? This was about him?" The pieces that hadn't been clear in months started flying together and forming a picture in my head.

"Well, yeah."

"So what? You left to what?" I searched for the words. "Save me?" I couldn't help the disdain I felt seeping in to my voice.

"Don't say it like that."

"I don't need saving. I'm not some fucking project."

"I know, but I'm dangerous."

"Now who's talking all crazy? You're about the only thing that's ever made sense in my fucked up world."

"Stop."

"Why?"

"Cause I can't. I won't be able to..." he trailed off.

"Rick, you are dangerous to me, but only because you make me feel. Yeah, that's tough when it comes to my father. But, god, these last few months without you.

That's been a whole new kind of hell."

"Kevin, no." He started to stand, but I gripped his wrist and kept him sitting next to me. "I can't."

"Don't go," I said, as he pulled against my restraining hand. "I won't survive without you."

"You won't survive *with* me. You can't stay focused."

"Really? This comes down to you or my father? He's out of the picture next week anyway. Who do you think I'll choose?"

"You don't have a choice," he cried, trying to pull his arm free.

"There's always a choice."

"You say that now, but what happens next time he's holding a gun to your head and your focus slips for a second because of some stupid thing I said or did? What if he tracks you down because of some mistake you make because of me? I can't be the cause of another person I love dying," he said, his voice cracking.

"I'd rather take that chance than live one more second without you in my life," I responded.

He pulled harder, finally standing up and breaking free of my restraining grip on his wrist. I followed him up, grabbing both of his hands in mine. Out of the corner of my eye, through the front window, I saw my father walking up the sidewalk towards the house. He wasn't supposed to be back until the next day. Why was he in the front yard, not the garage? Fragmented thoughts began to fly through my head. I looked at Rick, still trying to leave. I had to finish things with him. If I let him leave, he wouldn't come back. He thought he was protecting me. I looked at him and he had tears in his eyes. He was done. He was serious. Fuck! Why couldn't he see that he was wrong?

Glancing out the window again, I caught my father looking at us, shock on his face as he saw my fingers laced with Rick's. Without thinking, I reached for Rick's face and whispered, "I choose you," right before I kissed him. If he wasn't going to fight for us, I would. My father could fuck off.

"I'm so sorry," I cried as the words, "I love you!" came from my lips for the first time since my mom had left. Again my lips found his. I let my arms wrap around him, pulling him tight against me, kissing him, pouring my soul, my life into his. His arms enfolded me and I felt his body melt into mine. He had no idea what was about to happen. I held him and prayed that with him by my side, my father just might let me out of the house alive. I lost myself in his embrace, the movement of his lips, the way my heart felt so light and free, having finally admitted that I loved him.

My father clearing his throat ripped me from the light Rick was pouring into me. I spun, finding him standing in the room. I hadn't even heard him come in the door, let alone into the room. I wondered how long he had watched me lose myself in our kiss.

"Rick, would you mind heading home? I think Kevin and I have some matters to discuss," he said pleasantly.

I hoped my voice didn't betray my fear when I responded, "We are leaving together."

He paused at my blatant defiance, this being something I'd never done. After a slow breath, eyes locked on mine, he again asked Rick to leave.

"I don't think you heard me. We are leaving together." I counted a few beats, trying to calm my nerves and preparing myself for what I was about to say. "This is over. I am leaving. Do you understand?" I watched the anger flare in his eyes, something that had me automatically taking a few steps backward. I reached for Rick's hand, pulling him so he was directly behind me, shielded from my father. I prayed that my father's desire to keep what he did a secret would outweigh his desire to destroy me.

He took a step towards me. "You are not leaving here until we talk things through." He forced a smile, leaned to the side and turned his gaze on Rick, "Please leave. Now!" he said through gritted teeth. As fear rendered me speechless, Rick stepped forward, coming to my side.

"I won't let you hurt him anymore. We are leaving together." My father stared blankly at Rick, trying to comprehend his words. His eyes came slowly back to mine.

"He knows?" he growled at me. I was too scared to reply. I stood completely still, not breathing, knowing that a false move could have catastrophic results. My father took a step back and bowed his head, shaking it back and forth. "Rick, I am sorry Kevin was selfish and involved you in this. It was never my intent to have a witness to his disobedience." With a quick movement, my father turned and closed the curtains on the front window. As the meaning of his words and actions crashed over me, terror boiled through my veins, forcing me into action. Without hesitation I turned and shoved Rick towards the kitchen.

"RUN!" I screamed at him as I turned back to my father, not waiting to see if Rick listened to my command. As my father moved to take a step around me, following in the direction I'd shoved Rick, I pulled back my arm and threw a punch straight into his face. At the sound of his breaking nose, I threw another fist, landing right under his jaw. Shock flooded his eyes as he stumbled several steps back. Knowing he was stronger than me, and that the element of my surprise attack was my only advantage, I took several more swings, backing him up until he fell onto the couch. Adrenaline and my fighting instinct took over as I tried to buy as much time as I could for Rick to make his escape. As I climbed on top of him, I kept throwing punches until at last his strength kicked in and he flung me off him, tossing me into the coffee table. I groaned loudly as it gave way beneath me, sending sharp stabs of agony where the splintered wood dug into my body. Within moments, he was standing over me with fists flying at my face. I tried to shield the blows, but they rained down with such force that I was left defenseless.

From within my haze of pain, I heard Rick's voice cut through my fear as he screamed, "Leave him alone!" an instant before running into my father, which caused him to stagger several steps away from me. I tried to shake my head at Rick, pleading with him to leave but knowing it was too late. As he reached for me in an attempt to help me up, my father wrapped his fists into Rick's shirt, picking him up and slamming him against the wall.

"It really was a stupid decision for you to come back," my father said, smiling as he dropped Rick to the floor with a knee to the groin. He grabbed Rick's hair, hauling him up so he could slam the back of his fist against his face. As Rick rocked to the side he was met with another fist that spun him around, sending him crashing into the bookcase. I clambered to my feet in horror, begging my body to move faster than it was. Again, my attack from behind caught my father off guard, allowing me to connect several punches. Moments later, Rick was at my side, adding his own fists to the fight. I allowed myself to feel hope for our potential escape as my father reeled back towards the formal dining room. Just when I thought we were about to overtake him, he reached out to a nearby end table and in one swift motion grabbed a lamp, slamming the wooden base against the left side of Rick's head. As Rick lurched to the side, my father brought his swing back and the lamp collided with his right arm, sending Rick sprawling the other direction, collapsing to the floor.

Through my distraction with Rick lying motionless on the carpet, I felt my father yanking on my hair. I stumbled and grabbed onto his fist, waiting to be thrown into a wall. When I heard the door of the hall closet open, I kicked at him, desperate to free myself. Like a doll, he flung me into the tangles of coats and hangers and slammed the door. With the ease of experience, he locked it with the key that fit every closet in the house, explicitly designed for the purpose of confining me at his convenience.

I watched through the slats as he moved back towards the area he'd left Rick. I couldn't see them, but heard Rick moan as I imagined my father picking him up. I threw myself hard against the closet, hoping to break through the lock or the hinges, but despite my strength, it barely budged. He'd known what he was doing when he installed the doors. As my father intentionally brought the fight back into my view, I could hear myself screaming, but the words sounded foreign to me. As Rick struggled to withstand his fists, my father finally turned to the increasing sound of my cries.

"Shutup!" he grumbled as he dropped Rick to the floor, coming back towards the closet. I continued to bang and scream, anything to keep his attention off Rick. He unlocked the door and yanked it open. I tried to duck below his arm as he reached out for me, but his giant fingers closed around my neck and he lifted me several inches off the ground, thrusting me through the clothes and against the back of the closet wall. "I said shutup," he spoke quietly.

I watched through the hanging coats as Rick found his way to a standing position and made a weak attempt to rush my father from behind. I tried to shake my head at him, tried to communicate with him through my eyes that he should run while he could. Without even looking back, my father swung his arm and sent Rick flying towards the ground and out of my sight. I kicked and clawed against my father's hand as I fought for air. He glanced momentarily behind him and then turned his eyes on me. There was nothing there—no satisfaction from the destruction he was causing, not even anger. He was empty, deadly. As things began to get fuzzy, I tried to find Rick, to hear any sound that would give me a clue to his condition. I fought and struggled for breath. I thought I heard him moan as my father's fingers continued to cut off my air supply. I heard another crash, and it crossed my mind that it was my body hitting the floor as darkness swallowed me.

Years of waking up curled in a ball in the closet had me aware of my surroundings before I opened my eyes. I could feel the tightness of the cramped space as my body fought to stretch out the pain. I coughed as I took in a ragged breath, my swollen throat feeling tight and sore. I reached for the closet handle, not expecting it to be unlocked, and tumbled out as the door fell open.

As my eyes adjusted to the light in the room, the events leading up to my enclosure in the closet came rushing back. I struggled with reality as I observed the remnants of the attack. A majority of the furniture was either broken or smeared with blood. The bookcase was tipped over and items from the shelves were strewn about. Rick had put up a fight. I noticed the lamp lying against the wall with red covering the wooden base. I tried not to look at the blood on the couch, splattered on the wall...and, god almighty, the ceiling.

I started screaming, not knowing how the fuck anyone could survive the disaster I saw before me. Within moments my father came barreling into the room, slamming his fist against my face to quiet me. I rolled back and struggled to my feet.

"Where is he?" Hysteria cracked through my voice as blood dripped from my lip. A slow smile tugged at the corners of his mouth as he witnessed my distress.

"He's not here."

"Where is he? What happened?" I asked, stumbling

towards him, tripping over the shelves from the bookcase. "What have you done? Where is he?" He backhanded me and I fell over the broken coffee table onto the couch, landing in blood already turning the color of rust.

"It's upsetting that I couldn't continue his destruction with you watching, but you wouldn't shut up and then Jim Taylor showed up." I held my breath, knowing Jim was a cop. "Someone called the police, I suspect because of your loud mouth. As soon as I heard the knock on the door, it didn't take me long to guess who was there."

"What? What did you tell them? Where's Rick?"

"It was easy to convince them that I'd come home from my business trip and met Rick outside the house, looking for you. I invited him in, assuming you were inside, but you were nowhere to be found. Instead we came upon some home intruders. Of course, they attacked when they saw us. Sadly, your friend...," he let the word fall slowly off his lips, "got the worst of it before they ran out the back door. I told them I had tried to help him, to wake him, you know — to explain his blood all over me. Your absence was hard to explain, but I told them I had no idea where you were. It really is too bad they showed up. I was looking forward to letting you find his dead body when you woke up."

"What the fuck did you do to him? Did you kill him?" I screamed, lunging at him from the couch, but he easily tossed me aside with a swing of his arm.

"Watch your mouth. You better knock it off or I'll do the same to you," he growled at me, continuing his explanation. "On second thought, I bet it was your little friend Jeremy who called the cops. He was lurking in the front yard when I answered the door, stuck around eavesdropping until they left. We've had quite the guest list this afternoon."

I started inching towards the front entrance, planning to make a run for it. If he wouldn't tell me where Rick was, I'd find him myself. He grabbed my arm "Where do you think you're going? You need to stay here and clean up this mess." He threw me to the floor, and I felt pieces of glass from a picture frame cut through my skin. My mind raced. How could he have done this? What had he done? Had he killed him? I stood, rushing at him again.

"What have you done to him?" I insisted, and he startled at my rage. I threw a punch at him and then another. For the second time that day, he looked at me in shock, surprised yet again at my ability to fight back. "You better tell me what you did, or so help me god…" I hit him and he fell against the wall. I knew if he turned on me again I'd have no chance for escape. I had to get out of the house if I was going to live. I bolted out the door, running for Jeremy's.

"Is he alive?" I screamed as Jeremy opened the door.

"Kevin, what happened to you?"

"Alive? Is Rick alive?" I shouted, pushing at him.

"He was when they took him," Jeremy stammered, then continued when I demanded he tell me exactly what had happened. He told me how he'd come to the house looking for me. Even in the front yard, he could hear the screaming. From the sound of it he knew it was bad. Of course, he hadn't thought it was my father or Rick. He really had no idea what was happening. Jeremy had called the police and then waited until they showed up, hearing my father explain his side of the story.

"Your dad seemed pretty torn up about the whole thing. Where were you? Do you know who did this to Rick?"

"Where did they take Rick?"

"I'm not sure. Didn't your dad tell ya?"

I slammed my fist into a wall. "Fuck my father! Think, Jeremy, where is he?"

"Relax man, I'm not sure, ummm, maybe Alta View."

"Take me there."

"I can't, my parents are on their way home."

I grabbed his shirt and slammed him against the wall. "I'm not going to fucking ask you again." I glowered at him. "Take me there!"

He raised his hands, and said, "Fine, fine, let's go."

The hospital was only about ten minutes from the house. On the way, Jeremy pointed out the dried blood from my obviously broken nose. He gave me some napkins to clean up with, and a shirt from his gym bag in the back seat. I spent most of the time on the phone trying to get the nurses to tell me if he was there and if he was okay. I didn't get much, only that he'd been brought to the hospital after he'd been attacked.

Jeremy followed me into the hospital. I went straight to the emergency room front desk. They gave me the runaround, saying that I wasn't family and they couldn't give me any information. I saw his dad sitting with Sylvia and Emma in the waiting room, and I rushed over to them. His dad actually had the fucking nerve to look torn up.

"Where is he?" I demanded.

"He's still unconscious, in the ICU."

"Is he going to be okay?"

He hesitated, "I don't know. It's pretty bad. Can you tell us what happened?"

I paused briefly, calming myself and kneeling down in front of Emma, knowing it was something Rick would want me to do.

"Hey kiddo," I smiled. "You're bother's going to be just fine. I'm going to go check on him. Okay?" She nodded slightly, and a small smile crossed her lips before she reached up and gave me a hug.

I stood, looking away from all of them, trying to find someone who would know more than they did. Jeremy put his hand on my shoulder. "Maybe we should sit down and wait to hear from the doctors." I shrugged his hand off and hurried away. Desperate to find Rick, I burst through the doors to the ICU rooms.

"Can I help you?" a nurse asked me.

"No, I'm good." I knew I didn't have much time before someone stopped me. I started checking the names on the charts. Several rooms down the second hall I found Rick's name and threw the door open.

I nearly fell to my knees, reaching out to hold onto the wall for support. I knew I couldn't be in the right place. There were blood-soaked bandages everywhere. His face was purple with bruising and so swollen. No, it couldn't be Rick. I checked the name on the door again. Bile rose in my throat at the thought of losing him. I ran to the bathroom and curled over the toilet. Tears welled up in my eyes as I heard someone come into the room.

"I honestly don't think the kid's going to make it," a

female voice said.

"I've never seen a beating like this," a male said.

"The poor thing, so young."

"I'll be surprised if he makes it through the next hour."

The steady beeping from the monitor began a never-ending scream. "He's flat-lining. Get some help in here, now!" the woman called out. I came out of the bathroom unnoticed as doctors and nurses crowded around his bed. I was frozen, watching my life die in front of me.

"Rick, please don't leave me. I love you. I'm so sorry," I whispered. I was finally noticed and a nurse pushed me out of the room. As the door closed, I overheard someone say, "I think we should call it."

The time that followed was blurry. How I got out of the hospital and home was completely lost on me, but things came into crystal-clear focus as I found myself screaming at my father, "My god, you killed him!" while waving the gun he'd used to threaten my life. "I chose him."

"Kevin, listen to me," he said, holding up his hands.

"Shut the fuck up!" I leveled the gun to his face. "Don't you fucking say a word to me. Did you see his body? Did you see what you fucking did to him? My god, I loved him. This is your fault. He'll never know or understand…"

I sank to my knees, crying, my grip loosened on the gun. He took a few steps towards me, and I pointed it at him again. "Don't you fucking dare! He was the only good thing in my life. Why did you turn on him? Why kill him and not me?"

"Don't be stupid. I know you kissed him after you saw me. I told him as much—"

"You did what? You fucking told him that?" God, he'd never understand why I'd risked everything. How could he know that I only thought I was putting myself in danger, I never imagined my father would turn on him. "You don't understand. I loved him!" I shrieked. "Don't you get that? I loved him! You deserve to die for all you've done. You deserve to die for killing him."

I stood, taking several slow steps toward him. The safety on the gun released and my hand steadied. I stared into the eyes of the man I called father, the monster who had found pleasure in my torture and had killed the only light in my dark, fucked up world.

Then I felt it. I looked down at my arm and nothing was there, but I felt Rick's hand nonetheless, heard a silent plea, "This is not the part of you I fell in love with." I looked back to my father, hesitated, and then found Rick's words again. He loved me. He saw goodness in me. "Rick saved your life today, but one day you'll burn in hell for what you've done."

I dropped the gun and ran from the house, my mind racing with the images of Rick's beaten and bloody body. I hadn't been able to recognize him. I'd kissed him. I'd done this. I ran to Zarahemla. The wind on my face spread the wet tears as they fell, cooling my cheeks.

I tore into the abandoned barn and pulled up the loose floorboards where we kept the alcohol and pills. Opening a bottle of Wild Turkey, I started pouring it down my throat. "Rick" I screamed into the air, "Rick, my love, I'm so sorry." I grabbed a handful of pills and chased them down with more whiskey. I wanted to make my feelings go away. I wanted to disappear. I no longer deserved to be alive. I'd risked everything and I'd lost. I'd killed him. I drank more and coughed. I grabbed more pills, surprised at the peace I felt when I realized I wanted to die so I could join him. I couldn't be in this world without him. There was no light without his love. For once, I didn't want to fight.

The room was starting to get fuzzy. Another handful of pills and more whiskey, and I fell backwards onto the dirt. I could feel my legs and arms starting to go numb, my body shutting down, everything going slower, like my blood was trying to travel through mud, too much resistance. I let the pills and alcohol overpower my body. Finally, I stopped trying to control what was happing in my life, telling myself not to fight it. I welcomed it. I'd be with him soon. I'd be able to tell him that I loved him again and again. My eyes closed, and I thought only of his arms wrapped around me as I drifted into the peace of the darkness that would lead me to Rick's light.

Epilogue...

Rick

I nearly met death three times during the twelve hours following my attack. I obviously don't remember much those first few days except the comings and goings of doctors, and my dad always in the room. He didn't leave, which I think hindered my healing process. Regardless, he stayed. I do remember asking after Kevin and being met with vague answers.

I was told a story of home invaders at Kevin's, which at the time I didn't remember. They wanted to know who attacked me and where Kevin had been. I fought to piece together the events I could recall. I remembered the fight at the 24th of July party and going to check on him. My heart pounded every time I thought of his words of love, then his kiss. I didn't remember anything after that, and couldn't figure out who would've come and attacked me and why Kevin had left me alone. Everything after his kiss remained a blank until Kevin's dad walked into my room. Then the memories came crashing over me.

I started screaming and trying to get out of bed. When he joined with my dad in an attempt to restrain me, I fought with everything I had. I was convinced he'd try to finish what he'd started to keep me quiet. With some weird protective instinct, it was my dad who ordered Kevin's dad to leave. The doctors had to sedate me.

Even after I remembered, I kept Kevin's secret. I didn't understand why he hadn't come to see me, but I'd given up understanding him long before this. The police started coming around more, asking questions. To protect Kevin, I claimed I didn't remember the attack and left it at that.

I was surprised but didn't think much of it when two detectives asked my dad to leave my room. I was still a few weeks shy of eighteen and I was pretty sure they couldn't question me without him there. The first thing they asked was if either Kevin's dad or my dad had ever hit either of us. I clamped up immediately. They tried several different ways to get me to talk to them, but I refused to say anything. There was no way I was putting his life into the hands of two people I didn't know.

Not realizing I hadn't heard about Kevin's overdose, they inadvertently mentioned it during further questioning and I fell apart. The news destroyed me.

Jeremy found his body at Zarahemla, having gone looking for him after he tore out of the hospital. We later discovered that he'd been in my room when the crash cart was brought in, but he hadn't stayed around long enough to hear that they were able to revive me.

Hearing what Kevin had done, I knew I had to talk. His dad had caused enough pain. I tried to explain the attack without going into the kiss or what we felt for each other, but they kept asking me what I was leaving out, knowing I wasn't telling them everything. Finally, I told them how I figured that his dad seeing us kiss, and my refusal to leave the house was what had sent him over the edge. To their credit, they showed no judgment as they continued asking questions.

I'd recognized Kevin's kiss immediately as his attempt to prove to me that he was choosing me, and I loved him all the more for that. I knew that when Kevin kissed me he'd thought he was only putting himself in harm's way, counting on his dad's need to keep the beatings a secret, and I'd been the one to ruin his plan. In the end, Kevin made the choice to gamble his life on a chance to win love with me, and feeling guilty about my decision to stand by him minimized his choice.

The time I'd spent at the hands of Kevin's dad were some of the most terrifying moments of my life. His methods were far more sophisticated than my dad's, and I had no doubt that he intended to kill me. It took me over an hour to get through the details of the attack.

I then went on to describe to the detectives how I'd seen his dad punish him with the belt, and the three days he'd had to suffer being restrained at gunpoint. I retold the many stories Kevin had shared with me. The scars on his body and the evidence in his home validated everything. I hadn't planned on talking about my dad, but slipped up when I said that Kevin had always been there to help me with my dad, and I'd be willing to testify or do whatever it took to make sure the truth came out. They quickly threw in a question about my last beating. I was exhausted and emotionally spent, and without thinking I told them the truth.

Both of our fathers were arrested and our stories were splattered across the news for months. Everyone found out about Jason, the violence at home and, of course, our relationship. Sylvia stuck to the story she had told herself all along. She claimed she had no idea what my dad was doing to me, and that he had been under a tremendous amount of stress since Jason died.

It was weeks before I agreed to see Emma. I couldn't bear the thought of her seeing me beat up like I was. As soon as I felt it was okay, I asked to see her, but the visits were few and far between thanks to Sylvia.

Jessica was devastated to find out everything I'd been keeping from her. She decided to put off school for a year, and Derek stayed behind as well. Her parents insisted that I stay with them. Though I missed Emma, it was nice to have people around who cared for me, so I stayed with her family.

Mike and Jeremy turned out to be really great guys, and they came to a majority of the court dates. During the main trial they were there every day. I can't really say what happened to Brett. He disappeared with another group of friends.

The system wanted to restore my family the best they could, and since my dad had only started hitting me after the loss of Jason, they put him in counseling, along with some hefty fines and community service. I went to one family session with him because he asked. He cried a lot and said he was sorry. When he told me he loved me, I got up and walked out. I was beyond caring if he meant it or if it was all a show for the courts. I haven't seen or talked to him since that day.

Kevin's dad was so sure of himself, and thought he'd win at trial. But thirteen months after his attack on me, he was found guilty of seven charges, including felony child abuse and attempted murder. He is serving a life sentence in prison.

Just before my 20th birthday, I changed my last name to Kennedy and moved to New York, where we'd always talked about going. Since Jessica's brother was the same age as Emma, Jessica was able to keep tabs on what was going on with her, but for her own safety and mine, I haven't talked to her in years. I don't doubt that Kevin's dad could still hurt me, even from behind the bars of prison. For this reason, I lie low and have very little contact with those from my former life.

I finished college and work as a consultant for an HR firm. I have a small but perfect apartment in Chelsea, and I frequent local pubs where I play the guitar Kevin gave me, always closing with the song I wrote for him. I don't live a glamorous life, but I like the quiet routine. I still drink on occasion, but haven't smoked or used since the day his dad tried to kill me.

It's been ten years to the day since my attack and Kevin's overdose. I've heard that violence begets violence, but in my world, violence begat love. There's been no one since Kevin; I doubt there ever will be. We were able to find love in each other when both our worlds were riddled with pain. Violence only begets violence when we allow it to. We always have a choice. Kevin chose me.

The End...

DID YOU ENJOY READING *VIOLENCE BEGETS...* BY P. T. DENYS?

Please leave a review on Amazon or Goodreads!

You can write to the author directly at:

ChooseLove@PTDenys.com
www.PTDenys.com

Find PT Online:
Facebook.com/PTDenys
Facebook.com/PTDenysAuthor
Twitter.com/PTDenys

ABOUT THE AUTHOR

PT never imagined publishing a book. But, the story of Violence Begets… and the lives of Kevin and Rick had to be shared.

In addition to writing a sequel, PT spends times balancing family, work, attending theater and reading.

Above all else PT loves being a parent to 2 amazing daughters (a teenager and a toddler).

PT believes that no one deserves to be intentionally hurt (physically or emotionally) by another and that behind nearly every bully is a story.